PENGUIN BOOKS

One Winter Morning

lle Broom was born in Cambridge nine days before
980s began and studied Media Arts in London before
ag the ranks at *Heat* magazine, where she later became
ook Reviews editor. Always happiest when she is off on
renture, Isabelle now travels all over the world seek-
t settings for her novels, as well as making the annual
mage to her true home – the Greek island of Zakyn-
Currently based in Suffolk, where she shares a cottage
er two dogs and approximately 467 spiders, Isabelle
r writing around a busy freelance career and tries her
ot to be crushed to oblivion under her ever-growing
to-be-read books.

One Winter Morning

ISABELLE BROOM

PENGUIN BOOKS

PENGUIN BOOKS

UK | USA | Canada | Ireland | Australia
India | New Zealand | South Africa

Penguin Books is part of the Penguin Random House group of companies
whose addresses can be found at global.penguinrandomhouse.com.

First published 2019
001

Copyright © Isabelle Broom, 2019

The moral right of the author has been asserted

Set in 12.5/14.75 pt Garamond MT Std
Typeset by Jouve (UK), Milton Keynes
Printed and bound in Great Britain by Clays Ltd, Elcograf S.p.A.

A CIP catalogue record for this book is available from the British Library

ISBN: 978–1–405–93550–0

www.greenpenguin.co.uk

MIX
Paper from
responsible sources
FSC® C018179

Penguin Random House is committed to a
sustainable future for our business, our readers
and our planet. This book is made from Forest
Stewardship Council® certified paper.

For the brave, brilliant
(and utterly bananas) Ian Lawton

I

The morning began as so many do in winter, with low-hanging fog and a smattering of frost. For weeks the sky has been the muted silver of a much-thumbed coin, but today the sun has broken through, laundering my little Cambridgeshire village with light.

As I walk the ten or so minutes to the pub, I relish this new brightness which has brought with it so much colour – red berries in a thicket of holly, a battalion of purple pansies in a window box, and perched on the wall outside the church, a blue tit, its head cocked inquisitively to one side.

I see David as soon as I cross the threshold of the White Swan. He is easy to spot, with his round bald head and those John Lennon-style glasses, which he wears balanced precariously on the end of his nose. In all the early family photos of him, Anna and myself, David has thick, black curls, much like my own, but his hair started to thin rapidly the year he turned forty, and now, at fifty-eight, there's barely a strand remaining. Strangers used to comment on David's hair when I was a child, telling me how fortunate I was to have inherited it. I always smiled away and allowed them their assumptions – in fact, I enjoyed hearing them. In the eyes of those people, I was a normal daughter, from a normal family, living a normal life.

I once read that the average human life has seventeen possible starting points. Some believe it begins at conception, others the moment of birth, while for a few the transition into adulthood marks the real beginning. I suppose our life is a story, and we are its author – therefore it's down to us to decide which chapter means the most to us.

My own life began eight days after my fourth birthday – the day I found out I was adopted. I can't remember how it felt before that, just being Evangeline Nash, a child who had no idea she had been given away by the one person who was supposed to cherish her the most, a mother whose name I don't even know. In the quietest moments of the night, in that pause before the dawn arrives, I still search inside and try to find myself – the person I should have been.

'There she is!' David exclaims as I walk towards him. 'You look lovely – what a nice dress.'

'It's a jumpsuit,' I say, lifting one leg to the side like a tightrope-walker before accepting his enthusiastic hug of greeting. 'They're flattering, but an absolute nightmare when you need a pee.'

Stripping off in the ladies' loo aside, it made a nice change to wear something other than leggings and a sloppy jersey today, so I'm touched that he has noticed the effort. It has been a good long while now since I have ventured out for lunch, and I even went so far as to apply a smear or two of make-up.

2

We spend the first few minutes discussing the mundanities of David's life – his car MOT and the ongoing battle between the neighbour's dog and his rose bushes. I remark on the ludicrous number of Christmas decorations that are up in the pub, and we deliberate over whether to order the Swan's famous macaroni cheese or its triple-stacked BLT from the menu. I don't argue when he offers upfront to pay, even though it stings to accept. I will get back to a place where I am earning again, but at the moment, it still feels a long way off.

'So,' he begins, when we both have a Diet Coke in front of us, 'your big date is tonight, isn't it?'

'It is,' I agree. Then, seeing him arch an inquisitive brow, 'Why are you making that face?'

'I'm just happy for you, poppet, that's all. Billy is one of the good guys.'

David often makes these proclamations, telling me his opinion rather than asking me for mine. Anna told me once that he can't help it – before he became a full-time author, he spent so many years teaching that his mannerisms and speech patterns were altered.

'Well, don't get too carried away,' I inform him, allowing myself the flicker of a smile as I picture Billy. The idea of being on a date with him later is sending my mind down a helter-skelter, but it's too late to cancel on him now.

'It's just a drink,' I remind David. 'Not a Happily Ever After.'

'Yes, of course, I know that. I don't want you to feel that I . . . Well, that is to say . . . What I mean is . . .'

David coughs to mask his discomfort, then reaches into the inside pocket of his blazer and extracts a small cloth. When he removes his glasses to polish them, however, he promptly drops them on to the floor, then bangs his head as he begins rooting around beneath the table.

I would usually have been amused by such a display, but as it is, I find his obvious unease disconcerting. David was once the person I relied on to have the answers to all my questions, but nowadays, he falters whenever he speaks to me – even over a subject as benign as my date with an old friend. In his eyes, I have transformed from my robust self into something fragile, a delicate china ornament that must be handled with the utmost care at all times, just in case I crack.

Since Anna died in a horse-riding accident last Christmas Eve, it has felt increasingly like David's playing a part; he is A Father and Widow Who Is Coping, rather than his real, presumably wobbly self. Would it be different if he had fathered me in the traditional way? If we were related by blood, would we have a mutual understanding that allowed each of us to better support the other? I wish I could do more to help him, but then, I wish he could help me more, too.

Once the glasses have been restored to David's face, I do my best to steer the conversation away from the subject of my dating life, and the two of us end up sharing a laugh as we recall a comical habit from my childhood. I was very fond of pulling my jumpers up over my face and pratting around the house unable to see, which led to many a collision with not only the furniture, but also two long-suffering cats and, while seated at the dining room table once, a plate of macaroni cheese hot from the oven. That one was messy.

I have just put my knife and fork together across my empty plate when David drops his bombshell, beginning with the fairly innocuous comment that he's worried about me.

That makes two of us.

'I'm fine,' I say automatically, only to chastise myself for the lie. 'What I mean is, I will be fine. I just need a bit more time, that's all.'

I twist a thick wedge of hair furiously around one finger, wincing when it starts to shred.

'It's been almost a year,' David continues, and immediately I feel the all-too-familiar stinging sensation behind my nose.

'Oh, Genie.' David sighs and reaches across the table to pat my shoulder. 'I'm sorry, sweetheart. I shouldn't have brought it up.'

I shake my head and look down at my knees rather than at him. I have already learned that seeing my own pain reflected back in his expression does nothing at all to lessen it.

'It's OK,' I mutter. 'I don't want you to feel like you can't talk about it.'

David sits silently while I discreetly cry out this latest batch of tears, his fingers rubbing soothing circles on my hands. It's only when I stop and bring my eyes up to meet his that I see the fear in them. He has something else that he needs to tell me, but suddenly, I don't want to hear it.

I move my hands out of his grasp and lean back, gripped by an urge to flounce away from him, just as I would have done as a teenager. I tormented David and Anna from the age of thirteen right through to eighteen, sneaking out after my bedtime, drinking, smoking, even dabbling once or twice in recreational drugs. And I delighted in inviting boys home and locking my bedroom door behind us – a practice that was strictly against David's rules. How bold I felt, when really, I was lost. It's obvious to me now that I was oh-so angry at my displacement within the world, when what I should have been was grateful – happy to be as cherished as I was by my adoptive parents.

'I can't just sit here and watch while you allow your life to fall completely apart,' David says quietly, his tone sympathetic rather than severe. 'This is the first time you've been out for a meal in months,' he adds, gesturing around. 'And what about your job – are you ever going to go back?'

I shake my head once, the gesture unequivocal.

'I can't,' I say. 'I just can't be there. I can't be anywhere near there. I'm sorry that I'm not paying my way – I will get a job somewhere else.'

'Genie,' he begins, and I know what he'll say next: money is not the problem, never has been since he wrote all those books about another girl called Evangeline; since he turned my forlorn start in life into the *Evangeline And . . .* series for other children to enjoy. It's that Evangeline who has kept a roof over our heads, who settles the utility bills, puts food in the fridge and pays for the artwork on the walls of our home. She is the real star of our family.

'It's time we had a chat about your real mother,' David blurts out.

I feel the blood drain from my cheeks. Whatever I thought he was going to say, I never would have guessed it would be this. The official line regarding my birth parents has always been the same: that my mother was a friend of an acquaintance, a girl who got herself into trouble when she was too young to cope, while my father was simply some random that she hooked up with – perhaps even one of many – who was never in the picture and never wanted to be. David and Anna stepped in to help because they so longed for a baby. There has never been any suggestion she was a person they knew – or even met. I know her name must be on my original birth certificate, but I have never seen it, nor have I ever wanted to. The only one I care about is the reissued version, which has David and Anna down as my parents. For a moment, all I can do is mouth uselessly, my emotions veering violently from shock to anger to downright alarm.

David has turned pale at the look on my face – an expression that warns him to stop talking. I cross my arms and jut out my chin, my posture radiating anger. Before I can muster an appropriate reply, however, he takes another deep breath and adds, 'I know who she is and I know where she is, too. I have always known.'

'You WHAT?'

I can't believe that I am hearing this.

'You always said you had no idea where she went after I was born,' I storm.

'I know,' he agrees, looking sheepish. 'Anna and I told you that we didn't know any details, but we did. I'm so sorry, darling – but we thought we were doing the right thing, by her and you, by not revealing the extent of it all. But now that everything's changed, I think it's time you knew more. At least let me tell you her name?'

'What if I don't want to know?' I retort. 'What if I don't want to know anything about that ... that woman? It's not as if she can replace Anna, is it? Nothing and nobody can do that, and you shouldn't bloody well think they could!'

David sighs. He is not a big man, but my reaction has made him seem even smaller somehow. Despite my indignation, I feel something inside me give as I glare across the table at him. He has been so hurt already by my actions, yet here I go again, piling on more pain.

'Why?' I ask, and I have to clench my jaw to mask the tremble in my voice. 'Why now?'

David looks at me for a moment. I can guess what he is about to say, and brace myself.

'It's because of Anna,' he mutters, now close to tears himself. The waitress, who was approaching to clear away our plates, takes one look at him and veers off in the opposite direction.

'Because she would hate seeing you like this – seeing both of us like this.'

I close my eyes, and the image of my adoptive mother fills the dark space behind them. Her soft, lined face, her warm smile and those kind, fawn-coloured eyes. God, I miss her. I miss her so much that it makes my breath catch in my throat.

'The thing is, Genie, this is killing me – seeing you in this state. I feel like I've lost you, as well as her, and it can't go on. Things can't keep on the way they are, with you so miserable and shut off from the world, and the two of us tiptoeing around each other all the time. Something has to change, don't you see that?'

'No,' I reply sulkily, even though I know he's right.

'I know that meeting Bo—'

A glare from me makes him falter.

'Your birth mother,' he corrects. 'I know she won't become a substitute for Anna, but meeting her might help you find your way back to yourself. Haven't you ever wondered who she might be, or what she might look like?'

'No, I haven't,' I snap, although David knows as well as I do that I'm lying.

'And you do need to get out of the house,' he says gently. 'Get back into the world and remind yourself that there is still plenty to live for out there.'

9

'Why do I need some random stranger to help me do that?' I demand.

'She's hardly that,' he counters quietly. 'She's your mother.'

'I don't want another mother,' I tell him, my voice rising. 'I want *my* mother.'

The tears come back then, and I let them. I sit motionless as they trickle over my cheeks and down my neck. David's eyes behind his glasses are watery, but his expression remains determined. He has his educator hat on again, but the lesson he is trying to teach me is one I already know.

I can't have what I want, because what I want is Anna. And Anna died because of me.

2

I am fairly certain that, given the day I have just had, most people would probably cancel their evening plans. Finding out your adoptive parents have kept a huge secret from you throughout your entire life is catastrophic enough, but when you toss in the name and location of the woman who gave birth to you as well, it could surely be assumed that you would draw a line through any dates for the next month – let alone the following few hours.

At the very least, what I should be doing tonight is an online search for the woman who gave me up. Any normal person would be desperate to put a face to the name – especially if it's one they've waited almost their entire life to hear.

I am not most people, though, and neither am I normal. So, instead, I have come back to the pub to meet Billy, and so far I have done a sterling job of convincing him – and myself – that there is absolutely nothing wrong with me.

'Nice shot, Nash.'

Billy grins at me from across the pool table, and raises his half-empty pint glass in a salute. I have just potted three yellow balls off the break, and now I am limbering up for a fourth.

'She shoots, she scores,' I throw back, slamming the cue so hard against the white that it ricochets forwards and sends two of Billy's red balls hurtling across the floor of the pub.

'Whoa there!' Billy laughs as he tries and fails to catch them. 'Any harder and you'll take out the windows.'

It is not the first time the two of us have played pool together in this setting – it could easily be the two-hundredth – but none of the previous occasions was an official date. This is the first of those, and it's every bit as weird as I hoped it wouldn't be.

'Two shots,' I say, taking the opportunity to get stuck into my glass of white wine. I have been avoiding alcohol at home, but this evening it feels necessary. Anything that can ease this awful feeling of having the rug yanked out from under me is worth a punt – or a pint. Now if only they sold wine in those . . .

Billy always looks rather ridiculous when he is bent over the pool table. He has the body shape of one of those inflatable air dancers that you sometimes see outside car dealerships, all lanky limbed and square-headed. That is not to say that my old friend is not attractive, however, because he very much is. He has amiable pale-grey eyes, a liberal spray of Irish freckles and masses of conker-brown curls, not to mention the metabolism of an Olympic sprinter. Before we started this game, I watched him inhale a bacon double cheese-burger with all the sides, and now he's tucking into a bag of salt-and-vinegar crisps.

'Want one?' he offers.

My mouth is full of wine, so I decline with a shake of my head, deciding privately that there's no way he can be expecting a kiss at the end of the night. Not even Billy would be foolish enough to season his mouth with such a strong flavour if he thought there was any chance of it coming into contact with mine. He does keep glancing over at me, though, perhaps not in a suggestive way, but more with an expression of concern.

I made a pact with myself after my disastrous lunch with David that I would put on a stoic face during this date. It's not that I don't trust Billy or don't want to share things with him; it's more that I need to be the old me tonight – to prove not only to myself but to David, too, that I am getting on with my life. I don't need an intervention in the shape of my so-called real mother – I am going to get through all this grief and guilt on my own terms.

It would not have been fair of me to turn up and dump these latest woes on to Billy – he knows me as the girl who punctuates her sentences with laughter, the prankster who teaches the youngsters down at the stables how to bury the toes of their riding boots into the soft surface of the indoor school, then cartwheel right out of them. It's that Genie he fancies, not the shadow of what Anna's death has left behind.

'Genie?'

I look up to find Billy right beside me.

'Sorry – what?'

'Your go.' He gestures to the table. I have two balls left, he has three.

I line up the first shot, squinting along the cue until I'm happy with the angle.

'Shit,' Billy mutters, as the ball thunks into the corner pocket.

'Aaargh!' he adds, as the final yellow sails effortlessly in after it.

I only have one attempt at the black, but it's all I need.

'Victory!' I declare, downing the remainder of my wine.

Billy suppresses a belch.

'There I go again,' he says with a smirk. 'Being a proper gentleman and letting the lady win.'

'Best of three?' I ask, ignoring his comment, and Billy sighs.

'Oh, go on then.'

I head to the bar for refills, ordering myself a shot of tequila, which I quickly slam while Billy's back is turned. The alcohol is having the desired effect – my edges are beginning to feel fuzzy, and the awkwardness I felt when I arrived a few hours ago is slowly being extinguished. Perhaps I do fancy my friend the farrier after all? Maybe Anna was right.

My adoptive mother adored Billy. Whenever she and he happened to be at Mill House Stables at the same time, she would make a beeline for him, and I would often catch them talking about me. It was obvious from the way Anna giggled and looked over in my direction, and I knew what she was saying without needing to eavesdrop – she was telling Billy that he should persevere. That eventually, I would realise how great he was and fall madly in love with him.

My late mum was nothing if not a romantic fantasist, and I know that the real reason I'm here on this date – if I can even call it that – is because I want to make her happy in some small way. There is so much I have to make up for, but I have no idea how to begin.

Shrugging off my melancholy, I venture back to the table and listen while Billy tells me a funny story about his father's retirement plans, which to date have included pottery, ju-jitsu, birdwatching, and now, apparently, he's adding pond-building to the list.

'He spent all of Sunday digging the hole, then found out how much it was going to cost to line it with sand and scrapped the whole project. I think my mum might bury him in it!'

Billy's dad hung up his blacksmith's hammer in August, handing the reins of his business over to his eager protégé. I have known the family since I first started learning to ride, back when my legs were too short to reach the stirrups, and it has been a case of one amusing anecdote after another ever since.

I make it through three more victorious games of pool and two more illicit orders of tequila before my carefully constructed armour begins to chink. Knowing me as well as he does, it doesn't take Billy long to notice that I have fallen silent, and that I'm not biting my lip because I'm concentrating on the game, but in order to stop myself from crying.

'You're regretting saying yes to this date now, aren't you?' he asks.

'I would never regret spending time with you,' I tell him honestly. 'You're one of the people I like most in the world.'

Billy reddens at that, the colour spreading across his cheeks and down his throat.

'People you *like*?' he repeats, a note of reluctant resignation in his tone as I reach for my glass of wine.

I know what he wants me to say. He wants me to admit that I like him in more than a friendly way, that I agreed to come here tonight because I feel the same way that he does, because I want to be more to him than just that daft and haphazardly blundering lass from the stables with the hair that's nearly long enough to sit on. The girl who shares her Pot Noodle with him when he takes a break from shoeing the horses and makes him cups of instant coffee on cold winter mornings. I almost wish I did love Billy in that pure and passionate way, because then it would all be so easy.

The memory of my lunch with David hits me hard, landing like hooves in the centre of my chest.

'Genie?'

Billy has finished his pint and wants to know if he should get another. He is one of my dearest friends, but when I look up at him and see the unmistakable glimmer of hope in his eyes, all I want to do is run away, back to the security blanket of home, where I am free to wallow as much as I want. I feel uncomfortable here now, but it's not because I'm on a date with Billy – it's because I actually hate pretending to him that everything is fine. He deserves better than this fake version of me, and this clown act that I'm having to put on tonight is exhausting.

Lifting my glass of wine, I drain it forlornly.

'Come on,' says Billy, his fingers warm in the crook of my arm.

'I'm sorry,' I say, returning once again to the word I seem to use more often than any other these days.

Billy shakes his head, deflecting my apology.

'Don't worry,' he says. 'I get it, Genie – you don't have to explain.'

I'm not sure I would even know how, but I don't say as much to him.

Billy looks at me without a trace of disgruntlement. His concern, as ever, seems purely to be focused on how I feel, and what I want. Not for the first time, I feel lucky to have such an incredible friend. I certainly don't deserve him.

'To be continued, Nash,' he says, grinning at me as he pushes all the remaining balls into the nearest pockets. 'Get your coat on and I'll walk you home.'

3

It is the day after David pulverised me with his revelation, and Hayley is running late.

My best friend has many talents, but timekeeping is definitely not one of them – it's one of the many things we have in common, our chaotic disorganisation. She said that she would aim for just after four p.m., and it's almost five now, the December sky beyond my windows an inky black. As soon as I reach for my mobile to call her, however, I hear the distant chime of the doorbell, followed shortly by the muffled sound of David's voice, then feet on the stairs.

I have been friends with Hayley Thomas ever since the summer of our very first Pony Club Camp. Back then, she was saddled with a rotund and very greedy piebald pony called Boris, while Anna and David had arranged for me to loan out a chestnut gelding named Fox, who jumped like a stag but spooked at everything.

On day two, I was studiously warming up for the under-tens' showjumping competition when a bystander noisily opened a packet of crisps. Fox shot off sideways in fright, only to collide heavily with a rather exuberant Boris, who had also clocked the exciting packet and was determined to eat the contents. Hayley, who was up on his back, had pulled one of her reins to slow him down just as I yanked my own, and the two of us had collided in the air like skittles, our ears left ringing inside our hard hats as we struggled to regain control of our respective steeds.

From that moment onwards, we barely left each other's side at Camp. Hayley has always been able to make me laugh, but she has also listened, supported, berated and been there to hold my hand – or my hair back – as required, just as I have been for her. She is the only person I have told about my lunch with David. Immediately, she suggested that she should come over today so we could talk it all through.

'I'm so sorry!' she says now, giving me a repentant smile as she closes my bedroom door behind her and hurries towards where I'm sitting to give me a one-armed hug.

'The men came to remove the muck heap just as I was getting in the car, and I couldn't risk leaving them to their own devices,' she explains, pulling off her thick woolly hat with such vigour that strands of her hair stand up in the static.

Hayley is tall, lean and blonde, much like a sunflower, while I am petite, rounded and dark-haired, not unlike a blueberry.

'Don't worry about it.' I wave away her apologies. 'I bought a cake – do you want some?'

Hayley's eyes widen in delight as she eyes the box on my bedside table.

'Is that lemon drizzle?' she asks, grinning as I confirm that it is. 'Thank God for that – I'm bloody starving!'

Like Billy the burger-gobbler, Hayley is always hungry – a trait that I often tease her she inherited from Boris. But unlike her chubby first pony, my friend never seems to gain much weight. Then again, I never used to either – not until I stopped working at the yard. When you're putting in twelve hours of manual labour a day, only really sitting down when you're in the saddle, then you quickly burn off all and any calories you ingest – even those that originated in cake.

After I have cut her an enormous slice, Hayley tells me between mouthfuls that her younger brother Mike has quit his degree course for the third time in as many years.

'Honestly, I don't know why he doesn't just get a job like I did.'

Hayley and I both swerved university and went to agricultural college instead. Being riding instructors is all either of us ever wanted to do, so it seemed pointless to pursue anything else. Now that I can't see myself ever doing it again, however, I'm at a loss as to what else to try. It's been more than eleven long months since I turned my back on the job that I once loved, and I haven't so much as looked at an application form since. I know Hayley worries about me, just as David does, but I can't seem to motivate myself into doing anything about it.

'So, are you going to tell me how your date with Billy

the Kidder went?' Hayley asks, licking lemon icing off her fingers. 'Or are you going to make me guess? Hang on – I know! He's a terrible kisser? Or worse – he's terrible at the other stuff and you were forced to call a halt halfway through.'

'Stop!' I implore, lobbing a stuffed-dog toy at her. 'Nothing happened.'

'Boo to that,' she pouts. 'Since when do you kiss and not tell?'

'When I don't even kiss,' I reply, and Hayley cocks her head to one side.

'Oh dear,' she says. 'And there was me thinking he might have got down on one knee or something – we both know how bananas he is about you.'

'Perhaps not any more,' I reply with a sigh. Then, as Hayley gives me a questioning look, 'It's a good thing, really. Now I know for sure that we really are just friends – that's all we'll ever be, and that's fine.'

'Poor old Billy,' laments Hayley, helping herself to another slice of cake. 'But I suppose you can't force yourself to fancy him.'

Never able to sit still for more than a few minutes at a time, Hayley gets up off the bed and begins to prowl around the room, picking up and examining first a lipstick, then a necklace, before coming to a halt in front of my bookcase. Battered Jilly Cooper novels sit squashed beside the Enid Blyton adventure stories that I devoured growing up, while the shelf below groans under the weight of my *Evangeline And . . .* collection.

I watch as Hayley pulls out the first book in the series and flicks through the pages, smirking at the sight of my literary counterpart.

Right from the start, Anna and David wanted me to see my adoption as a positive thing, and he always made sure that I knew the character of Evangeline the time-travelling adventurer was based on me. Rather than paint her as someone tragic and lost, David had made her a pioneer. Evangeline had been chosen to lead a bigger life than the one she was born into, one where her intrepid spirit and natural courage could help others. This was all very well and made for a series of fun stories, but it also left me forever trying my best to match up to my literary twin.

I had enjoyed the notoriety at first. The *Evangeline And . . .* books began to take off when I was in my final year at primary school, a time when being the centre of attention suited me just fine. It was only when the film rights sold, and four big-budget movies were made during my tricky teenage years, that the comparisons started to rankle. I no longer wanted new acquaintances to know that this globally recognisable character was based on me, because they would inevitably look at me differently once they did. It felt almost as if they would stop trying to get to know the real me. I resented the assumptions they made, not to mention their misguided envy, and as the years passed, I started to dislike the character.

The larger the *Evangeline And . . .* brand grew, the

further I retreated. I went from being the noisy centre of a large circle of friends to spending every spare minute at the stables. Horses judge you purely on your own merits, and I found that most of the people working at the yard had little interest in stories about time-travelling children. There are no airs and graces when you spend the vast majority of your time shovelling manure, and while my family might have been well off as a result of my fictional frenemy's fame, I never acted as if I was, or took advantage of the fact. I think Anna and David did desperately want to spoil me, but aside from delighting in their decision to support my riding obsession with a series of ponies, I resisted their offers of holidays abroad and a new car. The way I saw it, I had a roof over my head, parents who loved me, a handful of trusted friends, a job I was passionate about and a horse, called Suki, that I adored – I didn't need or want anything else.

I look up to find Hayley staring at me, a look of concern beginning to take shape on her face. She has the lived-in skin of someone who spends every season outdoors, and her nails, like Billy's, are framed with the remnants of ground-in dirt. My own hands were not dissimilar once, but the past year's idleness has softened them.

'You've gone pale,' Hayley points out gently. 'Were you thinking about your mum?'

'Which one?' I reply bitterly, and Hayley comes over to sit beside me again.

I already told her the headline facts over the phone: that my birth mother is a woman called Bonnie, and that David and Anna met her before they adopted me. She doesn't know everything, though – I still have one last thing to reveal.

'You said that David knows where she is?' Hayley asks, and I nod.

'He thinks I should go and see her, that it might help me get back to myself somehow – whatever that means.'

'Wow.' Hayley's pale eyes are wide.

'I know.'

'That is huge. Are you going to go?'

My morning cup of tea is still sitting half finished on the floor, and I stare hard at the film that has formed across the top of it. Bringing my knees up to my chest, I wrap my arms around them in an attempt at comfort. When I woke up this morning, both my hands had pins and needles in them because I had been hugging myself so tightly in my sleep.

'Honestly?' I say, and Hayley murmurs encouragingly. 'I don't know. At first, I thought, "No, no bloody way." But now I'm not so sure. David is adamant that it's a good idea, and I do want to make him happy after everything he's been through. But part of me also wants to meet her just so I can shout at her for giving me away in the first place – I guess part of me needs to have it out with her. And maybe if I do, I will feel better. But then again, I could end up feeling even worse than I do now, if that's possible. Oh, I don't know . . .'

My words falter as I realise how weak they sound, and how feeble I'm being about the whole situation.

'This isn't about David,' Hayley observes. 'It's about you and what you need to do.'

'David thinks my life is stuck on hold,' I explain. 'He seems to think that this woman, this stranger, can help me feel normal again. But how can that be? How can meeting the woman who abandoned me make me feel better about losing the one who wanted me?'

Hayley is shaking her head.

'I don't know, Genes.'

For a moment, we just look helplessly at one another, neither of us sure what to say.

Hayley takes a deep breath.

'David is right about one thing, though,' she says quietly. 'About your life, I mean. It does feel like someone has pressed pause on it.'

There isn't anything I can say to that.

'Maybe meeting your birth mother is not what you need at all. Maybe what would really help you is coming back to work at the yard.'

'I don't think so,' I sigh, pleating my quilt between my fingers so I don't have to meet her eyes. 'I honestly don't think I could bear it. Too many memories, and too many empty spaces.'

'Don't you miss it?' Hayley presses. 'The horses, the people, the physicality of it all – me?'

All I can do is sit there, muted as I am by a mixture of exasperation at the situation and frustration towards my own emotions. I was three years old when I first sat on a pony, six when I began taking regular lessons, and nineteen when I began teaching others to ride. For so many years, horses were my passion, my main reason for getting out of bed in the mornings. But now, since I lost my own beloved Suki alongside Anna in such horrifying circumstances, I can barely bring myself to think about them, because it hurts too much.

Hayley jumps as a scatter of rain hits the skylight above us. It has been raining a lot recently, a series of downpours stripping the last of the late autumn leaves from the trees. Soon the landscape will look as it did the day Anna died, and I have no idea how I will bear it; how I will stand to feel the icy wind against my cheeks, and the sight of snow on the ground. My world has become a minefield of reminders, and I am powerless to escape it.

Or am I?

'I'm sorry,' Hayley says, looking from the skylight back to me, and I know how impotent those words must feel to her.

'Do you remember how we used to talk about going backpacking together?' I say then, noting her look of relief at the change of subject. 'We had that map stuck up on the wall at the yard, and we used to plan our route while we cleaned all the tack.'

'Of course I remember that,' she says. 'We ended up spending all the money we'd saved on those dressage saddles instead, didn't we? I left mine over Magnum's stable door and he chewed a hole in it, the cheeky beggar.'

I chuckle.

'Why do you mention that now, anyway?' she enquires, sliding a finger inside her thermal sock to scratch her foot. 'Are you planning on taking a gap year a decade too late or something?'

'Not exactly,' I begin. 'But there is something about this Bonnie woman that I haven't told you yet.'

'Oh?' Hayley lets go of her foot and gives me her full attention.

'She doesn't live here in England,' I tell her, pausing while Hayley takes this in. 'If I really want to find her, then I'm going to have to travel much, much further away.'

Thoroughly intrigued now, Hayley scoots along the bed until half her bottom is resting on my toes.

'How far are we talking?'

For a brief second, I look past her, towards where last year's calendar hangs like a confession of guilt on the wall, still open on December, the month Anna died. If I went away, there would be no memories waiting to ambush me. If I got on a plane, I would swap a cold and harsh winter for a warm and fresh new world. It would allow me the space to breathe, and to think, and maybe even to get some answers about who I am, and why I was given away in the first place. Because no matter what David and Anna told me so reassuringly over the years, the facts remain the same. My birth mother did not want to keep me, and I want to know the reason why.

'She is about as far away as a person can be,' I say. 'My real mother lives in New Zealand.'

4

One of the gifts Anna bought me for my twenty-first birthday was a five-year memory book. Bound in smart navy leather, it has gold lettering on the front, and is small enough to slip into a generous coat pocket. The idea is that you write a few lines each day, marking down anything of note, so that you are able to refer back to it later. So, rather like a diary, but with added meaning and fewer humdrum details.

I was useless at remembering to fill it in at first, but Anna never gave up encouraging me. David eventually joined in, too, merrily repeating what Dr Seuss said about never knowing the value of a moment until it is a memory. Thus inspired – not to mention keen for David to stop lecturing me – I started to fill it in every evening before bed. Soon it became a habit, like taking my multi-vitamin and applying night cream. If I ever went away from home, which was rare, considering how much I loathed to be parted from my horse, the little blue book would always come with me, and when I filled that one, I bought another the same.

Anna confided to me that she had been keeping memory books since she turned twenty-one, too, and would sometimes read me snippets as we sat curled up together on the sofa in front of the fire.

Given the limited space in the book, my adoptive mother had developed a real skill in summing people up in just a few words, and while they weren't always the most complimentary of descriptions, they were always amusing in their simplicity.

Her ex-boyfriend, who she spent two years with before she met and fell in love with David, was referred to as 'Bum bag beard' throughout, while the neighbour who lived in the flat above her first London home was 'Mr Anvil', on account of his clodhopping feet.

My favourites among Anna's memories, however, were the ones involving the two of us. She had scribbled down a memory for every single day we had spent together, and would delight in choosing pages – and years – at random, before recounting them to me.

'Oh my God!' she would cry, hooting with laughter. 'I had forgotten about the time you mistook a tube of mustard for one of toothpaste and chewed a hole in it.'

Apparently, as a baby, I liked nothing more than taking items out of her shopping bags one by one and testing them with my emerging teeth. Anna said she could leave me on the floor for hours, but that every single apple, banana or nectarine she ever put into the fruit bowl would be decorated with tiny fang marks.

At one of my little friends' fifth birthday parties, I was so scared of the clown they hired to do tricks for the kids that I squeezed myself into the airing cupboard up on their landing and got myself stuck behind the water tank. At the end of her memory for that day, Anna had written, 'Comic Relief may pose problems!' and later explained that my resulting terror of all-things red-nosed had even stopped me from wanting to visit Santa's Grotto at the local shopping centre that Christmas, for fear of running into Rudolph.

There were more recent memories, too, of trips to the cinema, dinners out, and even the odd line or two about arguments the two of us had. With the addition of both time and hindsight, both Anna and I were always able to laugh these away with ease, bickering instead over which of us had been the more foolish in said row, then getting the giggles as we realised the irony of what we were doing.

In the weeks after Anna died, I floated around the house like a leaf on the wind, tumbling down to howl in corners and weep across chairs. Occasionally, David and I would find ourselves in the same room, desperate to comfort each other but unable to find the right words. Instead, he would clutch me to him with a fierceness that frightened me, and I would stand there, stock still, my arms by my sides, immobilised by sadness, and with no idea how to bridge the metaphorical gap that had opened up between us.

I didn't forget Anna's memory book so much as not allow myself to think about it, just as I fought not to recall any details about her, or our life together. For a long time, it was easier to remain in a state of flux, somewhere between shock and acceptance. To give in to the grief was too terrifying a prospect, the pain it promised too devastating.

David must have agonised over how to give Anna's most recent memory book to me, but in the end, he did the simplest – and sneakiest – thing and slipped it into the bag I had packed for my flight to New Zealand. Anna had so many folded pieces of paper stuffed in amongst the pages that it didn't stay shut without an elastic band around it, and it was this that I fingered absent-mindedly as I waited to board. There was no way that I could bring myself to open it – not yet. If I turned to the last entry, would I see what Anna had written about that awful final day? A memory that was destined never to be amended by the passing of time, or by the simple beauty of hindsight. How would I ever bring myself to look at it – or at any of her words for that matter?

As well as the book, David had hidden an envelope containing five hundred New Zealand dollars, a credit card and a slip of notepaper bearing my birth mother's name and address. There was also a note from him, which read:

Darling Genie,

The enclosed is for emergencies, but if you run out of money, just call and I can top up your account. I know you're worried about leaving me alone over Christmas, but don't be. This year was always going to be a strange one, and I've had plenty of invitations to spend the day with friends. If at any time you want me to be there with you, let me know and I will get on the next plane. I'm so proud of you for having the courage to do this by yourself, my darling girl, and I know Anna would be too. I have sent her words and love along with you (see zip pocket), which I hope will help. If you feel afraid, just ask yourself what Evangeline would do – she is there with you, too, urging you onwards, as she always has been.

All my love,
Dad xx

If someone had taken me to one side a year ago, and told me that in twelve months' time, I would not only have lost one mother, but I would end up travelling to the other side of the world to find another one, I would have scoffed with disbelief. Yet, here I am, in that exact situation.

There is a crackle of static as a member of the Qantas staff steps up to the desk in front of the gate and leans over the microphone. It is time to begin boarding. As the business class passengers file importantly through the entrance to the jet bridge, I reach into my bag and extract my own memory book. I know without looking that my last entry was 23 December 2017. I know that it reads: 'Suki threw shoe, waited for Billy, so still no presents bought! Will go tmrw.'

And I know what came next.

Firmly folding over to a new, clean page, I note down today's date – 11 December 2018 – then write underneath: 'Fly to New Zealand.' I am about to close the book and stow it back in my bag, when I am struck by a need to acknowledge my missing mum somehow. I want her to know that she is with me in this decision, that she is always with me, and that she has been every moment since she wasn't.

Opening the book to the same page, I hastily scrawl: 'Days without Anna: 352.'

I hadn't even realised that I was keeping count.

5

Having a time-travelling literary character based on you brings with it a certain number of assumptions – the main one being that I myself am an avid traveller, just like Evangeline.

People meeting me for the first time just presume that I went off backpacking in my gap year. Because I must have, right? I am fearless and intrepid; I seek adventure; I wander the world without a backwards glance. I am Julia Roberts in *Eat, Pray, Love* and Leonardo DiCaprio in *The Beach*. Except that I am not.

In truth, I have always been content to remain in the small and secure pocket of my life just the way it is, close to where I grew up in a village outside Cambridge, with more fields and bridleways than buildings and pavements. I consider a two-hour flight to be extreme in terms of distance, so getting myself here to New Zealand has been quite a trial.

I boarded a flight at Heathrow Airport that took me to Dubai, where I wandered, bleary eyes stinging under the many artificial lights, until it was time to go back to the plane. I watched the safety video for the second time, raised polite eyes as the stewardess demonstrated which toggle to pull on the life vest, and wondered if anyone realistically believed that there would be time to place said item over your head in the case of an emergency.

Once we took off again and there was nothing beyond the oval window but blackness, I closed my eyes, twisting the jade-stone ring Anna gave me on my twenty-first birthday around on my finger as I listened to the whirr of the engines, the sporadic ping of call buttons and the muffled suck-whooshing sound of the toilet flush. Time had ceased to matter while I was up there, marooned as I was in the dark, my fate purely dependent on thousands of moving parts over which I had no control. Like life itself, it would only have taken one thing to go wrong for the rest to fall apart.

Now, the luggage carousel below me shuffles and groans into life, and I stare down at the scalloped pattern of the black rubber surface until suitcases, pushchairs and rucksacks begin to roll past. David gave me Anna's old backpack to use on this trip, which is khaki green and covered in sewn-on patches. Unlike me, she was quite the adventurer in her younger years, and explored most of Europe under her own steam. Anna and David's big retirement plan had always been to travel the world together; now they will never get the chance.

Shouldering the heavy pack with a groan, I make my way towards the exit. My journey so far has taken me from London to Dubai to Melbourne to Auckland, and from there down to Queenstown on New Zealand's South Island. I currently have no idea what time it is in the UK, or how many hours I have been in transit, but

I do feel relieved to have finally made it. I am here, I will do what needs to be done, and then I will return to whatever is left of my life back in England.

Outside, the sunshine beats down on me, so strong and sudden that it causes me to stop in my tracks. I know it's summer here in the southern hemisphere, but the ferocity of the heat still takes me by surprise. The jeans I travelled in feel all at once constrictive, and I peel off the thick pashmina that kept me snug on the numerous flights, bundle it up into an untidy ball and stuff it into my rucksack.

All I can see of New Zealand so far is clear blue sky, concrete pathways and the leaves on distant trees. The air is dry and crisp, and as I stand for a while, taking it all in, couples and families filter out past me. There are groups of older teens carrying backpacks, their tanned skin the colour of toffee and their wrists adorned with leather bracelets and coloured twists of string. They all seem to have somewhere to go, or people to meet, and watching them stride around so happily prompts a hollow lurch inside.

I know what David would say if he were here, his head on one side and his bespectacled eyes full of parental encouragement: 'Come on, Genie – think what Evangeline would do.'

That other Evangeline, the natural traveller, the version of me who has always been the bolder, brainier, better. She can sod right off.

*

The journey from the airport to the centre of Queenstown turns out to be a short one. The taxi driver chats away to me as we speed along, but I can barely muster up more than a few words of response because I'm so bowled over by what I can see through the windows. I have never seen mountains so large, or skies so vast. Trees and shrubs look greener here than those in England, the earth beneath them appears somehow richer, and there is a clarity to it all, as if Mother Nature herself has applied a filter to the landscape.

As we join the main highway, I glimpse a rapidly tumbling river far below the road, and high above it, a precarious-looking wooden structure that can only — shudder — be a bungee-jumping platform.

'There she is,' the driver announces, not without pride.

An enormous expanse of water has just come into view in the middle distance.

'That's Lake Wakatipu,' he informs me. 'People around here will tell you that she's the largest lake here on the South Island, but it's not — Te Anau is the queen.'

'Oh,' I say, and the man nods.

'Of course,' he continues, 'Lake Taupo is the real beast, up in the North Island — you could fit Singapore inside her.'

'Blimey,' I reply, trying and failing to envisage this. The driver smiles assuredly at me in the rear-view mirror.

Queenstown itself sits sprawled between Lake Wakatipu and the vast hills that overlook it, and I know already from my limited foray into the guide book that it's regarded as New Zealand's main party town, and that during the winter season, the area transforms into a bustling ski resort. Beyond that, however, I don't know very much about my home for the next two weeks, and while my desire to explore has never been that great, I'm nonetheless intrigued to have a poke around and acquaint myself with the place.

My rental apartment is situated on a steep road not far from the main hub of the town, and after collecting my key from a central reception area, I pop inside just long enough to dump Anna's backpack on the floor, text David and Hayley to let them know that I've arrived safely, and then have a quick shower and change into a simple black sundress. The loneliness that crept over me at the airport continues to linger like an unwanted house guest, and I don't waste any extra time bothering with make-up.

It's nearing five in the afternoon by the time I head off down the hill, but the sun is showing no signs of burning itself out. I was carefully liberal in my application of factor fifty, but I can sense it is a completely different heat here to the fuggy humidity that limps through an English summer – this sun feels almost abrasive in its ferocity. With my blue eyes and pale skin, I'm a prime candidate for burning, and by the time I reach Queenstown's busy Shotover Street, I have resorted to hurrying from one shaded patch of pavement to another.

Car horns honk, buses sigh under the weight of their

human cargo and mopeds weave around backpackers as they swarm out unsteadily from numerous bars. Crossing the street to avoid them, I get caught up in the tail end of a very long queue leading into a takeaway restaurant called Fergburger, and lose a few minutes trying to battle my way out of it. The town's party atmosphere is apparent at every turn, and it's impossible not to notice the mischievousness on the faces of the people I pass. I envy them their freedom and uncomplicated happiness, and it makes me wonder briefly what they see when they look back at me.

I need something to take the edge off what has been a very long and rather surreal day. Heading into the first pub I come across, which has a collection of tatty dark-wood furniture and the same sticky floor as my local back home, I approach a friendly barman who directs me up a set of stairs and out on to a wide, open roof terrace, which has been strung with multicoloured lanterns. There are around twenty people already seated in small groups around low tables, but the tall stools that run along the front of the terrace are unoccupied. Collecting a frothy pint of beer from the bar in the corner, I carry it to the seat furthest away from the other drinkers and clamber up, resting my sandal-clad feet on the metal rungs.

The sun is finally starting to weaken, and a warm breeze jostles the loose strands of my hair that have escaped my ponytail. I take one sip, and then another, enjoying the sensation of the cold beer as it slips down my throat. I sit there on my stool for what feels like hours, chasing away memories and watching as the sunlight streaming across the rooftops turns from the brightest white to the palest gold. More people arrive, and music starts playing from speakers that have been fixed to the walls. I wait until there's a gap at the bar to get up and order another beer. And then, as the volume on the terrace increases, another.

David went to see a grief counsellor after Anna died, and later tried his best to pass on some of the coping strategies she taught him. I was reluctant to listen, just as I had been adamant that I would not seek any help, but I find his words coming to mind now. There is no secret trick to combating your feelings of loss, but a good place to start is by doing something – anything – just to prove to yourself that you can. That could be as simple as cleaning your teeth, or vacuuming the lounge. With each action, a task has been completed. You may feel broken, but you are still there, still capable of movement and of achievements.

Sitting here now, I find that it is enough to simply sip my beer and watch the slanting sunlight. There is nothing else I need to do, and that is OK. For once, the nothing can be my something.

I'm still cast adrift in my own mind when a collective gasp snaps me out of it, and I look up to see a group of paragliders, each one swooping gracefully down from the top of one of the vast hills. They're so high that they could easily have been mistaken for birds, and as I watch them dip and swirl and buffet through the still air, I imagine how I must look to those strapped inside – how small and insignificant in a landscape bustling with life.

The sinking sun has cast a pale pink glow across the clouds above the lake – they look like candyfloss spun right out of the heavens. I stare out from my secluded spot and watch as a passing flock of real birds dives down to wash their delicate feathers in the shifting indigo water.

I don't know whether it's the lack of sleep, or the alcohol, but as I sit here, for once letting everything I'm witnessing simply settle over me, I realise that I am beginning to feel the whispers of something that I haven't felt for a long time.

Hope.

6

It is purely by chance that I spot him.

My first full day in New Zealand begins with a very large brunch at a café tucked away down a side street. I end up lingering far longer than I can make my second cup of coffee last to take advantage of the free Wi-Fi and scroll through each of my social media accounts in turn, scan-reading posts and double-tapping to like pictures. It occurs to me then that one of the best things about being this far away from home is the anonymity it offers, because surely nobody here in Queenstown will work out that I'm linked to the other Evangeline, even if we do share some of the same physical attributes.

After eventually settling the bill, I make my way towards the glistening sweep of Lake Wakatipu, wondering as I do so if my biological mother knows anything about the link between myself and my fictional counterpart – and if so, what she makes of it all. Would the fact that the stories are centred around an abandoned child cause her to feel guilt, or is she too self-centred to be sentimental about the baby she gave away? I have tried so many times to peer into the gaping hole that she left in my life, but never found anything there but emptiness. David and Anna played the role of parents with unfailing kindness and love, but they have only ever been able to fill up half of that wide-open space inside me. The rest remains vacant, waiting to be filled by something – anything – resembling truth.

I reach Queenstown's main harbour area and stroll down to the narrow strip of beach, where the curved tongue of the lake meets the shore. The sun is at full mast, and I watch a group of girls lay out their towels and strip down to their bikinis. I put on a blue-and-white striped sundress with oversized pockets on the front today, which is long enough to hide my pale thighs, but lightweight enough to prevent an episode of sunstroke. After bending myself into the shape of a paperclip this morning in an attempt to apply sun cream to my back, I gave up and instead unearthed a plain white T-shirt to wear under the dress as a cover-up.

According to the weather app on my phone, it's close to thirty degrees on this beach – and it feels it, too. Moisture is collecting on the nape of my neck, and I pause for a moment to tie my hair back into a ponytail. When I was small, Anna used to plait my hair for me before bed. I can still recall how comforted I felt under the gentle touch of her fingers, and I allowed my hair to grow longer as I got older in a bid to draw those moments out. Now, I can't bring myself to get it cut, even though it's almost long enough to sit on.

I distract myself by staring out across the lake, gazing with unseeing eyes at the jagged light dancing across the surface of the water and the vast irregular shapes of the Southern Alps, which are shimmering in the far distance. Anna would have loved it here. She would have been charmed by the quaint but bustling atmosphere of this town and she would have exclaimed over every little detail, pointing out all the things that I will no doubt overlook.

Feeling the familiar throb of unshed tears, I turn my back on the view and hurry across a small bridge, which leads me into a densely wooded park on the opposite shore of the lake. It is a relief to step into the dappled shade of the oak trees and breathe in their earthy scent, and I feel able to remove my sunglasses for the first time since leaving the café. I can hear birds chirping to one another in the canopy of leaves above me as I walk on, and every person I pass looks relaxed and contented. Whether it's the heat or the simple beauty of this setting, I don't know, but it doesn't take long before my emotions settle down again. There is peace here, the lake seems to whisper, and when I venture through the trees and down the stone-strewn bank, I see a sheath of clouds reflected in its surface.

The Maori people call New Zealand Aotearoa, which means 'the land of the long white cloud', and I am beginning to understand why. There is space for such natural creations here, room for everyone and everything to stretch and spread out. Perhaps that is why it feels so relaxed. Back at home, everything is jumbled and stacked together, including the clouds.

*

I see the minibus after I have finished exploring Queenstown Gardens and am making my way back through the centre of town. My heart leaps instantly into my throat when I clock the name emblazoned in bold green letters across its side. Those same two words – Koru Stables – are written at the top of the piece of paper that David gave me; the note bearing the address of my biological mother. I admit, I was immediately intrigued by the fact that my birth mother, similarly to me, had chosen to spend her life surrounded by horses. I had always wondered if I had inherited my passion from her, or even from my father, whoever he was – so when I found out about Koru Stables, I was grudgingly comforted to know that I had been right. Plus, I figured there was more chance of finding common ground with this woman if we had at least some of the same interests. If only I wasn't so afraid to face her.

A complex tangle of intrigue and fear keeps me rooted to the spot, and as I stand there, a group of people appear from the open doorway of a hotel a few yards in front of me. They are led by a tall, dark-haired man with the broad-shouldered build of a rugby player, who smiles widely as he unlocks the side door of the minibus and slides it open.

'In you get, folks,' he says, nodding at each of them as they clamber into their seats. Bringing up the rear is a teenage girl with a spread of wiry dark hair and a puppy in her arms the colour of apricots. She seems a bit unsteady on her feet, as if she's wearing shoes two sizes too big, and the same burly man offers her an arm so that she can lever herself up into the passenger seat more easily.

I know from a Google search at the café this morning that Koru Stables is in Glenorchy, which is close to Queenstown, but not close enough to risk bumping into my errant parent on the street. That element of distance had comforted me until now, and my plan was to spend a few days acclimatising before finding my way to the yard. I definitely did not expect to come across someone who is presumably a member of staff from the stables before I was ready, and now it feels as if the rug of perceived security has been yanked out from under me. All I can do is watch, open-mouthed and immobile, as the man steering the van toots its horn and drives away.

7

As soon as the minibus disappears from view, I'm struck with a powerful urge to run after it. I picture myself tearing along the pavement in my sandals, ducking in and out of backpackers, my hand raised while I shout for the driver to stop and let me on.

I am being ridiculous.

But then, perhaps I should go to the stables now? Get the whole uncomfortable encounter with my birth mother over with?

Buoyed by a sudden flush of courage, I hurry to the rank of idle taxis on the main road and practically throw myself into the back seat of one.

'Koru Stables, Paradise Valley, please,' I say, and the driver turns, eyeing my dress.

'Do you want to get changed first?' he asks. 'I can run you to your hotel on the way?'

'No, thanks,' I reply, my words rushing out across his. 'I'm not going there to ride, so don't worry.'

This seems to satisfy him, but I register definite confusion on his face as he puts the car into gear and drives us out of Queenstown. I sit quietly, taking one deep breath after another to steady myself, but when we reach the highway to the right of the lake, I begin to baulk.

What am I thinking, rushing in like this without a proper plan? This woman might well be my mother, but that doesn't mean she won't turf me out. The last time she saw me I was little more than a few hours old, according to David, and even if she does believe me when I tell her who I am, she may still want nothing to do with me. She has stayed away for all this time, and while things may have changed drastically in my life, her own might be nice and settled just the way it is, without my interruption.

Then again, I counter stubbornly, what does it really matter what *she* wants? The baby she chose to leave behind is a grown woman now – and that woman needs answers. Hell, I *deserve* answers. That is what I'll do – I will ask politely for a private word, then I'll tell her who I am and ask her what happened, why she gave me away, and who my real father is. I have to believe that the sooner I have these fundamental questions answered, the sooner I can begin to fill that empty space inside myself.

Almost as soon as I convince myself, however, I am assailed by thoughts of Anna, of what she would think if she could see me now. Am I being disloyal to her memory simply by being here? But even if I am, is that enough of a reason to turn and run? I can't do that now, not after coming all this way. I have to see this thing through, even if it does feel like a betrayal.

'Not far now,' the driver says cheerfully, half an hour later, his eyes flicking to the rear-view mirror as I fidget and fret in my seat. I hear loose stones crunching under

thick, black brows, a chiselled chin, wide nose and healthy spread of dark stubble. The white short-sleeved shirt he's wearing is branded with the same lettering and Koru Stables logo as the minibus, and his red shorts are streaked with dirt.

He's about to draw level with me, and I have yet to answer his question.

'Hey,' he says. 'Do you speak English?'

He's right in front of me now. His eyes are the faintest green.

'Yes,' I manage. 'Sorry, I just. I was just . . .'

I trail off clumsily, and the man's smile of welcome droops a fraction at the edges. He's looking at me now as if he recognises me, which makes me feel even more flustered than I was in the taxi. To buy myself some time, I feign a small coughing fit, then take a deep breath and force my features into what I hope is a confident expression.

'I wonder if you can help me?' I say politely, hearing the tremble in my voice. 'I'm looking for Bonnie, Bonnie Moon. I was under the impression that she works here.'

'That's right,' he says, folding his sturdy arms across his chest.

'Is she here?' I ask, standing on tiptoes in order to peer cautiously over his shoulder towards the yard. Half the assembled group from the bus have mounted their steeds now, and one of the horses has promptly carried its helpless rider over to a patch of grass and dropped its head down to eat.

'Pull one rein hard,' I want to instruct, but keep my tongue tucked firmly behind my teeth.

'You a friend of hers, then, eh?' the man asks now, and this time my reply is a sad sort of sigh.

'It's . . .' I begin, seeing him narrow his eyes. He doesn't look confused by my random blathering so much as curious, and I'm encouraged by the fact that his smile is yet to fade completely.

'She knows me, yes, but it's complicated,' I say, trying to appeal to him with my eyes. 'I just really need to speak to her – and I've come a long way,' I hasten, as if that much was not already obvious from my pale skin and British accent, which has for some reason become more like that of the Queen since I started talking to him.

'What's your name, then?' he wants to know, his arms still crossed. 'Might Bonnie have mentioned you?'

I very much doubt that she would have.

'Genie,' I tell him, offering my hand. 'Genie Nash.'

'Kit,' he replies, shaking it. His hand is so large that my own completely disappears within its grasp.

'And you're from England?' he checks.

I nod.

'Well, that's just plain weird,' he says, unfolding his arms and scratching behind his ear, 'because Bonnie actually left for England two days ago.'

8

Bonnie

Bonnie closed the bedroom door and sat down at the desk. The curtains were pulled across the window, but she could hear the lashing of rain against the glass and was grateful for its gentle disruption in the otherwise silent space.

She had got herself to England, and that alone felt almost unreal to Bonnie, because she'd sworn she would never come back. That was life, though – unpredictable, unfathomable and undeniable. All you could do was strap yourself in and hope for the best. Her father would have called it 'rolling with the punches', but Bonnie had never cared much for that phrase. Why was it that people so often plotted the route of their lives from one hurt to the next, rather than focusing on the moments of happiness, or love? She knew that she was guilty of the former, but while there had been darkness in Bonnie's life, there had also been light, and it was this that had taught her the most about herself.

When Bonnie had touched down at Heathrow Airport earlier that same day, the courage that had got her on to the plane deserted her, leaving nothing in her tank for what she had planned to do next. Instead of taking the Piccadilly Line to King's Cross, where she could catch a train up north to Cambridge, Bonnie had stalled for the best part of an hour in the arrivals lounge, before eventually opting for a taxi. A taxi that she instructed to drive in the opposite direction.

The gap between herself and her reason for coming to England still felt too great. She needed to bridge it somehow, create not an olive branch but a whole tree – one that she could then use to make her approach. Bonnie knew her time was limited, but she also knew that it would be foolish to rush something so important. This was the best chance she had at explaining herself, and she must take it.

Pausing a moment longer to gather her thoughts, Bonnie listened to the sound of the rain, and searched inside herself for a beginning. As the sky outside the house began to darken and the moon glowed bright among the stars, Bonnie picked up her pen and began to write.

I arrived in London for the first time on 5 October 1991. It was a Saturday, and the station concourse at Paddington was crowded with people rushing this way and that. I remember that I glanced instinctively up towards the vast glass ceiling as soon as I stepped off the train, searching for any remaining signs of the IRA bomb that had gone off in there a little under eight months previously. There were none – everything had been patched up – and I made a mental note to let my folks know when I next called them.

All I had heard for the past few months, you see, was scaremongering about how dangerous London was, and how terrorists were intent on blowing up the entire city and everyone in it. I wanted to reassure them that I was safe, but underneath that was a need to prove them wrong, too. I had insisted on taking this trip – no, strike that – I had pleaded and begged that they let me go. No way was I going to end up running home to New Zealand like they – and every other blighter – assumed I would.

There is something you should know about the eighteen-year-old me before we go any further with this story. That girl was impulsive. Now, you may think that's a good trait, but when you couple it with naivety, which I also had by the bloody shovel-load, then it becomes slightly more problematic. My folks knew this, of course – they suspected that my desire to go on a big adventure would only get me so far, before my lack of experience caused me to screw up in some monumental way. Either that, or homesickness would get the better of me.

In the end, of course, it was a combination of both those things – but I have never regretted a minute of it. I wanted to make that clear from the outset, before I tell you the story of what happened, because I know what you must think of me. Hell, I bet it's nothing I haven't thought about myself over the years. But the truth is, even after everything that went on, and all that I have gone through since, I would not change a single moment of it.

And that's because of you.

Bonnie paused, her pen hovering above the page as she read back over the words she had just written. Was she coming across as too flippant? Should she take out the word 'bloody' and replace it with something less crass? Then again, she mused, wasn't the whole point of this exercise to show her daughter who she really was – and didn't she use swear words on a daily basis, some far worse than the innocuous 'bloody'?

With a sigh, Bonnie sat up, dropping the pen on to the tabletop and stretching out her legs. She had barely slept on the multiple flights, too strung up by nerves to concentrate on any of the films or TV shows on offer. Eventually, she had found a playlist in the entertainment bundle entitled 'chill time', only to find that not even panpipes and gentle chanting could soothe her jittery heart.

She should sleep on it, that's what she should do.

There was a crash from one of the downstairs rooms, and Bonnie guessed that her host was starting to prepare supper for the two of them. Again, she marvelled at how accommodating her old friend was being. After all, it wasn't every day that a person you hadn't seen for over twenty-five years turned up on your doorstep without warning, then proceeded to bawl like an agitated baboon.

'Bon, love?'

She was calling up the stairs now. Bonnie got to her feet and trudged in her socks over to the bedroom door. The landing was painted purple and smelled faintly of lavender – probably thanks to the bowl of potpourri on the windowsill. The sight of such a chintzy and dated item brought tears back to Bonnie's eyes, and she blinked them away with a smile.

'Yeah?' she replied.

'Dinner in half an hour – and I've opened a bottle of red.'

Bonnie thought of her page of scribbled words, of how much more of the story she had yet to tell, and how much tougher it was going to get before she reached the end. She was glad that she was not alone, but then, she thought, as she switched off the bedroom light and made her way towards the inviting warmth of her old friend's kitchen, perhaps she never really had been.

9

It takes me a full minute to process what Kit has said. A whole sixty seconds where I simply stand, my mouth ajar, gazing at him in disbelief.

'Bonnie's gone to England?'

Kit makes a show of checking his watch.

'Should be there by now, I reckon,' he says. 'At least, I hope she is, otherwise it means the poor old coot got lost somewhere en route.'

He is clearly amused. I am anything but.

'Did she say why?' I ask, clutched with a sudden fear that the reason might be me. Could my biological mother be trying to find me at the exact same time that I am trying to find her? No, why on earth should she? But then why is she there? Why now, on this week of all weeks?

Kit puts his head on one side. He appears to be sizing me up, deciding whether or not I can be trusted with an answer. I feel too scrutinised to meet his gaze, so I stare instead at the lettering on his shirt. I hadn't noticed before that the 'O' of 'Koru' is a spiral shape, while the 'K' has been shaped to look like a horse rearing up on its hind legs.

'To tell you the truth,' Kit continues, 'Bon didn't

actually give me a reason as such – just told me she had something important to do and asked me to keep an eye on Tui.'

'Right,' I say, distracted. Kit shifts his boots through the dirt.

'Are you feeling all right there?' he asks as I sway to the right. 'Come on, let's get out of this heat, yeah?'

I follow him over to the shed-cum-office, keeping my eyes on his back rather than the nearby horses.

'Here.' Kit takes a can of Coke out of a small glass-fronted fridge and passes it to me.

'Sit if you like,' he adds, gesturing to a battered yellow sofa that has been pushed up against the wall.

I do as he says and sit down, while Kit perches on the edge of a wide wooden desk, folding his arms across his chest once again and looking at me in the same way Anna used to look at the cryptic crossword in the Sunday paper.

'Thanks,' I murmur after a moment, cracking open my drink and taking one sip, then another. I find that I'm very thirsty, and the sweetness of the cola brings me back to myself a bit.

'Sorry,' I say, 'I'm not usually like this. You must think that I'm a right weirdo.'

I try a smile, and he follows suit, unfolding his tattooed arms and sticking his hands deep into the pockets of his shorts.

'Bonnie knew me a long time ago, when I was a child,' I blunder on, wondering as I say it why I feel the need to explain myself to this man – this total stranger. Perhaps it's because there is an aura of kindness surrounding Kit, and for reasons I don't completely understand, I feel as if I can trust him. Just not enough to tell him the whole truth, of course.

'She knew my parents,' I tell him, the need to embellish my story fuelled by his silence. 'That's how I got this address, and I just, you know, thought it might be nice to surprise her with a visit.'

Kit takes this in, a slight frown casting lines across his forehead, and I wonder how much he knows. Is Bonnie the sort of woman who would be open about her past? Would she confess to giving up her own child?

'How long are you planning on sticking around?' Kit asks, only for the phone on the desk to ring. I wait while he answers, listening in silence as he jokingly chastises the caller about a late delivery of sugar beet.

'Where were we?' he prompts, replacing the receiver in its cradle and rooting through the mess of papers on the desk until he locates a pen, which he uses to write something on the back of his hand.

'You were asking me how long I was in New Zealand for,' I remind him, and he nods, giving me his full attention once again. Kit looks quite unlike any man I have ever seen before, and the more I take in his broad shoulders, pale green eyes and easy, relaxed manner, the more I warm to him.

'And?' he presses.

I lift my shoulders in a half-shrug. 'I was planning to stay for two weeks or so, but—'

Kit interrupts me with a laugh.

'Two weeks?' he exclaims. 'Strewth! You've flown all the way here from England and you're only staying for a fortnight? You can barely tickle the udders of this place in that time.'

I finish my Coke and start looking around the office in search of a bin.

'Well, I'm not really here to sightsee,' I counter. 'I came to see Bonnie.'

'Hell of a long way to come and a heap of money down the gurgler just for a visit,' he says, not unkindly. 'I'm guessing she must be pretty damn important to you.'

I emit a small, non-committal 'Mmm', and Kit leans across and plucks the empty can from my hands, crunching it effortlessly between his own.

'Well, if it's Bon you came for, I'd suggest you change your return flight,' he says. 'She told me she'd be away on her big OE for at least three weeks, if not longer.'

It feels as if he's just slammed a door shut in my face. 'OE?'

'Overseas experience,' he explains. 'Sorry, Kiwi lingo.'

'Right.'

I can't even muster up enough energy to feel despondent. I feel as if I could lay down my head on this tatty old sofa and sleep until Bonnie returns from England – perhaps forever. Giving in to weariness, I slump back against the cushions, shutting out the sight of Kit, of his consideration and decency. I wanted this to be simple; I wanted to get in, meet Bonnie, get some answers, and get out.

I feel the sofa shift and open my eyes to find that Kit has sat down beside me. He's far enough away that our legs aren't touching, but I can still sense the heat of him.

'Are you staying somewhere around here?' he asks, and I respond with a limp smile.

'In Queenstown,' I say. 'I got a taxi out here, but now I'm not sure what . . .'

I trail off yet again, and Kit's expression softens.

'Don't worry – I have to drive this latest group back into town in an hour or two, so you're welcome to hop in the gas guzzler at the same time, if you like?'

'Thank you,' I rush out, relief at his offer colliding with humiliation that I should have done something so dumb. 'That would be really helpful – if you're sure it's not a problem?'

As much as I want to get away from this discombobulating place and back to the relative safety of my little apartment, where I can lock the door behind me and pretend that this afternoon never happened, I'm surprised to find that I also feel forlorn at the idea of leaving. I really must be cracking up.

'No worries,' Kit replies cheerfully, standing up again before I get the chance to say anything else. 'I just need to head out into the yard and get a bit of graft done – you happy to hang out in here for a bit? Or,' he adds with a wry grin, 'you could always shovel some dung?'

I'm just about to reply when sounds of a kerfuffle filter in from outside, followed by high-pitched giggling, and the next second the teenage girl from the minibus erupts noisily into the room, the little caramel-coloured dog following closely at her heels.

'He's after me! He's after me!' she yelps, darting behind Kit and collapsing into peals of deep, throaty laughter. The little dog sits back on its haunches then springs forward straight through Kit's legs, and starts attacking the girl's shoelaces.

'B-B-Beeeea!' she cries, swatting half-heartedly at the puppy between bouts of mirth and loud hiccups. 'Don't bite me, Bea. Don't you do that. Naughty boy.'

Kit is evidently very amused, and I remain mute on the sofa as he bends over and scoops the offending mutt up from behind his ankles.

'Are you chewing Tui's shoes again, little mister?' he says in a mock-stern voice, waggling an authoritative finger as he lifts the dog up to his face. 'Now, what have we talked about?'

The girl stops laughing and gazes up at the puppy, her attention fully focused and her feet shuffling from side to side on the dusty floor. I had guessed her to be in her mid-teens when I saw her earlier, but her child-like behaviour suggests she is far younger. She hasn't looked at me once since bursting into the office.

'Oh, B-B-B Beeea,' she croons, holding out her hands for the puppy and then beaming when Kit lowers him gently into them. The dog looks up at his mistress and wags his stubby tail, licking her on the tip of her nose until she starts giggling all over again.

'Off you go, you pair of bitsers,' Kit jokes, pointing towards the open doorway and grinning broadly as Tui gallops back through it. 'And don't get into any trouble!' he calls after them, before turning back to face me. 'Sorry about that,' he says, fists on hips. 'Tui can be a handful, but she's a corker.'

'She seems it,' I say, standing up from the sofa. 'A corker, I mean.'

I'm smiling genuinely as I say it, but Kit looks thoughtful.

'I know Bonnie's struggled with her at times over the years,' he replies, his pale eyes narrowing. 'But she loves her so much, you know? The two of them make a great team.'

As the meaning of his words begins to penetrate, it feels as if all the warmth is being drained from the room.

'A good team?' I repeat nervously.

Someone shouts something in the yard, and Kit glances over my shoulder, giving me a precious few seconds to steel myself for what I know he will say next.

'That's right,' he confirms, giving me a look laced with even more curiosity than before. 'I guess you didn't know? Tui is Bonnie's daughter.'

10

I put the call through to David as soon as I shut the apartment door behind me, not checking or caring what time it is back in the UK. It takes him an age to answer, and he sounds half asleep when he does.

'Genie?'

'She's in England,' I say, my voice high and shrill. 'Bonnie is in England. She left New Zealand two days ago and now she's where I was and I'm here, on the opposite side of the goddamn world to her!'

There's a grumble of sorts from the other end of the line.

'It's five in the morning, Genie – hang on a minute.'

David dares to yawn.

I am powerless to stop the red mist from descending, and I begin to pace furiously around the apartment as I wait for him to come to his senses.

'I don't care what time it is!' I rant. 'For God's sake, Dad.'

I haven't called David 'Dad' since I was about nine years old, and the word causes us both to fall silent for a moment. He decides not to comment, instead telling me again to 'give him a minute'. There's a rustling noise as he presumably clambers out of bed, and a short while later, I hear the unmistakable sound of a kettle revving into life.

'I need coffee,' he croaks. 'Then I can think straight.'

'Why the hell would she go to England? Do you think it's because she wants to see me?' I am asking myself the question almost as much as I'm pleading with David to answer it. I can hear him clanking about in cupboards and picture him flat-footing around the kitchen. Anna redecorated that room not long before she died – she was so proud of it.

'Did you tip her off?' I demand. 'Did you write to Bonnie and warn her that I was coming?'

David sighs.

'Why would I do that, Genie? I want you to meet each other.'

There's another pause as the water finishes boiling, and David clears his throat.

'Even if I had, that wouldn't explain why she came here. Surely if she wanted to see you and knew you were on your way, then she'd just stay put.'

He's right, of course, but I am not in the mood to admit that I might not be.

'But do you think she's in England looking for me, though?' I say. 'The timing could be a weird coincidence.'

'I suppose it's possible, darling,' David allows. 'But it could be for another reason entirely – perhaps she has other friends here.'

He pauses then, as if something has occurred to him that he doesn't want to share with me.

'What were you going to say?' I demand.

'Nothing,' he assures me. 'I was just thinking out loud, poppet, that's all. I honestly don't know enough about Bonnie's life to give you a decent answer, but if she does happen to turn up here looking for you, then of course you will be the first to know.'

'What shall I do now, though?' I lament, frustration making me collapse on to the bed. 'Should I get a flight back? Or shall I wait? I just got here, though. Oh, I don't know what to do.'

The tiredness that came over me in the little office at Koru Stables earlier returns like a sullen thump, and I feel suddenly so weary that I can barely lift my head off the pillow. In the weeks immediately after Anna's death, I slept more than I ever had before. My unconscious state became my safe place, somewhere I could curl up and forget what had happened.

'Who told you Bonnie was in England?' David asks now, dragging me back to the present. 'Someone at the stables?'

'That's the other thing,' I tell him, fighting to keep my voice steady. 'It turns out that I'm not Bonnie's only child, just the only one she didn't want to keep. She has another daughter, a girl called Tui. I saw her today.'

There's a profound silence as David takes this in.

'Oh, gosh. Are you sure?' he asks. His voice sounds strange and constricted. 'It's definitely Bonnie's child? Not her stepdaughter or something?'

I picture Tui's wide grin and tangled black hair and

recall her joyful, mischievous nature. I assume the fact that she is my actual living relative, the first one I've ever met, is yet to properly sink in, because my response so far has been to remain stoic. Kit had no reason to lie to me about who she is – in fact, he doesn't seem to me to be the type of person to lie about much – but despite knowing that it's true, I can't feel it yet, or appreciate what it means. My lips can say the words and my ears can hear them, but my heart has simply slammed its doors. I came to New Zealand to find my mother – that in itself is big enough. I don't have it in me to take on anything more than that – not yet, anyway.

'As far as I'm aware, Tui is one hundred per cent Bonnie's real child.'

I feel guilty for being so overwrought. It's not David's fault this has happened – he's not to blame for Bonnie doing a disappearing act – but despite this, I can't seem to shake off my sour temper.

'It must have been very strange to suddenly be presented with a sister,' he allows, and I nod into the handset, a sob rearing up in my throat.

David then insists that I hang up to save my mobile-phone bill, and calls me back a few minutes later, when I've had time to compose myself. We talk for another half an hour or so, until he's sure that I've calmed down. I tell him a bit about Kit, Tui and Queenstown – but neither of us mentions Anna. I don't tell him how it felt to be so close to those horses today, either, because I know what he would say. He would tell me that it's time to get back in the saddle. He would say that it wasn't my fault I chose to go Christmas shopping that day instead of taking Suki out for a ride, and that it was in no way wrong of me to allow Anna to go in my place, as she so often had before. He would insist, as he had countless times over the past year, that I could not have foreseen my horse's catastrophic reaction to the car backfiring while she and Anna were on the road, and that it would have made no difference who was up in the saddle that day. He would tell me that Suki was just an animal, and that animals can be unpredictable and skittish. Anna falling off and landing badly was the fault of nothing but bad luck – the same cruel twist of fate that caused Suki to bolt away afterwards into the path of another car, breaking two of her legs in the process. It was not fair, but it was done, and neither blame nor guilt could change the facts or bring either of them back. He had said it all before, and I had listened and nodded. But I had never believed. David did not know what happened the day before Anna left for the yard; he doesn't know what I said, which I can now never take back. I would give anything to go back to that moment and shake some sense into myself. *Anything.*

'I think you should stay where you are,' David says eventually, answering the question I had asked him right at the start of our conversation.

'Bonnie is bound to head home at some stage, back to New Zealand. If you come here now, the two of you risk overlapping again and you might miss her, but if you stay put, you're guaranteed to find each other in the end.'

'I suppose that makes sense,' I allow. 'But Kit told me she would be away for at least three weeks. That means I will definitely have to spend Christmas here, and potentially New Year's Eve, too.'

'Is that such a bad thing?' he asks, and I think before I reply. It is true that the idea of being home for the festivities with David – but no Anna – filled me with enough dread to embark on this trip in the first place, but I am also unnerved by the prospect of being completely alone, too. Before I can say as much, though, David beats me to it.

'We can Skype on the day,' he suggests. 'And afterwards you can sunbathe. Think of that!'

'I never sunbathe,' I remind him, but I appreciate his attempt at jollying. I only have to get through two potentially difficult and isolated days, really – and Queenstown is a party town. There are sure to be places open on Christmas Day, so drinking myself into oblivion is a viable – if foolhardy – option.

'I can get through Christmas,' I say determinedly. 'But what am I going to do until then?'

I curse the words almost as soon as I utter them, because I know what David will say. I wait for the indulgent chuckle that always pre-empts any utterance relating to his beloved storybook character, then clench my teeth together in anticipation.

'Well, that's easy,' he says, all chirpy now. 'You just have to ask yourself what Evangeline would do.'

11

Bonnie

Exhausted from her long journey and soothed by half a bottle of very good red wine, Bonnie had forgotten to close the bedroom curtains before she got into bed the previous night, but it was not the light that woke her. A message had come through from Tui at around five a.m., saying that she loved and missed her – and that Beavis had chewed a big hole through the toe of one of her shoes, so could Bonnie bring her a new pair back from England. Bonnie had got her daughter a mobile in case of emergencies, and as far as she knew, Tui only had three phone numbers stored in there – her dad Simon's, Bonnie's and Kit's. No doubt Kit was mainly subjected to lots of texts telling him to bring her a 'surprise' from the shop. He had been treating her to toys, chocolates and trinkets since she was a toddler, and the habit had stuck.

Leaving Tui behind in New Zealand to come here to England was the hardest thing that Bonnie had ever had to do. Well, she countered internally – the second hardest. She had been absolutely fine, right up until the point when the plane began to taxi to the runway, and then she'd started to panic. A cold sweat had crept over her in seconds, and her hands had begun to shake so violently that the man in the seat next to her, presumably thinking that she had a severe fear of flying, offered her a sip of brandy from a hip flask in his inside pocket.

She had not expected to feel suddenly nineteen again, sitting on a different plane, but with the same overwhelming feelings of dread and regret. She knew it was instinct kicking in, and that it was only natural that she should feel nervous about leaving Tui – especially as she'd never done so before – but she could not shake the sense of wrongness that came with it. It had felt wrong to leave London all those years ago, and now it felt wrong to leave New Zealand.

Bonnie had replied to Tui's message immediately, reassuring her that yes, of course she would bring her some new shoes, but that it might be an idea to keep her existing pairs in a cupboard, or up on a shelf. Beavis the puppy had been a birthday present earlier in the year – one that Tui had begged and begged for until Bonnie gave in.

With a yard to run, lessons to teach and Tui to look after, the last thing she really needed was a tiny tearaway chewing up her house, but the change in Tui since having her own dog to look after had been remarkable. She took on the role of 'mummy' from the very first day, for once not minding when Bonnie chided her gently for being heavy-handed, and displaying a soft, nurturing side that Bonnie had not seen in her before. She quickly went from never letting the pair of them out of her sight to actively chasing them out to play unsupervised in the garden or the yard. Tui had friends, both at the stables and at school, but none of them expressed as much unbridled joy to be around her as Beavis did. Plus, being a dog, he was mercifully free from the pity or judgement that Tui, with her myriad difficulties, often faced from the humans she came into contact with. Beavis accepted and adored Tui just as she was, and Bonnie now wished that she hadn't waited so long to get him.

She had been left in the house alone today, as her host had errands to run, so Bonnie moved from the upstairs bedroom to the kitchen table, and once again read through what she had written the day before. The sooner she had everything written down and clear in her mind, the sooner she'd be able to embark upon what she really came to England to do. She wished she had come up with the idea of writing down her story before leaving New Zealand, rather than as an antidote to the crushing panic she'd experienced when she arrived in England. If she had, she would not only have been better prepared to face Evangeline, but she also wouldn't have had to spend so much time away from Tui.

With one final fortifying gulp of the coffee sitting on the table beside her, a re-energised Bonnie once again picked up her pen.

The first thing that struck me about London was how little space there seemed to be. In New Zealand, where I grew up, people tend to build outwards when constructing their homes, but in your capital city, everything felt to me as if it had been shoved one on top of the other. There were so many people, too, and so much bloody traffic. I wasn't so naive that I expected London to be quiet, but I still found the whole place a bit much, and that feeling never really left me, I suppose. I was in the country for over a year in the end, but it still felt alien to me by the time I left. I was like the odd piece of a jigsaw puzzle that has somehow ended up in the wrong box, so as much as I tried to fit myself in, there were always gaps around my edges.

I found a bed at a hostel on Euston Road and a job five minutes' walk from there at a little place called Sunrise Café. The owner, Tracey, asked me two questions – could I make a decent cuppa, and could I start straight away? When the answer to both was a resounding 'yes', she gave me the job on the spot. I had all these grand ideas about exploring the city on my days off, but in the end, I spent most of those first few weeks either out with my friends from the hostel, or picking up extra shifts. I enjoyed having a purpose, you see, and I loved spending time with Tracey, too. She quickly became like a mother to me, even though she couldn't have been more different to my own mum back home – she was twenty years younger than her for a start.

My mum was forty-five when she had me, which is the same age as I am now, and she and my dad had long before given up any hope of me coming along. They had done all *the tests, been poked and prodded and all that, but nobody could find any medical reason why a baby was not forthcoming. When my mum did fall pregnant, my dad was so terrified that she would miscarry that he refused to let her work, which I'm sure drove her around the bloody bend. I know it would have me, but then I was never that much like my parents. Not at eighteen, anyway. They were content never to travel beyond the boundaries of New Zealand, whereas I always craved adventure, and wanted to see as much of the world as I could. My plan was to begin in England, then travel through Europe and perhaps even America. Now, however, when I look back and try to remember why I wanted to do it so much, all I can conclude is that I didn't even know myself at that stage – not really. Now that I'm older (and maybe even a tiny bit wiser, although I am reluctant to roll out that ancient cliché), I know that I am somebody who prefers the security and comfort of home, and of things and people that I know and understand. Change scares me now, but when I was eighteen, it was what I wanted more than anything else.*

I've gone off on a bloody tangent again, haven't I? That is typical of me, I'm afraid. Let's get back to the story.

So, it was while working at Sunrise Café that I met the two people who were destined to change my life forever. One was called Seth, and the other—

Bonnie jumped as the back door into the kitchen opened, her pen skidding across the page and drawing a line through the final few words she had just written.

75

'All right there, duck?'

Tracey beamed across at Bonnie as she unwound her pink scarf. It looked as if the wind that was howling its way around the house had left a bright spot of colour on each of her cheeks, but as Tracey ventured further into the room, Bonnie realised that it was, in fact, a double helping of blusher. Tracey always had been a fan of the more-is-more approach to make-up and now, at the very respectable age of seventy, she still looked just as glamorous as she had all those years ago. The majority of the clientele at Sunrise Café had been workmen and engineers who came in for breakfast after their long night shifts, and Tracey used to joke that it was her duty to provide them with a pretty face to enjoy alongside their mugs of tea and bacon butties.

Bonnie held up her palms in a gesture of defeat.

'I'm getting there,' she said. 'But I think it's going to take longer than I expected. I keep losing track of the story I'm trying to tell.'

Tracey plonked a carrier bag down on the worktop and extracted first some milk, then a punnet of red grapes, which she put down in front of Bonnie.

'A treat,' she explained. 'Go on – they're good for you.'

Bonnie popped one into her mouth.

'Thanks. And thanks again for letting me stay. You didn't have to say yes, you know.'

Tracey gave her a look.

'I wasn't about to let you roam the streets now, was I?' she chided, and Bonnie chuckled.

'I would have gone to a hotel – I'm not bloody destitute.'

'Pah.' Tracey waved a perfectly manicured hand in the air as she put a packet of salmon fillets into the fridge.

'I was going to get steak, but my teeth aren't up to that any more,' she said regretfully. 'Honestly, love, I'm telling you now, never get old – it's a trap.'

Bonnie felt her smile falter, and plucked off another grape.

'I'm scared, Tracey,' she said in a small voice. 'I'm scared that I've come all this way, and she won't agree to see me.'

Tracey abandoned the shopping and pulled out a chair. Bonnie could see the foundation that had settled in the creases around her mouth – lines no doubt left there from that twenty-a-day smoking habit she'd had back in the nineties.

'Oh, pet.' Tracey placed a hand over hers. 'I'm sure she will. I would be willing to bet that she's every bit as interested in you as you are in her – how could she not be?'

'She probably hates me.' Bonnie let out a long sigh. 'I wouldn't blame her if she did.'

'Thoughts like that will get you nowhere,' Tracey said. 'Fact is, you're here now. You came for a reason, and you're going to see this thing through, even if I have to march you to that girl's door myself. And don't think that I won't.'

Bonnie had to smile at that.

'I know you would,' she agreed. 'Hopefully, after she reads this,' she added, motioning towards the sheaf of papers on the table, 'then it will help her to understand.'

'You were so young when it all happened,' soothed Tracey, letting go of Bonnie's hand and standing up. 'I'm sure she'll be sympathetic when she hears what you went through.'

Bonnie nodded, but the gesture belied the truth. Because how could she realistically expect her lost daughter to understand the reasons why she had given her up, when she, Bonnie, had yet to figure all of them out for herself?

12

I can't remember a time that I didn't think about who my real mother might be, but it was during my teenage years that I obsessed about her the most. I would sit at my dressing table and stare at myself in the mirror, trying to guess which of my features I had inherited from her. Did she have the same bright blue eyes as me? The same thick, dark hair? Was her Cupid's bow slightly asymmetric? Did she squint when she was concentrating? Was there a cluster of moles behind her right ear? Did she have to pencil in the middle part of each eyebrow, where they thinned inexplicably?

Whenever I lost my temper over silly things as an adolescent, I would pile the blame for my behaviour at my absent mother's feet. If I was being unreasonable, then it was because she had passed on the trait; if I was rejected by a boy that I had a crush on at school, it was her attributes that had put him off. It was easier to hang all the things I didn't like about myself on the shoulders of a stranger than to consider that they were down to me. It was my way of staying angry with this person, this unknown, shadowy figure who just happened to be my mother. Even when the hormones calmed down a fraction and I began to grow up and accept responsibility for my own actions, the ashes of that disgruntlement, once such a hot and furious furnace, continued to smoulder.

My head told me repeatedly that I didn't need to know anything about this woman – that I shouldn't want to know anything about her. But my heart . . . Well, that was a different matter. David and Anna admitted that my mother was young when she gave birth to me, but they knew far more about her than just that. They knew her name, for starters, so at any given time, I could simply have typed it into Google – although I am still yet to do so. They also knew that she lived in New Zealand – another fact that would have set me on my way towards finding her. David has assured me that the reason they never told me any details was because Bonnie had made them promise they would not – but I'm not so sure that's the whole story. I know how much I meant to the two of them – especially Anna – and it's not that much of a stretch to imagine that the desire to keep Bonnie and me apart could have come from her. But even if that was the case, it doesn't explain why Bonnie herself didn't come to find me. Why has it been left up to me to do the chasing?

What would Anna say if she could see me now, here in New Zealand, hunting for the woman whose daughter she had raised as her own? Would she understand my reasons for needing to do so, or condemn me for them? David has encouraged me to be here, it's true, but ultimately, the decision was mine and mine alone. I wanted to come; I can't deny that.

Deciding to try my best to push these thoughts to the back of my mind, I concentrate on getting ready for my second full day in New Zealand. I start by applying copious layers of high-factor sun cream, then laboriously twist my hair into a low bun and reach for my straw trilby. Despite covering up carefully yesterday, I still managed to burn both my nose and the tips of my ears – the heat here is like nothing I have ever experienced before. I feel like a jacket potato in a microwave.

I left my number with Kit, who promised to drop me a covert text if Bonnie turns up sooner than expected, so my plan for today is a simple one: locate a bench in the shade of a tree and read the novel I bought back at Heathrow Airport. I am determined to do something that takes my mind off Bonnie, off Anna, off everything that is causing my emotions to flounder, and getting lost amidst the pages of a good book feels like my best bet. There is a lot more of Queenstown I have yet to explore, but I figure that can wait another day or so. After all, it doesn't look as if I'm going anywhere anytime soon.

I pack my travel guide into a bag, along with some sun cream, an extra toggle – mine are forever snapping under the weight of my hair – and a bottle of water, and head off in the direction of Queenstown Gardens beside the lake.

It is not yet ten a.m., but already groups of young travellers are stretched out in rows on the tiny beach. It baffles me how they can lounge there all day. What was it Anna always used to say as she rubbed cream into my bare skin as a child? 'There's no such thing as a healthy tan.'

I reach the gardens and pause for a moment to gaze up between the branches of the red-and-black oak trees. The flat leaves are barely stirring in the calm, still air, and I can hear the insistent buzz of insects busily going about their days.

As before, the lure of the lake proves too strong to resist, and I pick my way slowly over the stony shore-line, passing an idle tyre swing hanging from a willow branch, before settling down on a clear patch of ground. I'm wearing pale-blue denim shorts and a thin green shirt today, which I've knotted at my waist. I haven't bothered with make-up, save for a light coating of mascara, and my only jewellery is my treasured jade-stone ring and some gold stud earrings.

How Anna would have loved this place, I can't help but think, just as I did the first time I ventured into these gardens. How cruel and unfair that she will never get to see it. If I could swap places with her now, be gone while she lives on, then I would.

I'm just about to take my book out of my bag when there's a loud shriek from somewhere behind the treeline and a girl erupts down the bank and runs with arms flailing to the water's edge, barely pausing for breath before jumping up and leaping on to the tyre swing. A moment later, a small dog follows suit, yapping excitedly at the girl's feet as she lifts them upwards.

'Tui,' I whisper in recognition, just as a loud male voice bellows her name, and the next moment Kit is through the trees, too, a grin on his face and a Frisbee in his hand.

'If you keep running off like a naughty little puppy,' I hear him say to Tui, 'then I'll have no choice but to put you on a lead.'

I should stand up, or call out to them, but before I have a chance to decide which, Kit turns his head and sees me sitting there.

'Genie?' he calls, and I nod, lifting a hand of greeting that turns into a wave.

'Hey.'

Kit's smile spreads even wider as he starts crunching over the stones towards me.

'Push me, push me!' yells Tui, and Kit stops abruptly in his tracks, raising his hands to the heavens.

'It's OK,' I call out. 'Wait a sec and I'll come to you.'

I stand up and brush the dirt from my shorts, feeling a flush of heat envelop my cheeks as I gather up my bag and slip my feet back into my sandals. As I straighten up from fastening the straps, I find that two more people have joined Kit and Tui beside the water – a man and a woman, both of whom stare at me curiously as I make my way over to join them.

'Genie,' Kit says again, offering me one of his big hands to shake. Turning briefly, he gives Tui's swing another gentle push.

'Tui you know,' he begins, then adds, 'this is Allie and her brother Griff.'

'Hi,' I say, my eyes flickering over each of the group in turn. Tui is the hardest to take in, because she's swinging around in circles so fast that her laughing face is little more than a blur. The man, Griff, who is even bigger and broader than Kit, but with straight blond hair instead of tight black curls on his head, steps forwards and offers me a hand.

'G'day,' he says, beaming at me.

The girl, who glanced at me briefly as she was introduced but has made no move to unfold her arms from across her chest, is tall and slim like Hayley. Her light-brown hair frames a neat, heart-shaped face, and she looks me up and down without speaking.

'Aren't you gonna say hello, Allie?' teases Griff, and the girl rolls her eyes.

'Hello,' she says. 'You're Bonnie's old friend, right? From England?'

'I was just telling the guys about you,' explains Kit. 'Saying what a 'mare it was that you showed up just as Bon buggered off.'

At the mention of Bonnie, I feel myself clam up, and mutter something about it not mattering, and that I'm happy to wait for her to get back.

Allie allows her arms to fall down to her sides. She

has a shrewd expression on her face, as if she's holding back from saying something.

Kit, who is watching both of us, stops pushing Tui and picks up the puppy.

'This little fella is Beavis,' he says, coming so close that the dog is able to give my nose a lick of greeting. 'He's much less of a nitwit than Allie.'

'Right charmer, this one, isn't he?' Allie deadpans in her Kiwi drawl, but she's definitely thawed a fraction.

Tui stumbles off the swing and reaches for her dog, noticing me properly for the first time as Kit places Beavis in her arms.

'Hello, Tui,' I say, choking out the words through the closed fist that my throat has become.

Tui peers at me through her lashes. She's around the same height as me, with very dark brown, rather wild hair, large almond-shaped eyes and the small, upturned nose of a Ragamuffin cat. She's no longer a little girl but not yet a woman, and her cheeks still carry the plumpness of youth, and I can see the indents of matching dimples on either side of her full lips. She is wearing a white vest top with a picture of Snoopy printed on the front, and tatty black shorts.

'You're a very pretty lady,' she announces, startling me so much that I laugh.

'Er, thank you,' I say, feeling hopelessly touched. 'I think you're very pretty, too.'

Tui shrugs and then nods her head up and down rapidly.

'Yes,' she says, apparently in agreement, before lifting Beavis up towards my face.

'This is my dog,' she informs me proudly, her voice slurring even as she takes care to pronounce each word correctly.

'He's lovely,' I tell her. 'Very sweet. And I like his name, too – did you choose it?'

Tui nods solemnly. 'No,' she says, and Kit chuckles.

'It's nodding for yes and shaking for no,' he reminds her, and Tui quickly shakes her head, making a low moaning sound as she does so.

'She doesn't like it when I point these things out to her, do you, Tui?' he explains, and Tui nods again, this time looking more mischievous.

'Who are you?' she asks a moment later, pointing right at me. Griff laughs at this, and I make a half-hearted attempt to follow suit – anything to give me time to formulate an appropriate reply. I can't exactly blurt out the truth, that I'm the half-sister she has never known existed.

'My name is Evangeline,' I say, settling for basic facts. 'But my friends call me Genie.'

'Gee-nie.' Tui tests the word a few times, drawing out the first 'e' sound. 'Genies live in lamps,' she says, turning to Kit so that he can confirm it.

Before I can reply, Tui starts cackling with amused laughter, so loudly that Griff puts his hands over his ears in mock-horror.

'Worse than that,' jokes Kit over the din. 'This Genie here lives in England!'

Tui bellows even more loudly at this, then steps forward and hooks her hand around the back of my head, pulling me against Snoopy and hugging me. She is surprisingly strong and, caught off guard, I wobble for a second, trying not to fall forwards.

'Come on now, put the poor chook down,' Kit says, prising Tui's hand away from where it's tangled in my hair. My hat has fallen off on to the ground, and he picks it up and gives it back to me.

Tui does as she's told and grins at me, her expression open now and accepting. I blink at her, trying to gather myself together, and cast an equally enthusiastic one back.

'Blue eyes,' she says wonderingly, her own brown pair focusing in on mine.

'The same as Mummy.'

13

'Did you say Frisbee golf?'

Kit's eyes crinkle up at the corners. 'That's right,' he says, reaching into his backpack and extracting three more plastic circular discs in various colours, one of which he hands to me.

'See that net?' he asks, pointing to a wooden post in the near distance. There's a wire-mesh contraption attached to the top, rather like a hanging basket without the chains. I nod.

'The aim of the game is to throw your Frisbee from each marker,' he explains, gesturing to a flat paved area twenty metres or so in front of the post, 'and get it in the net. You're after a hole in one, really, just like you would be in a round of golf, but those are a rarity.'

'Speak for yourself, bro,' Griff interrupts, flexing his fingers until the joints crack. 'Last time we came out here, I nailed you guys.'

'Oh, shut your hole,' Allie chides, pulling a face at him. I try to catch her eye, hoping to engage her in some form of female camaraderie, but she glances quickly away, giving Griff a light push and laughing when he stumbles over his own feet. Tui accepts a red Frisbee and clutches it tightly with both hands, her expression

88

one of excitement, while Kit has stooped down to clip a lead to Beavis's collar.

'Sorry, mate,' he says to the dog. 'Can't have you fetching all the Frisbees while we're trying to play.'

Tui shrieks with laughter. It's loud, throaty, and so full of unmistakable joy that I find it impossible not to laugh too. I notice that Kit, Allie and Griff are all grinning at her, too. I still can't quite fathom the fact that this girl is my half-sister. My real flesh and blood, a sibling, right here, standing in front of me. I keep waiting for the shock to render me speechless or even send me into a full-blown panic, but so far, all I really feel is curious.

'You go first, Gee-nie,' Tui says to me, as we reach the first marker.

I glance uncertainly at Kit.

'I think Griff should start us off, Tu,' he tells her, putting one of his big hands on her shoulder. 'Genie here has never played before, so she needs to watch us take a few turns, right?'

'Ohh,' Tui moans, clearly dismayed.

'Honestly,' I say quickly, smiling at her with as much reassurance as I can muster, 'Kit's right – I don't have a clue what I'm doing. I'll probably end up throwing this,' I hold up my blue Frisbee, 'into a tree.'

Tui bellows with laughter again and Kit's approving eyes meet mine. Griff, meanwhile, is limbering up to throw, making a big show of extending his arm and lining up the shot by squinting into the distance.

'Oh, get on with it, you great ape,' says Allie, and Griff swings around.

'Oi!' he cries. 'You'll give a guy a complex one of these days.'

'Will you two stop bloody bickering?' tuts Kit. 'They're always like this,' he explains to me. 'Makes me glad to be an only child.'

Griffin misses his shot and curses in good humour, and then Allie steps up to take her turn, throwing wide of the target and swearing with a gusto that makes Kit raise both his eyebrows at me. When he gets into position a moment later, Allie promptly moves in behind him and slips a hand into the back pocket of his shorts.

'Lay off, woman,' he says, wriggling away. 'You're distracting me.'

Allie pouts.

'If you don't want me to grab your backside, stop sticking it out,' she replies, tossing her hair over one shoulder. I decide that there's definitely an element of the stroppy mare about her, and wish I could placate her with a Polo mint as easily as I used to do with Suki.

Kit ignores the comment, and Allie only just steps out of the way in time to avoid being knocked over sideways by the swing of his right arm. The Frisbee soars through the air, curling up and around the trunks of several trees, before landing neatly in the net.

'Yes!' he yells triumphantly, unable to hide his delight.

'That,' says Griff, turning to me, incredulous, 'is how it's done.'

I'm not sure whether it's beginner's bad luck or a severe case of nerves, but it soon becomes humiliatingly apparent that I am utterly hopeless at Frisbee golf. After joking to Tui that I will probably lob my disc into the surrounding trees, I end up doing exactly that on more than one occasion during the first half of the game, and each time Tui finds my shambolic display hilarious. She is arguably no better than I am when it comes to technique, but unlike me, she has the benefit of Kit's guiding arms and gentle encouragement. Allie and Griff grow in confidence the further around the course we go, whereas the opposite is true for me. No matter what angle I bend my arm or which direction I throw the Frisbee, it stubbornly falls way short of the net. In fact, I'm so far behind the others by the time we reach the fifteenth target that they simply stop bothering to keep my score. As someone who regularly annihilates Billy at pool and never scores less than a spare at the bowling alley, my ineptitude cuts a deep wound in my ego, leaving me with no choice but to laugh uproariously at myself every time I miss. Which is every single time.

Kit is sympathetic to a point, but he's also amused by how useless I am. Griff, on the other hand, is positively angelic, going into raptures every time I get my little blue disc within ten feet of the net and berating his sister every time she makes a sarcastic remark. After showing such an interest in me at the start of the game, Tui hasn't said much else, preferring instead to stay close to Kit and pick up stones and leaves off the ground.

Beavis watches the four us with his little head on one side, puzzled as dogs so often are by the seemingly random behaviour of their human companions. David had suggested that we get a puppy about six months after Anna's accident, and I had not reacted well. It felt like such an obvious tactic, and in my head, he wasn't giving my grief the right amount of respect. How could he think that a pet would make up for losing a parent and my cherished horse? I had yelled at him and slammed doors and spewed forth a whole range of venomous retorts, but remembering that vile tantrum now makes me wince. David may have needed something new to love, too, and I should have factored in his sorrow. But I wasn't able to see past my own.

I force my mind away from the past and try to focus on the present. On the light-dappled ground and the sound of the leaves crackling in the wind; the sensation of warm sunshine on my bare limbs and the brilliant blueness of the sky above. Grief is black crayon scribbled across a painting, a cold empty room with a locked door. If love is the light, then grief is its shadow, and where there is one, there must be the other. I know that if I did not love Anna and Suki as much as I did – and still do – then I wouldn't feel their absence as keenly. But would I sacrifice that simple happiness so I could avoid the agony that later followed? No, I would not.

'Genie.'

Kit is standing right beside me. I didn't see him approaching.

'Sorry,' I say, blinking away tears. 'I was miles away.'

'A bit like your Frisbee,' he jokes, but his tone is tentative rather than teasing. The others are up ahead on the crest of a small hill, and as Kit and I stare up, Allie beckons an impatient hand at us.

'Chill out, woman,' he calls up with a frown, before turning to face me.

'She's in a right stinker today,' he mutters.

I wonder how I would feel if my boyfriend had invited a strange foreigner he barely knew to spend the afternoon with us, and decide that Allie has at least a smidgeon of justification for being a little put out.

'Have you two been together long?' I ask, as we stroll over to retrieve my errant Frisbee.

'Me and Allie?' Kit crinkles his brow. 'I reckon it's coming up to almost three years. Feels like longer, though,' he adds, with a snuffle of laughter.

'Gosh,' I say, unsure how to respond. 'That's a long time.'

Kit lifts one shoulder in a half-shrug.

'I guess. We all went to school together, me, Griff and Allie, and then she got a job at the stables at around the same time I started helping out. It kind of just happened, you know? But I tell you what, Griff was not best pleased when he found out that his best mate had started carrying on with his little sister.'

I glance up towards Griff, who is busy teaching Tui how to make Beavis jump up for a stick.

'He seems nice,' I remark, thinking as I do that 'nice' is a terrible word – so vanilla.

Presumably because he feels guilty for telling me his girlfriend was in a 'stinker', Kit then says, 'Allie is a cool girl. It's not like her to be so mardy, but maybe I deserve it. I'm not gonna win an award for boyfriend of the year anytime soon, that's for damn sure.'

I watch as he chews the inside of his cheek. Kit has so many tattoos decorating his arms that it's hard to tell where one ends and another begins.

A bird lets out a deep, echoing caw from amongst the trees, and Kit and I look up simultaneously into the dense tangle of branches high above.

'If it makes you feel any better, I've always been a useless girlfriend,' I confess, smiling when his eyes widen in surprise. 'I have always been too preoccupied with ho—' I falter. 'Hobbies – I have a lot of hobbies.'

Kit looks more puzzled now than anything, as well he might, but I blunder on regardless.

'I, er, knit,' I tell him, 'and I read a lot.'

At least the latter is true.

'You and Tui have that in common,' Kit says, starting up the hill.

'Oh?' I reply, following him, eager to hear more about my half-sister's interests. The others have moved away out of sight now, but I can still hear her infectious laughter.

'Not knitting.' He emits a low chuckle. 'She would never have the patience for that – but she loves her books. I used to read to her when she was younger, but these days she manages fine all by herself.'

The question about Tui's condition sits like a cactus in the back of my throat, prickling whenever I swallow. I used to run the Riding for the Disabled scheme back when I was still working at Mill House Stables, but none of the disabled teenagers who came along were as capable as Tui. It feels too soon to ask Kit about it – the subject too private. What is abundantly clear is that he cares about Tui very much indeed, and I don't want to say the wrong thing and risk damaging the fragile threads of our burgeoning friendship – not to mention ruin any chance I might have of spending more time with my new half-sister.

We reach the ridge of the hill to find Allie, Griff and Tui sprawled out on the ground, each of them pretending to be asleep. Tui, who is snoring loudly between bouts of giggles, opens one eye and peers up at us.

'I can't believe this lot fell asleep waiting for us,' exclaims Kit, playing along.

Tui, unable to stop her body from shaking with laughter, sits up and emits a hiccup so loud that it prompts Beavis to leap sideways in fright. Then, reaching up and grabbing my hand for leverage, Tui pulls herself clumsily to her feet and runs off ahead along the path.

'I've got dust all over my arse,' says Allie, brushing ineffectually at the offending patch of dirt. 'Help a girl out, will you?' she adds to Kit, and I avert my eyes as he attends to her bottom.

'You're my hero,' I hear her say, turning just in time to see her plant a kiss right on his mouth. And, was it my imagination, or did she just sneak a glance in my direction to make sure I was watching her do it?

It would have been more subtle if she'd lifted her leg and peed on him, I think wryly – and for a second or two, I consider taking Allie to one side and telling her that she has nothing to worry about. Not where I am concerned, at any rate. I'm not after a repeat of my disastrous 'date' with Billy a few weeks ago. That drunken sham of an evening proved to me that not only am I in no way ready for a romantic relationship with anyone, but that I have no desire for one full stop.

14

'So, let me get this straight,' Hayley says, taking a breath. 'Your mum is in England?'

'Yes.'

There's a pause on the other end of the line.

'And it turns out that you have a half-sister called Tui. Hang on, is that Tui as in the travel agent?'

'I think we can assume that it refers to something else in New Zealand,' I say, almost slicing through my hands-free headphone wire with the bread knife. While it's dinner time where Hayley is, I'm currently busy making my breakfast in the apartment block's shared kitchen.

'And,' Hayley goes on, 'as if all that wasn't complicated enough, you've also met a gorgeous man, who just so happens to know both of them.'

'Er, excuse me?' I protest. 'I haven't "met" a man – not in the way you're insinuating.'

'But you like him,' Hayley points out, and I grit my teeth.

'As a potential friend, yes.'

'And he's gorgeous,' she adds.

'I barely know the guy,' I insist, opening the fridge and replacing the carton of eggs.

'But you know enough to like him,' she teases. 'The first thing you told me after his name was how good-looking he is.'

'I did not!'

'OK, so I made that bit up – but I know for a fact that he's good-looking. I can tell from how gooey your voice goes when you talk about him.'

'Must be a poor connection,' I counter, and she cackles.

'Unlike the one between you and this Kit bloke, then.'

'Hayley!' I implore, opening a drawer in search of a whisk to mix up the eggs, but finding only a half-empty box of matches and a rusty vegetable peeler. 'I told you – it's not like that. He's got a girlfriend, for God's sake.'

'Billy will be so upset,' she adds. It's clearly a joke, but one with a sting in its tail.

'Can we drop the subject of Kit now?' I plead, choosing to ignore the mention of Billy.

Hayley sighs forlornly, and I give up on locating a whisk, fetching a fork from the draining board instead.

'OK, have it your way,' she says. 'But you can't blame a girl for hoping – a nice holiday romance might have cheered you up a bit.'

Now it's my turn to sigh.

'For the last time, you earthworm brain, I did not come to New Zealand to find a man – I came here to find my real mother.'

'I know.' Hayley's voice is smaller now, her tone more contrite. 'I'm sorry.'

'So, what do you think I should do?' I ask, cursing as the toast pops up. I haven't even ignited the gas under the egg pan yet.

'Hmm,' Hayley begins, and I hear her tapping her fingers on something as I hunt in vain for a reheat button on the toaster. 'That depends. How are you feeling about your mother now? You know, now that you're there, and you've seen where she lives?'

'Well, I guess if she's horsey then she can't be all bad,' I allow. 'And Tui is an absolute sweetheart, so I have to give Bonnie some credit for raising her. But I still feel like I know hardly anything about what she's like as a person, you know? And there are no photos of her anywhere at the yard – not that I saw, anyway. She's still faceless to me.'

Hayley makes sympathetic noises while I pour the beaten eggs into a pan and pick up a wooden spoon and scramble them. It's not going to be the best breakfast I have ever made, given that I forgot to buy butter, salt or pepper.

'It must have taken serious guts to just walk on in there,' Hayley allows. 'But you did it – you faced your biggest fear on the very first day.'

What I haven't yet admitted to Hayley is how strange it felt to be so close to horses again. I stay away from the stables at home because I can't bear to be around so many reminders, not just of my life before the accident, but of Anna, too, and my poor darling Suki. I thought it would be the same at Koru Stables, that those familiar smells, sights and sounds would invoke that terrible, gasping grief again – but they hadn't. Or perhaps I hadn't let them. I had kept my eyes averted and my hands firmly to myself.

'I suppose I might be a bit braver than I thought I was,' I agree. 'But I have to admit, the whole thing felt like one long, extended moment of madness.'

'Not madness,' Hayley tempers lightly. 'Courage.'

The eggs are cooked at last, and I take the pan across to my plate and scrape the contents unceremoniously on to the cold toast. Hayley and I continue to talk as I eat, her chatting loudly to mask the sound of my chewing. She's seen David, she tells me – they bumped into each other in the Co-op.

I know I should really be calling my adoptive dad every day while I'm here, but for some reason, I don't feel ready to share the details of my Frisbee golf game with Kit, Tui and the others with him yet. For a few precious hours, as the five of us sweated and laughed our way around Queenstown Gardens, the coal-dust blackness in my heart was swept away into the corners. The memories of Anna were still there, of course, but they didn't feel as all-consuming as they usually did, and because I was not with anyone who knew me, or anything at all about Anna's accident, thoughts of her had receded quite naturally to the back of my mind for once. That was yesterday, though, and with each breath, that gloom is stealing back through me. I may be pretending to Hayley that everything is more or less fine – even joking around with her about Kit – but the truth is, I feel like I'm on the edge of an emotional precipice.

'So, what are you up to today, then?' Hayley asks, as I finish the last of my meal.

'Probably just go for another wander around,' I say vaguely. 'Maybe book a skydive.'

'Funny,' she deadpans. Then, so quietly that at first I think I may have misheard her, 'You could always go back to the stables, you know.'

The first time I headed out here to Paradise Valley, I at least had a purpose for coming. This time my reason is simply that I have a very persuasive best friend, one who pointed out to me that getting to know my new half-sister better was the only thing that really made sense. It certainly made more sense than jumping out of a plane, even though, as I laughingly informed her, I was definitely not serious when I suggested that.

Hayley wasn't wrong, but now that I'm back here, facing the gate with the long stony driveway beyond it, I realise that I need a different excuse for anyone I might encounter at the yard. I can't very well roll up and tell the truth – but where does that leave me? With a lie, and I hate lying, even when I have no choice.

Deciding to leave it up to chance, I push through the trees and make my way towards the office to the right of the main yard. Perhaps I can pretend to have lost my purse and have come back to see if it's here? That feels plausible . . . ish.

Before I can get there, however, I catch sight of Tui over in the largest of the outdoor schools. She is up on the back of a stocky chestnut pony, her reins knotted to stop them trailing, and as I draw nearer, I see that her stirrups are crossed over the front of her saddle, too. Allie, who is standing in the middle of the arena holding a long lunge rein and whip, sees me and inclines her head in a brief greeting. Feeling thus encouraged, I pause to watch for a few minutes, my elbows up on the fence.

'Try to deepen your seat,' Allie instructs, cracking her whip on the ground so that the pony begrudgingly shifts into a loping trot.

Up in the saddle, Tui begins to bounce and flail, her usual merriness punctured by a frown. Gripping the pommel until her knuckles turn white, she starts to slip helplessly to one side, and Allie is left with no choice but to pull the pony up.

'You need to relax,' she tells Tui soothingly. 'Don't grip the saddle with your knees, make your legs go all floppy.'

'All right, all right. Jeez!'

'Now, shall we try that again?' suggests Allie, and Tui promptly nods, which I remember could very well mean no. Before I have time to call out to Allie, though, the whip has cracked yet again, and this time the startled gelding sets off with more gusto, almost unseating Tui and bringing her rapidly to tears.

That's it. I've seen enough.

Ducking under the fence and striding briskly to the centre of the school, I take the lunge rein from a shocked Allie and ease the chestnut pony to a walk.

'Halt,' I command.

The pony halts.

'Tui, are you OK?' I ask.

After wiping her cheeks with the bottom of her bright yellow Pokémon T-shirt, Tui shakes her head.

'Yes, I think so, Genie, yes.'

She remembered my name.

'Good,' I say, wrapping the rein more tightly around my fingers. Allie is yet to say anything, but I imagine the hostility is radiating off her like steam off a pudding.

'Now, wriggle your bottom backwards until you feel comfortable – that's it. Then lift up that chin until you can see the clouds. Can you see them?'

'Uh-uh.' Tui shakes her head again.

'Right, now I want you to imagine that there's a really heavy stone in the heel of your boots – can you do that?'

Tui closes her eyes, her tongue poking out through her teeth as she concentrates, and as I hoped, she drops both her heels and lifts her toes into the correct position.

'That's brilliant!' I say. 'Now hold on to the saddle, and we'll try a walk first – OK?'

I give the little cob his head, and after a few hesitant steps, the pony begins to relax and lengthen his stride. Tui's knees are still pressed against the saddle like a vice, but after a few more circuits, she, too, begins to soften. Whenever she drops her chin, I ask her to tell me which clouds look like animals, and when I sense her beginning to wobble, I simply remind her of those magical weights in the heels of her boots. After ten minutes, during which time Allie has sat down on a plastic jump block behind me, I call out to Tui that we're going to try a trot again.

'This time,' I say, before she has the chance to feel scared, 'I want you to imagine that there's a big spring at the top of your legs, like a slinky. Do you know what a slinky is?'

Tui shakes her head with enthusiasm.

'When your pony starts to trot, the only thing that needs to move is those springs. Everything else on your body can stay still, OK? Shall we give it a try?'

'OK, Gee-nie,' Tui sings, but I notice that she tenses up a fraction. Tossing Allie's proffered whip to the floor, I click my tongue against my teeth until the pony takes the hint, then let the rein go slack again, so he isn't left fighting for his head. Enjoying this new freedom, the sturdy little pony slips effortlessly into a slow, comfortable trot, and Tui, quite miraculously, finds and deepens her seat.

'Better?' I call, as she's on her sixth rotation, and this time, as she says yes, she's nodding.

'You clearly know your stuff,' Allie remarks. I expected her to be annoyed with me for muscling in, but she seems genuine in her praise – a fact that strangely makes me feel even more of an imposter.

'Not really,' I say, glancing down at my sandals.

'It's bloody clever of you, to use imagery like that with Tui,' Allie continues. 'I've been trying to get her basic seat better for months, then you come in and nail it in fifteen minutes.'

'I'm sorry,' I begin, but Allie holds up a hand.

'Don't be – I'm stoked that Tui's finally enjoying herself up there. Isn't that right, Tui?'

'What?' bellows Tui, causing both of us laugh.

'Right, come on, Missy.' Allie takes the lunge rein and tows Tui and the chestnut pony back towards the stables. 'And you, too, other Missy,' she calls over her shoulder.

Feeling all of a sudden light-headed with happiness, I set off after them through the dust.

15

Bonnie

It had been a very long time since Bonnie had let herself think about Seth Cooper. Back in 1992, when she had returned home to New Zealand from England, forever changed but determined not to let on why, both Seth and baby Evangeline had plagued her thoughts on a daily basis. She had veered from regret to sadness to relief to guilt and back again – it was a seemingly never-ending cycle of confused emotion, and far from dissipating along with her post-pregnancy hormones, the feelings had intensified, building up to a crescendo of catastrophic misery.

It was during those days of total and utter despair that Bonnie had come the closest to confessing everything to her elderly parents, but fear always stopped her in the end. She told herself that they would be angry and disappointed, but what scared her the most was the possibility that they would want her to take it all back. And she couldn't do that, not even if she wanted to. She had made her decision, and she was adamant that she must stick to it no matter what.

Now, however, Bonnie had to try and recall all

those mixed emotions. She had to go back even further, back to the day she had first met Seth Cooper, and try to make sense of what followed. She wanted her daughter to understand, but she, Bonnie, needed to understand, too.

Tracey had just brought her up a cup of tea, and Bonnie took a fortifying sip, trying her best to cast her mind back to that fateful afternoon. Closing her eyes, she pictured the cosy but cluttered interior of Sunrise Café as it was then, with its scrubbed Formica tables and polished wooden floor. She remembered how the coffee machine used to hum when it was idle, and how the smell of frying bacon would waft up the back stairs from the kitchen. There was a bell above the door that jangled whenever customers came in, and Bonnie knew that sound would have heralded the arrival of Seth. She would have looked up in greeting, perhaps smiled the only genuine smile that he would ever see on her face. Because after that she was always too self-conscious, aware of how he saw her, and how her gestures would be interpreted. She never had been able to fully relax around him.

That was it, she thought, reaching at last for her pen. She had her starting point.

I was attracted to Seth as soon as I saw him. I guess you're a bit too young to remember the band Nirvana, but I bet you know who Kurt Cobain is, right? Well, imagine a slightly less grubby version – that is what Seth looked like. The fact that I was a massive Nirvana fan at the age of eighteen definitely helped when it came to his allure, but it was also eye-opening to meet a man so unlike the boys I had grown up with back in New Zealand. They were all big meatheads — or so I thought then — but Seth was slim with long hair. I had never met anyone who looked quite like him, and as such, he caught my attention straight away.

Sunrise Café was not far from the University College London campus, so we often had students popping in for coffee or toasted sandwiches. I used to eavesdrop on their conversations as I cleaned the tables, and they all seemed so knowledgeable and worldly-wise, with their fashionable clothes and their packets of Silk Cut. Seth intimidated me just as much, but unlike the other students, he used to come in with one of his professors. The two of them were Friday-afternoon regulars, and over the weeks that followed, I got to know both of them quite well. Tracey had a soft spot for the young professor, and would give him free custard tarts, but for me it was all about Seth.

Dating wasn't something I had ever done before at home. My parents were overprotective in the extreme, and aside from the odd kiss at a school dance or something, I hadn't had much experience with boys. That's not to say I didn't want any — I did — it just wasn't worth the row that I would face at home. I think Mum and Dad must have known that I would start meeting boys once I went travelling, but I guess they figured what they couldn't see wouldn't worry them as much. Or I thought so then. Now, of course, I know better. When you're a parent, you are always bloody worrying.

Anyway, as you can see, I was quite an innocent eighteen-year-old — and very naive, too, even if I pretended that I wasn't. I wanted everyone to believe that I was as self-assured and mature as all those other girls my age that came into the café — and I especially wanted Seth to believe it. Have you ever liked a boy so much that he occupies your every waking thought? Getting a flash of the teeth from Seth would keep me going for days, and I would spend the hours that I wasn't around him plotting what I would say when I was.

But nobody was more surprised than me when he turned up after closing one evening and asked me out. Tracey had left early for the day, and I had the radio turned up full blast and was dancing around like a right dafty. When he walked through the door, I was so shocked that I whipped round with my cloth in my hand and swiped him right in the eye. Oh my God, I was bloody mortified — I almost cried. But Seth just laughed and made some joke about it being better than a wet fish. He was like that, you see, so confident and funny with it. I couldn't understand why someone like him would choose me, and therein, I suppose, lay my biggest problem.

Our first date was three days later. Seth took me to the National Gallery — you know, the big one in Trafalgar Square? What am I thinking? Of course you know! You're British, after all. Anyway, we talked a lot about the history behind the paintings. I had no clue what he was even on about half the time, but it felt like such a grown-up way to be spending a Sunday afternoon. I barely spoke when we were in there, in case I ended up saying something stupid and putting him off.

Afterwards, we went for a meal at a little pub in Soho, and Seth even ordered a bottle of wine for the table. I had never even tried wine before, and I don't mind admitting to you now that I thought it was the foulest-tasting thing I had ever put in my mouth – but I couldn't let on as much to Seth. I wanted him to think that I was sophisticated. Silly, isn't it? Even writing it down now makes me feel like a prize wally. I want to be honest, though. That's the whole point of this story, to tell you the truth of how it was, and how I felt – I promised myself when I started this that I would be nothing but truthful, no matter how much it scares me, and so that's what I will continue to do.

Bonnie paused as her mobile phone vibrated with a message, and put the pen, the end of which she had been furiously chewing, down on the desk.

It was Tui, and Bonnie felt her chest swell with affection as she read her daughter's cheerful update.

'Did sit's trot today mumy.
A Geenee helpped me.'

Tui had clearly been watching her Disney *Aladdin* DVD again. She often became fixated on things, and would watch her favourite films over and over, sometimes for days on end, until she could recite them by heart. It had started when she was very young, and Bonnie had assumed she would grow out of it eventually, but Tui was fourteen now, and still just as hooked on her cartoons.

Bonnie thought for a moment before tapping out a reply.

'That's brilliant news! Did
the genie come out of a
lamp?'

A message came straight back.

'No a hairplaine mumy.'

Well, that was a new one. Bonnie grinned. Tui could become agitated when she was corrected for making a mistake, but sometimes she made them on purpose to be funny. She must be trying to catch Bonnie out.

'Silly me! I forgot that all
genies come from planes.'

There was no response to this for a while, and then when Tui did reply, instead of words, she sent two rows of pony emojis, three blue hearts, an Easter Island head, a Spanish flag and the dancing lady in the red dress.

Oh, hell, thought Bonnie as her eyes misted over with tears. She missed her little girl so much. This was the first time the two of them had been apart for longer than a weekend, and the absence was beginning to take its toll. She toyed briefly with the idea of calling Kit to check in, but then thought better of it. She hadn't even been gone a full week yet, and he would have been in touch if there was anything to worry about. And anyway, she reminded herself, her focus was supposed to be on the task in hand. The more distractions she let in, the longer it would take to get this story written.

Bonnie knew the next few weeks were going to be some of the toughest of her life, but at least she could feel comforted by the knowledge that everything back at home was exactly as it should be.

16

There is no sign of Kit or the Koru Stables minibus as I follow Allie and Tui back into the yard. Several horses are tethered to the same wooden post as they were on my first visit, but none of them are tacked up. Instead, they rest quietly with one back hoof tucked up, their tails dancing away the flies and their eyes closed in a half-snooze.

There's a wheelbarrow propped outside one of the open stable doors, and every few seconds, a forkful of soiled woodchips soars out and lands inside with a thud. The air is ripe with the scent of ammonia, but I breathe it in greedily, allowing my senses to drink in the familiar smell that I have missed so much. The office door is shut, but I can hear sounds of a radio playing inside. It is all so reminiscent of Mill House Stables – there is even a ginger tabby cat, which is now rubbing itself luxuriantly against my bare shins. It feels wrong to be wearing a dress in a yard, and now that I'm here, I wish I'd opted for shorts.

Tui has dismounted using the block, and I watch as she carefully leads her chestnut pony into a loose box, closely followed by Allie. Unsure whether or not to head in after them, I notice a broom resting idly against the wall beside the taps, and quell a strong urge to pick it up and begin sweeping. Instead, I follow my nose into a feed room, opening one barrel lid after another and inhaling the sweet smell of pony nuts, sugar beet and chaff, aware that I must look like a weirdo, but not caring enough to stop.

In the tack room next door, I'm greeted by yet more gloriously familiar scents, this time of saddle soap, brass rub and leather, and I can't resist running a finger over the patterned brow bands and polished reins. It has been more than a year now since I picked up a bridle or slung a saddle over my folded arm, but I know instinctively that my hands would know what to do, and that my body would know to stand beside the horse's shoulder, facing forwards with the headpiece gripped in my right hand. I would lift the bridle up over the pony's firm, teardrop ears, slip my finger into that secret place inside their mouth, and then, when they obediently parted their thick, bristly lips, slide the metal bit under their tongue, fastening first the noseband and then the cheek strap, turning two fingers outwards to check that it was not too tight. Perhaps a few strands of the forelock would have become tangled. I would ease those out with care, combing the coarse hair until it fell neatly from poll to lashes.

Suki had such a full, thick forelock. She used to doze as I ran my fingers through it, the lovely weight of her head against my chest, my beating heart so full of uncomplicated love for her, and for the moment we were sharing. I know I should be grateful for every single one of them, but all I feel is anger that there will never be any more.

'Genie?'

Letting out a yelp of fright, I leap away from the bridle I was examining so fast that I promptly hit my head on an empty saddle rack.

'Ow!' I cry, rubbing the spot. Kit lurched forwards at the same moment I screamed, but he stops short of actually touching me.

'Sorry,' he says, looking amused. 'Didn't mean to scare ya.'

'It's my fault,' I reply, still rubbing. 'I shouldn't have been lurking in here like an ogre.'

'Nah.' He grins. 'I'd say you were more urchin than ogre. You know, small and spiky.'

'Gee, thanks,' I drawl, but I'm smiling.

'If you're looking for Bonnie,' he says, 'she's still not here.'

'I wasn't,' I hasten, before adding, 'I was looking for you – and Tui, of course. I thought I might have left my purse here, which I hadn't, as it turns out. Plus, I didn't get to see much of the place the other day, so I thought I'd come and take a look – if that's all right with you?'

'Free country,' he replies, still amused. 'But you're not going to see much of the Dart River Valley from inside here.'

I'm just about to throw back a witty retort when Allie appears behind him.

'Oh, there you are,' she says to me. 'Tui was asking for you.'

'She was?' I feel all at once puffed out with happiness. 'I'd best go and find her then.'

'Sweet,' she replies, then, turning to Kit, 'Can you help me tack up for the midday trek, please? Tammy didn't show up again and I've got all the other girls mucking out.'

It's on the tip of my tongue to offer to help them, but I decide it's probably best that I don't. Teaching Tui a few basics from the far end of a long lunge rein is one thing, but actually touching the horses is another. I'm not sure what my reaction would be.

Kit steps around me and uses one hand to scoop up two saddles as if they're feather pillows, before using the other to feed four bridles up on to one of his big shoulders.

Outside, the sun is steadily climbing, but I'm gratified to see that there are at least a few clouds jostling for position across the sky. The minibus has appeared along with Kit, and is parked in the shade of a large tree not far from the outdoor schooling area. A new group of tourists is lined up behind a makeshift fence, each one looking rather out of place in their brightly coloured leggings and borrowed riding hats. Turning so that the sun is behind me, I spot Tui perched up on the highest step of the mounting block, holding a stick up in the air and bellowing with deep, throaty laughter as Beavis tries unsuccessfully to reach it. When she catches sight of me, however, she leaps down, almost falling in her haste to cross the yard, and throws both her arms around my neck.

'Gee-nie!' she croons delightedly into my ear, before bringing up a hand to stroke the side of my face.

Taken aback, I find that I have absolutely no words, settling instead for a smile.

'Stop groping the guests,' remarks Kit, who is passing with another two saddles.

Tui removes her hand from my cheek, but she doesn't stop staring at me.

'Hello again,' I say, putting a somewhat rigid hand on her arm. 'How are you feeling after your ride?'

'Great,' she says, then begins to hum quietly.

'It's very nice to see you again,' I add, thinking as I do how much I genuinely mean it. Tui doesn't say anything, but she nods in agreement, then slides one of her hands into mine. Her skin is as soft as a baby's and clammy to the touch.

'Gee-nie,' she says again, almost in wonderment, and I grasp around for something to say.

'Do you know the names of all these horses?' I ask, nodding towards the stalls, and again she nods.

'Mm-hm.'

'Will you tell me them?'

Tui considers this for a moment.

'Maybe later, Genie,' she says, swinging my arm backwards and forwards with a giggle.

'I bet they all have nice names,' I continue, trying another approach.

Tui hums again, but this time I can sense her irritation and worry that I may have pushed her too far. Yet again, it is a nearby Kit who comes to my rescue.

'Why don't you give Genie a tour of the yard?' he suggests, as he tightens the girth of a large bay horse with a white blaze across its face. 'You can show her all your favourite ponies.'

This seems to do the trick.

'Jeez, Kit. All right, all right. Jeez,' Genie complains, rolling her eyes in an exaggerated fashion before dragging me by the hand over to a row of stables.

'Merlin,' she calls sweetly over the first half-door, her hand still tightly gripped in mine. 'Merlin, baby.'

A very small and very fat white pony bustles importantly over from his hay net.

'Hello, Merlin,' I say, ignoring the frantic pounding of my heart as I reach out to stroke his hairy chin. This is officially the first pony that I have touched since Anna's accident.

Beside me, Tui makes a kissing sound, and Merlin promptly curls up his top lip, showing off a neat collection of yellow teeth.

'Did you teach him that?' I ask her, and Tui nods through her giggles.

'No,' she says.

'Is he your favourite?' I ask, as Merlin, realising that neither of us have brought him any food, turns on his nimble little hooves and continues to chomp away at his hay.

'I don't think so, no,' Tui says, thinking for a moment. 'I'm not sure.'

There's a smear of something green across her Poké-mon T-shirt and her leggings have the beginnings of holes on both knees. Her thick, dark hair, which looks as if it hasn't been brushed in weeks, is sticking up at the back as if birds have been squabbling in it, and there are felt-tip stains on her hands.

Going to the next door along, Tui makes a clicking sound with her tongue, and the chestnut pony she was riding earlier appears, gently butting her with his head.

'What's this handsome boy called?' I ask, peering into the box and admiring the pony's stocky legs and neat quarters.

'Keith.'

'Keith?' I splutter in disbelief. 'Are you sure?'

'Mm-hm.' Tui shakes her head from side to side.

'Keith is a funny name for a pony,' I say, and Tui bursts out laughing.

I was lucky that Suki came with her perfectly accept-able name already well established, because it's supposed to be bad luck to change them. It was how we ended up with a Trevor and a Mildred back at Mill House Sta-bles. Now, I don't have anything against the name Keith, per se, but it's a decidedly lacklustre choice for such a striking animal.

Tui continues the tour with her trademark buoyancy, and with every horse or pony I encounter, I'm aware of my anxiety beginning to lessen. I always did know how to behave around animals, and I'm relieved to discover that my instincts haven't abandoned me. I thought that touching another horse would feel like a betrayal – or worse, that it would send me into some sort of catatonic state – but the opposite is true. I am starting to relax.

All the horses are beautiful, but there is one in particular that stands out. Her name is Ekara, and with her glossy walnut coat and tempestuously flared nostrils, she reminds me acutely of Suki. Tui seems more wary of the highly strung mare than any of the other ponies, and tells me solemnly that Ekara once bit her on the bottom when she went into her stable.

'I had a bruise,' she explains, and is about to pull down the back of her leggings to show me her bum when a nearby Allie shrieks laughingly at her to stop.

Once the morning riders have been helped on to their mounts and are following Allie out of the yard, Kit strolls over to join us, confirming my immediate query about the name Keith and explaining that they also have a Pete, a Tim and a Bob.

'No Kits?' I ask, and he shakes his head.

'Far too exotic.'

'It's a great name,' I tell him honestly. Then, turning to Tui, 'But I like your name even more.'

'Bonnie reckons she named her Tui because she looked so much like a baby bird when she was born,' explains Kit. 'All pink and wrinkled, weren't you, eh?' he adds, and Tui cackles, as if she can recall the image herself.

'Mm-hm.'

'Oh, so Tui is a bird?' I say, finally understanding.

'I guess you might not have them in England,' Kit replies, ruffling Tui's already ruffled hair. 'The best thing about a tui is their impersonations – they have two voice boxes, too, a bit like this little chatterbox,' he adds, and Tui wriggles out of his grasp.

'Bonnie told me that when Tui was a baby,' he adds, 'she would sit her in one of those bouncy chairs by her feet in the indoor school, and teach riding lessons while Tui just chirped away to herself.'

I become aware of a dull ache inside my chest. Anna must have done similar things with me – perhaps even more so, because she gave up her teaching job to raise me full-time, and I know she made a special effort to take me out to interesting places and play exciting games. But it still hurts to know that my birth mother did not deem me worthy of the love and attention she later showered on to her second child. What was it about me that was so hard for her to love?

'She sounds like a perfect baby,' I say, my tone thankfully betraying none of the torment that is going on inside my head.

'Well . . .' Kit pauses while Tui chases off ahead of us after Beavis. The little dog has pinched a dandy brush from somewhere and is carrying it proudly between his teeth.

'I guess so,' he says. 'Until it became clear that she wasn't like all the other kids, anyway.'

'Why exactly is that, if you don't mind me asking?' I say quietly, and Kit stares for a moment into the distance.

'You'll have to ask Bonnie to be sure,' he says. 'But I know she has mild dyspraxia, some physical disabilities and a communication disorder – and that's not all,' he continues. 'She has a complicated range of learning difficulties, too, you see, but nothing concrete enough for a solid diagnosis. The thing is,' he adds, still not looking at me, 'Tui is smart in many ways. She can tell you the name of every single flower, plant and bird in New Zealand, but then she can't be trusted to cross the road by herself.'

'Right,' I say, not really understanding.

'I like to think of her mind as a sponge,' he explains, cupping his hands together. 'Most of the knowledge that goes in is absorbed, but there are holes, and so other bits go straight through. Tui was put on a pony before she could walk, but she still can't remember to keep her heels down, or how to hold her reins properly. But when it comes to directions, she's better than a satnav. It must be so frustrating for her, but she rarely ever complains. She just gets on with it as best she can, you know?'

I nod, not trusting myself to speak. My feelings towards Tui are far too messy for me to articulate, even to myself. I do feel sympathy towards her, but there is also a trace amount of jealousy there. It's a hateful thing to admit, but there it is, as solid and undeniable as the mountains I can see beyond the boundaries of the yard.

Kit has stopped talking, too, and the two of us watch on in silence as Tui skips around the mounting block, her cheeks pink with exertion and Beavis yapping at her heels. There's a thud as somewhere a horse kicks over its water bucket, and from behind the closed door of the office, the telephone begins to ring.

Kit puts a brief hand on my arm.

'I'd better get that,' he says. 'But when I get back, how about you, me and Tui take a walk?'

What I should do is head back to Queenstown and let him get on with his day, but I'm aware of the fact that my time with Tui could be limited. There is a strong chance that these precious encounters will come to an abrupt end the moment Bonnie returns from England, and suddenly I know that all I want is to be here; I want to spend more time with my sister.

Reaching down, I twist Anna's jade-stone ring around on my finger, torn between the 'should' and the 'could', and then I think of David, and of those four little words he's been saying to me since I was a child.

What would Evangeline do?

I know what that Evangeline would do, and for once, I am happy to follow her lead.

17

Kit, Tui and I leave the stables and head along the same path that Allie and her group of tourists took, following a stony lane past several paddocks of grazing horses before banking left through a gap in the treeline. Tui is up on Keith the handsome chestnut's back again, her face a mask of concentration and her hands balled into fists on the reins.

Kit, who has attached a lead rope to Keith's bit, is strolling along on the pony's near side, while I keep to the right. It feels safer with Tui positioned between the two of us, just in case something were to go awry. However, I do have to keep reminding myself that Suki was a flighty, spooky mare, liable to jump at her own shadow, whereas Keith is very much a riding-school plodder. Tui is probably safer up in his saddle than she would be walking next to him.

'Don't worry,' says Kit, as he clocks my somewhat apprehensive expression. 'He's as soft as anything, this one – wouldn't hurt a flea.'

He must assume that I am scared of Keith, rather than simply concerned about Tui.

'I'm sure he is,' I say quickly. 'I just haven't been around horses in a while, that's all.'

'So, you used to ride?' he guesses, and I think for a moment before replying.

'Yes . . . once upon a time.'

'Let me guess,' he says. 'You had a fall?'

I shake my head, but Kit continues regardless.

'You should get back in the saddle,' he says, as if it's the simplest thing in the world. 'That's what you're supposed to do when you fall off – isn't it?'

'That's what they say.'

If he can tell that I'm answering him through gritted teeth, Kit doesn't show it. Stripping a nearby twig of its leaves, he sprinkles them on to the ground.

'I don't ride myself,' he adds. 'Never found a horse big enough for starters.'

He laughs as I pull a face at him.

'I'm king of the odd jobs,' he continues. 'I don't think Bon has ever given me an official job title, but I like to think of myself as the yard manager. I would argue that you don't need to get on a horse's back to understand it, just like you don't need to ride a dog to be its best mate.'

'Merlin is a good boy,' pipes up Tui. 'I rode on him when I was a baby and very small.'

'My feet would touch the floor if I sat on him,' I point out, and Tui chirps with amusement. Looking up, I notice that her hard hat has slipped down over her eyes.

'Here.' I beckon her downwards until her nose is beside her knee, then reach up and readjust her cap.

'Thank you, Gee-nie. Oh Gee-nie, darling,' she calls in her singsong voice, gathering her reins back up. She would find it much easier if someone simply knotted them together.

Kit has mercifully decided to drop the conversation about getting me on to a horse, and is instead talking me through the route we're following. Koru Stables, he explains, is situated in the gateway to Mount Aspiring National Park and the famous Routeburn Track. The Dart River feeds its way across the area like a silver braid, its glacier-fed waters icy cold even during the summer months. The closest town to us is called Paradise, and it is here that Kit currently lives, although he confesses to spending most nights at Allie's apartment just outside Queenstown.

'I rent a room at Bonnie's,' he reveals, holding aside a low-hanging branch to make way for Keith and Tui. 'It's partly why I'm so close to this one.'

'Kit is my roomie,' Tui tells me proudly. 'He lives in the big room, and I live in the tent.'

'A tent?' I query, glancing at Kit.

'She means in the extension,' he corrects, grinning up at Tui. 'For some reason, we have a bit of trouble with that word, don't we?'

Tui shakes her head. 'Yes.'

'Tui's staying with her dad, Simon, while Bon's away, and I don't really like being at the house alone. It feels too big and too quiet.'

'How big is it?' I enquire.

'It's only a bungalow,' Kit tells me. 'Bonnie's parents left it to her, but she's made some modifications over the years, added a few rooms here and there, you know.'

Bonnie's parents, echoes my brain. My grandparents.

'Did they move away?' I ask hopefully, dreading the answer.

'They went to the next place,' Tui says happily. 'Where Kit's daddy went, that's all.'

Kit doesn't say anything, but his expression is tinged with sadness. So, he has lost a parent, too, but unlike me, Kit doesn't seem to wear his sorrow like a second skin.

For a moment, neither of us says anything, Kit unwilling or unable to meet my eye. Even Tui is quiet, distracted by a bird that is hopping from branch to shrub behind us, its tiny head cocked to one side. There is barely any wind, and the only sound is the gentle tread of Keith's hooves across the dry ground. It is so peaceful here, and so still. It should be soothing, but instead I feel stirred. Not for the first time, I wish that I was able to extract my emotions, take them out and examine them objectively. And what would I find, in amongst the hurt and the pain? There would be anger, shame and foreboding, but there would also be the murmur of something else – something less abrasive. I'm finding it hard to work out where one feeling ends and another begins, but maybe that is my problem. There are no single emotions inside me, just mashed-up scraps, left over from that initial outpouring of grief.

Lost in my own thoughts, I don't see the rotting clump of nettles until I stumble right through it, almost slipping over in the process. It is the solid bulk of Keith that keeps me upright, and I lean unthinkingly against his warm flank for a moment. Horses and ponies, even relatively small ones like Keith, are such noble and powerful creatures. I can still remember the first time I went riding, how I felt a head and shoulders taller than everyone else, not just literally but figuratively, too. Nothing and nobody could hurt me up there, and I drew such strength from that feeling.

The path has grown so narrow now that Kit has no choice but to walk ahead, and before long we are heading down a small hill towards a glittering ribbon of water. The muddy earth is littered with white pebbles that crunch pleasantly underfoot, and Keith's red-gold ears stand to excited attention as we arrive at the river's edge.

'Can I go in – please, please, please?' Tui asks Kit, bouncing up and down in the saddle.

'Only as far as the lead rope will stretch,' he replies, giving Keith's rump a gentle tap to encourage him forwards. The pony walks boldly into the shallows, lifting his hooves like a Lipizzaner and snorting with pleasure. Tui, who has now abandoned her reins completely, begins clapping her hands in delight as the pony lifts a front leg and begins splashing water all over her and himself.

'Keeeeeeith,' she croons, between her giggles. 'You're getting me all wet!'

Kit matches my enchanted expression with one of his own, his pale-green eyes alight beneath his tight black curls. I notice for the first time how small and neat his ears are, and how thick his neck. Just like a horse, he exudes power and strength through his size, but there is also a softness to this man, an innate sense of safety and of care. Everything about him says that he is a good person.

'It's so beautiful here,' I remark, looking around as Tui and Keith continue to splash about in the river. 'The space and the scope of the place – and the colours.'

'Glad you like it,' Kit replies, squinting at me as shafts of sunlight hit the surface of the water. 'I've never been to England, but I've heard it's not that different to here.'

'From what I can tell, New Zealand is a lot like England . . .' I pause. 'If you fed England a hefty dose of steroids. We have all the same ingredients as you guys, just on a far smaller scale.'

'New Zealand is one of the safest countries in the world, you know,' he says, with patent pride. 'You could go and live in the woods if you wanted to and nothing would eat you. We don't have wild lions, bears or wolves – and none of those big ugly crocs that the Aussies have to put up with.'

'What about poisonous plants?' I ask, and he shakes his head triumphantly.

'Nah, and the water is safe to drink, too. Help yourself to any river or stream you like.'

Keith lifts his hoof and makes an almighty splash of approval, causing Tui to laugh even louder.

'Is that why you have so many extreme sports on offer here?' I joke, stepping backwards to avoid getting soaked. 'To redress the balance a bit?'

A flicker of amusement crosses Kit's face, and he folds his arms before replying.

'Why sit at home growing your gut when you could be jumping off a bridge?' he jokes. 'You know, now that you're here, you should do it.'

'What – a bungee?' I laugh with incredulity.

'Why not?' he says. 'You don't even have to jump – you can sit in a chair or be strapped to a tricycle. I even saw a dude leap off with a barrel over his head once.'

'Utter lunacy!' I exclaim, lifting a hand to wave back at a thoroughly overexcited Tui. Keith has stopped splashing now and has dropped his head to drink. The Dart River is so clear that I can see its stony bed, and the bubbles collecting around Keith's fetlocks as the water rushes past his hooves. The shoreline is littered with the gnarly carcasses of rotting plants, but when I point them out in dismay to Kit, he merely shrugs.

'I think there's actually a huge amount of beauty in decay,' he says. 'I take comfort from it, I guess. Because as sure as you know these plants here –' he aims a foot at a nearby husk – 'will eventually die, you know another seedling is sprouting under the ground. Everything has its time; its own moment to be and to exist.'

'Some things don't get enough time,' I mutter, feeling myself flush.

Kit waits for a moment before replying. I don't dare look at him.

'Who did you lose?' he asks, so quietly that at first I am not sure if I heard him right.

I can't tell him the truth – not yet. And not in front of Tui.

Aware of my discomfort, Kit allows the lead rein to go slack and moves towards me. For a fleeting moment, I think he might put his arm around me, but instead he raises a hand to rub across the stubble on his jaw.

'How long ago?' he asks, but all I can do is shake my head.

'Ah, shit,' he mutters. 'Recently, then? I'm sorry. I lost my dad when I was eighteen. Sent me off the rails there for a while, but I pulled it back.'

I wish I could respond, but my desperate need not to cry in front of him and Tui has rendered me mute. No matter how kind Kit is, or how much he might well understand, my grief is private. I don't want to share it with anyone yet.

'Time is the only thing that really helps,' he goes on. 'I know that sounds like a bloody obvious thing to say, but it's a fact that every single day that you get through is another day towards feeling less crook. In the beginning, all I did was rage and shout and drive my poor mum near crazy, but after some time had passed, that all receded, and I was left with a quieter kind of sadness, I guess. It's not that I don't feel sad any more, or don't miss my dad every day, I've just learned how to carry it with me.'

I am still unable to do much more than nod and make sympathetic expressions. Thank goodness Tui has been distracted by a butterfly landing on Keith's neck.

'You should talk to Bonnie about it when she gets back,' Kit adds then, and immediately I feel my chest constrict. 'Her folks passed on not long after Tui was born, so she knows what it feels like to lose someone. Plus, she's a great listener and—'

'Didn't you say we had to be back within the hour?' I interrupt, and Kit looks at his watch.

'I did – shit. We had better rattle our dags or Allie will string me up like cured meat.'

Thank God for Allie's strict schedule, I think silently, as he tows Keith and Tui back to shore.

'I want Genie to lead me!' Tui cries, her legs flapping against Keith's sides as she attempts to urge him forwards.

'I don't really think that she—' begins Kit, but I am already reaching across to take the lead rope.

'It's OK,' I say, surprised to discover that it genuinely is. 'I'd like to.'

'Only if you're sure?' he checks, and then, as we turn to head back up the hill, 'I'm right here if you need me.'

I may not be able to talk openly about the fall that killed my mum, or how I feel so wretched about it that sometimes the guilt knocks me physically to the ground, and I might not be ready to envisage sharing anything meaningful at all with the woman who gave me up, but I am able to walk along this pathway leading a pony. What's more, I want to, and that has everything to do with the girl up in the saddle.

18

Bonnie

Jet lag had woken Bonnie in the early hours, her eyes scratchy and her throat parched from the two glasses of wine she had indulged in over yet another excellent dinner. Tracey had refused all Bonnie's offers of help, or of money, insisting that it was a pleasure having someone to cook for again. Like Bonnie herself, Tracey had never married, but she'd had a number of live-in boyfriends over the years, the most recent of which, she told Bonnie, she'd had to boot out when he started seeing another woman behind her back.

'The cheek of the fella,' she fumed to Bonnie, as she tossed a handful of frozen peas into a pan of boiling water. 'Leaves me at home, ironing his underpants, while he buggers off to swing jive classes at the town hall with her from number ten.'

'Sounds like you're better off without him,' Bonnie had told her, then confessed that she, too, was now single, having been unable to make things work with Tui's father Simon. Far from being hurt by their eventual break-up, though, Bonnie had felt relieved when he packed his things and moved out of the bungalow.

That had been almost ten years ago, and she hadn't felt the inclination to date anyone else since. She had learned from her very first relationship just how damaging it can be to have your trust abused, and it was a lesson Bonnie had been unable to forget. She and Simon had always made it work with Tui, right from the minute he left, and Bonnie still considered him a friend. He had cheated out of desperation, he told her – he thought that it might get her attention. If she had loved him in the way he wanted her to, then perhaps his ridiculous plan might have worked. But she didn't – she never really had. Simon was better off with his new wife than he had been with Bonnie, and Tui was happy to spend time at both her homes, with both her families.

It was no good, Bonnie thought to herself – she was never going to get back to sleep – not now the cogs of her mind were whirring. Crossing the room to the desk and collecting her biro and paper, she folded herself back under the covers and began to write.

Seth did everything right in those first few weeks. He was the personification of charm, but he was such good fun, too, taking me out to parties all around London and introducing me to all his friends. One of them, a girl called Lavender, took me under her wing as soon as we met. She was one of those effortlessly cool girls – you know the ones I mean – all dyed hair, alternative fashion and scary-looking piercings in unexpected places.

She would tell me not to worry about other girls approaching Seth, because she would be there to keep an eye on him, and would report back if anything dodgy happened. There was this one girl, Cece, from his university. She made it pretty bloody clear that she had the hots for him, and I was so jealous of her. Cece was all the things that I wasn't, you see: skinny, blonde, rich and so confident. I couldn't work out why a boy like Seth would choose dumpy, lumpy little me over someone like her, but Lavender would laugh at that and tell me how pretty I was, and how Seth was lucky to have me. She very quickly became the person I confided in the most.

I thought that I trusted Seth, too, but looking back now, of course I didn't. Jealousy and trust are like oil and water – they do not mix – and I was so scared of Seth getting bored of me, or finding someone better, that I would have done anything to keep him interested.

Of course, there were lots of happy moments in those heady first few weeks, too. When Seth walked me back to the hostel at night and kissed me under the streetlights, or when he turned up at the café with flowers, just because he thought I'd like them. At night, I would lie in bed and picture our wedding, right down to the dress and the speeches. I imagined my dad clapping him on the back, and my mother crying because she was so happy. Seth would write the novels he was always talking about and I would keep horses, and we would live happily ever after, back in New Zealand. It was all there in my head, the life I thought I wanted, and the focal point of it all was Seth Cooper.

As well as Tracey and Lavender, there was one other person that I confided in. Remember how I mentioned that Seth came into the café with his professor? Well, one evening he turned up at Sunrise as I was closing down, and he looked so sadly through the window that I let him in and made him a hot chocolate on the house.

At the time, I thought of him as being so much older than me, but actually, he was only in his early thirties. He had all this wild hair that stuck out at all angles, and his glasses were held together by Sellotape. He fitted my idea of a mad English professor perfectly, and I liked him not only because of his friendship with Seth, but also because of how much he made me laugh without really meaning to. The professor always had an anecdote, and usually it consisted of something funny that had happened to him. Once he told me that he'd driven halfway to work with his nosy neighbour's cat clinging on to the roof of his car, and another time he had Tracey and me in stitches over a story involving his mother-in-law and some out-of-date prawns.

I'm telling you all this so you'll understand just how much of a shock it was that evening, when he slumped into a chair and started crying in front of me. I had never seen a grown man sobbing before – my dad would certainly never have wept in front of me – and I had no idea how to handle it. I knew that Tracey kept an emergency bottle of brandy under the café sink, so I offered him some of that, and after a while, he started talking.

He told me that his marriage was in trouble, that he and his wife had been arguing non-stop and that she had *threatened to leave him. I tried to ask why, as gently as I could, but all he kept saying was that he wasn't able to give her what she wanted, and that he felt helpless. I didn't know what to say to comfort him, so I just kept pouring the brandy, but the more he drank, the sadder he seemed to become. To distract him, I started to confide my own worries, explaining how I was struggling to get over all my awful jealousy and trust Seth. He gave me some advice, and it helped, it really did. Lavender said all the right things, but she wasn't an adult – not really, not compared to the professor anyway. His words meant more to me than hers, and after that first night, the two of us began talking a lot more.*

It wasn't in any way romantic between us – nothing like that at all – but I did start to care about him. He was like a best friend and a big brother rolled into one, and I felt special knowing that I was the one he had chosen to turn to at his time of need. It wasn't very long before the professor knew more about me and my life than anyone else in London – even Seth.

But, of course, there were things that I didn't tell him.

Bonnie closed her eyes for a moment to consider which part she should tell next. Everything back then had felt as if it happened all at once, but it was important now to separate those events as coherently as she could.

She tried to imagine what her daughter would want to hear, but that was impossible when she knew so little about her. She knew bits, snatches that she had picked up over the years, through letters she had received and searches on the internet. Evangeline Nash was a private person, but Bonnie had found a few traces of her online: photos of a sullen-looking teenager on the red carpet at a film premiere, her hand enveloped tightly by her adoptive mother's; a local newspaper report detailing her first prize win at a dressage event. Her Facebook profile picture was of a striking dark bay horse, and further exploratory clicks had led Bonnie to a more recent photo of Evangeline with her arm wrapped around the shoulders of a laughing blonde girl.

That one had jolted her in its familiarity.

Would Evangeline slam the door in Bonnie's face as soon as she realised who she was? Would David and Anna? It was no more than she deserved. Then again, if Evangeline was anything like Bonnie, she would have an incurable need to know all the facts, no matter how horrid and hurtful. Bonnie had always been that way, had perpetually chased and probed and nettled until she got the truth. Some facts had to be known, whether you sought them or not, and it was one of those that had convinced Bonnie she must finally make this trip. Because in order to face her future, she must first confront her past.

19

Not since my days at the stables have I had to set an alarm to go off so early in the morning.

It is amazing what the body gets accustomed to, but also how quickly habits can fall away from the fore if you don't keep up with them. Since I quit my job at the yard, I often sleep in until past ten, and I have gone from being almost continually active to not moving much for most of the day. My once-firm thighs have softened, and my bottom is now the consistency of blancmange, where previously it was barley sugar. I even feel out of breath climbing the stairs nowadays, and I used to bound up them two at a time. I know it's not good for me, and that I have done that dreaded thing and 'let myself go', but it's only really now that I am starting to notice, let alone care much.

My legs are still aching from my long walk with Kit and Tui a few days ago and I'm keen to do something about my lack of fitness. New Zealand is not a country for sitting around – there is too much to see and do here, too much beauty outside to waste any time festering away indoors. Being here has given me a new hunger to explore and ramble, and it is this that I focus on as I rub the sleep out of my eyes and blunder across the car park.

'Morning!'

Griff greets me from the open door of a coach, a clipboard in his hands and sunglasses pushed up into his tufty blond hair.

I was happily surprised when Kit suggested after our walk that I join him and Tui on this day trip to Milford Sound – even more so when my half-sister started jumping up and down with excitement at the prospect. As it transpires, Griff operates a number of tours out of Queenstown, and he happened to have a few extra seats going spare today. Allie wasn't able to join us because someone had to stay behind at the stables, and the girl who had covered for her and Kit on the day we'd all played Frisbee golf had the weekend off to attend a wedding. And anyway, Kit added, Allie had seen it all before, whereas I was a genuine tourist, and Tui a big fan of the seals that we were apparently guaranteed to see.

'Hey,' I say, glancing at my watch. 'I'm not late, am I?'

'Nah,' Griff grins. 'Kit only got here a few minutes ago – him and Trouble are already on board.'

Clutching the coffee I picked up on the way here, I head quickly into the cool air-conditioned interior of the bus. Tui, who is sitting about halfway down by the window, spots me straight away and calls out my name, her eyes screwing up in delight as I make my way along to join her and Kit. He taps his takeaway cup against mine in greeting, his expression communicating that he feels exactly the same about the early start as I do.

As Tui chatters away, telling me a story about how Beavis chased a rabbit and got himself stuck in its burrow, Griffin does a final headcount and, with a merry toot, manoeuvres the coach out through the deserted streets.

It is nearing six a.m., and the only people I see as we drive out of town are those opening their cafés or shops for the day. The sky is a faded navy blue, and the sun is tucked away behind the distant hills. It is undoubtedly going to be another scorching-hot day, but for now the heat is quiet, soothed into submission by the damp fingers of dawn.

'So, we're now on the eastern shore of Lake Wakatipu,' Griff announces, his microphone crackling slightly as he clears his throat and starts to tell us all about the area.

The view out across the water is staggering. It is the sheer scale of the lakes and mountains here that so enthrals me. They make me feel smaller in size, but stronger in myself somehow. The flat Cambridgeshire countryside back home is isolating by comparison. Anything feels not only possible here, but probable, too. It is, simply put, incredible.

Tui falls silent as we continue further along the highway, passing bleached snatches of grass, dense patches of undergrowth and the occasional dwelling set back from the road. The Remarkables loom grandly above us, their jagged peaks silhouetted against the still-rising sun. I stare, my eyes glassy, trying not to think about

Anna, and the clever words she would have chosen to describe this place. I still haven't been able to face opening her memory book, but with every day that I spend here, I can sense myself becoming braver. Perhaps the fact that my birth mother is not here is fortuitous rather than disastrous. It has meant that I have been able to spend time getting to know Tui without the added pressure of her knowing that we are related, but it's also given me some much-needed space for myself – something that I did not realise I needed until I had it. David was right, after all – getting away from home has been a tonic for my battered heart, even if the circumstances are a very long way from straightforward.

We stop for breakfast in the pretty lakeside town of Te Anau. Tui takes my hand and practically drags me down the steps into the sunshine, and the two of us wait under the shade of a bakery's awning while Kit and Griff pop inside to pick up some goodies. She is wearing duck-egg-blue leggings today and a red Mickey Mouse sweatshirt, which she promptly yanks off and attempts to tie around her waist.

'Shall I help you?' I offer, but she nods her head and says no.

'I can do it, Gee-nie,' she assures me through gritted teeth, but it's hard to simply stand there and watch while she struggles. When I move towards her to help, however, Tui emits a shrill squawk of indignation and scurries away out of reach.

'Don't mind Miss Grumpy Pants,' says a returning Kit, handing me a paper bag containing some sort of warm pastry.

'She can be very stubborn, this one,' adds Griff, who is making short work of an enormous sausage roll. 'Tui the mule, I call her.'

'Hmph!' Tui crosses her arms in an exaggerated gesture of disapproval. 'I'm not a mule, Griff. Jeez! I'm a puppy, that's all.'

'You are?' Kit exclaims. 'Well, then,' he says, holding up another bag, 'you'd better not have this muffin – it's got chocolate chips in it, and those are poisonous for dogs.'

'Mmmm,' croons Tui, sticking out her chin and opening her mouth in a wide grin. 'Chocolaaate.'

Deft as a cruise ship magician, Kit gives Tui her muffin whilst somehow managing to unknot and retie her jumper around her hips at the same time. When he clocks my look of admiration, he laughs.

'Not my first time,' he says.

The four of us take our assorted breakfast bits down towards the shore of the lake. The water here looks as thick and dense as gloss paint, and is the deep, bruised blue of a thunderous sky. Griff sits down on a wooden bench and closes his eyes, luxuriating in the warmth of the sunshine as he absent-mindedly rubs sausage roll crumbs out of his beard. Tui, meanwhile, has finished her muffin at a speed that would impress even chief-of-the-cake-devourers Hayley, and is busy selecting stones to chuck into the water, the first of which sends a lurking gull scuttling away in noisy alarm.

'Quite something, right?' Kit remarks, between mouthfuls of bacon roll.

'It's so serene,' I tell him, assuming that he means the view and not the bird. 'Even in the quietest spots back home, you can usually hear the rumble of traffic, but here, there's barely a sound. It's so peaceful.'

As if on cue, Tui lets out a very long and loud burp, before collapsing into shouty hiccups of laughter.

Kit rolls his eyes.

'You were saying?'

I grin back at him.

'She's brilliant,' I say simply. 'A comedy genius.'

'That girl is the sweet potato of Bonnie's patch,' Kit agrees. 'I reckon she would do literally anything for her – you know?'

'Of course,' I mumble, momentarily winded by his words. Little does Kit realise how much of a gut-punch it is to hear how cherished Tui is by her mother – by the same mother who felt unable to cherish me. Unable or unwilling – I don't yet know which. But I find that I cannot resent Tui, even if I am a bit jealous of her. Because how could I? She absolutely deserves all this abundant love that everybody seems to shower her with – Bonnie's most of all.

I look down at my napkin, which I have begun shredding into pieces in my hands, then back out across the water. Now that Tui has ceased lobbing her stones in favour of hunting for shells, the surface of the lake has returned to a glassy calm.

'Time to get back on the road, kids,' Griff says, stretching out each of his arms like a scarecrow. His eyebrows are so pale that the sunlight makes them appear translucent.

I take one last, lingering look across the lake, squinting until the scene begins to blur. I wish I could keep this moment as something other than just a memory, and then I would be able to return to it during times of need. I want to remember how it felt to be here, to be so close to something resembling contentment.

'Come on, Gee-nie, come on,' sings Tui, and this time when she presses her hand into mine, I squeeze her fingers back just as tight.

20

The closer we get to Milford Sound, the more enthralled I feel.

There is such a lot to know about this country, and I marvel at Griff's humorous commentary as he entertains the coach with interesting facts and anecdotes, telling his captive audience more about Fiordland National Park and sprinkling in general titbits about New Zealand. No wonder Kiwis are so proud of their homeland – I would be, too. But then, of course, I suppose that my own heritage is linked to this place. Is that why I feel so at peace here? Or would the same have been true if I had embarked on a backpacking adventure, as Hayley and I originally planned years ago, without knowing anything about my roots?

For so many years, I have been content to fill my mind with only the stuff that I considered to be important, none of which ever reached as far as New Zealand. In truth, much of it did not reach past the gates of Mill House Stables. How sheltered I have been, and for so long, too. How could I have been so fulfilled by such a minuscule existence? It feels utterly baffling to me now that I'm here, learning and uncovering so much with every passing hour, and my previous life is starting to feel increasingly small.

We have only stopped twice more since breakfast – once to stroll past the jaw-dangling splendour of the Mirror Lakes, and again while we waited in line to drive through the Homer Tunnel – and Kit and I agree that it's a relief to get the circulation going again via a short walk from the coach to the waiting ferry.

The vast white vessel has an upper and lower deck, but everyone – including Kit, Tui and me – heads immediately up the metal steps, keen to be in the best spot for both scenery and sunshine. It's invigorating to be out in the clean air, and as the engines rumble into life and the boat moves slowly out into the water, I grip the railings with cheerful anticipation.

The only thing I know about Milford Sound is that Rudyard Kipling once referred to it as the 'eighth wonder of the world' – a fact that David repeated to me multiple times before I flew out here. As the boat chugs on, however, I soon understand why Mr Kipling was so overawed by what he saw.

Vast peaks the colour of ash burst up out of the dark, swirling water of the fiord, while veils of mist cling like toddlers to their jagged sides. Waterfalls tumble down from the clifftops, each one tossing its load into the deep basin below with a powerful yet light-hearted abandon that both thrills and astounds me. The sky above is a faultless Tiffany blue, blemished only by the merest suggestion of cloud, and I lift up my chin to gaze at it, overwhelmed yet again at its colossal breadth. It's as though my senses are lined up one by one, like soldiers on parade, each one ready for action. I can see and hear the awesome beauty of this place – but I can feel it, too, just as I can taste the spray in the air and feel the wind rushing through my hair. It is impossible not to be moved by Milford's might and magnitude, inconceivable not to feel privileged simply to be here.

I tear my eyes away from the view in order to steal a glance at Tui. Like me, my half-sister has been wowed into stillness, the frothiness of her irresistible personality temporarily subdued by wonder. Beyond Tui and also with his eyes trained on the water, Kit looks utterly lost in thought. But as if he can feel the weight of my scrutiny, he looks round and catches me staring at him, the sides of his mouth dancing upwards in an easy smile before I have time to turn away.

Around Billy, I often feel as if I am the one driving the conversation forwards, and that to a certain extent, at least, he reacts to my remarks, rather than vice versa. Our friendship trots along with the ease that comes only once you have spent years in another person's company, and are therefore privy to all their foibles. With Kit, however, the opposite is true, because although he is easy-going and approachable, I still can't read his expressions, or those little tics that so often give people away. When he fixes me with a look like the one he is giving me now, so genuine in appearance yet so disarmingly kind, it makes me feel strangely bashful and unsure of how to react.

Further embarrassment is avoided thanks to a sudden collective shriek. The ferry driver has aimed the bow of the boat right under the largest waterfall, soaking two thirds of the top deck in the process.

'Tui!' It's Griff, calling across from the opposite railings.

'Come and see what I've found,' he says, beckoning with a hand, but Tui is already slipping and sliding her way across the wet boards towards him.

'Watch out!' I shout, just as Kit yells, 'Bloody hell!' and the two of us leap forwards and catch one of Tui's arms each at exactly the same time, saving her from an almost certain collision with the floor.

'Jeez,' she grumbles, shaking us off without a word of thanks.

'Well,' exclaims Kit. 'That's charming. Of all the ungrateful little toads.'

I am about to reply, when Tui calls out my name, her frantic hand flapping even harder than the ferry's red, white and blue flag.

'What's the matter?' I begin, hurrying over and then letting out a cry of delight. Because there, lounging below us on an outcrop of flat rocks, is a whole little tribe of brown seals.

'They're amazing!' I say, beaming first at Tui then at Griff.

Lifting my camera, I zoom in until I can see the

small, inquisitive faces in more detail, delighted by their black beady eyes and short grey whiskers. Despite the proximity of the boat, most of the seals appear to be fast asleep, and I point out as much to Tui.

'Lazy bones,' she says laughingly, but I can see that she is enchanted.

'Actually,' I tell her, 'seals are nocturnal – do you know what "nocturnal" means?'

Tui shakes and then nods her head.

'Well,' I continue, happy to put my lifelong animal fascination to some good use for once, 'it means that they are active at night time. That's when they prefer to catch fish for their dinner, and it must be quite hard work, because they are so tired afterwards that they sleep nearly all day.'

'Wow,' she says, her eyes wide.

'Brown seals like those have got fingernails, just like us,' I tell her, wiggling my fingers and feeling hopelessly touched when she follows suit. 'They use them to climb up on to the rocks.'

'Will they bite me?' Tui wants to know. She looks so serious as she says it that my heart almost breaks.

'They can be a bit stroppy, Tu,' says Kit, who has just appeared behind us, 'but you'll be OK as long as you don't get too close.'

'They're extra aggy at the mo,' Griff puts in. 'It's mating season.'

As the boat pulls away and heads out into open water, Tui rubs her stomach and announces that she's hungry enough to eat three sandwiches, two chocolate bars and a seal, prompting a laughing Kit and me to venture down one deck in search of lunch.

'So,' he says, as we join the back of a very long queue leading up towards a kiosk, 'Tui has not stopped going on about that riding lesson you gave her. Allie reckons you must be a pro?'

'Tui is much better than she gives herself credit for,' I reply honestly. 'You said she first sat on a pony as a baby, right?'

'I think it pretty much goes with the territory if you're Bonnie's daughter,' he says, not noticing me wince. 'But as you know, she's nowhere near confident or able enough to go out alone yet. Her balance is a bit off – it's part of her condition.'

'She's so great,' I enthuse. 'It feels so unfair that she has all these issues to contend with.'

'I know,' Kit agrees, his expression pensive. 'She's such a sweetheart, despite it all. She never lets her condition stop her from doing what she wants. Bonnie's raised her so she understands her limitations, and she accepts that she's not like most of her friends.'

It's the casual 'Bonnie's raised her' that stings the most, and I'm assaulted by a wave of both sympathy and disgruntlement. Of course I feel sorry for Tui, but I don't want to make any allowances for the difficulties that Bonnie must have faced. Dismay has always been my go-to emotion where my biological mother is concerned, but now those clear waters are being muddied by all this new information, and these people, and this place. I'm not even sure how I'm supposed to feel about Bonnie now – or if I want her to make an appearance. Can I still resent her when everyone else seems to love her so much? Is she really as great as Kit makes her out to be, or has she simply done a good job of fooling him? Maybe he doesn't know her as well as he thinks he does. And then there is Tui – can I have affection for her that is not linked to our shared mother? And will I lose one if I refuse to forgive the other?

I am still mulling it over an hour later, long after lunch has been eaten, chasing the same questions around in my mind as I stare out at the view across Milford Sound. Perhaps somewhere in this dark, churning mass of water, I will find the answers I crave. I don't want to have to face all this on my own – I want someone else to take over and tell me what I should do, and how I should feel.

And not just anyone, I realise, closing my eyes as it comes to me.

I want my mum.

21

Anna's memory book lies open on the bedside table – it's the first thing I see when I open my eyes. The leather is cracked along the spine, and the ribbon bookmark frayed at its edges. I remember that Anna used to play absent-mindedly with it as she scribbled away, caressing the soft material with the fleshy part of her thumb.

She had busy hands, my adoptive mother, and each finger was laden with the rings that she had collected during her years spent travelling. Her favourite was the vintage diamond engagement ring that David had blown his first proper month's salary on, but I always preferred the jade stone. When she gave it to me on my twenty-first birthday, I was so touched that I cried genuine tears of joy.

After we disembarked from the ferry at Milford Sound four days ago and got back on the coach, Griff explained that the early Maori people had discovered jade stone in the area, although they called it *pounamu*, and that spiritually, it was very important to them. Anna never told me where she got the ring from originally, or perhaps I didn't think to ask, but now it feels important to know. This memory book does not go back as far as the year she gifted me the ring, sadly, but I have decided to begin reading it again anyway, mostly because of how much I am missing her.

It was difficult at first, seeing her neat, rounded letters. She had a funny way of curling the tails of her 'Y's and 'G's, and her buoyant spirit has been captured by her fondness for an exclamation mark – or three. That was Anna, though – always laughing, forever positive, perpetually bubbly. I had not realised what a light she was, until that glow was snuffed out, leaving David and me stumbling around in the darkness that followed. Reading her little observations, quirky remarks and insightful musings is bringing back the mother I miss, and although it hurts when the inevitable loss comes knocking, I have discovered over the past few days that the gain is more than worth the pain.

I have not been back to Koru Stables since Sunday. Tui is at school during the week, and despite Allie welcoming me last time, I doubt she would appreciate me turning up again for no apparent reason. I know how busy a yard can be – and Kit and Allie are filling in for Bonnie as well. It still feels utterly bizarre to me that my biological mother ended up flying to England the very same day that I came out to New Zealand, and I have been over the possible reasons for her trip multiple times in my head. I checked in with David yesterday, but he is adamant that he has not heard from her. What could she be doing – and with whom? If I wasn't such a coward, I would ask Kit to find out for me, but then I would have to explain why I couldn't simply contact her myself. Plus, I am actually beginning to dread the thought of her returning and finding me here – the result of that is too uncertain, and her reaction could unravel all the calm I have gathered around me since I arrived.

It is such a mess, this whole bizarre situation, yet I can't deny that some good has come from it. Namely meeting my half-sister and, my subconscious whispers, it has been nice to be around horses again, too.

I have no plan for my day, just as I hadn't for the past few, but actually, I quite like that. Back at home, I am always aware of David down in his study, clacking away on his keyboard as he sends poor old Evangeline off on yet another time-travelling adventure. His action fuels my own inaction, and makes me feel doubly guilty for doing nothing. I did try to work as a receptionist at Hayley's mum's dentistry practice in the village, but all the patients recognised me, and the pity in their eyes quickly became too much. I managed three weeks, before retreating to the safety and solitude of my bedroom.

Here, however, it's different. Nobody knows me, nobody expects anything from me, and nobody but me gets to choose how much or little I achieve in my day. As a result, I have found myself exploring Queenstown and the surrounding area tirelessly – I even toyed with the idea of booking a ziplining trip, for heaven's sake.

Thinking that I might take Anna's memory book

down to Queenstown Gardens for a day of reading, I am just chucking a few essentials in my bag when there's a knock at the door.

'G'day.'

I stare up at Kit, my first thought being that Bonnie must have returned earlier than expected, and that maybe she is even here with him now, in the passenger seat of that red jeep parked down by the kerb, come to tell me that I'm not wanted here, not in her town and not in her life.

I must have stuttered out a few words of response, because Kit's friendly expression swiftly changes into one of bemusement.

'What was that?' he asks, folding his arms in the same way he did at the stables on that first day. They're so large – more like felled logs than human limbs.

I cough.

'Hey,' I manage. 'What brings you here?'

'Well,' he begins, waiting for me to cease my awkward fidgeting, 'I was supposed to be spending the day with Griff, but the big, yellow-headed idiot had to work. I was in the area anyway, so I thought I'd pop by and see if you fancied a hike?'

'A hike?'

When did I turn into a parrot?

'Yeah, that's right.' Kit removes a speck of lint from the front of his grey T-shirt and drops it on to the wooden floor of the patio. 'I've got the day off, and seeing as how you're here alone and probably don't know much about what there is to do around here, I thought I could show you around a bit, you know.'

'Oh,' I say, tucking away an imaginary strand of hair and fiddling furiously with the strap of my bag. What is it about this man that makes my entire vocabulary vanish into a black hole?

'Before I worked over at Koru, I used to be a tour guide like Griff, believe it or not,' Kit explains. 'So, I do know my stuff. And Queenstown has got a lot to offer – I'd feel damn awful if you'd come all this way and I didn't help you to make the most of it.'

It's a very generous offer, but how will Allie react? Will she be angry if she finds out that the two of us spent time together alone, without Tui? The last thing I want to do is cause friction between them – especially not when they have both been so nice to me. But then, I can't ignore the fact that it would be nice to have a companion for the day – and surely Kit would never do anything to deliberately upset his girlfriend? He's too decent for that.

'I guess I could,' I begin, still hesitant. 'I mean, as long as you don't mind?'

'You'd be doing me a favour,' he assures me. 'If I don't have something planned for the day, I only end up in the boozer – or worse, back down at the yard, and then I'll get roped into working. There's a truckload of new wood chippings waiting to go down in the indoor school, and the paddock fences aren't going to fix themselves.'

'Only if you're sure?' I check again, and this time Kit blows exasperated air into his cheeks.

'I'm very sure, right? Now, do you have any shoes that aren't those girly stilts?'

I look down at my wedge-heeled espadrilles.

'These are hardly stilts,' I protest. 'I can walk in them fine.'

'Along a catwalk, maybe,' he drawls, rocking back on to the heels of his far more sensible boots. His calves above them are thick and laden with muscle, and he is dressed in simple cargo shorts and an ash-grey shirt.

'If you're really going to experience the best that Queenstown has to offer,' he adds, 'then you're going to need something a bit sturdier.'

'OK, in that case . . .' I give in, leaving him on the doorstep while I venture back into the apartment. By the time I've swapped my beloved wedges for the deeply unattractive pair of chunky walking shoes that David insisted I pack and made my way back outside, Kit is standing down on the pavement, a rucksack slung over one meaty shoulder and a large bottle of water in his hand.

'Much better,' he says, appraising my footwear as I clomp down the steps like a Clydesdale.

'I feel like a shire horse in these,' I mutter, and Kit starts tapping the pockets of his tatty dark-green shorts.

'Ah, bloody hell – I'm all out of sugar lumps.'

'Funny,' I retort, but I'm smiling.

We set off in the opposite direction to the town

centre, and even in my walking shoes, I have to jog to keep up with Kit's huge strides. The incline of the road becomes increasingly steep the further away from civilisation we get, and after ten or so minutes, I have to stop and lean over to catch my breath.

'You all right there?' Kit asks, glancing over his shoulder.

'I'm fine,' I splutter, my hands on my knees as I try not to think about how red and shiny my face must be. 'It's just the heat – I'm still not used to it.'

He regards me for a moment or two.

'Are you sure you're OK?' he asks again. 'Because this hike is not going to get any easier.'

'I'm sure,' I insist, unwilling to appear any more unfit than I have already.

Kit looks as if he doesn't quite believe me, but he chooses not to comment, instead pointing ahead at a huge, overgrown hill.

'We're going up there next,' he says, watching me for a reaction.

I laugh, certain that he's not serious, only to realise from his expression that he very much is.

'All the way up there?' I repeat, not even pretending to sound anything but aghast.

Kit nods once.

'Yep, we're going to take the Tiki Trail and then head right the way to the top.'

'How high is it?' I want to know, but he shakes his head.

'If I tell you, you'll wimp out on me. And it's not as high as it looks – you'll breeze it. You'll be skipping up there.'

'I'm not some sort of mountain goat,' I grumble under my breath, and Kit snorts with laughter.

'No,' he agrees, looking me up and down. 'I reckon goats are way uglier.'

As we continue towards the base of the hill, I find myself smiling away for no apparent reason. I must be more relaxed around Kit than I thought, and it's heartening to know that the two of us have slipped effortlessly into the same game of banter tennis that I play with Billy. Back home, where everyone has known me for years and has witnessed my transformation from bubbly and sociable into brittle and closed off, I don't feel one hundred per cent authentic with anyone – not Billy, not Hayley, and not even David, not one hundred per cent. If anything, my adoptive father is the person I feel least comfortable with. We were so close once, the three of us, in our tight family unit – but Anna's accident has shattered the bonds between us, the same ones that I always believed to be unbreakable, and now I have no idea how to mend them. Kit knows nothing about this, or about the accident, or about me – not really. I can be a different version of myself with him, one that is perhaps more like the old me.

I had an idea of how things would be when I reached New Zealand – how I would feel and what I would do and say – but never for a moment had I factored in a

Kit or a Tui. I had envisaged getting some answers and finally putting a face to the empty space that I had in place of my birth mother, but I never imagined that I would make a friend or discover that I have a sibling. Kit has listened to and accepted me, and now he's here, choosing to spend his free time with me, his friendship offered freely and seemingly without complication.

It's as if I'm beginning to wake up after a very long sleep, and for the first time since that awful day, I am able to be present in the moment again. I feel alive.

22

Bonnie

Despite being as big a fan of parties as she was of wasp stings, Bonnie had been told that she must come downstairs and attend Tracey's annual mince pies and mulled wine soiree. Her unflinching host had also insisted that Bonnie put on a frock for the occasion, giving her house guest the benefit of a pained expression when she wondered aloud what was wrong with her old jeans and oversized jumper.

'If you don't already know the answer to that, duck, then I can't help you.'

Now Bonnie was trapped between the arm of Tracey's sofa and the pale, limp form of Mr Gregory from three doors down, who had breath potent enough to puncture a parachute and was wearing sandals with his battered corduroy slacks, despite the below-freezing temperatures outside. For the past twenty minutes, he had been talking earnestly about the properties of volcanic soil – a fact that was making Bonnie wish she had never told him where she was from. New Zealand had acres of the stuff.

'It's all about the nutrients and minerals, you see,' he

enthused, scooping up a handful of salmon blinis from a nearby dish. When he then started extolling the virtues of phosphates, Bonnie found herself sprayed with damp, fishy crumbs and, deciding that enough was bloody well enough, mumbled something about needing a top-up before politely, but firmly, shouldering her way past him.

Once in the relative safety of the kitchen, she filled a glass with water from the tap and leant against the work surface to down the whole lot in three satisfying gulps. She was wearing the only dress she had brought with her, which was black, shapeless and had a hole in the right armpit – but Bonnie could not have cared less. Glancing at the clock on the opposite wall, which was shaped like a cat and had a swinging black tail in place of a pendulum, she reflected that at least now she had put in an appearance she could surely spirit herself back upstairs to the spare room and hide. The story was not going to write itself.

'You all right, love?'

Tracey had just bustled in for another bottle of fizz, and Bonnie jumped forwards guiltily.

'I came for more snacks,' she muttered, picking up a half-empty bag of tortilla chips.

'Poppycock.' Tracey pulled her chin down against her chest. 'You forget how well I know you, love – you never were that comfortable around lots of people. Remember how your hair used to practically stand on end whenever the caff had more than four customers?'

Bonnie went to protest, but she knew Tracey was right. She did hate parties, and concerts, and airport terminals – basically anywhere that you would expect to find a large number of people. How she had ever dealt with so many months in London, she didn't know. Nowadays, Bonnie managed her crowd phobia by barely leaving the stables. Aside from the busloads of horse-riding tourists ferried in daily by Kit, not many people tended to pass by the yard. One of the things she loved most about her place of work was its remote location. Bonnie knew the names of everyone booked in to ride, so in theory, surprise arrivals were a rare-to-non-existent occurrence.

England, in sharp contrast, felt like a minefield. Tracey lived in Kent, which Bonnie knew was many miles away from both Cambridgeshire, where Evangeline lived with her adoptive parents, and London, where everything had happened – but she still didn't feel safe. Coming back here had made the intervening years fall away, and Bonnie felt increasingly as if she was reverting back into her eighteen-year-old self – that lost, scared and homesick girl who was so desperate to please and fit in.

'Tracey,' she said, as her old friend free-poured an alarming quantity of rum into a pan containing mulled wine, 'what else do you remember about me from those days?'

'Well . . .' Tracey considered this for a moment. She had pulled out all the festive stops for her party, dressing in floor-length purple sequins and sweeping her streaked blonde hair up into a chignon. She had joked to Bonnie earlier that she resembled a Christmas bauble, but Bonnie preferred to think of her as an eccentric fairy. Tracey had certainly granted her a good few wishes over the years they had known each other.

'You were determined,' Tracey decided, bending forwards to sniff the pan appreciatively. 'You used to do this adorable thing where you jutted out your chin and clenched your teeth together, as if to say, "I want that and I will damn well have it." And you were capable, too, much more so than I think you realised. Aside from the times when the café was overrun with workmen, nothing seemed to daunt you. Well, nothing until . . .' She paused in her stirring.

'The baby,' Bonnie said quietly, and at this, Tracey nodded sympathetically.

'Yes, love – the baby.'

And it was true. The pregnancy had hit Bonnie hard and sent her cowering into a corner, terrified to face what was happening, yet scared to undo what had been done. When she left little Evangeline behind and went home to New Zealand, it wasn't simply her swollen, leaking breasts and topsy-turvy hormones that rendered her miserable; it was what she had lost – not just her daughter, but herself. That girl, who Tracey remembered as being such a go-getter, had remained on the tarmac of Heathrow Airport, while the embattled new version flew to the other side of the world, forever changed.

It was only when Tui was born thirteen years later that Bonnie began to regain her lost strength – and when it became clear that her new baby daughter was not like all the other children, and that she was going to face more challenges than most, Bonnie had no choice but to step up and woman up. Tui needed her mum right there next to her, ready and willing to fight any of the battles that she could not, and as the years passed, Bonnie's gutsiness had begun to re-emerge.

That was what she needed to channel now, Bonnie thought. She must find that strength – the same determination that had got her through all those hospital appointments and tests with Tui, the bravery that she'd had to show in the face of others' pity – and utilise it.

'I need to—' she began, making to leave the room, but Tracey was already smiling.

'I know, duck. I know.'

23

Kit barely breaks a sweat as he leads me along the steep and winding trail. He seems to be impervious to both the intense heat of the day and the arduous gradient of Queenstown's Tiki Trail, but the opposite is unfortunately the case for me. The relief I felt when we moved from the unsheltered pavement into the tree-shaded undergrowth turned out to be short-lived, and before long, I'm plucking the damp material of my T-shirt off my back and dabbing ineffectually at the sweat on my forehead.

The muddy uphill footpath is littered with exposed tree roots and the air is thick with the scent of vegetation. Birds chirp, fallen leaves crunch under our boots, and columns of sunlight filter through the branches of the towering Douglas firs, dappling the ground with white-and-gold speckles. It feels like being inside the vast cave of a treasure-hungry dragon. Kit chats away amicably as we continue to climb, offering a casual hand of assistance whenever the going gets particularly tough and pointing out large throne-like chairs that have been sculpted from the wide stumps of felled beech trees. Further up, we pass a narrow roped-off area that Kit explains is a mountain bike trail and tells me matter-of-factly that he once broke both his collar-bones trying to ride down it 'at full tit'.

It's difficult to imagine anything causing damage to a man of Kit's size, and I tell him so.

'Fragile as a fern frond, me,' he says with a laugh, plucking a leaf from a nearby bush and shredding it between his fingers.

'Have you ever had any other injuries?' I enquire.

Kit frowns, his gaze flickering upwards as he seeks out the small gaps of blue sky visible through the treetops.

'Smashed up my nose playing rugby at school,' he says, tapping it. 'Destroyed a few ribs on a ski trip a few years back, munted my coccyx jumping into a river when I was about fifteen.'

'Bloody hell, man,' I retort, resting my hands on my thighs. A couple of around my age are making their way down the hill, and as the two of us stop to let them past, I notice that the man has a prosthetic leg. That, and the fact that, like Kit, he has clearly found the climb no bother at all, makes me feel even worse about my shambolic fitness levels.

'That's what the olds said at the time,' Kit jokes, his voice cracking with amusement. 'Then my mum, she followed it up with a few more, less polite words.'

'Your poor mum,' I say, wincing inwardly as a pain-ful memory of Anna sitting by my hospital bed slices through me. When I was ten, I had fallen from a bolt-ing pony and managed to break my wrist badly enough that it required surgery. Anna's tearful face was the first thing I saw when I came around from the anaesthetic.

'What about your folks?' he asks, glancing at me as we continue upwards. 'Are they the protective types?'

Where to even begin? I settle on a non-committal 'I guess so', remembering how wobbly I had become down by the Dart River, when it was on the tip of my tongue to tell him about Anna. The mood between us is so light at the moment, I don't want to dampen the cheery spirit of the day by touching on that subject.

Even Kit begins to perspire as we puff and pant our way up what looks to be the final section of the trail. I can see a crescent of sweat on his back and marvel again at his generosity in offering to show me around. Unlike me, Kit also had the foresight to bring a bottle of water along with him, and he offers it to me every few minutes, pulling a face when I shake my head.

'You need to stay hydrated,' he points out after my third refusal, thrusting the bottle towards me. 'I don't want you passing out on me.'

When we finally, blessedly, emerge from the trees on to a flat expanse of road beside a large café, I contemplate weeping genuine tears of exhausted relief. It still feels beyond bizarre that it's essentially summer in December. Just five days now until Christmas, and only four until the anniversary of Anna's death. I have now spent 361 days without her, yet somehow I am still here. The world is still spinning, the sun rising and setting, my senses still reeling from all these sights, sounds and smells. Everything has continued without her, and it's not fair. It's not right.

'Quick breather here, then we'll carry on up, yeah?'

I turn and stare at Kit, feeling the blood draining from my cheeks.

'This isn't the top?'

Kit looks around, as if surveying the area for the first time.

'Er, nope, sorry.'

'But the luge starts from here,' I say, pointing to a sign behind him. 'And over there is the gondola drop-off.'

'This is just the Skyline,' he states. 'The tourist summit, not the proper one. If you want the true Kiwi experience, then we're going to need to go a bit higher.'

'How much higher?' I ask, but Kit merely shrugs.

'Ben Lomond is a good three or four hours' walk away, but I reckon it will only take us an hour or so to reach the point where the hang gliders take off. Maybe two hours at your pace . . .'

'Oi!' I admonish, and he grins at me.

'Oh, come on – I'm only pulling your pisser.'

'I beg your pardon?' I reply.

Why does my frightfully posh voice keep insisting on coming out?

'Pulling your pisser. You know – tickling your tootsies, taking the royal mickey.'

'Tickling my tootsies?' I repeat incredulously, and Kit's wide mouth lifts into another smirk.

'Could have been worse,' he says. 'I could have said

titties. Now, I dunno about you, but I reckon I have earned myself an ice cream.'

Once we're inside a small café area, I offer to treat him, and after grumbling half-heartedly about chivalry being a lost art, he agrees, making me laugh when he promptly opts for a triple-scoop cone with extra lashings of fudge sauce.

'I'm a growing man,' he quips, patting his flat stomach.

I choose a small ice lolly the shape of a watermelon slice, which starts to melt as soon as we step back outside. I have no real choice but to insert the entire thing into my mouth, but it doesn't seem to faze Kit in the slightest. He merely grins, and then devours a good third of his own in a single bite before leading me around the café to a narrow wooden gate. Pushing it open with his foot, he waits until I have passed through the gap to follow.

'Wow,' I breathe, strolling across the wide platform to take in the view. Low-slung clouds drift like soapsuds across a clear, bright sky, while far below, the vast deep-blue puddle of Lake Wakatipu plays affable host to their reflections. Houses as small as Monopoly pieces sit strewn around the shore, and thimble-sized boats chug across the water, each leaving a faint sliver of white in its wake. What really draws my eye, however, is the Remarkables, so mighty and self-assured as they stand like sentries on the far horizon.

'Quite something, right?' says Kit, his gaze following

my own. 'And they look even better topped with snow in the wintertime.'

'I can imagine,' I mumble, lulled into quiet by the scene spread out below us. There is something undeniably ethereal about New Zealand – it has a spiritual atmosphere. There is so much space and apparent peace up here, and I feel all at once uncaged, as if I could step over the railings and simply float away into the endless blue, up and away from all the confusion and the hurt.

I only realise that I have started to cry when Kit's concerned face blocks out the view.

'Hey, what's up with you?' he asks, crinkling his pale-mint eyes in sympathy as I accept his proffered napkin.

'I'm fine,' I sniff, rubbing furiously at my face. 'Just being a cretin as usual. Sorry.'

Kit takes a deep breath, and I stare down at the ground, willing him not to pry any further. I never know once I give in to my tears how long they will last, or how wretched I will become.

'I'm a pretty good listener,' he offers. 'Obviously, you can tell me to go away and get stuffed, but I would like to help you, if I can.'

His expression is so genuine that for a second or two I waver, imagining how it would feel to tell him the truth – and not just the facts, but the secret. The one that has anchored me here in this harbour of sorrow.

'Genie.'

I look up, blinking away a fresh batch of tears.

'Whatever it is,' he says, 'you can tell me. I'm not going to judge you or anything like that.'

I almost laugh at that, because how could he not?

'I know you lost someone that you cared a lot about,' he continues, his hands resting on the wooden rail of the balcony. 'It helps to talk about it, you know. I swear on this.' He raises a pinky finger.

'Another two hours uphill, was it?' I say, giving my cheeks a firm wipe.

Kit nods, but his smile is at half mast.

'At least.'

'Well, how about I bet you a beer that I can do it in under one?'

'A beer?' he exclaims with delight, limbering up in a ridiculously over-the-top manner. 'Now you're talking. I will absolutely take that bet!'

24

Kit clinks his bottle against mine and grins before taking a swig.

'Come on, 'fess up,' he says. 'You were hustling me on that first trail this morning, weren't you?'

I shake my head as I swallow my own sip of beer.

'Not at all. I just got into my stride, that's all.'

'Hmmm,' he says, one thick, dark eyebrow slightly raised.

'I'm even faster across a flat surface,' I joke, and he barks out a 'ha' of amusement.

'A regular little Road Runner, you are,' he proclaims.

'Meep, meep,' I reply lamely, and again he laughs. It's a nice sound – deep and authentic.

The two of us are sitting on a large patch of grass not far from the lake, a liquor-store carrier bag on the ground between our outstretched legs which Kit has pinned down with the same bunch of keys that he used to prise the tops off our bottles. I left the choice of ale up to him and was surprised when he returned from the shop with a four-pack of the tequila-flavoured variety. I would have had Kit down as more of a standard beer man.

It's a relief to be off my feet. The climb up Bob's Peak

today was as tough as Kit had warned it would be, but I do feel good for it. Tomorrow, I will no doubt wake up to delayed onset muscle soreness and be forced to limp around clutching the furniture for support, but for now, I'm perfectly content. It is just after six p.m., and the fierce heat of the day is beginning to mellow. The wide Queenstown pavements are busy with the usual groups of backpackers – many of them sporting Santa hats – as well as families and older couples heading out for an early supper. Christmas songs filter out from the open doors of bars and restaurants, and the surrounding trees have been strung with hundreds of fairy lights.

Kit has finished his first beer and is now lying down flat on his back, his hands laced behind his head and his eyes shut. He is so comfortable in his own skin, this man. I have never met anyone so utterly at ease with the world and their place within it.

'So,' I say, watching a gull swoop down and pinch an abandoned chip from one of the outdoor tables of a nearby pub, 'what does everyone do for Christmas in New Zealand?'

Kit opens one eye.

'Goes to the beach,' he replies. 'There's always a right big party down here. Some folk go out to Lake Wanaka for the day, and everyone has a barbie, no matter where they end up.'

'Sounds fun,' I comment, and Kit props himself up on one elbow. There's a fine layer of dust all down one side of his shirt.

'I'm spending the day itself with Allie, Griff and their olds,' he explains. 'But I was chewing over the idea of a barbie at the yard the day before. We always close up around lunchtime on Christmas Eve, and I reckon Tui's dad will be cool with her coming along. Would you be up for it?'

'Me?' I exclaim.

Kit gives me the same look he always seems to give me, the one that says, 'Of course I mean you, you flaming goof.'

'It'll be a right hoot, I reckon,' he adds, reaching into the bag and extracting another bottle. After giving the top a cursory bite, he shakes his head and uses his keys to get it off instead.

Christmas Eve, the anniversary of Anna's death – a day I should by rights be spending alone, thinking about what I've lost, and the part I played in it. But the thought of being alone in my rented apartment, in a different time zone to my friends back home, is unbearably bleak. I can dwell after the barbecue – I will have the entire night to dwell.

'I'd actually really love to come,' I tell him, pausing to down the rest of my own beer. 'But you must let me contribute some food and stuff.'

'Just bring plenty of beer,' Kit says. 'Griff will get through a keg on his own.'

I excuse myself to pay a visit to the very clean public lavatories on the other side of the green, and when I return, Kit is tapping away on his mobile.

'Bonnie,' he says, by way of explanation. 'Should I tell her you're here after all?'

It is a fair question, and in any normal circumstances, it would make perfect sense for me to say yes – but this situation is very far from being anywhere close to ordinary. I wonder why Kit hasn't already shipped me – why he wouldn't have called Bonnie to tell her about me the very minute I was out of range.

'Er, no – don't worry,' I blurt, scraping hurriedly through my unhelpfully empty brain in search of some words – any words. 'Like you said, she'll be back soon. I kind of wanted my visit to be a surprise.'

A surprise, I think bitterly, as if me turning up to confront my long-absent mother is something fun and exciting.

Kit still has his phone in his hand, his fingers poised to type.

'If that's what you want,' he says, seemingly unfussed. I feel a rush of relief.

'Is she having a nice time in England?' I ask, feigning casual interest.

'She didn't really say,' Kit replies. 'Never has been a big one for texting. Truth is, Bon's a bit old-fashioned. I don't think she'd have a mobile phone at all if it wasn't for Tui demanding one, and you should see her trying to use the yard computer – it's like watching a baby seal trying to tap-dance.'

Despite my inner wariness, I chuckle at the ludicrous image.

I guess this explains why I could find no trace of Bonnie Moon on social media when I finally looked her up, and why Googling her name brought up no helpful results. The Koru Stables website, meanwhile, is rudimentary at best and looks as if it hasn't been updated in years. It seems the woman who gave birth to me is a future-phobe, and actually, we have that trait in common. Growing up in the shadow of the famous Evangeline has made me wary of putting too much information about myself out into the ether, and I am very strict about who I follow and befriend. I am far more likely to lurk than ever comment or share, and the only posts I look at on Instagram are those relating to horses.

I'm just about to say something intelligent-sounding about the toxic effects of too much technology, when Kit's phone lights up with a message.

'This'll be Bon again,' he says, only for his brows to knit together as he swipes a finger across the screen.

'What now?' he mutters under his breath, and my paranoid heart starts to beat a little harder.

'Is everything OK?'

'Yeah.' Kit looks up. 'I think so. I mean, I hope so.'

'Oh.'

Kit grimaces.

'Yeah.'

For a moment he appears to deliberate, then in one fluid movement, he is up on his feet and strolling slowly away, his phone now pressed to his ear. I gaze at his back view as he talks into the handset, noticing how

179

the material of his shirt strains across his shoulders, and how tanned his bare calves are below the baggy shorts. Perhaps because I have grown up with him, or maybe because of his slim build and lack of stubble, I always think of Billy as a boy. Kit, in contrast, is very much a man, and way more of an unknown entity. And while he is most definitely – and undeniably – attractive, I'm also slightly in awe of his size and obvious power. It is border-line intimidating – or would be, if he wasn't such a softie.

A steam boat with a large Christmas tree on its upper deck is chugging into shore beyond where Kit is still standing, and I can see couples lined up by the harbour wall waiting to board. How nice it would be to have dinner out on the lake. Even before my 'date' with Billy a few weeks ago, I hadn't been wined and dined by any-one for years. Any boyfriends I have had are men I happened to meet on nights out with Hayley – drunken snogs that became short-lived flings. In my experience, most men don't appreciate coming way below a horse on their girlfriend's priority list – but that is always where they have ended up. Well, it was until the acci-dent. Since Anna died, I have barely even thought about my love life, let alone actively gone out and sought one. Why I thought Billy was the solution to my sexual stalemate, I really don't know.

Still lost in thought, I start as Kit flops back down beside me.

'That was Allie,' he explains, looking forlornly at his bottle of almost-full beer on the grass. I go to ask him what she said, then think better of it, settling on an encouraging smile instead. If he wants to open up to me, then he can, but I'm not going to force the issue.

'She wants us to leave,' he says gloomily.

'Leave?' I reply. 'Leave where?'

'Here.' He sweeps a big arm around. 'Queenstown.'

'She just told you that on the phone?'

For a moment he looks confused.

'Eh? Nah. She just said we needed to talk, and I know what that means. She's been trying to bring it up with me for weeks and I keep making excuses.'

'Where does she want you to go?' I ask, aware that the thought of a Koru Stables with no Kit is a very sad one.

'Wellington,' he says simply, spitting out the word with disdain. 'The big city.'

'And you're not keen?' I prompt, filling in the blanks.

Kit shakes his head.

'Thing is,' he admits, looking sheepish, 'I promised her that if she stayed here for another year, then I would try living in Welly for a year.'

'And how long ago was that?'

Kit clenches his teeth together. 'Two and a bit years.'

'I see . . .'

Poor Allie, I think, watching as Kit runs an agitated hand through his hair. But then, what about Tui? How would she cope if Kit were to move away? He is clearly one of the closest people to her – she adores him.

'I thought I'd be ready to go by then, you know?' Kit laments. 'I would never have said it if I didn't believe that. The thing is, the longer I work at Koru, the more I realise how much I like it. I'm happy where I am, and Allie's happy, too, really – she just tells herself she isn't.'

'Do you really think that?' I ask. 'Or are you just saying it to make yourself feel better?'

His eyes are wide now with bemusement at being challenged, but I don't back down.

'Because,' I continue firmly, 'it would be easier for you if Allie agreed to stay, wouldn't it?'

Kit agrees rather reluctantly that it would.

'And she knows that, which is why she's let you get away with claiming another eighteen months.'

'I told you.' Kit is now picking the label off his bottle. 'She's a good person.'

'I would say that you're both good people,' I point out, but Kit shakes his head.

'A good man would quit whingeing like an old coot and do whatever it takes to make his girlfriend happy.'

'But if that doesn't make you happy . . .' I let the sentence hang unfinished in the air, and Kit looks at me, his mouth set in a grim line.

'Right,' he mutters. 'Now you see my problem.'

'You know what my mum always used to tell me?' I say, and find myself smiling at the memory. 'That it's important to make others happy, but in order to do that, you must start with yourself.'

Kit doesn't miss a beat.

'Used to tell you?' he says softly, and I feel myself wince.

'Yes.'

'Your mum is the one you lost?'

Kit scoots across the grass as I drop my chin, and puts one of his vast arms around me.

'Ah, come here, you,' he says, pulling me against him for a moment.

'I'm fine.' I shake my head, surprised to find that for once, the tears have not automatically appeared. I can hear the opening bars of 'Last Christmas' by Wham! playing in the nearest bar, and wonder if my own heart will ever mend enough for me to give it to someone special.

'How long?' Kit murmurs.

'Almost a year.' It comes out as a croak.

'Bloody hell.' He squeezes me a bit harder. 'You poor little mite.'

'It's OK,' I say, even though we both know that it's anything but. He is so close to me now that I'm practically resting my head on his shoulder, but as soon as I become aware of the warmth of him, I feel his phone vibrate in his pocket.

'Ah,' he says, extracting it with some difficulty. 'Bon. Oh, good stuff – she says it's grand to have a barbie at the yard.'

'Hooray,' I declare, but my delivery is weaker than a daddy-long-legs faced with a hairdryer.

'I'm really sorry,' Kit says. 'About your mum. That fucking sucks, if you'll excuse my language.'

'I do,' I assure him, and with a sudden eruption of laughter, I realise that he's right, too – it does absolutely fucking suck.

'FUCK DEATH!' I shout, causing several people to glance around in alarm. Kit, however, looks thrilled.

'Yeah!' he cries, getting to his feet and pulling me up to join him. 'Death, mate, you are a right shithouse – now why don't you swivel on THIS?'

I splutter with amusement as he holds up an index finger.

'I am literally laughing in the face of you, Death!' I bellow, letting out a scream as Kit grabs both my hands and starts to spin me around. The bars, restaurants and lake all merge into a blur of colour as we whirl, and while I am dimly aware that I must look totally bananas, for the first time in a while, I don't care. I feel like myself, like the old Genie, the one who thought nothing of dancing as if nobody was watching, and of laughing until she could hardly breathe.

'Stop!' I protest, falling into an exhausted, giggling heap on the grass.

Kit joins me, reaching for his beer only to find that he's drunk it all.

'Balls,' he declares, but shakes his head when I offer him a sip of mine.

'I shouldn't – I have to drive back to Koru.'

Panting slightly, overcome with a sudden, crushing embarrassment, I find that I have no idea what to say to him. The resulting silence drags on for an uncomfortably long time and, just like that, the moment Kit and I shared slips away out of reach.

25

The day has arrived.

Anna has been dead for a whole year. Twelve long months, 365 arduous days, and too many agonising hours, minutes and seconds to fathom. One winter morning she was there, alive and glowy-cheeked in my bedroom doorway, then, just a few hours later, she was gone.

It is still the previous day in England, but I call David anyway.

'Darling.' He answers on the second ring.

I open my mouth to reply, but all that comes out is a strangled sort of gasp.

'Oh, Genie.'

I can't stand his sympathy. It makes me feel worse. It makes my horrible snarling guilt intensify. I wish he would shout at me – somebody needs to shout at me.

'I'm sorry,' I say, but he cuts across me before I can continue, always so ready to reassure and comfort. What he doesn't understand is that I don't deserve either of those things.

I'm not sure exactly when I decided that I must tell David the truth – whether I came to it gradually, or I blinked and the notion was there – but once I knew that

I was going to do it, I became almost impatient, as if it wasn't the most terrifying thing imaginable. No, strike that, the most terrifying thing imaginable had already happened – and then some. All I know is that I have to tell someone. I can't keep holding on to it while it erodes me from the inside out.

Guessing that talking about Anna is only making me feel worse, David cautiously changes the subject. He is now telling me a story about some party he went to at his publishers' in London. His editor gifted him a specially made Evangeline ornament sculpted from glass. Sales of his latest book, *Evangeline And . . . The First Father Christmas*, have surpassed all others in his genre, and there is talk of an animated TV series. My adoptive dad is very much the golden boy of the moment.

'That's great,' I say, staring hard at a scuff mark on the wall of my little apartment. It is still early, but the sunlight is already splashing through the open curtains in great golden waves.

'David,' I say, but he isn't listening.

'Did I tell you who they've got to do the audiobook, darling? Only the girl from that period drama we used to watch on Sunday nights – you know the one. Anna fancied the lead actor something rotten, that Irish fellow with the preposterous hair. What was the name of it again? Anyway, it doesn't matter, but she is very popular, apparently – won a Bafta last year, or so they told me, and then—'

'David!'

'Yes?'

'I need to tell you something.'

'What's happened – are you hurt? Did someone hurt you?'

'No,' I say patiently, then almost add, *It's me who did the hurting.*

I went through some more of Anna's memory book before I rang him. I have been doing so every morning and night for the past few days, and each time I open it, I am edging closer to her final entry, her final memory. Will telling David the truth now help me to face it?

I have discovered that Anna almost always wrote about me. Sometimes it's just the briefest of mentions, things such as 'Genie let me plait her hair today. It reminds me so much of when she was a child', while other entries are full transcripts of a conversation we may have had, with her thoughts pencilled in carefully underneath. Anna was not the type of woman to agree with something just for the sake of it, but she was not argumentative either – not for the most part. That was the thing about Annabel Nash – you had to really push her to make her angry.

David has fallen silent now; for once he is waiting for me to speak. I close my eyes for a moment to steel myself, and am surprised to see an image of Kit, of his wide, kind face and sleepy-edged eyes. What would he say if he could see me here, on the verge of confessing it all? Would he urge me to get it over with, or warn me to keep it to myself? I already know the answer, and just that simple fact alone gives me the final bit of courage I need.

Despite the abundant decorations in Queenstown and the familiar music belching out from the taxi radio as it hurtles along the highway towards Glenorchy, I have yet to feel festive. Christmas with sunshine just doesn't feel right. I'm wearing a summer dress, for heaven's sake – with no tights, and no slippers – this is all wrong.

Forty minutes later, however, when I push my way through the treeline at the bottom of the stony pathway and head towards Koru Stables, it looks as if Santa himself has set up his grotto right in the middle of the yard. There are colourful paper chains pinned up above each stall and swathes of fake snow covering the outer walls and windows. Baubles hang from the bolts of the open half-doors, and I exclaim with delight when Keith sticks his whiskery chestnut nose over the top of one to reveal a jaunty Christmas hat, which some enterprising staff member has attached to his headcollar.

I can smell but not see the barbecue; a faint plume of smoke is drifting up from one of the paddocks behind the indoor school. The radio in the office has been cranked right up, and as I make my way over, I spot an enormous Christmas tree inside, its branches covered in a tangle of fairy lights. It has just gone four p.m., and the earlier fug of the afternoon has been tempered by the gentlest breeze. As I always do when I venture out here to the Dart Valley, I take a minute to admire the view of the mountains and the vast, endless blue of the sky.

The skin on my face feels sore from my earlier tears, but I also feel cleansed, as if the weight that has been sitting so heavily and for so long on my chest has lessened somewhat.

David was silent at first, for once allowing himself the time he needed to absorb what I was telling him rather than rushing to reassure. I had feared disappointment – perhaps even anger – but in the end, my adoptive father was pragmatic. His measured response to my tearful confession had been almost a let-down, because in my mind, at least, my crime deserved a far greater punishment. That's the thing about David, though – he is kindness and forgiveness personified. If only he really was my father, then perhaps I would have inherited those same admirable traits.

As for Anna, she is still very much in the forefront of my mind, but keeping her there is not as painful as I suspected that it would be today. Of all the days, this should be the very worst, but as I am beginning to learn, if that pain is not already there, I don't always have to go rooting through myself to find it.

I'm just wondering whether or not to drop off my bag of presents in the office, when Tui and Allie emerge from the same direction as the barbecue and, seeing me, wave and head across. Tui is wearing a bright red dress festooned with yards of tinsel – there's even a piece threaded around her messy ponytail. When I tell her that she looks like a Christmas fairy, she beams with pride, and puts up a hand to self-consciously pat at her updo. Allie, who is looking extremely chic in a skin-tight black dress and flat silver sandals, blushes at the compliment. It turns out that she is responsible for Tui's hair, while my sister is the mastermind behind the additional tinsel.

'Where's Beavis?' I ask Tui, and she replies with a roar of laughter.

'Tell her! Tell her!' she cackles, and Allie raises an amused eyebrow.

'Beavis is sitting in a puddle of his own drool by Kit's feet,' she explains. 'There are bangers on the barbie, and there is no way that little dude is leaving until he gets one.'

'Sensible,' I concur, then, holding up a clanking carrier bag, 'Where shall I put the booze?'

'Straight into my brother, probably,' Allie says dryly.

I follow the two of them around the side of the indoor school and find Kit and Griff – both clad in comedy reindeer antlers and snowman aprons – cooking the meat, each with a bottle of beer in their free hand. A table bearing bowls of various salads, sliced buns and condiments has been set up alongside the paddock fence, while another table the same size is groaning under the weight of bottles, cans and a huge ice box. Several groups of people are milling around – some I recognise as staff from the stables, but there are quite a few that I have never seen before, who I presume are Kit and Allie's friends. Everyone seems to have a drink in their hand, and nobody seems to care that there is a relative stranger in their midst.

I had worried that I might be left stranded on my own today, but of course, that was never going to happen with Tui around. Before I've had time to help myself to a drink or say more than a quick 'hi' to Kit and Griff, my half-sister is dragging me across to a makeshift seating area built from bales of straw.

'Daaaaad,' croons Tui, coming to an untidy halt at the elbow of a dark-haired and dark-skinned man. So, this is Bonnie's ex – the man she chose to have and keep a child with. Is this my birth mother's type? And if so, should I expect my own father to look or have looked similar? Or perhaps not, given the fact that he – whoever he is – was presumably found to be lacking. It could be that my real father doesn't even know that I exist, and I'm not sure whether to be comforted by that notion, or disturbed by it.

When Tui's dad turns to face me, an expression of adoration already in place for his daughter, the likeness to my half-sister is apparent immediately, and I find myself warming to him straight away.

Simon, as he quickly introduces himself, has allegedly heard a lot about me over the past couple of weeks.

'Really?' I'm touched. 'All good, I hope?'

'Very much so,' he says, before confiding in a half-whisper, 'I think Tui is a bit besotted, to be honest.'

'Hey!' Tui is indignant. 'Jeez, Dad.'

Simon pokes her playfully in the ribs until she squawks. Then, noticing that I don't have a drink, he suggests to Tui that she fetch me one, ignoring my assurances that I'm fine.

'This is your first Kiwi Christmas barbie, right?' he checks, and I confirm that it is.

'In that case, drinking is a requisite must, I'm afraid. Grab her a beer, Tu – the same as mine, yeah. Sorry, Genie – is beer OK?'

'Perfect.' I beam at her. The prospect of a cold beer genuinely is thrilling.

We both watch with affection as Tui gallops off trailing tinsel, then Simon turns his attention to me. He is older than I originally thought – or perhaps his weathered complexion is more to do with New Zealand's UV rays than the toll of time passing. Tui has inherited his wiry hair, smudgy-hazel eyes and rounded nose, but the rest of her must be pure Bonnie. That determined, heel-shaped chin is something we both share, and seeing it on Tui has made me like my own more. I have to accept that if I like all of Tui's features – which I do, very much – then it only stands to reason that I allow my own the same courtesy.

'So, Kit tells me you're an old mate of Bonnie's?' Simon says now, and I hesitate before replying – impossible not to when you're trying your best not to trip over the lie.

'My parents knew her,' I reply. 'A long time ago.'

'In England, right?'

'Right.'

Tui bounds back with a beer for me, half of which she must have spilled on her clumsy canter across from the table. I take it gratefully from her and swallow such a huge mouthful that most of it spills down my chin. Glancing unthinkingly over at Kit, I grin as I see him sneaking a burnt-looking sausage into Beavis's eager mouth.

'You know,' Simon adds, as Tui hurtles off yet again, 'I was shocked when Bon told me she was going back there – to England. She never had many nice things to say about it when we were together.'

'How long did she live there?' I ask idly, my skin prickling.

'Quite a while – at least a year, I'd say,' Simon replies. 'She went from there to Australia for a month or two, and that was it. She told me that she had set out thinking she'd explore the whole world, but that England had put her off. Made her realise that she had everything she wanted or needed right here at home.'

'England isn't all that bad,' I protest, ignoring the tightening fist of resentment in my stomach. The implication is clear: Bonnie hates the UK because of what happened to her while she was there – namely me. But that's not the only reason I'm rankled – like most Brits, I am very happy to moan about my home country, but I'm not all that keen on anyone else doing so. It's basically an English law, like drinking tea in a crisis and apologising to people that walk into you.

'I'm sure it's very nice,' Simon allows, about as con-vincingly as an art critic would be if faced with a stickman. 'But whatever happened to Bon over there, it changed her. She admitted as much to me herself.'

'What did happen?' I ask, playing dumb, but Simon is shaking his head.

'She's never said. Whenever I brought it up, she'd go all quiet on me, you know? Shutters would come down over her eyes.'

He frowns as he recalls it; I sip more of my beer.

'I see,' I say eventually. 'So, that's why you have no idea why she would go to England now, because she hates it so much?'

Simon shrugs expansively.

'Not a dicky of a clue,' he says with a sigh. 'But I hope she's gone there to make her peace with it all, you know? Something's been haunting that woman, and I think whatever it is has held her back. She's never really let herself be happy, or let anyone in very far. Me and my wife – ' he points towards an elegant blonde over by the food table – 'tell each other everything, but I worry that Bon has never had that. She just resists it, and I don't even think she knows why.'

Simon looks pensive now, lost in his own memories – presumably of the relationship that he and Bonnie once shared, which did not end up working out for whatever reason. Of course, I know something that he does not about what happened to Bonnie in England – *I* happened. Could the mere fact of my existence be the reason she shut Simon out – even after they had their own child together? Or did something else happen all those years ago to cause my birth mother to close herself off from everyone? Something worse and even more life-changing than giving up a child?

And if so, what?

26

Bonnie

After she left London in 1992, Bonnie had tried her best not to think about Seth Cooper. Even if she had wanted to contact him, she wouldn't have known how. Nobody had a mobile phone in those days, and the only number she'd ever had for him, which was the landline in the shared flat he rented in Shadwell, was out of service the one time she had tried it.

As the years progressed and everyone moved their lives online, Bonnie had begun a search for him, but it had been half-hearted at best. The fact of it was, she didn't really want to locate him. She just needed confirmation that she had not dreamt the whole thing.

But it was Seth she was thinking about now, as she sat in the hard-backed chair in the corner of the library, her notebook and pen on the table in front of her. She had told Tracey that she would write in a café for once, but it was Christmas Eve, and every coffee shop in the local area was teeming with stressed-out parents, excitable children and groups of insolent teens. Seeking solitude, Bonnie had wandered the streets of Boughton-under-Blean until she discovered this place.

It was morning now, not yet ten, but the woman behind the desk had warned her that they would be closing at midday. Bonnie had two hours in which to tell the next chunk of her story, which should have been plenty, but she found herself delaying. She had reached the part where everything had begun to spiral out of control, and reliving it now, trying to recall all the emotions she had felt, was making the pitter-patter of anxiety tap-dance its way through her chest. Picking up her pen, she wrote, 'Isn't it extraordinary how much power love can have over you?' And then scribbled it out.

Because it wasn't love that was to blame for what happened; it was someone else's abuse of it.

Seth and I had been dating, I guess you'd call it, for about a month when he invited me to spend a weekend with him in Brighton. It was quite a big deal, because the two of us had yet to actually sleep in the same bed together, and I had yet to sleep in a bed alongside any boy. There was just no way my folks would ever have let me do such a thing, and I guess I wanted to wait to respect their wishes — at least that's the excuse I used. I didn't want Seth to think that I was frigid and lose interest, but I was also reluctant to do the deed with him in case he then worked out how inexperienced I really was.

Doesn't that sound absolutely bloody dreadful? I know it does — but at the time, that warped logic made sense to me. And anyway, Seth didn't put all that much pressure on me – he told me that he was happy to wait. But I knew once we were in Brighton, then he would expect something more than a smooch, and I admit, the idea was scary. No, it was terrifying. But in the way that so many frightening things are, it also exhilarated me. I knew the day it was finally going to happen, and I could prepare myself.

In the end, however, I never did go to Brighton.

Tracey had a fall, bless the clumsy old thing, and so I had to take over running the café while she recovered. It all happened the night before Seth and I were supposed to go off on our romantic weekend for two, and when I met him at Euston Station and told him I wouldn't be able to come, he was furious. It was the first argument the two of us had ever had, and he was swearing and all sorts, telling me that it was only a stupid job in a café and that I should walk out. Well, that pissed me off, because I had been raised better than that. I knew that I had a duty and that I owed Tracey my loyalty. I would never have dreamt of letting her down when she needed me – not even for Seth – and looking back now, I think it was that which annoyed him the most. In his eyes, I had put the needs of my boss above the needs of my boyfriend, and before he stormed off and left me crying in that station, he told me that I was immature, and disloyal and – worst of all – a tease. I was devastated.

Off he went to Brighton, while I stayed behind and worked, but I could barely concentrate all weekend for thinking about him, and whether he would ever forgive me. But then, when Monday rolled around, the weirdest thing happened – Seth turned up at Sunrise Café just after lunch, fresh off the train and looking damn awful, with dark circles under his eyes and his hair sticking out all over the place. He told me that he'd been feeling like a bastard the whole time he'd been away, and that he was sorry for everything he said to me. Of course, I was over the bloody moon – probably the moons of Saturn. And so relieved not to have lost him that I would have agreed to anything.

And I did.

That night turned out to be 'the' night – and afterwards he told me that he loved me, and I said that I loved him, too. And I believed it, I really did. I remember heading to work the next morning and feeling as if the clouds billowed more joyfully. All the dirty pigeons suddenly looked like birds of paradise. I reckon I was skipping, perhaps even singing – the boy I loved, he loved me back, and I was a proper woman at last. I was going to get what I wanted after all and Seth and me would live happily ever after.

That feeling lasted a good fortnight, too. The more time Seth and I spent together, the harder I was falling. I was addicted. I needed my daily fix of him or I would start to twitch. And nothing seemed to faze me then, not Tracey's injury, not how busy it was at work and how out of my depth I was, not my homesickness – nothing. I felt as if I owned the bloody world.

The only thing that did dent my love euphoria was my mate the professor. He came in one afternoon looking totally ghastly and told me that his wife had moved out. The rows had become too much, he said, and he didn't know if she would ever come back. There I was, this naive girl, trying her best to comfort this man with all the wisdom of one who has had sex about twelve times in her whole life. How little I knew then about life, and relationships, and marriage. I mean, Jesus, I didn't know a goddamn thing – but because I was floating around in such a love bubble myself, all I wanted was for everyone else to be the same.

I encouraged the professor to make a grand gesture, to tell his wife that he loved her above all else – because in my mind, it was that simple. Love was mightier than petty arguments – it was an all-conquering force that could heal any rift.

I don't know whether the professor even listened to me, but he did seem to cheer up when the two of us talked. I even told him about the Brighton row – I probably compared it to his own troubles, which of course only goes to show how young and dumb I was. But that was the thing about the professor – he never made me feel foolish. He treated me like an equal, and I admired him for that. I was so accustomed to being treated like a child by my parents and their friends that it felt nice to be welcomed into the 'proper adult' pool, even if I was flailing about in the bloody deep end.

It was during one of our deep and meaningful chats that the professor offered me a room at his house. He and his wife had always taken in student lodgers, but the latest had quit university in the middle of her course, so the room was going spare. It wasn't much more in rent than I was paying at the hostel, and when he told me that Seth would be allowed to stay over, I practically jumped up and down with excitement. It wasn't as if I had much stuff to pack, so *moving in was easy. By the following weekend, I was living there, and the friendship between me and the professor became even stronger. He was a mate, a good guy. I thought he was one of the best people that I was ever likely to meet.*

So, to summarise: I was happy. I had a new home with a landlord who was also a great mate of mine, I was dating a boy I loved, who loved me, and I was enjoying being in charge of the café for a while. Everything was on the up.

Until, one night, when everything came crashing down.

27

'I don't think I have ever been so full in my entire life.'

Kit grins as he stretches out on the straw bale next to mine, his feet crossed at the ankles and his head resting against the wooden rails of the fence. Both of us are sipping at bottles of beer, only this time there is no added tequila.

'Nah,' he replies. 'Today's tucker was nothing. You should have seen the spreads my old man used to put on.'

I rub my swollen belly.

'He clearly taught you well.'

'Thanks again for my gift, by the way,' he says. 'Really sweet of you.'

I had no idea what to buy him, but getting him and Allie a little something gave me the perfect excuse to get a present for Tui. In the end, I opted for one of those silly, nodding-head dogs to sit on the dashboard of the minibus – only this one isn't a dog, but a Gollum. Kit had creased up as soon as he opened it, before proceeding to reel off a repertoire of surprisingly good Gollum impressions, and telling me that from now on, he would only be referring to me as 'my precious'. Allie, who had thanked me politely for her basket of toiletries, did not look very enthused by the latter prospect.

The temptation to spoil Tui had been extremely strong, but in the end, I settled on a gorgeous stuffed-dog toy that looked as if it could have been modelled on Beavis, a T-shirt with a Keith lookalike pony printed on the front and – best of all – a slinky.

'I thought it would help with your riding,' I mumbled, as Tui flung her arms around my neck, and Kit smiled at me with such warmth that I felt compelled to scurry away from him on the pretext of getting a second helping of potato salad.

'I feel bad,' he says now. 'For not getting you anything. I'm not very good with gifts for girls – just ask Allie.'

'Oh God, don't be sorry,' I assure him. 'I don't need anything – all that food was gift enough.'

'How about a free ride?' he asks, suddenly looking animated. 'There's a trek booked in for the day after Boxing Day with only a few people on it – you could ride out with them if you like?'

'No, thanks.'

'Oh, go on – silly not to take advantage of all these horses,' he says, gesturing towards the paddocks. 'And we both know that you can ride. I know what horsey folk are like – they're obsessed. You must be itching to get in the saddle by now.'

'I'm not,' I reply, detecting the note of panic in my voice. Kit doesn't seem to notice. Or if he does, it doesn't deter him.

'Bon always says that the longer you wait after a fall,

the harder it is to get back on. If you're worried about that, I can come with you. I'll even lead you, if you like.'

'I'm not scared,' I tell him truthfully, my tone now almost pleading. I don't want to have to lie to him, but I can't explain my reasons for not riding any more without telling him about the accident. And perhaps I could do that one day, but not on this day – not on the anniversary.

'Well, then,' he says. 'That settles it. I'll just tell Allie to—ALLIE!'

'No, don't!' I implore, but Allie is already on her way over.

When Kit explains his plan, she turns to me, head cocked in enquiry, and I shake my own, trying to convey through expression alone how much I need her not to push me. Miraculously, it works, because a moment later she says to Kit, 'You heard the poor girl – she said no and she means no. Stop being a bully.'

'Hey, I'm not bullying anyone!'

'Listen,' I say, my hands raised in an attempt to defuse, 'it's OK. Honestly, Kit, it's really generous of you to offer, but I haven't got any of the right clothes or anything with me and—'

'You can borrow some of Allie's.'

This man is not one to be easily deterred.

'No.' This time I make sure that I'm being firm. 'But thank you.'

Allie folds her arms and looks at each of us in turn. She really does look nice today in her dress, and she's curled her hair, too. All I did was scrape my ridiculously long locks into a bun and apply a token amount of make-up. I have caught so much of the sun now that I don't need any foundation, and there's little point bothering with perfume when you are going to be surrounded by horses and all their associated aromas.

'Just think of your fear as a plaster,' Kit says now, and I could swear that Allie rolls her eyes. 'The faster you rip it off, the less it hurts – getting back on a horse is the same thing.'

'It's really not, you dickhead,' Allie chides. Then, addressing me, 'Kit has only been on a horse once in his life, so he's talking out of his backside.'

'I'm just saying,' he protests noisily, 'that you can't go through life being cautious all the time. If you fell over as a kid and never dared walk again, then where would you be?'

'I didn't fall off,' I can't help but argue. 'That's not the reason I don't ride any more.'

'Then what is?' he asks, and this time Allie doesn't come to my rescue. She is just as intrigued to hear the answer, I realise; I can see the curiosity in her eyes just as my own fill with treacherous tears.

Almost immediately, Kit senses that he has pushed me too far and, getting to his feet with an apologetic murmur, announces that he's off to check on Tui, although it's obvious he is going purely to give me some space.

'Sorry about him.' Allie sits down on the vacated

bale of straw. 'He can be like a seal with a crayfish, that one – bloody relentless.'

'You look really nice today,' I tell her, my keenness to change the subject making me more direct than I usually would be. Allie looks self-conscious for a beat or two, before giving in to a smile.

'I thought I should make a bit of an effort,' she confides. 'Given that it's the last time I'll get to party with a lot of these guys for a while.'

'Oh?' I swallow nervously.

'Yeah,' she says, picking out a piece of straw and twisting it around her finger. 'Didn't Kit tell you? We're off to Wellington in the New Year. Well, I am, anyway. Kit is gonna wait for Bonnie to get back, but then he'll come and join me.'

'That's great,' I say, then start coughing as my sip of beer goes down the wrong way. Allie pats me hard on the back, but this only seems to make it worse.

'Shit!' I gasp, struggling to breathe as my eyes fill with water. 'Sorry. Shit!'

'Drinking really is bad for your health,' she remarks, but her face is all concern.

It takes me a few minutes to fully recover, during which time Allie has fetched me a soft drink and some napkins, which I use to mop my wet cheeks.

'Won't you miss all this?' I ask her, when I'm able to speak again. 'The horses, the people?'

As she goes to answer, I realise it is exactly what Hayley asked me, not long before I came out here. She knew what I would say in response, just as I know what Allie will say now.

'Of course,' she agrees. 'But they'll all still be here. It's not as if Wellington is on the other side of the world.'

I wonder what Bonnie thinks about her head girl quitting. I wonder if she even knows.

'In fact,' Allie adds, 'I was going to ask you a favour.'

'Oh?'

'I need a few days to pack and sort stuff out for the move, and I was wondering if you'd help out here. Don't worry,' she hastens, seeing the look on my face, 'you won't have to take out any rides – just help with the general chores, do a bit of tacking and untacking, maybe teach Tui . . .'

It's the last that persuades me.

28

'Hang on a minute – you're working there?'

Hayley is surprised, as well she might be.

'Not working, just helping out,' I explain, switching her on to speakerphone so I can finish getting dressed. 'Lending an extra pair of hands while Allie gets stuff organised.'

'And you'll be OK?' she asks. 'You know, being around the horses all day long?'

'The first time I walked into that yard, I felt as if I was going to have a full-on panic attack,' I admit. 'But the more time I've spent there, the less strange it feels. And it's only a bit of mucking out and stuff – gives me something to do, gets me off my butt. I just spent the last two days wandering around on my own, and it's making me go doolally.'

'Oo-de-lally?' Hayley laughs.

'That too.'

'Weirdo,' she proclaims. Then, more seriously, 'I'm so sorry you ended up spending Christmas by yourself. Nobody should have to do that.'

'I didn't,' I say. 'I had you and then David on Skype, remember? And I saw about four thousand drunk people when I went out into Queenstown.'

'I know, but it's not the same.'

'I was fine,' I assure her. 'I am fine – but I'm also glad to finally have something useful to do.'

'What about riding?' she asks hesitantly, and I freeze with one leg through my shorts.

'I'm not doing that.'

Hayley starts to say something, but then thinks better of it.

'What was that?' I ask, shaking a bottle of sun lotion before squeezing a dollop out on to each thigh.

'I was just wondering if you'd told your dad?'

'I haven't yet,' I tell her. 'I don't want him to get his hopes up that I'm suddenly cured, so please don't say anything if you see him.'

'I wouldn't,' she replies. 'But don't you think you should?'

'Why?' I counter, sitting down on the bed to put on my boots. The minibus will be arriving to collect the morning riders from town soon, and I need to get a move on if I want to catch a lift back to Koru Stables with Kit.

'I think it would make him happy,' Hayley says in a small voice. 'To know that you're enjoying yourself over there.'

'He knows that,' I counter lightly, feeling slightly guilty at the lie. I think back to how quiet David had gone when I told him my awful secret. 'He thinks I'm enjoying myself by sightseeing.' The last is partly true – he was happy when I told him that I'd made time to visit Milford Sound.

'But I don't understand why . . .' Hayley begins, and I snatch up the phone.

'If I tell him, he'll be bound to push me to go back to Mill House when I get home,' I explain. 'Even more than he already does, and I'm just not sure I can face it. I still need more time. Being around horses again is one thing – being around them in that place . . . well, I just don't know if I can do it.'

Plus, Tui and Kit won't be there to hold my hands.

'OK, OK.' Hayley is contrite now. 'I won't mention it again, I promise.'

'Thank you,' I say, smiling in the hope that she'll hear it in my voice. 'Enjoy the rest of your weird "day after Boxing Day" – eat lots of cake for me. I have to go now, or I'll miss Kit.'

'Ah, the delectable Kit again,' she teases, suddenly gleeful. 'Now he really does deserve an oo-de-lally.'

I'm still on a buoyant post-Hayley high three hours later, as I empty the final wheelbarrow of droppings on to the muck heap and pause to stretch the knots out from my back. It feels good to be working hard again and using my body for something other than walking.

After Anna's accident, I went from strenuous twelve-hour days at the yard to doing absolutely nothing except lying prone on my bed, or on the sofa, staring into space. I thought then that if I got up and did anything, I would somehow shift the weight of my grief, or be distracted from it, and I didn't feel as if I deserved that.

I took on the mantle of suffering and embraced it, never even questioning whether or not it was the right thing to do, because at the time, it felt like my only option. But now that I'm here, sweating and puffing and aching from exertion, all I can think is how wrong I have been. While I may not be able to face going back to Mill House Stables, perhaps I could make peace with working at another riding school when I get back to England? The simple and inescapable fact is, I like being useful. Rotting away in my bedroom was not getting me anywhere.

It is also nice not to have the burden of responsibility that I had at Mill House, where I was second in command and seemed to spend most of my time chivvying up the younger members of the team. With Allie away, nobody really seems to be in charge here at Koru, but all of us know what we're doing. When I arrived this morning, I simply grabbed the nearest fork and barrow and got stuck in, only stopping to chat for a while to Tui, whom Simon had dropped off not long after the first ride of the day went out.

My habitually boisterous half-sister is quieter than usual today, and instead of tearing around the place with Beavis yapping at her heels, I find her curled up on the sofa in the office, her nose in a book.

'What are you reading?' I ask, only to be struck dumb with surprise when she lifts it up to show me.

'*Evangeline And ... The Time Machine*,' she reads, her words succinct but laborious. Then, when I simply gawp and say nothing, she adds, 'Can you read it to me, please, Gee-nie?'

'Oh, I'm not sure if I—' I stop myself before the lie comes out. Of course I'm not too busy to read my new favourite person a story, even if it happens to be one starring a character based on me.

'Budge up, then, Beavis,' I say, and Tui chuckles affectionately as she lifts the little dog on to the floor. Then, almost as soon as I've sat down, she snuggles herself against me and pops a thumb into her mouth, the fingers of her other hand already searching for strands of my long hair to play with. It takes some effort, but I manage to push my voice far enough past the emotion that has gathered like a lump in my throat to begin the story. It is the first *Evangeline And . . .* book that David ever wrote, and it's also my favourite.

'Once upon a time, on a day soaked by rain, something very peculiar happened on a train.

A baby was born, right there on the floor, as if she'd appeared through a secret trapdoor.

Her hair was dark and her eyes were blue, but she wasn't like me and she wasn't like you.

This child was special, a wish come true, and boy did she have some things to do . . .'

'Eyes like yours,' Tui says, removing her thumb from her mouth as she gazes up at me. 'Blue eyes.'

'That's right,' I croak.

'And like the sea,' she adds, almost as an after-thought, but instead of replying, I continue to read.

'With a whoosh from the engine and a squeal from the brakes, the great chugging train gave a groan and a shake.

Passengers hopped off and scurried away, everyone in a hurry, no time to delay.

The station fell quiet, and darkness arrived, when suddenly the silence was shattered by cries.

"What's that?" cooed a pigeon, who had stopped to eat crumbs.

But nobody answered, no dads and no mums.'

Tui starts laughing again, hiccupping over her words as she points out, quite rightly, that pigeons cannot talk.

'What do you think they would say if they could?' I ask, and she screws up her eyes as she thinks it through.

'Give me food?' she suggests, and I have to laugh because she looks suddenly so serious.

'Shall I read more?'

'Uh-huh.'

'Mr and Mrs Poppet saw the story on the news: a baby had been found and there was no time to lose.

They rushed to the shops to buy toys and games, made a list on paper of possible names.

Evangeline was chosen and it suited her just fine – its meaning is good news, so they took that as a sign.

But even though the Poppets raised her as their own, Evangeline was destined to strike out all alone.'

If Tui remembers that my full name is Evangeline, she doesn't say so. Every now and again, while I have been reading, she has reached out and stroked the illustrated face of my literary twin, as if she genuinely cherishes her.

'Six years went by, two more made eight. By now Evangeline had learned how to skate.
    She whizzed along pavements, and skidded around trees; more often than not, she had scrapes on her knees.
    One day in the springtime, while zooming through town, Evangeline heard thunder, and rain poured down.
    The ground was slip-slippery, she needed to hide, so when a train pulled up, she climbed right inside . . .'

'That silly old train again!' giggles Tui, and I nod, thinking how much like this Evangeline my half-sister actually is. If anyone spends their time whizzing and skidding around, then it's Tui. I think today is the first time I have seen her sitting down for more than a few minutes, aside from the long coach trip out to Milford Sound. She seems so at home, nestled in beside me, and the closeness is comforting. It has been a very long time since I was cuddled by anyone, and Tui has made me realise how much I needed to be.

'With a beep and a whistle the doors slid shut; Evangeline got a funny feeling in the depths of her gut.

She looked on in horror as the city sped by, biting her lip so she wouldn't start to cry.

The next stop, she thought, that's what I'll do. I'll hop off this train before you can say "choo, choo".

A tunnel then brought darkness and a flash of bright light, but what happened next was the really big fright . . .'

Just as I'm getting into my reading-aloud stride, Beavis decides that I have monopolised his mistress for long enough and promptly snatches the book right out of my hands, before trotting out into the yard with it in his teeth. Tui bellows with laughter.

'B-B-Beeeea!' she calls, haring off after him and almost crashing into Kit, who is coming the other way.

'Watch out, you little scamp,' he says, swerving to the side so fast that he collides with the doorframe. 'Ow, you absolute tos—' he swears, then, seeing me, 'toad.'

'Don't mind me,' I say with a grin. 'I'm sure I've heard worse.'

'What, than "toad"? Surely not?'

I pull a face.

'What you up to?' he asks, heading behind the desk and yanking open a series of drawers in turn. 'Skiving?'

'Er, no!' I exclaim, getting up from the sofa. 'I'll have you know, I was actually reading Tui a story.'

'Good one, was it?' Kit is enjoying this. 'I don't suppose it was about a guy who'd lost his mobile phone and couldn't remember for the life of him where he'd left the bloody thing?'

'No,' I confess. 'But I did see a blue phone in the tack room earlier.'

'You did?' Kit stops rifling. 'Oh, you beauty!'

Before I am aware of what is happening, Kit has stepped around the desk, placed his big hands on either side of my face, and planted a kiss right on my lips.

Laughing with shock, I stumble backwards and almost end up on my bottom, but Kit reaches out and catches me, letting go only when he's sure that I'm upright again.

'Sorry about that,' he says, looking mildly surprised, as if someone other than him had boldly decided to kiss me. 'You know what it's like when you lose your bloody phone,' he adds.

I have barely looked at my phone over the past year – and didn't use it much even before then – but I agree with him regardless, keen to follow his lead and gloss over what just happened. I'm glad he hasn't said anything else about me riding, or let the slightly heated discussion we had about it a few days ago interfere with our friendship. I haven't mentioned to Kit that I know about his decision to move to Wellington after all, and I certainly haven't mentioned it to Tui. I think if she was aware that her favourite man was leaving, then she would be gutted, and it's certainly not down to me to be the one to break it to her. Then again, aren't I planning on doing the exact same thing? Haven't I allowed myself to get close to Tui knowing that I will soon be gone from her life again? The realisation upsets me enough for Kit to notice.

'Hey,' he says, raising a hand towards me, 'less of the long face, yeah? We've got enough of those around here as it is.'

'Funny,' I deadpan, but, as always, he has managed to cheer me up.

Changing the subject, he asks what I made of the Christmas present he got for Tui, and I have to admit that she hasn't even mentioned it to me.

'That's gratitude for you,' he laughs. 'I'm taking her up to a place called Oamaru in a few days' time, to visit the blue penguin colony.'

'Oh, wow – that does sound like an amazing present.'

'She's wanted to go there forever, but Bon never has the time and, well, I reckon Tui deserves a treat, you know, what with having to do Christmas without her mum.'

I know only too well how awful that is.

'Sounds like fun,' I tell him, but Kit is looking thoughtful now, his index finger rubbing at the groove in his stubbly chin.

'I know,' he says. 'Why don't you come with us?'

I open my mouth, but Kit immediately starts to talk over me.

'Before you make up some lame excuse, it would really help me out. Tui loves spending time with you, and it would mean I have someone to drink with in the evening, after she's gone to bed. And you need to see more of this bloody beautiful country,' he adds. 'I owe you a Chrissy present anyway, and how often do you get an invite that includes penguins?'

I have to agree that it's not very often.

'Go on, then – come with us. We'll have a hoot, I'm telling ya.'

I can't help but think back to my conversation with Hayley that morning, and how she keeps joking that Kit sounds 'delectable'. God only knows how she'll react when I tell her this.

'OK,' I agree, my smile of acceptance mirroring his own of victory. 'But only if Tui agrees.'

'Oh, she will.' Kit is already on his way back into the yard to ask her, and calls out the rest of his sentence over his shoulder.

'Tui bloody loves you.'

29

Bonnie

Moving from the hostel into the professor's house had been a revelation for Bonnie. She no longer had to shower in a communal bathroom, or queue up to use a microwave, and her new landlord didn't mind if she stuck up her photos on the walls, or put a load of washing through the machine. And then there was the television – something Bonnie had missed since the beginning of her trip, although she would have been loath to admit as much to anyone other than the professor himself. Bohemian backpacker types are not supposed to care about what's happening on *Neighbours*, but Bonnie was only too aware of the fact that she was not, in any way, cool. Quite the opposite, in fact. What she was, she had quickly discovered, was a big fan of home comforts, and now that she lived with the professor in his charming little terraced house in north London, she had those in abundance.

Seth was not quite as happy about the new arrangement, however, and while he never asked her outright to look for somewhere else to live, he did refuse to stay over, or even to visit. It would feel weird, he said, because the professor was his teacher, someone with whom he shared a mutual respect, and so Bonnie continued to spend at least three nights each week at her boyfriend's overcrowded shared house instead, which had grubby plates piled in the sink, overflowing ashtrays on every surface and a collection of bras pinned up like streamers in the lounge – trophies from his flatmates' various sexual conquests.

As she wrote all of this down for the daughter she had not seen since birth, Bonnie couldn't help but reflect on how much the world had changed. She was glad that Tui was far more interested in reading books than staring at her phone all day, and hoped that her first daughter would turn out to be the same. Given Evangeline's adoptive father's profession, there was no way she wouldn't have been encouraged to read a lot as a youngster, but Bonnie had always wondered if the pressure of having such a famous character based on her would have affected the girl negatively.

The popularity and success of David Nash's *Evangeline And . . .* books was so widespread that it was impossible even for Bonnie, sheltered as she was from the wider world out in Glenorchy, not to have become aware of them. She had bought the first few for Tui, who she hoped would meet the real Evangeline someday. If Bonnie could just get this next bit right, then perhaps her elder daughter would consider a visit. The idea of her two girls being together in the same room or, even better, becoming something close to friends, made Bonnie's heart leap. But that was all a long way off. First, she had to face Evangeline and explain not only why she left her behind, but why she had chosen now to come back. There was a very real chance that her daughter would refuse to listen, that she might be too screwed up by resentment to even hear Bonnie out. It was a terrifying prospect, but Bonnie knew that she must at least try – if not for herself, then for Tui. Because the future was uncharted territory, its waters dark and choppy, and she knew that everything could change in a single moment.

Bonnie shifted her position on Tracey's sofa. Like many of the furnishings in her old friend's home, it was the faded pink of marshmallows and easily as squishy. Continuing this theme, the Christmas tree, which was standing proud in the front bay window, was also decorated solely in pink tinsel and baubles. The overall effect should have been garish, but actually, Bonnie found it to be oddly soothing.

Tracey had popped out to, in her words, 'smash and grab the sale rails', leaving Bonnie alone to finish her story. And she really must finish it today – she had already encroached on too much of Tracey's time and hospitality – and she was missing Tui – and home – with an ache that had begun to keep her awake at night.

Pulling her notepad across her folded knees, Bonnie continued to write.

On the evenings that I didn't see Seth, I would usually stay in with the professor. His wife was still trying to decide what she wanted, and I felt sorry for him spending every night by himself. He must have had other friends, but perhaps they felt awkward given the circumstances, or maybe they didn't even know what was going on. Either way, he seemed content to just hang out with me – and he started teaching me how to cook. I'll admit, I was bloody useless back then – could barely bake myself a spud – but the professor taught me how to do a traditional Sunday roast, and how to test if spaghetti was done by throwing it against the kitchen wall.

We used to eat dinner off our laps in front of the box, then he would get stuck in to the red wine. I sometimes thought that he might be drinking a bit too much, and it used to make him maudlin if he had more than a glass or two, but I didn't feel like I could tell him off. The professor was a grown man – who was I to educate him on how to deal with his marriage problems?

It took him a few weeks to open up about the reasons behind their estrangement, and actually, when I think back, it was probably an accident that he told me at all. We had gone into his study because he wanted to lend me a book, and when I was in there, I spotted a whole shelf of baby books. There were titles that covered everything, from eating the right diet while pregnant to anthologies of names, to self-help stuff about falling pregnant in the first place. I was curious as to why there was such a massive collection, and when I asked the professor about it, the whole story came tumbling out.

He and his wife had tried for a baby for years without success, he told me. They'd done all the tests, been poked

*and prodded and whatnot, only to find out that a baby
would never be on the cards. The professor had assumed it
would be down to him, but in fact, it was the other way
around. His poor wife didn't have the capacity to carry a
baby – not even if they went through IVF. And while the
professor had made his peace with the idea of not becoming
a parent, his wife had not and would not. It was this that
had caused all the rows, and was the reason behind her decision to walk out.*

*I knew a little bit about this, because my own parents
had struggled to conceive me. I arrived a long time after they
had given up on me, and so I knew how much I meant to
them, and how treasured I was. I had yet to meet the professor's wife, but my heart went out to her. It still does – even
more so now than then – because now I know what a wonderful privilege it is to bear a child. And it is you who
taught me that, Evangeline.*

Bonnie stopped as her tears hit the page, the ink
below them smudging as she wiped a hasty finger across
the paper. It was hard, reliving all of this, trying to get
back inside her mind as it was then. She recalled how
happy she had been when she discovered she was expecting Tui, and how that initial euphoria had been tempered
by an almost immediate redoubling of guilt. Tui was
wanted from the moment of her conception, and that
love which burned like an insistent flame within Bonnie had only grown in size and ferocity since. She knew
that she loved Evangeline just as much, but it was a

more confusing type of love. Because while Bonnie did not know her firstborn daughter, Evangeline was still part of her. For a long time now, that had been enough, but now Bonnie wanted more. She needed her daughter to know her, and to know Tui as well.

30

The strangest thing happened when I woke up this morning – I felt happy.

Not the shiny-new-coin type of happy, but I do feel lighter somehow, as if something has lifted off my shoulders for good this time. And, in the spirit of lightening the load, I have decided that it is finally time to get my hair cut.

'It's a lot to take off – are you absolutely sure?'

The young stylist is standing behind me, scissors raised, and our eyes lock in the mirror.

'Very sure,' I tell her. 'It's only hair, right? It'll grow back.'

'It's the most hair I've ever seen,' she admits, but it's obvious that she's more excited than concerned.

'It's time,' I say simply, because it is. I have kept on growing my hair for years now because Anna loved it so much, but since she died, all it's really become is a reminder that I have lost her – and a big, heavy, difficult-to-dry one at that. Very soon it will be long enough to sit on, and being here in the heat has made me realise how completely ridiculous that is. Even Anna would agree – I'm sure of it. She would probably laugh at me for letting it get this straggly in the first place.

'Are you ready?'

The hairdresser is poised to cut, my curtain of dark locks draped over one of her arms.

'Do it!' I urge her, then shut my eyes as she begins, relishing the sound of the blades as they saw through the strands, slicing and snipping and freeing me of all that weight.

Just as I did as soon as I woke up this morning, I smile.

'You've cut your hair.'

Kit looks so surprised that for a moment I falter, bringing my hand up to self-consciously pull at the chin-length strands.

'Not me – a hairdresser did it.'

'Well, yeah,' he says, picking up an empty water bucket and walking with me over to the stable tap. 'I didn't think you'd taken the shears to it yourself.'

'You don't think it's too short?' I ask, cringing as he uses his spare hand to ruffle it.

'Nah.' Kit grins. 'It suits you.'

'Is Tui around?' I ask him, dipping my chin so he won't see how much his compliment has pleased me.

'Last seen causing trouble in the hay barn.'

I find Tui playing chase with Beavis up in the rafters, and splutter as a great wave of dust floats down to greet me. The hay smells sweet and pungent, and I don't mind that it stirs up my memories today. Being around the horses is becoming easier with every day I spend here, and while Kit told me to aim for around ten this morning, as we would be leaving for Oamaru not long after that, I decided to come early on the off chance that Tui fancied another riding lesson.

'Genie!' she exclaims, sliding down over the bales on her bottom. 'New hair. Wow.'

'I had it all cut off,' I announce proudly, bracing myself as she runs over and throws her arms around me. She's always so ready to cuddle, and I'm always so grateful to receive said hugs.

I have learned that my half-sister is straight-forward when it comes to her likes and dislikes, and if she didn't want me around, then I would soon know about it. Tui is not capable of being false – she simply isn't made that way – and I find being around her refreshing as a result. Adults are so good at pretending, and since Anna's death, most of them have been tiptoe-ing around me, acting as if they want to be there, when in reality my misery chokes them. I grew sick of being treated like an invalid months ago, but then it still angers me if anyone tries to make light of my situation or – even worse – tells me that it's time to 'move past' my grief. They can't win, I don't let them, and so I guess it's easier for them to be fake. That's on me as much as them.

But Tui has no idea that Anna ever existed, and so she behaves exactly as she wants to around me, regard-less of what I think. Kit isn't all that different, either. While he is aware that I've lost someone I was close to, he hasn't automatically smothered me in pity. I believe that he treats me exactly the same way he treats everyone – I'm not getting any preferential allowances made simply because my mum died, and I'm very grateful to him for that.

'You look like a famous lady,' Tui informs me now. Her own rather wild-looking hair is full of hay.

'That's very kind of you,' I say, feeling the morning's lightness flit up yet another notch.

'I got you another present,' I tell her, holding up a carrier bag, then laugh as she makes an unashamed grab for it. Beavis, who took slightly longer than Tui to make his cautious way down from the top tier of hay bales, wags his tail at the sound of crinkling plastic.

'No, Bea, it's not for you,' sings Tui, holding the bag high up out of reach. Beavis puts his little brown head on one side, and wags his tail through the dust.

'Go on, open it,' I urge, and Tui promptly closes her eyes tight shut and reaches in a hand.

'Oh!' she exclaims, pulling out the box. 'Gloves!'

I hadn't been able to resist when I spotted them in an equestrian store back in Queenstown.

'They'll help you to hold the reins better,' I say, as Tui shakes her head.

'Great.'

'Are you sure you like them?'

'Uh-huh.' Tui extracts each maroon riding mitt and gazes at them in awe. 'I love them, Genie. Thank you, oh, thank you, darling.'

Wrapping an arm around my neck, she pulls me towards her and plants a great big wet kiss on my cheek.

'Steady on!' I laugh, extracting myself. 'Now, shall we ask Kit if I can give you a lesson on Keith? We can put him on the lunge rein if you like?'

'Yeah! Yeah! Yeah!' cries Tui, jumping up and down with such exuberance that Beavis scuttles sideways to avoid being squashed. Then, grabbing my hand, she pulls both of us out of the barn.

After a bumpy start, Tui settles into her sitting trot and even feels confident enough to try one loop at a canter. Whooping with delight as Keith swooshes his chestnut tail and lengthens his stride, Tui lets go of her reins to wave at Kit, who has come to check on our progress.

It feels miraculous to watch her up there enjoying herself, so much more confident than she was even a week ago. Far beyond the boundaries of the outdoor school stand the jagged silhouettes of the mountains, each one surrounded by an ocean of blue sky. A gentle breeze carries the whisper of birdsong, insects hum their busy tunes in the trees, and I drink it all in – the sounds, the sights and the sense of peace that has been building inside me all day, in this country of such beauty, and space, and quiet.

Looking again towards where Kit is standing, his thick tattooed forearms resting on the fence, I note that he is also captivated by the sight of Tui. The two of them have an uncomplicated closeness that would be easy for me to envy, the kind of connection that can only be built over time, on a foundation of trust and familiarity. Tui is lucky to have him – they are fortunate to have each other.

'Ready to try a little jump?' I call out, and Tui shakes her head with such passionate agreement that she almost falls right off into the dirt.

'Whoa!' I cry, just as Kit shouts the exact same thing, and Tui looks at each of us in turn before bursting into fits of laughter.

'I scared you!' she cackles, laughing so hard that I find myself joining in. Kit, who has now vaulted the fence and is strolling towards me, smirks wryly at the two of us.

'Flaming pair of crazy chooks,' he remarks, patting Keith's hot neck as I pull Tui and the pony to a standstill.

'Have a quick breather,' I tell her. Then, turning to Kit, 'Can you help me build a few jumps?'

We collect the blocks that are stacked in the far corner, then Kit returns to fetch the poles, while I count out the correct strides.

'I can't believe how much she's already improved,' he says, using his foot to lever one end of a pole into its slot. 'You've worked wonders with her.'

'I didn't do anything, really,' I say, throwing in a shrug for good measure. 'She just needed to think about it in a different way.'

'That's true of a lot of things in life,' he replies,

sounding thoughtful. 'Often, I find that if you turn a problem on its head, it tends to solve itself.'

If only that were true, I want to say, but I'm unwilling to put a dampener on such a positive day.

'All set?' I ask, as Kit bends down to arrange the final set of poles into a crossbar. Tui flaps her legs ineffectually against Keith's sides.

'Just squeeze with your ankles,' I call. 'That's right — perfect.'

The chunky pony shuffles forwards and I note with pride that Tui has remembered to gather up her reins, and is holding them correctly with her thumbs balanced on the top. Keith is arching his neck like a dressage champion now, which reminds me unavoidably of Suki. My horse was as far removed from a riding-school plodder as it is possible to be, and was more likely to prance sideways than trot in a straight line, but she did like to stay on the bit and flutter her eyelashes at everyone. A shameless flirt, but so beautiful with it. She was only eight when she was killed. No age at all.

'Jumps! Jumps! Jumps!' Tui choruses, and I hear Kit tutting at her good-naturedly.

'Come on, then,' I say, crossing the outdoor school. I swap the lunge rein for a shorter one and clip it on to Keith's bit.

'I'll jump them with you on the first go.'

Tui's whoop of joy as we clear the first fence together is so loud that Kit claps his hands over his ears.

31

The drive up the coast to Oamaru takes a little under four hours, and as luck would have it, Griff is taking a coach that way, dropping a few travellers off in the town before heading towards Kaikoura for the night, returning the following day, so Kit, Tui and I are able to sneak a lift there and back. Tui insists that I sit next to her, choosing seats just behind the middle exit, while Kit stays up at the front with his friend.

As before, Griff spends a portion of the journey talking into the microphone, telling stories and pointing out local landmarks, and I listen with interest as he explains more about Maori history, and how many of the areas that we are driving past were named. A trail of clouds is smeared like icing sugar across the sky, and when I point them out to Tui, she solemnly proclaims that they look like 'fluffy Frisbees'.

She seems a bit tired after her triumphant morning ride, her usual cheer dampened by a pensiveness that I haven't seen from her before. When we stop for a toilet and coffee break an hour or so into the journey, I take Kit to one side and ask him if she's OK.

'Just narked off because she had to leave Beavis behind,' he explains. 'And I think she's missing her mum.'

I swallow hard to remove the lump in my throat.

'Of course she is.'

'I reckon Bon'll be home in a few days,' he adds, too distracted by a gesticulating Griff to notice the wan expression on my face. 'I got a text from her this morning, just checking in.'

'Oh?' I stuff my clammy hands into the pockets of my denim shorts.

'Yeah, she said she's almost done over there.'

I wonder for at least the thousandth time what my birth mother has been doing in England all this time. Could she really be there looking for me? And if she is, why hasn't David been in touch to tell me? Then again, I have screened a few of his recent calls, and I'm not even sure why. Perhaps it is because I am getting through each day by allowing myself to live in the moment, rather than thinking too much about the consequences, and I am enjoying my state of denial too much to risk anyone questioning it. I know I will have to go home eventually, but the more time I spend here in New Zealand, with Tui and my new friends, the less I can imagine leaving.

Once back on the road, I suggest that we play I-Spy, which seems to perk Tui up – especially when I go along with her outlandish choices of 'V is for very big tree' and 'A is for almost-red door'. Needless to say, she wins every game by a landslide, and is still hooting with amusement about the fact when the coach rolls into Oamaru.

'Penguins!' cries Tui, as she spots a sign advertising the colony, twisting her fingers together and humming with excitement. She has an adorable way of rocking from side to side when she is especially animated, and she does this now, her untidy plait swinging in tandem. She's wearing blue leggings and a white Koru Stables polo shirt today, the front pocket of which is trailing a thread, and there are Velcro-fastened trainers on her feet. I already know that she can't quite manage to undo the fiddly straps of a bridle, so I imagine shoelaces are a stretch too far. I don't look all that different to her today, opting for casual attire of shorts and a plain black vest top, plus my trusty walking boots. I have gone from hating them to practically living in them, and I now feel like a dimwit for packing two pairs of heels – I haven't so much as looked at them since the day Kit and I climbed the Tiki Trail.

I keep forgetting about my shorn hair, and it's odd to reach up and find my neck completely exposed. Not odd in a bad way, though – in truth, I feel about two stone lighter. I only wish I hadn't waited so long to get it done.

Tui predictably wants to go straight to the blue penguin Colony as soon as we have waved goodbye to Griff, and it takes all of Kit's immense patience to stop her throwing a tantrum in the middle of the street. 'The penguins are all out at sea now, they don't come back to their nests until night-time,' he reminds her, promising her an ice cream if she behaves herself.

'You can have one, too,' he jokes to me. 'If you're a good girl.'

We check into a cosy bed and breakfast overlooking a horseshoe bay, then stroll down the hill into the centre of town. A four-lane high street is dotted with shops, cafés and meandering pedestrians, and as we wander further, I take in the limestone architecture and cobbled lanes. It's obvious even to a non-history buff like me that this North Otago town has embraced a Victorian theme – an assumption Kit confirms as he leads us past a steampunk museum.

He must have been here many times before in his tour guide days, because he seems to know exactly where everything is, and takes me and Tui into antique shops and a retro toy store, before nipping into the New Zealand Malt Whisky Distillery to pick up a bottle.

Tui is transfixed by the yards of flapping bunting draped between the buildings, while I'm charmed by a minuscule lending library that someone has thought-fully set up on a small wooden shelf. Peering along the row, I'm jolted by the sight of a familiar book, but before I have time to react, Tui is stretching out a hand to pick it up.

'*Evangeline And . . . The Angry Queen*,' she reads aloud in her careful, low voice. Then, looking from the draw-ing on the cover of the book to me, then back again, she says, 'Evangeline looks like you, that's all.'

'How funny,' I say, attempting to take the book from

her so I can have a closer look. But Tui does not want to let it go.

'Can I have it?' she asks doubtfully, scanning the instructions pinned to the shelf.

'I think you have to swap it for another book,' I point out.

'Hmmph,' grumbles Tui, nodding her head and clasping the book tight to her chest. She really must love Evangeline – apparently much more so than I ever have.

'Is it a good one?' I ask, and after eyeing me cautiously for a few moments, Tui hands it over. It's the second in the series, set when Evangeline is nine years old, and follows her back to the Victorian era on her time-travelling train. I finger the lettering on the cover, tracing a path over the pleasant swoop of David's 'D', before stroking the 'N' of Nash.

Why shouldn't Tui have a book that she wants – especially a book that I know is full of adventure and learning?

'I say we take it,' I whisper, smiling as Tui starts clapping in earnest. 'Shall I carry it in my bag for you?'

I have just zipped it away out of sight when Kit reappears, a clanking carrier bag in one of his vast hands.

'For later,' he tells me, holding it up.

Having exhausted Oamaru's town centre, the three of us take our hokey-pokey ice creams – a New Zealand speciality of vanilla with butterscotch toffee pieces – down to the seafront and sit for while on a low wall, dangling our legs and ducking to avoid the huge gulls that hang like puppets on strings above us, waiting to gobble up any leftover crumbs of wafer. The water in the bay is the bright turquoise of a swimming pool in a glossy holiday brochure, the pale gold rocks and shingle beach warmed by a high, ferocious sun. Kit points out what he calls 'shags' paddling through murky patches of seaweed, and while I tell him that we find the same birds along the coast at home, I choose not to mention the alternative meaning for the word shag, which he might not be familiar with.

Tui finishes her ice cream first and bounds off towards a park, which is set on a grassy lawn not far from the wall on which Kit and I are still sitting. Once satisfied that she is staying within range, Kit starts to relax, swinging his legs round to face inland and crossing his feet over at the ankle.

'She's in her element, that little monkey,' he remarks, watching as Tui clambers untidily up a slide that has been built over the structure of an elephant. The park has been designed with the Victoriana steampunk theme in mind, and as well as the strange elephant slide, there's a vast penny-farthing swing set and a roundabout adorned with disembodied horse heads. Oamaru has a very different feel to Queenstown, which is all bustle and noise. With the exception of the sea and the vibrant purple lupins sitting in clusters along the shore, the palette here is mostly greys, greens and muted variations of beige.

'She's an amazing girl,' I say, not for the first time, and Kit smiles.

'Yeah, she certainly is. And she really likes you, you know? I meant what I said about you being good with her. It usually takes Tui time to trust new people, but there's a bond between the two of you – I reckon it's been there right from the start.'

I don't trust my voice not to wobble, so instead I simply nod.

'Maybe it's an only-child thing,' he muses. 'You, me and Tui all have that in common, hey?'

Not any more, I think.

'Do you want children?' I'm amazed to hear myself ask. 'Sorry, I mean – that's probably none of my business.'

'That's all right,' he says easily, popping the last piece of his ice cream cone into his mouth and allowing himself a moment to chew. 'I guess the honest answer is that I don't know. I know I should – I'm gonna be thirty-five next year, and I know Allie is pretty keen on the idea of having a few ankle-biters about the place one day, but I'm not sure if that's the next step for me just yet, you know?'

'I think I do know,' I say, watching Tui emerge from the bottom of another slide. This one is higher and curled around some sort of pyramid-shaped structure made from scaffold poles. 'I'm not sure if I want any either.'

'Is that because you lost your mum?' he guesses, only

238

to quickly apologise when he takes in the expression on my face.

'Don't worry,' I assure him, chewing my lip. 'It's not that. I don't think I have ever really wanted kids, but I never haven't wanted them, if that makes any sense? Maybe I'm just not the maternal type.'

'Tui would disagree,' he says, and it's ridiculous how happy his words make me feel. My half-sister has definitely brought out a protective side of me. Tui just has a way to her that is irresistibly uncomplicated and easy to love – there is no pretence to her, no games, no real Tui lurking underneath. What she puts out into the world is who she is, and she makes no apologies for the fact. I love her because of her free spirit, and her big open heart. If only I had inherited those same traits from our mother, but in contrast to Tui, I have always kept my guard right up to my hairline. Most people have to earn my trust, and my love, but not Tui – she has both.

'Do you think she would like a brother or a sister one day?' I ask Kit.

'Oh yeah, I reckon so,' he says. 'A playmate is what she craves the most. Bonnie is always so busy – that's why Tui started hanging out with me all the time, and why she was allowed to have a puppy. There's so much affection in that girl – I think she would love the whole world, given half the chance.'

'She's amazing,' I say again, and this time Kit touches a hand briefly to my arm.

'I think she would say the same about you.'

32

Steampunk HQ is without a doubt one of the most bizarre yet brilliant places I have ever been in my life. From the enormous steam engine crashing through the ground by the entrance to the gloomy, cavernous room full of artefacts and oddities inside, the whole place is deliriously inventive and brilliantly entertaining.

'I feel like I've walked on to the set of *Mad Max*,' I remark to Kit, my mouth falling open as I spy an enormous metal beetle mounted against a wall. Tui runs off ahead to bash the keys of a makeshift organ, shrieking with amusement as each key plays a different creepy note or sound effect. There are ghoulish heads, a gorilla and frog made from the scraps of old cars, a fossilised wheelchair with a cracked leather seat and TV screens that have been tuned in to static fixed high on the walls. It is difficult to know whether all the flashing lights and strings of tinsel are part of the decor, or simply there for Christmas, but it is all completely bonkers in the best way.

After exploring a backyard area full of even bigger and weirder creations, Kit beckons Tui and me towards a doorway with 'The Portal' written in lights above it.

'You have gotta see this,' he says, looking more

animated than I have ever seen him, and after pressing a large red button on the wall, he quickly ushers us inside.

Almost immediately, the dark chamber is illuminated by hundreds of strings of flashing lights. Eerie singing begins, low and soothing at first, but then, as the lights begin to change from red to blue to green to yellow to pink and back to white, the pitch of the woman's lilting voice goes up. The three of us are standing one behind the other on a metal platform caged in by two horizontal bars, and the walls, floor and ceiling around us are mirrored, creating the impression of a much larger, higher and deeper space. Upon closer inspection, I see that many of the lights are encased in plastic skulls, the effect hauntingly beautiful.

Tui has fallen silent ahead of me, her gaze on the lights and her hands raised as she twists her fingers together, utterly enthralled. I wish we could stay here in this magical portal, the three of us. Perhaps if we did, it would whisk us away to another time, like Evangeline's train, a time where there were no lies and no secrets, where I had not lost so much, nor had so much to lose.

I don't want to lose Tui, not now that I have found her. With a deep sigh, I take a step backwards, only to tumble against Kit. Instead of righting me, however, he simply puts a hand on my waist, steadying me but making no move to distance himself. It's such a simple gesture, but it almost brings me to my knees.

The music stops.

'Again, again!' says Tui, turning to face us as the over-head lights go up. She is unwilling for the show to end quite so soon. For Kit and me, though, the moment has passed.

We grab a very late lunch at a steampunk-style café constructed from rust-coloured sheets of corrugated iron, then make our way back down to the water. In the same way that I can never resist the gently lapping shallows of Lake Wakatipu, Kit appears to be drawn to the sea, and now that Tui is full of burger, fries and an extra-large chocolate milkshake, she's very happy to skip along beside us, picking up stones and great slimy lumps of seaweed, which she uses to chase Kit around in circles.

Following the curve of the bay, we pause to admire a large stone statue of a penguin, which Kit insists that Tui and I pose beside for a photo. Another yellow sign further along warns us to go slow, because we have entered a Penguin Crossing zone – a fact that prompts a clumsy cartwheel of joy from my sister.

'The colony is up ahead,' Kit explains, pointing towards a red-roofed building. 'The ticket says we should turn up around eight, though, so we've got a while to wait yet.'

'Oh.' Tui pouts, but Kit simply laughs at her.

'Put a boot in it, you cheeky wotsit,' he says, and Tui blows a raspberry at him before haring off along the stony path ahead of us.

'Don't go too far,' he calls after her in exasperation. 'Wait by the pier!'

I assume that he's worried about Tui falling into the sea, but when we reach the long stone jetty, it becomes clear that there is a different and unexpected danger.

'Seals!' cries Tui, grasping my arm.

Unlike those we saw from the boat in Milford Sound, which were a good fifty feet away, these whiskery creatures are lazing only a few metres from where Kit, Tui and I are standing. The nearest is lying prone on its back, with its eyes closed and its mouth slightly ajar. We are close enough that I can see the pattern of wet fur across its head, and a jagged scar running across one of its hind flippers.

'What do you have to remember about seals?' Kit asks Tui, putting a calming hand on her shoulder.

'No touching,' she replies.

'And?' prompts Kit.

'No running.'

'That's right.' He pats her on the top of her head. 'Just walk past slowly and don't make any noises that might scare them.'

The three of us make our way stealthily past the first seal, which opens one eye to stare at us but doesn't move. I'm watching it so intently that I don't see one that has just lumbered up over an outcrop of rocks behind us, and yelp in fright as it barks loudly. Kit, who now has one arm around Tui and the other wrapped around me, pulls both of us against him.

'Strewth!' he exclaims. 'This one's a big fella.'

The seals are about the same size as the soppy black Labradors back at Mill House Stables – albeit without legs – and look faintly ridiculous as they roll and heave themselves into comfortable positions on the stone walkway. There's a dicey moment when two begin to jostle for position on the same ledge, each one rearing up and grunting aggressively at the other, but Tui thinks they're hilarious, and cackles so loudly that she distracts them. By the time we reach the far end of the T-shaped stone pier, most of the younger seals have slithered down into the sea, miraculously transforming from helpless lumps into graceful dancers as they do so.

Taking out my phone, I start filming a pair that are swimming together in a neat loop, mesmerised by the way they turn over and over, letting the water skim gently over their glossy brown bellies. I have seen seals in a zoo before, but never out in the wild like this, enjoying the freedom that all this space allows. Aside from the occasional trampling feet of a tourist or two, they must have a pretty relaxed existence, and it is a satisfying notion. It's nice to know that my grief has receded enough to allow me to feel happy on behalf of others again, because for a while, I seemed to lose that ability altogether. Anything and anyone who was not me, I resented. I wanted to portion away my pain, while at the same time I did whatever I could to load more of it on to myself. I clung to it, using it as an anchor to halt the progression of my life.

I lift my chin and close my eyes for a moment while I bask, seal-like, in the heat of the sun. How astonishing that I should be here, on the edge of one of the furthest tips of the world, where the days begin and end before so many others. How can it be fair that I get to feel the rough surface of the concrete beneath my feet, smell the salt in the air, and have the ripple of the wind lift the hair from my cheeks? Why me, when it could just as easily have been her?

'Pretty bloody nice here, right?' says Kit at my side. Tui is sitting down on the edge of the pier a few feet away, carefully taking photos of a sunbathing seal with Kit's phone.

'Bloody beautiful,' I agree, grinning at my own terrible attempt at a Kiwi accent, before turning my eyes back to gaze across the water.

'I spent a few weeks here after my dad—' he begins, stopping when I glance at him. 'I needed to get away from all the reminders at home, and this felt like as good a place as any.'

'There's something very wild about it,' I say, thinking how different the craggy rocks and crashing waves are to the placidity of Lake Wakatipu.

'At the time, it matched my mood right about perfectly,' he explains. 'I was even angrier than one of these fellas.'

'At least you still had your agility,' I joke, as a particularly rotund seal tries and fails to lumber out of the water.

'What did you do after?' he asks, and a beat of silence stretches between us.

'Nothing. Nothing at all for the longest time,' I admit, not looking at him. 'Then I came here.'

'You know,' he continues, 'there's a Maori proverb that my dad used to say to me, whenever I was feeling down about something. He would take me outside and make me look up at the sun, just like you're doing here now, and he would say, *Hurihia to aroaro ki te ra tukuna to atarangi kia taka ki muri i a koe* – turn your face to the sun, and the shadows fall behind you.'

A small noise escapes from the back of my throat.

'I always reckoned that it meant your sadness doesn't always leave you, but that you can put it behind you. The sunshine represents the future, and all the pain of your past is in the shadows.'

Again, all I can do is nod.

'Ah, shit.' Kit notices the tears on my face. 'Genie – I'm sorry. I didn't mean to upset you. I keep doing this, don't I? I'm a flaming idiot.'

'It's OK,' I mumble, forcing myself to laugh instead of sob. I know that he's right, and that I should be trying my best to turn towards the sun, but there is so much shadow behind me. The space I'm in now is on the ledge between the two, and it feels precarious.

'Hey,' he says again, and this time he puts both arms around me and pulls me forwards a few steps until my cheek is on his chest. Kit is so tall that he can rest his chin on the top of my head, and I let myself relax into his embrace, feeling helpless as I weep more silent tears on to the front of his T-shirt.

'You're allowed to be sad,' he says quietly, being careful not to alert Tui to my distress.

'I know,' I mutter. 'I'm just so tired of it, that's all. Sadness is so exhausting.'

'You poor bloody thing,' he soothes, stroking my hair. I can hear his heart beating, feel the warmth of his strong arms around my back, and the firmness of his stomach against my chest. I want to curl up inside his embrace. Hibernate here until the leaves darken and fall, until the peaks of Mount Aspiring are white with snow, and the plants down by the Dart River complete their cycle of decay and rot, and new buds spring up. I would be safe here, hidden away. I wouldn't have to face Bonnie or see the deep lines that grief had dug around David's eyes or the guilt in my own.

'You know, I reckon that your mum would hate seeing you like this,' Kit says then. 'She would want you to be happy, right?'

If only it were that simple. Perhaps I could strive for something close to happiness again, if I wasn't the one to blame for Anna's death, if I had behaved better, pushed less and apologised more quickly. Anna loved me enough to forgive, but I don't love myself in the way she did. I never have. That is at least one thing that Bonnie and I will have in common, I think dully – neither of us loving me.

Kit doesn't let go of me until Tui begins to clamber

back to her feet, and then he uses his thumbs to wipe any remaining tears from my cheeks. I rest my face gratefully against his hands, not caring what he thinks, or how it might look, just needing the comfort.

'Penguins now?' asks Tui hopefully, jiggling on the spot.

Kit drops his hands from my face to check his watch.

'Not long now.' He puts his head on one side and regards her for a moment or two. 'But first, perhaps we should head back to the guesthouse and change?'

'Hm-mm,' giggles Tui, and shakes her head before grabbing for my hand.

'No running!' yells Kit, but his voice is carried away by the wind as Tui and I set off back along the pier, dodging lounging seals and squealing as one barks at our heels. By the time he catches up with us, my earlier sorrow has evaporated. I know a few near misses with some wild seals are not the reason I feel better, though – that has far more to do with the people standing here beside me.

33

We return to the bed and breakfast to change into warmer clothes for the evening, because even though the day was scorching, it is supposed to get chilly down by the sea at night. Plus, as Kit explains to me and Tui as we share a pizza in a restaurant near the town centre, there is a lot of waiting around when it comes to the art of penguin spotting, and you must stay as quiet and still as possible, so as not to startle them.

We arrive at the colony just before the doors open at eight p.m., then make our way along a winding board-walk path to a small grandstand. Kit has splashed out and bought the best seats in the house, which will give us a front-row view of all the blue penguins as they waddle up from the water. What began as just a few nests amongst the rocks here has expanded into a thriving blue penguin community, with the petite sea birds free to come, go and breed as they please.

Such is the anticipation of the crowd that there is a collective intake of keyed-up breath as the first cluster of penguins comes into view, each one padding with quiet stoicism from one flat foot to another with their pointed little flippers held out behind them. As they pass by right below us, Tui gasps out loud with awe, and Kit and I exchange a smile over her head.

Some of the birds hurry straight under the protective cover of the wooden walkway, while others stand in groups, squawking away as if they're having a good old gossip about their day out fishing. It is not just Tui who is gazing down at them adoringly now, all three of us are, and when the first batch have all scuttled into their nests, another group comes ashore, and then another, and before long there are hundreds of penguins just distinguishable in the dusk. The racket they are making, as well as the smell coming off them, is quite something, and Tui pointedly holds her nose.

'They're so noisy,' I whisper to Kit, and he chuckles.

'I might start calling Tui a penguin from now on,' he replies, prompting an indignant and clearly audible, 'Hey!' from the girl in question.

'Shhh,' hisses a woman sitting behind us, and Kit rolls amused eyes to the sky.

Looking down, I notice that Tui is holding Kit's hand as well as mine, but the next moment she almost pulls the two of us over as she shoots up from her seat, leaning right over me so she can see the newest arrival of penguins more easily.

'Sit down!' demands the angry woman, and I tap Tui gently on the leg.

'Jeez!' she complains, her shrill voice echoing around the silent grandstand. At first I think Kit is going to tell her off, but instead he shifts round in his seat.

'Chill out, would ya?' he says to the woman, his voice low. Then, reaching across me, he grabs the waistband of Tui's leggings.

'Bottom down, bouncy pants,' he instructs. Tui sits, landing not on the bench but on my lap, causing her to lurch sideways, blocking the view yet again. There is another snort of annoyance from the row behind, and I scoot quickly out of Tui's way, my thigh ending up rammed against Kit's. I assume that he will move, but he doesn't, and I can't, squashed in as I am by a grumbling Tui. The longer I sit here, the more I become aware of Kit, and how being this close to him is making the murmur of something close to pleasure creep through me. It has been so long now since I have experienced even an inkling of desire. I thought that feeling had been cauterised by Anna's death, and until this moment, I hadn't dwelled on it very much. It didn't seem important enough. Trust me to have my desire reawakened by a man who not only lives on the opposite side of the world to me, but is also very much involved with another girl. I shouldn't even be thinking these things – it's not fair on Allie.

More penguins arrive, and my nose begins to tickle from the cloying aroma of fish.

'Yuck!' declares Tui loudly, as yet again she makes a big show of holding her nose. Next to me, I feel Kit's shoulders beginning to shake with suppressed laughter.

'I think we had better get going before someone gets

us booted out,' he murmurs, and I nod in agreement, reaching for Tui's hand.

'Come on,' I tell her. 'We'll be able to see the penguins going into their nests from the walkway.'

In the end, we get a better view than we could ever have hoped for, because halfway back along the coastal path towards town, a single rogue penguin appears without warning from the long grass beside the shoreline and flatfoots it across the road less than a metre from our feet.

'PENGUIN!' screams Tui, hurling herself towards it at speed, both her arms outstretched.

It is only Kit's rapid-action reflexes that prevent her from scooping the little thing up into her arms and bringing it back to the B&B with us.

'I still can't believe she tried to pick up a bloody penguin.'

I have just returned from helping an exhausted Tui into bed in our shared room, and find Kit sitting at the kitchen table. The bottle of whisky he bought earlier is open and partially decanted, and there is an empty glass beside his own, which he lifts as I approach.

'You mean p-p-p-pick up a penguin,' I correct, nodding to accept his offer of a drink.

'What was that?' Kit looks confused.

'It's from an advert that used to be on for Penguin chocolate biscuits,' I say, pulling out the chair next to his. 'I keep forgetting you're not British.'

Before I can sit down, however, Kit nods towards the open balcony door.

'We could go and drink these outside? It shouldn't be too cold now that we're up here.'

'Sounds good,' I agree, and Kit pushes back his chair. Pouring several fingers of whisky into my glass, he slides it towards me.

'You might need a splash of water in there,' he warns. 'It's right strong enough to leave scorch marks on your tongue, this stuff.'

Reluctant for him to think I'm a lightweight, but also not keen on the idea of passing out drunk anytime soon, I take my glass over to the cold tap, before joining Kit and his bottle out on the balcony. The owner has left a few beanbags out here in lieu of furniture, and I collapse gratefully into one with a contented sigh.

'Long day.' Kit holds up his glass.

'Great day,' I reply, clinking my own against it.

The diluted whisky burns a fierce trail down my throat, and almost as soon as I have swallowed it, I begin coughing violently.

'Oops.' Kit pats me on the back. 'I should have grabbed us some beers instead. I can go out to the liquor store now, if you want? It'd be no bother.'

He is already halfway to being on his feet again, but I stop him with a raised hand.

'Don't worry,' I say, coughing again. 'This is honestly nice – I just haven't drunk whisky for a while – I forgot how strong it is.'

He doesn't need to know that by 'a while', what I actually mean is 'ever'.

'Tui behave OK?' he asks.

'Out like a light. I didn't even get to finish her bedtime story.'

'I could tell she was bushed.' Kit tips back his glass. 'She gets all worked up when she's tired – Bonnie warned me of that before she left.'

'And you don't mind looking after her?' I ask, already predicting his answer.

'Not at all.' Kit takes another sip. 'I feel a bit sorry for the kid, you know? Not because of her issues so much as her olds being separated. That can't be easy on her – it wouldn't be easy on any of us.'

'Was Tui a planned baby?' I ask, and Kit frowns.

'I've never asked Bon that – doesn't seem like my place, you know? But I do know that she and Simon were never married or anything like that. My mum told me that Simon was torn up when they split – he was bats about Bon, but I guess she felt differently.'

'That's sad,' I say, thinking back to what Simon had said to me at the barbecue, about Bonnie being reluctant to let anyone in.

'I guess.' Kit is more pragmatic. 'But it can't have been easy on either of them to deal with Tui's prognosis. It's still not easy now.'

He shifts into a more comfortable position on his beanbag, his eyes black pools in the darkness.

'Tui is amazing. We all love her. But she can never be

left completely alone. There are things that she just can't seem to learn, and unfortunately, many of them are things that could land her in trouble, so we have to keep on watching her.'

He stops, looking at me for a reaction.

'She can learn a bit,' I say hesitantly. 'She's improved her riding loads recently.'

'Perhaps you have the magic touch?' he says, but I am already shaking my head.

'I just made a few lucky guesses.'

'Why do you keep doing this, woman?' Kit implores. 'Why do you put yourself down all the bloody time?'

'I don't mean to,' I insist, taking such a fortifying glug of whisky that I almost choke again.

'Well, you shouldn't,' he persists. 'You're a choice girl, Genie – and I'm not the only one who thinks it. Tui downright idolises you, and Allie and Griff both reckon you're great.'

I'm about to ask him how he's feeling about moving away to Wellington, only for the question to stall like a knackered car. It is none of my business, but there is also a part of me that doesn't want the news confirmed.

Feeling horribly disloyal towards Allie, I force down yet more of the whisky. If only Kit wasn't always so kind to me, if only he hadn't kissed me that day at the stables. I know he only meant it in a platonic way, but I can't help reliving it in my head, over and over.

'Griff is brilliant,' I say, settling on a safe topic. 'He looked after us so well on that Milford Sound trip.'

'Well, yeah, of course he did.' Kit is smirking.

'Why do you say it like that?'

'No reason.' Kit stirs the ice around in his glass with a finger. 'Just that it's been a while since Griff talked about a girl, and he's been yacking about you something chronic.'

For a brief second, I try to imagine myself in the arms of Griff, with his curls of blond beard and his large broken nose.

'That's very flattering,' I concede. 'But he's not my type.'

'Poor old Griffster,' Kit laments, sounding in no way sad for his friend whatsoever.

'What is your type then?' he asks.

'Oh, you know, the usual,' I say, pausing to take another sip. 'Tall.' I raise my eyes to his. 'Dark.' I take in the sweep of his hair. 'Handsome.' I let my gaze linger a dangerously long time on his face, before trailing my eyes deliberately down across his broad chest.

What the hell has got into me? I wonder, too light-headed to realise that the answer is, in fact, swilling around in the bottom of my glass.

Kit looks away first, using the excuse of refilling our tumblers to break eye contact. I can hear the muted chirp of crickets coming from the garden below us, while high above the balcony, stars lie like ribbons of tinsel across an indigo sky. The air is still now, this afternoon's breeze hushed by the night, and I can hear the distant swoosh of the waves as they buffet the rocks, displacing pebbles and carrying debris back to shore. If only a force as great as an ocean could scoop up the debris of my life and put it back where it's supposed to be.

'I'll have to buy Griff some dye for his hair,' Kit says into the silence. 'But there isn't much even I can do about his face.'

'It took you all that time to come up with *that*?' I exclaim, and Kit laughs.

The whisky continues to go down as we talk, trading stories about our childhoods and coming back time and time again to Tui. The more time I spend with Kit, the more carefree I feel with him, although I know the alcohol probably has something to do with it, too. He is just so easy to talk to, and before long, I find myself opening up in ways I haven't for a very long time. Without giving away the truth about my adoption or my connection to Evangeline in Tui's favourite books, I do confess that I struggled with my own identity, and that I went from being loud and outgoing to more of a mousy introvert as I grew up.

Kit puts his head on one side.

'I knew there was a lively spirit lurking under your surface,' he remarks. 'I see flashes of it from time to time.'

'Alcohol clearly unleashes it,' I joke, holding up my glass.

'I figured it was losing your mum that made you retreat into yourself,' he adds, and I slump back into the beanbag as if I've been punctured.

'It did,' I admit, my voice low. 'But I can't blame that

entirely. Truth is, I used to be a person who liked being looked at and noticed, but now . . . Now I'm the opposite.'

'I notice you.'

It's too dark now for me to read Kit's expression, but I am aware of the tremble I felt earlier at the penguin colony returning. He is sitting so close to me; it would be so easy to lean forwards and kiss him.

'I noticed you today,' he says. 'I saw how brave you were being.'

'I'm not brave,' I counter automatically, but he hushes me with a look.

'I have a confession to make,' he says, his gaze so intense now that I feel compelled to stare down at the floor. 'I invited you out to Oamaru with us partly because I thought it would help. There is something about this place – I felt it when I came here after my dad died, and I wanted you to feel it too.'

Whisky tears well up in my throat.

'Did it work?' he asks, and I manage to nod.

'I thought it had, at least a bit. You always look so haunted usually, as if you carry the dead with you every-where you go. Today you seemed more, I dunno, alive, I guess, as if you were living properly in the moment, rather than hovering on the outside looking in.'

'Are you some sort of magician?' I say, desperate to lighten the mood. I cannot believe how much of a measure he has of me, or how closely he has been pay-ing attention.

'Nah.' Kit levers the bottle of whisky down, but I put a hand over the top of my glass.

'Any more of that and I'll end up sleeping out here.'

'Wouldn't be so bad.' Kit stretches his long legs out and knits his hands together behind his head. I am curled up like a hedgehog on my beanbag now, chilly despite the musty old blanket I found in the bedroom wardrobe.

I am still unsure how pleased Anna would be about the idea of me meeting my birth mother, but I know without question that she would have adored Kit – and Tui, for that matter. All this time, I have felt traitorous to my adoptive mum, but perhaps I have been doing her memory a disservice by ever doubting her capacity for forgiveness, understanding and love. Because the truth is, Anna was full of love, and if she were here, she would urge me to follow my heart no matter what.

34

Bonnie

The day I found out that Seth was cheating on me was also the day I told him I loved him.

We had woken up at his place, all limbs entwined and sheets tangled up, and I was feeling woozy with happiness. He had a lecture to go to, but I remember that he missed it. He told me that I was teaching him more about love than anything Shakespeare had written could possibly hope to, and I thought that was so romantic.

I had never told anyone that I loved them before except for my folks – and it wasn't even something that I said to them all that often. So, when I blurted out those three words to Seth that morning, it was a big deal.

A really big deal.

The rest of that day, I floated around London. I felt invincible, you know? Like I had worked out the entire meaning of life, and wanted everyone else to feel as good as I did. Hell, I probably even sang, I was that happy.

After I'd finished work that evening, I got on the bus and went straight to Camden Town. I had arranged to meet Seth in the World's End pub – an ironic choice of venue, as it turned out – but bumped into Lavender on the way in.

I knew something was up right away. She seemed so twitchy, like she had a whole nest of ants in her smalls, and she couldn't look me in the eye. We got ourselves a couple of ciders and went to the table where Seth and his other mates were, and right away Lavender starts goading him, making all these snide little remarks under her breath, saying stuff about all the lies he told, and that he owed her because of the trouble he'd got her into with her parents.

It was so weird, because the two of them usually got on great. I mean, she often teased him and told him off, but it was always in good humour. I became aware very quickly that she was right raging angry with Seth for some reason. And I wasn't the only one who noticed — everyone was looking at each other as if to say, 'What the bloody hell is her problem?', and I'll be honest, I didn't really know how to handle it. I just knew that something was wrong, really wrong — I could feel it in my gut.

After this had been going on a while, Lavender got up and went to the toilet, so I followed her. I thought I'd try to cheer her up, you know? Snap her out of it. I was still trying my best to hang on to the happy mood I'd been in all day, but as soon as I asked her what was up, Lavender started going in on me, saying how stupid I was, and how Seth was making a laughing stock out of me.

Well, that really wound me up, and I'd had a few drinks by this point, so I argued back for once. I told her that Seth would never do that to me because he loved me, and that he'd told me as much that very morning. When I said that, her face seemed to crumple in on itself. I had uncovered — and shredded – her last straw. From the look of her, I thought she was going to start crying, but instead she just laughed, and it was this really cruel and hard laugh.

I went cold all over. I'm cold all over now just remembering it. Her reaction had scared me, and so when she tried to keep on talking, I ran right out of there. I went back to Seth and told him that we had to go, that I needed to leave. I just wanted to get him away from Lavender before she said anything else, but he wouldn't listen to me. He was drunk, and showing off as he always did when he'd had a few too many jars. Talking rubbish while all his so-called friends rolled their bloody eyes at him.

Lavender came back from the bathroom with this dangerous air about her. She'd not long ago dyed her hair bright blue and that night she had spiked it up like Jack Frost. She was all sharp edges and icy colours that night, and she fizzed with self-righteous anger. I could feel it coming off her. Seth apparently couldn't, or didn't want to, because he just laughed at her, all scornful and dismissive. I will never forget the look on her face when she turned to me and calmly told me to ask Seth what had happened in Brighton.

I was confused, because as far as I knew, he had gone off to Brighton on his own when I couldn't go with him. It was after that weekend that he'd started being really sweet to me. I told Lavender to shut up then. I was fed up with her for ruining my day, and I was too frightened to have any desire to hear Seth's answer. In the end, though, he didn't say a thing. Lavender sighed, and said that she had to tell me – and she did. She told everyone at that table how Seth had invited her to Brighton at the last minute, and how they had spent pretty much the entire weekend in bed together.

I almost hurled. The blood just drained right out of me, and I tried not to cry, but it was as if I had been possessed. I was wailing and screaming and shouting at both of them. Seth tried to grab my arms, but I found some superhuman strength inside me and managed to pull away from him. All I could think was that I had to get away from both of them, from her need to hurt me so inexplicably, and his pathetic lies as he tried to persuade me that she was playing a trick on me — that the whole thing was some sort of sick bloody joke.

I ran out of the pub without my jacket, and the bus was right there at my stop, so I got on, and I saw Seth out of the back window, chasing up the street behind me. I loved the guy so much that I wanted nothing more than to get off, but I knew that Lavender was telling the truth.

The signs had been there all along, but I had allowed myself to become blind to them. Even when I knew Seth was manipulating me in order to get his own way, I excused his behaviour. I thought that's what love must be, and that his need to control me was fuelled by genuine affection, but there was always a small voice telling me that things weren't quite right — that I should want to have sex with him rather than feel as if I owed it to him. My worst fears had come true, and having all my horrible insecurities confirmed in such a cruel way had upset me, of course, but it had also made me angry. I was fuming.

I went straight back to my home away from home, where

I knew I would be safe and looked after. The professor, who I'm sure by now you have worked out is David, was shocked when he saw the state of me, and then he was furious. I didn't know he had it in him to be so cross, but it made me feel better, seeing him so affronted. It made me feel as if I was worth something after all, even if Seth clearly didn't think so.

Once I had stopped my crying and we were talking it all through, I started to feel even angrier – this time on David's behalf. I was pissed off with his wife for the first time. Because how dare she walk out on him? How could she blame him for something that was nobody's fault? I told him what I thought, too. I said that she was stupid – even more stupid than I had been to put my trust in Seth – and he did the oddest thing. He started laughing, then he picked me right up and swung me around, said I was the first person to ever take his side, and that me being cross meant that he could be cross, too. He needed to shout – we both needed to – and that's what we did. We yelled and we swore and I think we even smashed a few glasses. It was cathartic, and even though it was the worst day of my life, it somehow became one of the very best.

Bonnie took a breath. She had been writing so fast that sweat had beaded on her upper lip and under her arms. Tracey must have switched the heating up to tropical again. Her friend could not bear to be cold, and there were soft pink blankets draped over the back of every chair in the house.

It felt good to have reached this place in the story – it was a poignant memory that Bonnie had been dreading delving back into, so she was glad to find that it hadn't upset her as much as she'd feared. And it was all true, anyway – that day had turned out to be one of the most pivotal of her life.

Putting the lid back on her pen, Bonnie collected up her empty coffee cup and went down to the kitchen, where she found Tracey weeping over a copy of the local paper.

'Shit.' Bonnie was beside her in seconds. 'What's the matter? What's happened?'

'Oh, nothing.' Tracey dabbed her eyes with a corner of her Pink Panther apron. 'Just this horrible story, that's all. I'm just being silly as usual, duckie.'

Bonnie scanned the headline. A young child had been left orphaned after a traffic accident.

'That is awful,' she agreed. 'So sad.'

Tracey's voice cracked. 'I just feel so sorry for the little darling,' she sobbed. 'No child should have to lose their mum and dad.' Then, glancing sideways at Bonnie, 'Oh God, I'm sorry, love – I didn't mean that as a dig at you.'

'It's fine.' Bonnie gave her shoulder a reassuring squeeze. 'That's why I'm here, you know? To make up for the past.'

Tracey shuddered as she closed the newspaper and folded it in half.

'It reminded me of this terrible story from last

Christmas,' she told Bonnie. 'That one really upset me. Tea?'

Bonnie nodded as Tracey made her way towards the kettle.

'This woman was killed while she was out riding her daughter's horse on Christmas Eve, and the pony had to be destroyed, too. Imagine that, right before all the festivities, all the presents under the tree that would never be opened. My heart broke for that girl and her dad.'

'That is tragic,' agreed Bonnie, the thought of anything happening to her horses dropping like a stone through her insides. 'Where did it happen? Around here?'

Tracey paused as she separated two tea bags.

'No, I think it was over in Cambridgeshire or somewhere. The woman's husband was some sort of famous author, if I remember rightly, so it made all the papers.'

Bonnie suddenly felt as if a fist had closed around her throat. Picking up her phone, she opened the internet search function and typed in a few key words. The stories and photos that came up made her cry out in such horror that Tracey dropped the mug of tea she was holding so it smashed into pieces all over the tiles.

'What the hell is going on?' she cried, but Bonnie was already running from the room.

35

Despite enduring a two-day whisky hangover that would have measured a strong ten on anyone's 'what the hell were you thinking'-o-meter, I have felt pretty good since my trip out to Oamaru. Queenstown is even busier now than it was in the run-up to Christmas, as backpackers and holidaying New Zealanders alike converge on the South Island's party capital, ready to see in the New Year.

I haven't seen Kit or Tui since they dropped me off back at my apartment, but I have been thinking about them – mostly about how much I will miss them when I eventually go home. It has been eighteen days now since I landed here, but I feel as if I have been here for so much longer, and with no return flight yet booked, I feel pleasantly untethered. And it's not just the winter sunshine warming me up, it is the people that I have met, and the person that I have started to become once again – someone less brittle and more at ease, someone who is able to find the funny in every situation. I didn't realise how much I had missed myself, how much I needed to feel something other than sad and hopeless. My main concern now is what will happen when I go back to England.

To give myself a task for the day that will hopefully go some way towards distracting my freewheeling mind, I set my alarm early and leave the apartment before the sun is fully up, going directly to the bus station and buying a ticket out to Wanaka – a picturesque area about two hours north of Queenstown.

Like many of the towns in Otago, Wanaka boasts a quaint sprawl of houses, shops and businesses, but its defining feature is the lake. As the bus pulls in, I spy the Southern Alps in the distance, glaring down like proud parents at the landscape below, and admire the tribes of colourful flowers bursting out from window boxes and pots. There are a handful of cafés on the opposite side of the road to the water, but instead of eating in as I usually would, I order a flat white and a muffin to go, keen to keep moving after the long drive.

The sky above the lake is part obscured today by a swell of donkey-grey clouds, the sunshine subdued for once behind them. Crunching underfoot, the shore is nature's button box of colourful stones, interrupted at regular intervals by tree roots, bursts of emerald-green mountain grass and untamed thickets of wild flora in radiant yellows and harmonious mauves.

I walk along slowly, sipping coffee and breaking off pieces of muffin, my tatty old Converse finding easy purchase on pebbles long since softened by tides. Gnarled trees bend over like crooked old ladies, caressing the water with their fingers of fronds, and I smile at a black dog as it splashes through the shallows, a stick almost as long as me clamped triumphantly between its jaws. Red and orange kayaks litter the shore, their oars poking up like diffuser sticks, and further along, small wooden rowing boats lounge belly up like sunbathers, displaying cracked patches of paint that were once perhaps white.

There is a rawness here in Wanaka that is absent in the more polished Queenstown, and as such the beauty feels more authentic somehow, less intrusive – a morning after rather than the night before, a place where dust settles rather than being kicked up.

I could not have chosen a better location to stop for a while in order to think.

I came to New Zealand in search of my mother, but instead, I have found a sister. And I met Kit, too. I am not sure what to call him. Certainly, he has become someone I consider to be a friend – but will that still be the case when Bonnie returns, and Kit finds out who I really am? Any day now, Kit said – any day now I will finally have to face the woman who chose to give me away. I could have grown up surrounded by all of this, but because of her, I am only just discovering it now.

I watch a flock of birds sweep out across the water, their little bodies gliding in perfect harmony, unknowing skywriters as they soar first up and then down. How lucky they are to belong to one another; how simple it must be to fall in line and become part of something far bigger than yourself. David would argue with that notion if he were here – my adoptive father would tell me that being an individual is far more important, and that one person can harness just as much power as a thousand if they so choose. That may be true of some, but not of me. I'm tired of being the only one. I do better with other people around me – and it is here in New Zealand, more than anywhere else since I lost Anna, that I feel as if I really belong. If I go home, will I lose that feeling? Will I be alone again?

At this moment I look up and see the lone tree in the middle distance. One that has strayed away from its companions up on the shore and set down its roots in the shallows of the lake, as if it is a child that has been ushered forwards to paddle. There are a handful of people crowded around taking photos, and with the backdrop of the mountains and the clouds now breaking up overhead, the little tree looks lost and vulnerable.

Charmed that such a kindred spirit should emerge on my horizon, I venture closer to examine the tree in more detail, taking in the rustic knots in the bark, the freshly uncoiled leaves of dazzling green, and the jaunty way it bows reverently to one side, as if curtseying to Mother Nature. It is the lone pawn that heads out to confront a queen, the bugle player on a battlefield, as brave and foolish as any soul that dares to face the world alone.

I understand then that I have a choice: I can see myself as lost and alone, or I can find the courage to step out and accept the hand that I have been dealt. Isn't that what Evangeline would do? Isn't that what Anna and David have wanted me to do all along?

I continue walking until I reach an impassable section of the lake. There is a fallen tree not far from where delicate waves are tickling the shoreline, and I sit down on the bleached husk of its splendidly decaying body. Only a few weeks ago, I would have been uncomfortable to be this close to death, but Kit has made me remember that life goes on, that old makes way for new, that a future can be altered but not destroyed – he has managed to turn his face towards the sun and let shadows fall behind him, and now I am finally starting to believe that one day, just maybe, I might be able to do the same.

Thanks to this place and these people, I am starting to find ways to be less bitter, and less afraid. I was fearful that being around horses would be too painful, but my desire to spend time with Tui was strong enough to carry me through. I started this trip by only giving away the tiniest pieces of myself to those around me, and now I want to scale one of those distant peaks just to scream from its tip that I have a sister – and that she is the best and bravest girl I know.

Whatever happens now, I know one thing for sure – I must keep Tui in my life. I want her to know what she means to me, and that I will always be there for her, no matter what. If I have Tui, I know that I can cope with anything – caring about her has made me stronger. As fast as the thought occurs to me, so follows another: that I don't want to wait any longer for Bonnie to return – I want my sister to know who I am now.

I don't even realise that I'm crying until the tears land on my bare knees, and I smile as I wipe them from my cheeks. For once, I don't feel sad to be shedding them, because I know that this time they have nothing to do with sorrow at all.

36

Having made the decision that I want to tell Tui the truth about who I really am, I find myself impatient for it. The temptation to hurry straight back to Queenstown and jump in a taxi to the stables is an ardent one, but I know that the more sensible option would be to sleep on it. Plus, I want to tell David first. I feel bad for the way I have shut him out since I've been here, and I worry that he will be upset to learn about it all after the event. Anna and I had so many shared interests and spent so much time together that David inevitably ended up being left out, which must have rankled a tiny bit, even if he never showed it. I want to start letting him in again. We used to be so close when I was young – surely we can get back to that place again?

When I take out my mobile to call him from the bus, however, there is no answer. David's voicemail informs me cheerfully that he is 'probably reading, writing or sleeping', while the house phone simply rings out. I know it's only around seven a.m. in the UK – and a Sunday, granted – but my adoptive dad is an early riser. He always has been.

Frustrated and beginning to worry, I put a call through to Hayley instead.

'Hello.' She sounds bleary.

'It's Genie – did I wake you?'

'Yes.'

'Shit, I'm sorry, but I need a favour.'

'Hang on a minute.'

I hear the ruffling sound of a duvet being lifted, then what appears to be a male voice asking if everything is OK. Hayley has not had a boyfriend for years, and for a moment, I am so surprised that I almost forget why I was calling her in the first place.

'Who's there with you?' I ask, as soon as she comes back on the line.

'What? Nobody. You must be hearing things.'

'The thing I heard was a man – in your bedroom!'

There is a pause.

'No comment,' says Hayley, and I respond with a 'hmm', before filling her in on my MIA dad.

'Maybe he's still asleep,' is her response.

'He never sleeps past seven,' I argue. 'And he never switches off his phone either. I tried both – the mobile and the landline.'

'What can I do?' She sounds more resigned than concerned.

'I guess, if you don't mind, you could maybe drive over there? Just to make sure he hasn't fallen over or something?'

'He's not even sixty yet,' she chides. 'I doubt we're looking at a slip and fall situation.'

'Pretty please,' I plead, closing my eyes and willing

her to agree. 'You know I wouldn't ask you unless I thought it was absolutely vital.'

'Oh, OK then, as it's you.'

The next half-hour passes like a week, and not even the stunning swathes of scenery rushing past the window can distract me. It's stupid, but I keep envisaging David submerged under his bath water, or in a crumpled heap at the bottom of the stairs. I check my phone to see the date of his last text – three days ago. Before I went to Oamaru. I didn't even tell him that I was going. Now, suddenly, I want to tell him everything.

I'm still holding my phone when Hayley calls me back, and the shrill ringtone makes me jump so much that I almost drop it.

'Talk to me,' I say, not bothering with pleasantries.

'Well, it's really weird,' Hayley says, sounding far more awake now than she did during our initial conversation. 'I'm outside your place now, and there are no lights on or anything. I've been knocking and calling through the letterbox, but he hasn't answered.'

'Shit! Can you see anything through the windows?'

'The curtains are drawn,' she says, and I hear the sound of gravel crunching underfoot as she makes her way around the side of the house. 'No, no sign of him in the kitchen either.'

'Try chucking a stone at the front bedroom window,' I say, but Hayley isn't keen.

'If he didn't hear me shouting, he's not going to hear a stone. Hang on – I've got another idea.'

All I can hear is her feet on the driveway, and I hate myself for being so far away. It's been days since I called – he could have been trapped for ages.

'Oh,' Hayley says, and I clutch the phone.

'What?'

'I've just had a look through the letterbox again, and I can see a pile of mail on the mat.'

'He must be in there!' I cry, attracting curious stares from other passengers on the bus. We're not far from Queenstown now – I can see a glimpse of Lake Wakatipu in the distance.

'I think the alarm's on,' Hayley says. 'I can see the light flashing.'

The icy fingers of dread that had wrapped themselves around my airways ease off a little.

'Are you sure?'

'Well, the only way to find out is to try and break in, and I don't really fancy being arrested at this time on a Sunday morning – or ever, for that matter. Oh, hang on, Mrs Gilbert is coming.'

Our nosy-but-nice neighbour must have heard the commotion. I can just imagine her padding importantly down the drive in her pink slippers, her Highland terrier Boris taking the opportunity to lift his leg on David's rose bushes.

'I'd better speak to her,' I allow, and Hayley passes me over.

'Hello, Genie darling – is that really you? I thought you were in New Zealand?'

'I am,' I say. 'They do have phone reception here, though.'

'Yes, of course they do, silly me.'

'Sorry to have woken you up so early,' I begin, 'but I'm trying to find my dad. Have you seen him this week?'

'Yes, dear, he popped over yesterday morning to give me his spare key.'

'Why?' I demand, aware that I'm perhaps not being as polite as I could be.

'Well, he always leaves me a key when he goes on holiday,' says Mrs Gilbert. 'Didn't you know he was going away?'

Obviously not.

'I don't think so,' I reply warily, second-guessing my own memory. Did David mention that he was going somewhere? Where would he even go at this time of year – to a friend's?

'Is everything OK?' asks Mrs Gilbert.

'Yes, of course – thank you,' I say, wracking my brain for any further clues as she mutters something about time zones.

'There you go,' Hayley declares. 'Problem solved. Can I go back to bed now?'

'David didn't tell me he was going away,' I grumble, standing up as the bus groans to a halt on Shotover Street. It's odd how much coming back to Queenstown feels like arriving home.

'Perhaps it was a last-minute thing?' suggests Hayley,

who is now back in her car. I can hear the swish of windscreen wipers.

'God, I'm sorry I dragged you out of bed. I just panicked when I couldn't get hold of him.'

'It's fine,' Hayley hushes. 'Don't worry about it. You would do the same for me.'

'I wonder where he's gone?' I say, leaning against the wall beside the NZone Skydive Centre, where two girls with Thailand tans and braided hair are daring each other to go inside. Anna and I had a conversation about skydiving once, and she made me promise that if I ever did it, I wouldn't tell her until afterwards, when I was safely back on the ground.

'Somewhere sunny, if he's got any sense,' muses Hayley. 'It's vile weather here.'

I look up towards where the sun has just emerged from behind a small, tufty cloud, and decide not to rub my friend's nose in the fact that it's glorious where I am.

'David hates the sun,' I say insistently. 'He has the same complexion as me – we're not made for it. And anyway,' I add, thinking, 'he wouldn't just swan off without telling me – he knows that I worry since—'

It is then that an exceptionally horrible thought occurs to me. Maybe David really is angry with me after what I admitted to him on Christmas Eve. At the time, he had reassured and comforted, but perhaps upon reflection, he has realised that what I did that winter morning was as reprehensible as I had always feared, and now he doesn't want to see or speak to me, because he can't bear to.

'David would never do anything to deliberately upset or worry you,' Hayley says then, as if I had blurted out the words instead of merely thinking them. 'There must be a good reason.'

'There will be an explanation,' I decide, reassuring myself more than her. 'You should go – this call will be costing you a fortune.'

It's only when we have said our goodbyes and I'm walking distractedly back up the hill towards the apartment that I remember the man's voice I heard. Lucky Hayley, I think, despising my envy almost as soon as it manifests as a scowl on my face. I am happy for my friend, and even more so for whoever she woke up with this morning, because he is a very fortunate man. It's just that it has been such a long time since I have been close to anyone in that way – and when Kit comforted me on the pier in Oamaru, it only served to make me realise how long. I had felt a yearning in that moment, even though I was flooded with mournfulness, and the same stirring of desire had been there amongst the eerie lights of the portal, too, when Kit stood so close behind me. When we sat on that balcony, sharing stories of our lives in between sips of whisky, that longing intensified yet more, until I had no choice but to excuse myself and go to bed. It was either that, or risk giving in to the need that the alcohol was coaxing out of me. Because that was surely all it was – that is all it can ever be.

I know it makes no sense to hanker after that which you cannot have – it's all I have done for the past year, and even before that. I guess I have always been craving a missing something, or someone. Tonight, however, as I pull the covers up around my chin and wait for sleep to sneak in and rescue me, not only from my own confusion but from my increasing concern about David's whereabouts, there is only one person whose arms I would like to be wrapped around me.

37

Bonnie

For the first few moments after he opened the door to find Bonnie standing there, the professor just stared at her. Bonnie took in the absence of hair, the lines around the kind eyes, the bags underneath them. Here was a man who had been through a terrible ordeal, but even if she hadn't known as much, Bonnie would have guessed it as soon as she saw him.

'Bonnie,' he said at last, letting go of the breath he had been holding in. 'It's . . .'

He paused, visibly overcome by a surge of feeling so potent that Bonnie felt herself move forwards to comfort him. It was how their friendship had begun, all those years ago. The professor had been upset, and she had supported him. It was the thing that bonded them together.

'Sorry,' she said, hanging her head. 'I should have called first, I know, but I was afraid that you would tell me not to come. I only just found out about Anna, and, oh bloody hell, Dave, I'm so, so sorry. I can't believe it.'

David nodded, just once, his bottom lip tucked behind his teeth as he fought tears.

'I can't either sometimes,' he said with a sigh, looking past her and along the driveway. There had been a frost that morning, and the front lawn still glittered beneath a tepid sun. Bonnie could see her breath in the air between herself and David, and shivered.

'Those days are the worst, in a way,' he said absently. 'I wake up and, for a blissful minute, I forget that Annabel's gone – sometimes I even reach out for her. But then reality lands on me again, and . . .' He trailed off, his expression articulating far more than any words could ever have done.

'I'm so sorry,' Bonnie said again, feeling as if she was being no help at all. 'I wish I'd known sooner. If I had, I would have—'

'Don't worry.' David pushed his spectacles up on his nose. 'There was nothing anyone could have done. It is what it is.'

'I would have come sooner if I'd known,' protested Bonnie, although even as she said it, she wondered how true it really was. Would learning of Anna's death have been enough of a reason to persuade her to get on a plane? She liked to believe that it would have. And as soon as she had read the first few lines of the article about Anna's accident in Tracey's kitchen, all she could think was that she had to get here as quickly as possible. She had been packed and in a taxi to the train station inside ten minutes.

'Please come in,' David said then. 'Sorry, forgetting my manners. Must be the shock of seeing you again after so many years. You look well, by the way. Did I say that already?'

He had taken a step back and opened the front door a fraction more, revealing a wide tiled hallway and a side table piled high with unopened post.

Bonnie hesitated.

'Is Evangeline . . .?' she began, but David shook his head.

'She's not here, and you won't believe it when I tell you where she actually is.'

Bonnie was about to ask what he meant, when her phone beeped with a message. Recognising the tone as the one she had allocated to Kit, she fished it out of her handbag, apologising to David as she followed him inside.

'Mission Penguin a big success,' she read, then gasped as she took in the photo that Kit had sent along with it. There was Tui, smiling broadly beside a large statue of a penguin, one hand waving up towards whoever was taking the photo, and the other clamped firmly in the hand of— No, it couldn't be! The young woman had chin-length thick dark hair and a neat, rounded chin. She was gazing down at her half-sister with nothing but adoration in her eyes. Evangeline was in New Zealand.

Bonnie came to an abrupt standstill in the hallway, her hand over her mouth.

'Everything OK?' David came back towards her.

Unable to speak, Bonnie simply handed him the phone.

'Oh, gosh!' he exclaimed, pushing his glasses up from where they had slipped down his nose. 'Is that Genie? It is! Oh, she looks well. She's cut all her hair off. And who's that with her?'

'My daughter,' Bonnie croaked. 'Tui.'

'Aha.' David looked again. 'Yes, Genie did mention that she'd met her. They seem to be getting on rather well, don't they?'

How could he be so calm about this? Bonnie was struck dumb. But then she remembered, David Nash always had been difficult to shock. He was practical-minded – a man with solutions rather than problems. And he'd presumably had advance warning. Evange-line must have been in touch with him regularly, filling him in on Bonnie's life back in New Zealand. But did this photo mean that Tui was aware she had a sister? No, it couldn't – Kit would have called her if that was the case – or Simon. Evangeline must have become friends with Tui and Kit without coming clean about who she was. And who could blame her? Certainly not Bonnie – the queen of omitting truth.

'Genie really does look well,' David remarked con-tentedly, handing Bonnie her phone back.

'I thought she was called Evangeline,' murmured Bonnie, who thought she might fall over if she didn't find a chair to sit on soon. David, perhaps sensing this, led her into a very modern kitchen and pulled out a stool.

'Oh, she is,' he said cheerfully. 'But we call her Genie

for short. She always felt like she made a wish come true for me and for Anna, so it made sense. Now, would you like coffee or tea? I can make a pot of either.'

He was reaching for the kettle as if all this were completely normal, as if women he hadn't seen for almost thirty years regularly showed up at his front door in search of the children they'd given him.

'Tea,' she managed, easing herself into a sitting position and gazing again at the photo of her two daughters. How could this be happening? How could Evangeline be there in New Zealand, casually hunting for penguins with Tui and Kit, while she, Bonnie, was here? Evangeline had gone to find her at exactly the same time as Bonnie had sought her out – it was enough to make her head spin.

David filled the silence by putting the water on to boil, readying two mugs and fetching the milk from the fridge. Bonnie watched him with unseeing eyes, envious of him for having tasks to complete while all she could do was sit there, trying to make sense of everything.

'How long has Genie been in New Zealand?' she asked, and David frowned mid-stir, then referred to the calendar pinned up by the back door.

'She flew out on the eleventh,' he said, blowing air into his cheeks. 'Gosh, that was quite a while ago, wasn't it?'

'That's the same day I flew here,' Bonnie replied numbly.

'I assumed it must have been.' David put a steaming mug down in front of her. Bonnie had been shivering pretty much non-stop since she found out about Anna, and now she wrapped both her hands around the cup in an attempt to extract some much-needed warmth.

'Genie went to find you the day after she arrived,' David explained, levering himself on to the stool opposite her own. 'Someone told her you'd come here, but she decided to stay and wait for you to return.'

'What a bloody mess.' Bonnie was shaking her head now in disbelief. 'I mean, what are the chances that, after all this time, we try to find each other at exactly the same bloody time?'

'Where have you been since you arrived?' David enquired.

'I came to see Evangeline,' Bonnie said. 'But when I landed, I couldn't make myself come here. I was terrified, and I needed some more time to get my thoughts in order, so I went to stay with Tracey.'

'Sunrise Tracey?' he exclaimed, and Bonnie smiled for the first time.

'The very same.'

'Gosh! How is she?'

Bonnie filled him in, explaining how she had come to learn about Anna's accident.

'Of course.' David sipped his tea. 'Tracey never knew my surname, did she? She used to call me "The Professor".'

'I can't even begin to imagine how awful it's been for

you,' she said in a small voice. 'For both of you.' Bonnie fiddled with the cuffs of her thick winter coat, which she had yet to remove. Despite the artificial heat in the kitchen, she still felt chilled right through to her bones.

'Genie took it very badly,' David said, rubbing at his eyes so rigorously that his glasses fell right off. 'It was my idea that she fly over and try to find you – I thought that perhaps it would help. I should have written or called, but like you, I was afraid that you would refuse to see her. We never wanted to close that door completely, and I'm ashamed that Anna and I allowed it to happen. Annabel was so bowled over by love for Evangeline, and she used to worry herself into a fury imagining that you would come back one day to claim her. In the end, I guess it became easier to distance ourselves. But Genie always knew that she had a mum somewhere – we never lied to her about the adoption.'

'Did she never ask to see her original birth certificate?' Bonnie asked, because she knew that if it were her, she would have peered under every pebble in the world until she found out the truth.

'Quite the opposite,' David admitted, staring resolutely down at his moccasin-style slippers. 'We told her there were no adoption papers because you were a friend of a friend, and that it was easier to simply put Anna's name down as her mother and my name as her father to avoid the headache and expense of going through official channels.'

'And she believed you?'

David shrugged. 'I guess she did – she asked me once about who her real father was, but I simply told her we didn't know.'

Bonnie took a sip of her tea, unable suddenly to look at him.

'And you never heard from . . . you know who?'

David shook his head. 'No – not a peep. But then, none of us expected that he would get in touch, not after what he did.'

'So, why now?' Bonnie couldn't help but ask. 'Why does Genie want to know me now?'

'Anna dying left a hole that was far too large for me to fill,' he said. 'In the past, Genie had been quite dismissive about the idea of seeking you out, but now I'm wondering if that was more to do with Anna than Genie herself. She was fiercely loyal to Anna,' he explained. 'She would have known that expressing an interest in locating you would have hurt her mum, so she talked herself out of it.'

'I suppose that makes sense,' Bonnie allowed. 'You never want to let your parents down, do you? It's why I never told my own about Evangeline – I foolishly convinced myself that it would devastate them, when in fact, the opposite was probably true.'

David looked ashen.

'I'm so sorry,' he said. 'I should have supported you better back then – offered to tell your mother and father myself.'

'No.' Bonnie was adamant. 'It wouldn't have made any difference. I was damn stubborn, and I wanted

Evangeline to have the best chance at happiness. That was you and Anna. And she has been happy, hasn't she? My girl?'

Bonnie's voice had cracked as she said the last, and David waited a moment or two before replying.

'I think we made her happy,' he confirmed, nodding as if to reassure himself. 'But she is definitely not happy now. The thing is, Genie blames herself for the accident – which is ridiculous, of course – but she can't seem to move past it. Until she went out to New Zealand, she had barely left the house in a year. She gave up her job – a job she loved – and only saw a handful of her friends. It's been terrible for her.'

Bonnie was about to offer more comfort, when David surprised her by smiling.

'That's why it was so nice to see that photo just now,' he went on. 'She looks like her old self again – and happier than I can recall her being in a very long time.'

'Tui has that effect on people,' Bonnie told him, smiling now herself as she pictured her rambunctious daughter. 'It's impossible to feel sad around her for long.'

'She sounds like her mum,' David said quietly. 'You always had that same effect on me, if I remember rightly. Before Anna came back, I leant on you so much. I never forgot that.'

'I can barely remember what I was like then,' Bonnie told him honestly. 'I have been trying to, over the past few weeks.'

Reaching into her bag, she produced a sheaf of lined

paper and held it up. 'I started writing down the story of everything that happened back then, to give to Evangeline.'

'*Everything* that happened?'

David was staring at her, his gaze intent.

'I haven't got to the end of the story yet,' she said carefully. 'So no, not everything.'

'Have you had any breakfast?' he asked.

Startled by the abrupt change of subject, Bonnie stammered an incoherent reply.

'I'll make us some eggs,' he decided, hopping down off the stool and crossing the room. 'How do you like them – fried, poached, scrambled?'

'David.'

'I could do us an omelette, if you fancy? I have some posh cheese left over from Christmas. Do you like Stilton?'

'David, please.' Bonnie was standing up now, frustrated by the fact that he had begun flapping about the place. She had been consumed by such a tidal wave of anxiety on the journey here that she felt suddenly deflated. All this time she had been holed up in Tracey's guest bedroom, wasting precious time that she could have spent with her daughter – with both her daughters. She was frustrated with herself, and that in turn made her annoyed with David. It had been almost three decades since she last saw him, since everything had happened, and here he was discussing which cheese to add to her breakfast.

'I need to go home,' she told him. 'Back to New Zealand. As soon as possible.'

'I understand.' David lowered the frying pan he was holding in a gesture of defeat. Then, as if the thought had only just occurred to him, he folded his arms and gave her an enquiring look.

'You haven't told me everything,' he stated. 'You're hiding something.'

'Like what?' Bonnie began packing her stack of paper back into her bag.

'Like the reason you came here to England,' he said. 'You said you only found out about Anna yesterday.'

'That's true.' Bonnie was aware of her heart beginning to beat a little harder. The anxiety had returned, and was smashing its way through her like a bolting pony.

'So, why now?' asked David, repeating Bonnie's earlier question back to her. 'What made you want to see Genie again after so long?'

Bonnie rested her hands against the worktop, closing her eyes as she steeled herself. She thought about the compassionate green eyes of the doctor, and the family portrait the woman had propped up in a frame on her desk. She had talked about time being the most precious thing, about how life finds a way to show you what you need to do, why it is so important not to let your fear get the better of you.

Bonnie was yet to tell anyone her real reason for coming to England. She didn't know whether it was the shock of seeing her two daughters together for the first time, or if it was simply the comfort of being in the presence of such a good and trusted friend once again, but suddenly, she didn't want to lie any more.

Taking a deep breath, she told David everything.

38

I arrive at Koru Stables a little after eleven a.m. to find the yard crowded with riders. There is no sign of Kit or Tui, but I notice that the minibus is parked in its usual spot underneath the big tree. I'm just about to wander into the office when Allie, who has returned after her few days off to pack for Wellington, emerges from the tack room, her cheeks and bare shoulders sunburn pink.

'Hi,' I say, then swallow my next remark when she stares right through me as if I'm not there.

Unsure how to react, I follow her over to where two horses are tethered, waiting to be tacked up. Keith wickers with recognition when he sees me, and promptly wipes his velvety nose on my T-shirt.

'Lovely to see you, too,' I exclaim, but any amusement withers and dies when I see the look on Allie's face.

'Are you OK?' I ask, and she nods at Keith.

'Can you tack him up for me?' she replies, strolling away before I have time to pry further. She doesn't seem upset so much as distracted. Perhaps the fact that she's nearing the end of her time here at the stables is making her feel out of sorts. By the time I have tightened Keith's girth and fastened his noseband and cheek piece, Allie has vanished into the office to deal with payments, so I sneak a mint from my pocket into the chestnut pony's grateful mouth, laughing as he curls up his lip and flashes his big yellow teeth at me. Heading towards the hay barn a minute later in search of Tui, I spot her in the outdoor school, playing chase with Beavis. With her head thrown back and her arms and legs flailing with carefree abandon as she runs from left to right, she is such a wonderful sight for my sore eyes that instead of calling out to her, I simply stand and drink her in.

My sister.

'Have you ever seen a human being look so much like a windmill?'

It's Kit, looking typically handsome, despite being red in the face and reeking of the muck heap.

I sing a few chorus lines of 'Spinning Around' by Kylie Minogue back at him, and Kit grins.

'Don't go giving up the day job.'

'Too late,' I reply, thinking of Mill House Stables. Kit, however, must assume that I'm still in joke mode, because he merely pulls a face.

'How many days were you hungover after that bottle of whisky we chugged?' he asks, looking suitably impressed when I admit that it was two.

'I'm pretty sure I'm still munted now,' he admits. 'This is what old age does to a man.'

'Kit!'

We both wheel around to find Allie about to mount a large skewbald cob.

'I'm taking the ride out now – we're doing the longer route, so expect us back in about two hours or so.'

'Got ya.'

Is it my imagination, or is Kit looking decidedly sheepish? And Allie is definitely a bit on edge today – perhaps they had a row. The two of us watch on in silence as the riders file out of the yard. I can still hear Tui whooping and laughing over in the outdoor school, and it reminds me again why I am here. I want to tell her the truth – and the same goes for Kit.

Maybe it makes more sense to tell him first, but I have no idea how to even begin. I was so gung-ho yesterday, but now that I am faced with him, being open and kind as he always is, I have been rendered mute by trepidation. What if he's angry – or worse – disgusted?

I follow him across the yard to the barn on the pretext of helping him fill hay nets, trying my best to ignore the fact that my insides are churning.

'Any big New Year plans for tonight?' I ask, flushing as I notice the dark flash of his back and stomach that emerges from below his shirt when he pulls down a bale.

'Nah.' Kit doesn't quite meet my eyes. 'I was gonna hang out at Allie's, but—'

'Geeee-nie!'

Tui is calling for me.

'In a minute, Tui – we're busy,' Kit shouts back.

'Genie!' she calls again, this time with more urgency.

'I should go and see if she's OK,' I begin, but he stills me with a frown.

'She's fine,' he says. 'She's got a surprise for you – that's all.'

For a fleeting, gut-punching second, it occurs to me that the surprise could be Bonnie, but then Kit adds, 'But you might want to change first.'

I look down at my shorts and vest top.

'Why? Don't tell me you two have rigged up a hot tub in the feed room or something?'

'Chance would be a very fine thing,' Kit replies wryly, finishing his first hay net and throwing it to the floor. 'Nah, it's more physical than that.'

'Not more Frisbee golf?' I groan jokingly. 'I'm bloody awful at that game.'

'I wouldn't put myself through that again – let alone you,' he says with a laugh. 'Nah, guess again.'

'Geee-nie!'

'She sounds fed up,' I point out to Kit, who steps from the barn into the yard and yells at Tui to 'stop crowing like a rooster'.

'She's just excited for the surprise,' he says. He definitely looks shifty.

'Just tell me!' I exclaim, still amused but also growing exasperated.

'Tui wants to go for a ride,' he explains.

'Oh. OK . . .' I hedge, unsure where he is going with this.

'With you,' he continues, forcing a hefty helping of enthusiasm into his voice.

'She wants me to teach her?'

He shakes his head.

'Lead her? Out to the river again?'

'You're getting warmer.'

'Come onnnn, Genie. Jeez!'

Tui is still calling for me. I wish Kit would hurry up and spit it out – he is enjoying toying with me far too much.

'That's it.' I drop my half-finished hay net. 'I'm going to find Tui – she'll soon tell me.'

Kit stops me with an outstretched arm so large it could be a drawbridge.

'She wants you to ride with her, you daft old coot,' he says, matter-of-factly. 'On horseback. Allie tacked up Ekara for you before she left.'

'But I can't,' I protest, my high spirits plummeting to Earth faster than a hailstone. 'I don't ride any more.'

'But you can,' he argues gently. 'You know how.'

'So what?' I snap back tersely, not caring when he recoils at my harsh tone. 'I'm guessing this was all your idea, right? You wanted to trick me, so you told Tui to pretend that it was her plan.'

'It was all her idea,' Kit replies, his total cool making my stroppy reaction seem even more unreasonable. 'I'm serious.'

'Oh, for God's sake!' I exclaim, flouncing away out of his reach. 'Why are you so obsessed with getting me back on a horse? I told you, I don't do that any more.'

'You did tell me,' Kit allows, his folded arms the only sign that he's feeling defensive. 'But you never gave me a good reason why.'

'I don't because I can't,' I tell him, my voice rising. 'Because I don't deserve to.'

'What do you mean, you don't deserve to?' Kit looks baffled. 'Of course you deserve to – if riding makes you happy, then you should do it. Jesus, Genie, you should know better than most how short life is. Why are you punishing yourself for no reason?'

I open my mouth to reply, but the words tangle up with a frustrated sob. When Kit comes towards me to offer comfort, however, I step hurriedly away.

'Please don't.'

He looks so crestfallen to have been rejected that I cannot bear to look at him, so instead I turn and flee, running across the yard and slamming the tack-room door shut behind me. How can I explain to him that riding *is* what I want to do, more than anything, but that is exactly the reason I choose not to? I caused Anna's death because I was too lazy and disorganised to exercise my own horse. My poor darling Suki, whose life was also lost because of her mistress. My punishment for not riding on the one day I should have is never riding again, no matter how much it pains me to stay away.

'Genie.' Kit is hammering on the door.

'Just give me a second,' I plead.

'Is Tui in there with you?' he asks, and I realise that he no longer sounds concerned or even cross, but scared. I slide the bolt back across, his expression when he rushes into the tack room sending an awful coldness through me.

'Shit,' he says, scanning the corners of the room. 'When did you last see her?'

'I didn't,' I say, beginning to feel frantic myself now. 'I only heard her – and that was a good ten minutes ago.'

'Don't worry.' Kit touches a hand to my shoulder. 'Search the yard. I'll check the paddocks.'

We split up and head off in different directions, both of us calling Tui's name as we run from feed room to indoor school to office and back again. I start to yell for Beavis, too, hoping that wherever the little dog is, his mistress won't be far behind, but there is no sign of either of them. Ekara is tethered to a wooden rail in the centre of the yard, and on my fifth fraught circuit, I pause for a moment and press my forehead against her dark brown neck.

'Any sign?' Kit emerges from the outdoor school looking harassed.

'Nothing,' I say, biting my lip. 'Where else would she go?'

'I don't know.' Kit runs an agitated hand through his hair. 'She knows not to run off without someone with her, but if she was annoyed . . . Oh, shit.' He looks suddenly frantic.

'Keith is missing,' he says. 'He was right here tacked up for Tui, but he's gone. Oh, bloody hell! You don't think she would have – '

'She must have ridden out in the direction of the river,' I interrupt, more with hope than conviction. The alternative is the highway, and I can't let myself entertain that idea.

'Let's go then,' says Kit, starting to move, but I stop him.

'We'll never catch up with her on foot.' I turn towards Ekara. 'I'll have to go on horseback.'

'But what about – ' he stutters, but I'm already yanking down the stirrups.

'I'll go on ahead,' I say. 'You check the road, then follow us.'

There is no time to look for a hat. Snatching up the reins and turning once more to throw Kit a look that I hope conveys far more confidence than I feel, I take a deep breath and vault quickly up on to Ekara's back.

'Are you sure you'll be OK?' Kit grabs my hand. He looks so terrified that I almost bend down to give him a reassuring kiss. Someone I love is out there, alone and in danger, and this time I am here to help. This time I can do something.

I wrap my fingers around his and squeeze.

'I will be,' I say. 'But only if my sister is.'

Then, before Kit has time to reply, I am kicking Ekara into life, and the two of us are thundering out of the yard without a backward glance.

39

The gate at the far end of the drive is fastened, but instead of slowing down to open it, I dig my heels determinedly into Ekara's sides and she leaps fearlessly into the air, clearing it by a foot. Gathering up the reins into one hand, I drop the other to the brave mare's gleaming neck and give her a pat of thanks. Pausing for only a moment to check my bearings, I veer right and gallop up the hill towards the tree-lined path that leads down to the Dart River.

I am aware of the sound of Ekara's hooves as they pound against the dry ground; I can feel brambles tearing at my bare legs and arms and the wind whipping through my hair, twisting and turning and flattening it against my head. My senses are reeling, my body slotting effortlessly back into the position that it knows so well, but all I can think is that I must find Tui. She is out here somewhere, most likely scared and upset because Kit and I both disregarded her cries for attention. The thought of anything bad happening to her is enough to make me urge Ekara on even faster, my lower legs pressing hard against her heaving sides.

As we crash our way through a partially concealed gap in the undergrowth, I only just spot the low-hanging branch in time, ducking my unshielded head until my face is pressed into the horse's flying mane. I can only hope that Keith, the pony Tui's presumably riding, is not going at this speed. Every time I turn a corner, I expect to see her sprawled out unconscious on the ground, the thought making me whimper with fear.

We reach the Dart River and I slow Ekara only long enough to canter her around in a circle, scanning the area for any sign of Tui as I go. Frustrated, I throw out the reins yet again, giving Ekara her mouth and urging her into the running water with my heels. There's an almighty splash as the mare gallops in right up to her belly, throwing up her head so fast that my nose collides with her neck. Blinking away river water, I reach up to wipe my face and encounter blood.

'Shit!' I swear, standing up in my stirrups and leaning forwards to squint into the distance. There is nothing, just river and mountains and trees and that never-ending sky. For the first time since landing in New Zealand, I curse the landscape for its size and sparsity. I hate the lack of fences and the endless parkland, I hate how easy it is to get lost, and to lose someone.

'Please,' I say aloud, gritting my teeth. 'I can't lose her – not Tui. Do you hear me? Not her.'

I am properly crying now, and Ekara, with her sweet, kind wisdom, seems to sense my distress. Slowing to a tidy trot, she heaves herself up the riverbank on to dry land, then stops to shake off the excess water, her nostrils bright red from exertion. The pause is enough to help me regain some control, and as I glance up ahead to where the trees seem to converge together, I see a small gap that could lead to another pathway.

'Come on,' I say, turning Ekara with one hand while I attempt to stem the flow of blood from my bashed-up nose with the other. Encouraged into a canter, she reaches the opening in less than a minute, and this time when we burst through to the other side of the treeline, I let out a yell of relief, because standing there, looking a bit lost and forlorn but still in one piece, is Tui.

'Gee-nie!' she calls, waving frantically with the hand that isn't clutching Keith's bridle. While she is clearly pleased to see me, I can tell that something is wrong, and trot quickly up to the edge of the river to join her.

'We didn't know where you'd got to,' I say breathlessly, sliding quickly off Ekara and pulling Tui against my chest for a hug. My arms, hands and legs are shaking, but it feels so good to have her back, to have her right here next to me.

'I came to find that silly boy Beavis, that's all,' she says, looking at me with her doleful dark eyes. I am still so overwhelmed with relief that at first her words don't register and, frustrated, she says them again.

'Beavis?' I repeat, looking around for the little brown dog. 'Where is he?'

'I don't know,' Tui says, and then she bursts into tears.

'Hey,' I say, cradling her head against my chest. Her hair is flattened and hot from wearing a riding hat, and

I send up a whisper of thanks that she had the foresight to put one on.

'It's OK,' I soothe. 'Don't cry – we'll find him.'

'But what if he drowned in the river?' she wails, quite distraught now.

'Dogs are very good swimmers,' I assure her, hoping I'm right where Beavis is concerned. The water is moving alarmingly fast, and it would be very deep for a little mutt like him.

'He chased a rabbit,' Tui tells me, tears all over her cheeks.

'So you followed him?' I guess, and she nods.

'I thought he would get lost, that's all.'

'And then you got lost?' I ask, and she shakes her head. She must have been calling for me and Kit back in the yard to help her with Beavis, I think with a stab. She did the right thing, but nobody came.

'I'm so sorry I wasn't there when you needed me,' I tell her, smoothing away the matted hair that is stuck to her wet cheeks. 'I promise that will never happen again – not ever.' And I mean it, too, even if I have no clue how I can keep the promise. If Bonnie decides that she doesn't want me in her life, how can I remain in Tui's?

'Uh-huh.' Tui starts biting one of her fingernails, then, as if noticing Ekara for the first time, she says in surprise, 'That's Allie's horse.'

'I thought you wanted me to ride her,' I say with a grin.

Tui looks at me with bemusement.

'You forgot your hat,' she states, bellowing with

unnaturally forced laughter as I put a hand on my head and feign shock.

'So I have,' I exclaim, untucking my T-shirt so I can use it to wipe my face. At least my nose has stopped bleeding. 'Silly me!'

'Silly Genie,' Tui crows with delight, rocking from one foot to the other. She clearly didn't have time to change for our planned ride, because she is dressed in shorts and her Snoopy T-shirt, and I wince as I see the red weals on her bare thighs from where Keith's saddle must have rubbed.

'How about we walk back to the yard?' I suggest, but she nods her head in furious disagreement, moaning loudly.

'B-B-Beeea,' she croons, her voice cracking as she remembers that her dog is missing.

'Beavis!' I call, my voice far louder than hers. Getting Tui back to the stables without him is going to be difficult, if not impossible, and I also have two horses to think about.

'Can you wait here and be in charge of Keith and Ekara?' I ask Tui, offering her both sets of reins. She looks unsure, so I put a hand on her shoulder.

'I'm going to look for Beavis,' I explain: 'But I won't go far – just over there, see?'

I point into the distance, to where the river hurtles around a bend obscured by large, grey rocks, and Tui eyes me distrustfully, before slowly shaking her head.

'OK,' she says, but I can sense her reluctance. I am

loath to leave her, but there is no other choice. She is safer on the ground than on horseback, and if I hurry, I can scour most of this area within half an hour or so.

'I'll be back soon,' I assure her. 'You can let the horses eat the grass if you like.'

She watches me go, and I turn to look back at her as I make my way along the edge of the water, watching her dear little form shrink the further I go. Now that I have found her, I feel like I can breathe again, but I'm conscious of how frantic a pursuing Kit must be. Even if he runs all the way here, it will take him at least another twenty minutes, and that could be too late for Beavis if he is trapped or in trouble. The sooner I can locate the dog and get him, the horses, and Tui back to the stables, the better.

I am calling Beavis's name so incessantly that I fail to hear his little bark at first, only making it out when I spot him on the opposite side of the river. The water here is just as fast-flowing and looks deep, but in his excitement at seeing a familiar face, Beavis doesn't even hesitate. Picking his way almost daintily over the white stones, I watch in mounting horror as he lowers his little pink nose to sniff the water, and then promptly jumps in and goes under.

'BEAVIS!' I yell, hurrying so fast down the bank that I slip right over and tumble down through a sticky mix of mud, clay and rotten tree roots. Clambering to my feet, I race along to where the current has swept the puppy, his little black nose just visible as he frantically tries to swim across to me.

Just as I didn't stop to think before vaulting on to Ekara in the yard, I don't give myself time to reconsider my actions now, and start to wade out into the water. It's so cold that I catch my breath in a shocked yelp, but I can see Beavis struggling only a few metres away now. I must reach him – I must not let Tui lose the animal she cares about most. I know how it feels, and it is a loss I will not let her bear – not while I can do something about it.

'Come on, little one,' I call encouragingly over the roar of the river. Water pummels against my legs, knocking them out from under me and rushing into my eyes and down my throat. Using a superhuman strength that I didn't know I possessed, I fight the current and manage to stand up again, but now I realise in horror that I can't see Beavis anywhere.

Holding my nose, I duck down under the water, keeping my eyes open and desperately searching around for any sign of him. It's impossible to see anything, but again I go under, clutching a tree root to balance and feeling around with my free hand, grabbing at loose stones, twigs, sticks, anything that could be the leg or tail of a little dog.

'Beavis!' I cry, wading further out into the river. I'm just about to submerge myself yet again when I hear a shout and turn, catching my ankle between two rocks as I do so and falling down heavily on my side.

I have lost the tree root, the water is rushing over me, I can feel myself moving but I can't stop, I can't see,

I can't breathe. Opening my mouth to scream, I choke as the river floods in. My chest burns in protest and my eyes sting. I am going to die here, I think numbly, and again it is Tui's face that I see.

I can't let this happen – I can't be someone who breaks their promise to her.

'Help!' I shriek, raising a hand above the surface, and somehow, another hand is there to grasp mine – a hand that is strong and dry and warm. A hand that is steadying me against the bottom of the river, and sliding down to cradle my elbow, and now the underside of my arm. With a great bellow, the owner of the hand pulls me up out of the water, then a second hand is wrapping around my other arm, and I'm being half lifted and half dragged out of the river, up on to the muddy bank, where I roll on to my back and frantically gasp in the air.

'Genie!' Kit is bending over me, his face an inch from my own. 'Genie, can you hear me? Say something.'

'Beavis,' I croak, coughing up more water. Rolling me briskly over on to my side, Kit pats hard on my back until there is no more water to cough up.

'I need to get Beavis,' I say again, trying to get back to my feet, but Kit pushes me gently down.

'You mean this Beavis?' he asks, pointing up the bank to where an inquisitive furry brown face is watching us both with interest.

'He got out?' I cry. 'Oh, thank God for that.'

'Sod the bloody dog!' Kit looks amused. 'Are you sure you're all right?'

'I think so,' I say, looking down at myself. My clothes are soaked through and clinging to me, there are scratches all over my arms and legs and a nasty gash on my ankle, but other than that, I seem to have survived.

'Oh,' I say, when I lift both my hands to check for damage.

'What?' Kit turns them over in his own, searching for wounds.

'My ring,' I say. 'It must have fallen off.'

Kit checks the ground around us, his mouth set.

'I can't see anything,' he says. 'Was it expensive?'

'It's not that,' I say, taking a breath. 'It was my mother's.'

'Ah, shit.' Kit crouches down on his haunches. 'I'm really sorry.'

'That's OK,' I say weakly. 'It's only a ring – I'll get over it.'

Kit helps me to my feet, and we walk back to where an overjoyed Tui has been reunited with Beavis. I can't seem to stop shaking, and after helping Tui back up on to Keith's saddle, Kit removes his shirt and wraps it around my shoulders.

'You don't have to,' I argue feebly, only to be silenced by the sight of his bronzed and muscular torso. The tattoos that start on both his arms extend right across his chest, to where an image of an eagle stands proud and noble, just like Kit is now.

'Aaaah, hunky Kit. You hunky man,' announces Tui, looking at me with great amusement. The only thing to

309

do is to laugh. Kit joins in, too, and Tui cackles with trademark abandon. She has been allowed to carry Beavis up on Keith's back, while Kit and I lead both him and Ekara, and as the six of us make our slow way back towards the stables, she keeps lifting him up and kissing the end of his nose. Seeing her happy and safe is worth every single thing I have just endured. I would do it all over again in a heartbeat.

Neither Kit nor I say much to each other, but every time I look across at him, our eyes meet. There is so much I need to tell him, about who I am and why I'm really here, but for now it is enough to simply relish this moment with the two of them, the half-sister I didn't even know I had, and the man I didn't even know I needed. Because the truth is, I have grown to need Kit – it is time to stop pretending that I don't.

When the slate-tiled tops of the stable buildings finally come into view up ahead, I am weary with fatigue. The ride and the river have stripped me of energy, and all I want to do now is find a soft bed somewhere and lie down. Perhaps I will curl up like a cat in the loft of the barn, rest my head on a bale of hay and sleep, secure in the know-ledge that my sister is safe and back where she belongs.

'Mummy!'

Tui has shot right up in her stirrups, holding Beavis tight under one arm and waving the other energetically from side to side.

'Mummy! Mummy, look at me – I'm riding. Mummy!'

A woman is standing at the far end of the long

driveway, her black hair shining in the dipping light of the sun. She had raised a hand to wave back at her daughter, but seeing me, she lets it drop. My legs are still propelling me forwards, but I can't feel them. My knuckles are white on Ekara's reins.

Bonnie takes a step towards us, but as she moves, a man comes into view behind her, shielding his eyes from the sun with a hand. I can see the glint of his glasses, the smooth sheen of his bald head, the familiar slant of his shoulders.

The two of them wait together side by side, and somehow, I continue to walk. I try to draw strength from Tui and Kit, but the truth is, I am in this alone. The secret is out, and everything that I have built since I got here is about to fall into disarray.

David is smiling at me, but Bonnie remains still, as if she cannot quite believe that I am here.

As we reach them, I open my mouth, determined to be the first to speak, but my birth mother beats me to it.

'Hey,' she says, her smile untethering as I return her gaze. 'It's nice to see you.'

'And me, Mummy!' interrupts Tui.

Bonnie softens as she glances from her first to her second born, then she looks back at me. Her eyes are so like my own, the same bright blue as the ever-reaching sky above us, the colour of possibility, and of hope, of everything I have come to believe since I arrived here.

'Yes, Tui darling,' she agrees. 'I've been waiting a long time to see you both.'

40

Before I can turn the hopeless jumble of emotions inside me into coherent words to use in reply to Bonnie, Kit has reached across to take Ekara's reins from me, and Tui has slid untidily off Keith's back to fling herself into her mother's arms.

'Mummy, oh Mummy!' she cries, covering Bonnie's face with kisses. 'Where have you been, Mummy? I missed you. Did you bring me lots of presents and surprises?'

Bonnie hugs her tightly, unfettered happiness creasing her face. I hardly dare look at her, but I also can't seem to drag away my eyes. I am acutely aware of David standing to one side, awkward discomfort radiating off him in waves, and wish that he would say something – anything to make this situation less weird. Feeling desperate, I turn towards Kit, who has folded his big arms across his bare chest and is peering at my adoptive dad with friendly intrigue.

Mumbling something about needing to clean myself up, I begin to move away, only to feel a hand on my arm.

'Wait,' says Bonnie, her confidence wavering when I don't return her proffered smile. 'Please don't run away before we have a chance to talk.'

'OK,' I croak, stepping out of her grasp. My limbs feel stiff. David falls in beside me as we all begin walking slowly towards the yard and starts saying something jolly about how much he likes my hair, but I barely register his words. While I am glad to see him and relieved that he is OK, I can't deal with him being kind to me – I'm only just holding it together as it is. All I want to do is collapse against my dad and beg him to make it all go away, but I also want to know how he came to be here in the first place. Did he come with Bonnie, or is it purely a coincidence? And if it is the former, why didn't he warn me? Why did he disappear and not reply to any of my messages, knowing how much it would worry me?

Despite the solid heat of the day, my teeth begin to chatter, and I wrap my arms around myself, trying to draw warmth from Kit's huge shirt. Everything is going to change again, I think despondently. Bonnie might be curious now, but once she's met me properly and satisfied her curiosity, she may not like the idea of me hanging around, taking up space in her life. I will probably have little choice but to return home to England and never see Tui – or Kit – again.

David and I reach the office first, and I sit wordlessly down on the threadbare yellow sofa, my hands knotted together and my shuddering jaw set. I can hear Tui reeling off details of her adventure outside, informing Bonnie importantly that she remembered how to do a rising trot, even when Keith started 'running really fast'. It would be adorable in any other circumstances, but as it is, I can't even conjure up a smile. My mother is on the other side of that door – the woman who gave me away. I keep waiting for the age-old resentment to engulf me, hold me in a tight-chested grip as it always used to, whenever I thought about her and what she had chosen to do. There is nothing inside me now, though – not so much as a murmur.

David shifts from one foot to the other on the concrete floor, and I stare hard at his pale, hairy shins, unable and unwilling to meet his beseeching gaze. It's agonisingly reminiscent of our behaviour in the waiting room we were shunted into at the hospital on that cold Christmas Eve. David had got there before me, but he was too poleaxed by shock to offer me any comfort or reassurance when I arrived, and the two of us circled one another instead, each one wary of tipping the other over into the abyss. When the doctor had finally joined us and relayed in a calm, sympathetic manner that the news was not good, she was the one – not my adoptive father – who had caught me in her arms when I collapsed to the ground.

After what feels like hours, but can only be a few minutes, I hear Bonnie telling Tui to go with Kit, reassuring her daughter that she won't be long. The door creaks open, and I take a deep breath, forcing myself to look up as she comes into the room.

Bonnie is taller and slimmer than me, but our dark hair is the same, as are our determined chins. She is wearing faded jeans tucked into brown boots and a green plaid shirt with a Koru Stables logo on the breast pocket, and while the bags under her eyes hint at tiredness, there is an ease to the way she moves fluidly into the office, her hands going straight to the kettle. This is her space, of course. Her home – the place where she feels the safest and the most self-assured. I recognise it, because I have grown to feel the same way.

'Shall we start with a brew?' she checks, and David replies with an eager 'please'. When I say nothing, Bonnie looks over her shoulder.

'Would you prefer coffee?' she asks, as if I am simply a tourist who came a cropper while out on one of her horses. How can she be so relaxed? How can she even be thinking about whether I want tea or coffee to drink? I shake my head in irritation, then, taking Bonnie, David and myself by surprise, I get abruptly to my feet.

'I need to wash my face,' I mutter. 'Back in a sec.'

Pulling the door shut behind me, I run across the yard, aiming blindly for the hay barn, and once inside, clamber over the bales until I reach the wooden rafters right at the top.

I still feel cold all over and my hair is matted with river water. The scratches I got from all the brambles and stones are stinging, but there is a far worse pain coming from deep inside, from where my anxious heart is smashing against my chest. The enormity of it all is raining down on me – the desperate race through the undergrowth, the leap into the river, Kit's arms hauling me out, the sight of my mum, and of David. My throat closes up and I start to gasp. It's as if I'm underneath the water again, but this time it's a current of pure panic dragging me down, twisting me around and around in the dark. Black spots swirl in front of my eyes, and I fall backwards against the scratchy hay, letting out a muffled cry of fear.

'B-B-Beeeea!' sings a voice, and the next thing I am aware of is a rough, dry tongue licking me all over my face. Opening my eyes, I find Beavis standing on my chest, his little head cocked to one side with concern, his tail wagging with excitement at having found me. Taking a very deep breath in through my nose, I exhale it out through my mouth and sit slowly back up just as Tui's face appears below me.

'Beeeea!' she says with a giggle. 'Where did you go to, Bea? Don't you run away now.'

'I think he came to find me,' I tell her. 'Returning the favour, perhaps.'

Tui frowns, not understanding, then crawls across on all fours to sit beside me.

'Are you feeling OK after your big adventure?' I ask, and she shakes her head happily from side to side.

'Yes, Genie,' she trills. 'I got lost, didn't I?'

'You worried me, running off like that,' I tell her. 'You know how scary it is when Beavis runs away and you don't know where he is?'

Genie shakes her head, her eyes solemn.

'Well, that's how I felt when I couldn't find you – I was scared.'

'Sorry.' Tui looks at me through lashes that are lowered by shame. 'I won't do it again, OK?'

'OK.' I grin to perk her up. 'Do you promise?'

'Yes, jeez!' she exclaims in a high-pitched screech, making me laugh. This girl never fails to gild even my gloomiest clouds with silver.

Beavis is busily licking his mistress's feet now, which I have just noticed are bare.

'Tui,' I remark in mock-horror. 'Where are your shoes and socks?'

'I don't know!' she says, bellowing with laughter.

I should convince her to go back down into the yard and find Kit, in case he's worried, but a selfish part of me wants to keep her here with me. The moments that I thought I had lost her were some of the worst of my life, and now it's taking all my powers of self-control not to pull her furiously into my arms and never let her go again.

Tui seems charmingly unfazed by the morning's misadventure, and is now picking hay seeds out of my hair like a chimpanzee and flicking them into the air. If only I could stay up here with her forever, in a bubble of untroubled happiness.

'Whose little piggies are those that I spy?' calls a voice from below.

While I immediately tense up, Tui starts laughing helplessly, wiggling her toes to taunt Bonnie, who I can now see making her way up to join us.

'I assume these are yours?' she says, thrusting a pair of grubby, rainbow-striped socks towards us.

Tui nods in delight, pursing her lips together and giggling like Muttley from *The Wacky Races*. Bonnie, who is almost level with us now, reaches across a hand and tickles Tui's bare feet, causing her to shriek and fall into me.

'Help me, Genie!' she cries. 'Oh no – Mummy's trying to get me!'

'Genie can't help you,' Bonnie says warningly, but her expression is all warmth. 'If I want to eat your bare toes, then nobody can stop me!'

Tui jumps up so fast that she cracks her head on one of the wooden beams, and without thinking, I leap up to see if she's OK.

'Silly donkey,' Bonnie says from Tui's other side, rubbing her daughter's head. 'You know I wouldn't really eat your feet.'

She catches my eye as she speaks, and this time I find that I can hold her gaze. Now that I'm closer to her, I realise that her features are, in fact, much more like Tui's than my own, and the resemblance catches me off guard. I had been so ready to judge my real mother, but during these past weeks where I have essentially lived inside her life, I have come to understand and appreciate that she is more than simply a woman who chose to give me away – she is also the person who raised Tui.

The three of us sit back down and Bonnie hands Tui her socks, telling her to get them back on before she steps in some dung.

'It's happened before,' she tells me, rolling her eyes. 'Quite a few times.'

'Shit happens,' I murmur, and Bonnie laughs.

'You're not wrong there – and that is exactly what Kit would have said. I can tell you've been spending a lot of time with him.'

'He's been great,' I tell her, my voice wobbling.

'He is one of the good guys,' Bonnie confirms.

Tui has got her socks back on and is lying on her back in the hay, Beavis held aloft in her outstretched arms.

'Thank you,' Bonnie says to me, stroking a hand through her daughter's wild hair. 'For finding her. Kit says I have you to thank for saving Beavis, too.'

'It was no trouble,' I mumble, but Bonnie quite rightly scoffs in disbelief. To be fair to her, there is no denying the state of me. I am a horror.

'Did you say thank you to Genie for rescuing you?' Bonnie asks Tui, who sits up with a great beaming smile on her face.

'Uh-huh.'

'You love her, don't you?' Bonnie surmises with pleasure, and Tui shakes her head.

'I think so, yes,' she replies, appraising me with her big dark eyes.

'Shall I tell you a secret?' Bonnie asks, looking not at me but at Tui.

'Uh-huh.'

'Genie is your sister.'

There is a pause as Tui takes this in, frowning at her mother in confusion. Beavis has padded across on to my lap, and I pat him mindlessly, unsure what to do or say. There is a great torrent of emotion building behind the dam of my senses, and I'm afraid that if I open my mouth, or blink, or even move, then it will erupt.

Tui scratches at a scab on her ankle and hums tunelessly to herself. Then, turning to me, she traces a finger over my forehead and across my cheek.

'The same eyes as Mum's,' she says wonderingly.

'That's right,' Bonnie says. She sounds choked, close to tears herself now, but I can't muster the courage to look at her. I had been preparing myself for the moment she said she wanted nothing to do with me – but this proves that she must. Now that I am faced with acceptance and genuine welcome, I feel thrown, and I'm not yet sure whether it's a good or guilty feeling.

'Oh Gee-nie, my sister, what are you sad about?' demands Tui, pulling me into a fierce, one-armed hug. 'Don't cry. There, there.'

I cling to her, to this wonderful girl that I love so much, and I cry for all the years of her life that I have missed, and for all the times that I longed for her before I even knew she existed. Tui only lets me go when my sobs have ceased, and even then, she holds Beavis up to my face so he can lick away what remains of my tears.

'Sorry,' I mumble, wrapping myself up even tighter in Kit's shirt. 'It's been a weird day.'

'You can say that again,' replies Bonnie, and Tui titters uncertainly.

'I need to do a poo,' she announces.

I can't help it, I start to laugh.

'Right,' says Bonnie, feigning seriousness. 'Well, in that case, you had better scarper.'

'OK, Mummy.' Tui gets to her feet. She is about to slither down the hay bales on her bottom, when she stops and turns once again to me.

'Don't be sad any more, Genie,' she instructs. 'Me and Mummy will look after you now, OK?'

And with that, she is gone, disappearing in a cloud of hay dust and excited giggling, Beavis not far behind. Bonnie and I say nothing at first, both of us listening instead to the sounds of the yard, to horses pawing the concrete with their hooves, to one of the stable hands shouting something about a missing noseband and the distant ringing of the telephone. I remember David down in the office, abandoned. He is no doubt wondering where we are, but is too awkward and polite to venture outside.

'I'm sorry I ran off like that,' I say finally, glancing at Bonnie.

'I think you get that from me,' she says, lifting an apologetic shoulder.

Another silence blooms.

'I don't know what to say,' I admit after a pause. 'I had it all planned out a few weeks ago, but then you weren't here when I arrived.'

'Sorry about that.' Bonnie grits her teeth. 'I always did have bloody awful timing.'

'Did you go to England to see me?'

'Yes,' she says, then turns to me. 'But when I got there, I wimped out. I went to stay with a friend instead, and then I found out about Anna. I am so sorry.'

'Thanks.' I try out a smile.

'You are a lot braver than me,' Bonnie adds. 'Coming out here to the yard almost as soon as you'd got off the plane.'

I shake my head. 'I'm not brave.'

'Oh, come off it,' she protests gently. 'Not only did you come here alone, you also saved Tui. Your dad told me that you haven't been on a horse since—' She hesitates.

'Since Anna died,' I finish. 'He's right. Not until today, anyway. I thought I wouldn't be able to do it, but in the moment, it didn't even occur to me that I couldn't. I was so worried about Tui that I acted before I had time to think it through.'

'And yet you say you're not brave?' she chides softly.

I think about galloping underneath the low branches and leaping into the river.

'OK,' I allow. 'Maybe I am a little bit.'

'I really am sorry,' Bonnie says again. 'About Anna. She was a lovely woman, and what happened is just horrible.'

'It was,' I manage. Then, as her words sink in, 'You knew her?'

'Enough to know what an amazing mother she must have been.' Bonnie confirms. 'She kind of became like a mother to me for a while.'

'She did?' I sit up straighter in surprise.

'I lived with her and David while I was pregnant with you,' she explains.

My brain feels like a washing machine that has been set on continuous spin.

'What?' I splutter. 'You lived with them? I know they met you, but not that you *lived* with them? I don't . . .' I begin, mouthing with confusion. 'I don't understand.'

'There is so much I need to tell you,' she says. 'That's what I've been doing all this time in England, I've been writing down my story for you.'

I shake my head as I try to take in what she is saying.

'You wrote it down? For me?'

Bonnie nods.

'I thought it would help, and make it easier.' A pause. 'For both of us. You can read through it all, and then we can talk properly.'

'Sorry,' I say, talking over her. I am unable to articulate quite what I'm feeling, which is an odd mixture of fear, relief and bewilderment. 'I just . . . I don't know where to begin with all this.' I had thought it would be me leading the interrogation, that I would be the one calling the shots of our first conversation, but Bonnie is way ahead of me. I feel like a sprinter who's been overtaken in the final seconds of a race.

'How about you start at the beginning?' suggests Bonnie. 'I think it's about time you heard the whole story – if you want to, that is?'

I wish that Anna were here, that she could give me a comedy thumbs-up like she always used to and tell me that everything is going to be fine, and that no matter how tough the truth is, I need to hear it. I deserve to hear it. But she isn't, and that means it is up to me to do the brave thing. This is my story, after all, and nobody but me can make the decision to hear it.

'You're right,' I say, turning to face my mother. 'It is definitely time.'

41

It is mid-afternoon by the time Bonnie and I emerge from the hay barn. A persistent sun is casting lazy shadows across the yard, and horses doze over the open half-doors of their stables. Tui is up on the mounting block with Beavis, the two of them lost in a make-believe game, while Allie sponges down the ponies that have not long returned from the last ride. She seems to be in better spirits, and gives me a friendly wave as I pass.

Realising that I am still wearing Kit's discarded shirt, I peel it off as he approaches, holding it out to him like a peace offering.

'Ta.' He sniffs it. 'On second thoughts . . .'

Immediately consoled by his teasing manner, I glance sheepishly towards Bonnie and then back at him, trying to say with a gesture what I can't even begin to explain with words.

'It's OK,' he says. 'I had a good chat with your dad and he filled me in.'

'Oh.' I can feel my face burning. I thought Kit would be angry with me for keeping my identity a secret, but on the contrary, he doesn't seem any different. If anything, he looks rather pleased with the situation. He has unearthed a T-shirt from somewhere, but it is at least two sizes too small.

'I'll just go and get that stuff for you,' Bonnie says to me, heading off in the direction of the minibus, which I now notice has a battered red car parked beside it.

'So . . .' Kit rests his chin in one of his big hands.

'So . . .' I reply, chewing the inside of my cheek.

'So, this has been quite the day,' he remarks. 'I know there are supposed to be fireworks on New Year's Eve, but usually they start going off towards the end of the day, not at the start.'

'I think I've had as much drama as I can handle for one day,' I admit. Then, when Kit says nothing, 'I'm so sorry I wasn't honest with you from the start – I didn't mean to lie, I just panicked and then I—'

'Hush up, you silly old coot,' he chides. 'I had guessed you were related to Bon, you know.'

'You had?'

'Of course.' He puts his head on one side, examining me with those pale mint eyes of his. 'You look just like her.'

'Why didn't you ask me outright?' I exclaim. 'Or call Bonnie and ask her?'

Kit pushes his lips together. 'None of my business,' he says simply. 'I figured you and Bon would sort it out when she got back, and I didn't want to scare you away by poking my noggin in. The thing is, I kind of like having you around – and Tui loves you,' he adds quickly, clocking my look of incredulity.

Bonnie is making her way back towards us now, a folded sheaf of papers in one of her hands.

'I should—' I begin, and Kit flashes me a smile.

'Of course. Well, Happy New Year, I guess. You're certainly seeing this one out in style.'

I dredge up a laugh. 'And to you – and thanks again for fishing me out of the river.'

'Anytime,' he retorts cheerfully, and I find it impossible not to stare at his departing back as it vanishes into the tack room.

'Here you are.' Bonnie pushes the papers into my hands. 'I hope you can read my handwriting – it's bloody dreadful.'

'Something else I get from you,' I say lightly, and register relief in her eyes.

David is still in the office where Bonnie and I left him, reading a battered Penguin paperback and eating a chocolate biscuit that he must have unearthed from the tin behind the desk. Leaping immediately to his feet, he asks if I am OK, which of course I'm not. My emotions are tied into even more knots than my ratty nest of half-dry hair.

Bonnie, who is still maintaining a respectful distance, offers to drive the two of us back into Queenstown, but David insists that she call us a taxi instead, pointing out that Bonnie must also be tired after such a long flight, and that the best thing all of us can do is get some rest.

I can tell that my adoptive dad is nervous, because he prattles on about all manner of nonsense throughout the entire journey back, starting in on the driver when he fails to elicit more than a murmur from me. I listen with only half an ear as they discuss the local sights, and David points out of the window as the mighty Lake Wakatipu comes into view.

I have been in New Zealand for weeks now, but that is still not enough time to feel blasé about its beauty. The far-flung mountains still enthral me, just as the lakes and verdant hillsides draw me in. The air flooding in through the open car windows is as clean and rejuvenating as it was on that first day, while the sun still beats down as adamantly. I am so far from home, yet home is where I am. The thought is enough to make me smile in spite of it all and, closing my eyes, I whisper a thank you to whatever it was that brought me here.

I think of Kit in his too-tight T-shirt, and the image is so substantial that I can almost smell the earthy scent of him. He has become as much a home to me as New Zealand, and Tui, and even the horses – all of them have played their part in piecing me back together again. I was broken when I arrived, but now I feel more whole than I ever have before – even without Anna. Losing her left me with a wound that I feared would never heal, but now I see why it has been gaping open for so long. Because I allowed myself to fill it with bitterness, fear and self-loathing, when what I should have tried to do was knit it back together with love.

There is something I must do before I read Bonnie's story, something that I should have done a long time ago. I wait until the taxi has dropped us back at the apartment, then prevaricate by sending a quick text message to Hayley while David carries in his case from the boot. He is famished, he tells me, pointing out that I must surely be too. He wants us to eat together, and then he says we can talk. Properly talk.

Scribbling down a rudimentary map on the back of a flyer advertising ziplining, I pack him off in the direction of Fergburger, feeling slightly guilty because I know the queue will keep him occupied for at least an hour. I need some time, though – I don't want him to be here while I do this.

The shower rejuvenates me, and once dry, I dress quickly in leggings and the biggest, comfiest hoodie I have, then take Anna's memory book and a cup of tea to the sofa. I can already feel the jitters of cowardice starting to build, so before I can talk myself out of it, I flip open the book to the page bearing my mum's final entry and begin reading.

42

Anna

Saturday, 23 December 2017

It's almost Christmas Eve again – how did that happen? I swear the older I get, the faster time passes. It felt like I blinked and Genie went from a newborn to a five-year-old, then a teenager, and now she's a beautiful young woman. Not that she believes me when I tell her so – according to Genie, nobody's bottom has ever been bigger, or chin more shaped like a canoe. I wish she could see what I see – that she is practically perfect in every way, just like Mary Poppins.

We had the silliest row earlier. In true Genie fashion, she has left all her shopping till the last minute. Honestly, she and Davey are like one of a kind – he has been known to buy my present on Christmas Day before! So, she now has to spend tomorrow shopping instead of exercising Suki, a job which has now become mine. I don't mind, of course – I love that dear little horse – but poor Genie got herself in such a snarl about it.

She does this when she feels guilty about something – lashes out at me and Dave – but I know she'll feel really crap about it by tomorrow, the nitwit. I must admit, I did snap back at her, something about her being so far beyond my tether that I would need a telescope to see her. She hates it when I get smart with her, and she really lost her temper after that, said all sorts of nasty things that I know she didn't really mean. Honestly, it was very hard to keep a straight face. I had to pretend to be all stern and disappointed, when really I was caterwauling with laughter inside. I'll tell her when I get back from the stables tomorrow, and we'll have a good old giggle about it. And a ride will be lovely. I'm going to sneak Suki a whole packet of Polos to make up for not being Mummy.

Maybe I will pick out another gift for Genie, too – a necklace to match her ring. It's sweet that she never takes it off, and Davey was right, it doesn't matter a bit that it once belonged to Bonnie. I thought it would upset me, but actually, I like seeing it there on Genie's finger – it makes me feel as if Bonnie is still here with us in some way. I think of her often, and the sacrifice she made. Perhaps I need to stop being selfish and tell Genie more about her. I should have more faith in her. Yes, I will talk to Davey about it tomorrow.

Wouldn't it be wonderful if tomorrow's memory was that time I decided to be brave for my daughter's sake? I owe it to her, after all, and I owe it to Bonnie, too.

43

All this time. All these months that I have spent believing Anna was angry with me when she died, that I had hurt her with those horrible things I said to her when we argued, that the residual upset had contributed to the fact that she wasn't paying proper attention to the road, or to Suki.

And all along she had found it funny?

I don't know whether to laugh or cry, so I do both, loudly and hysterically and without a thought for how berserk and deranged I must sound to anyone who might be passing.

How could I have been so stupid? Why did I ever think that Anna was capable of holding a grudge against me, when all logic said she wasn't?

I know the answer, but it's an unpleasant one to admit, even to myself. The truth is so clear to me now: I believed it, because it allowed me to make sense of Anna's death. When I could levy the full blame for the accident at myself, then I became the reason she was gone – *me*, not some dumb bad luck, or fate, or anything else intangible, but me.

If I was at fault, then I could punish myself; I could stop doing the things I love and shut myself away from the world. I thought it would make the grief easier to bear, but my thinking has been so warped by misery. All I did by clinging on to all the blame was prolong the agony.

And that is what it has felt like: agony.

David returns with a large paper bag stained with burger sauce and a clanking carrier from the liquor store to find me curled into a foetal position on the bed. The crying has ceased, but my skin feels sore and my throat throbs. Taking one look at me, David drops his purchases on the floor and rushes towards me.

'Whatever is the matter?'

Numbly, I hand him Anna's memory book, pointing to the entry I have read and re-read so many times now that I could probably recite it verbatim. David rubs at his eyebrows as he scans the page, his expression softening as he takes in his late wife's words.

'Oh, Anna,' he sighs. Then, almost as an afterthought, 'God, I miss her.'

'I do, too.' The words are barely audible through our crushing misery. Or is it misery? Perhaps it is no longer that simple. It used to be sorrow at what happened, but now it feels more like frustration. I am so tired of the sadness, so very weary of carrying the weight of such a gigantic loss.

'I can't believe it,' I tell him, gesturing to the book. 'She wasn't cross with me at all, just like you said she wouldn't have been.'

'Of course she wasn't.' David is smiling at me, but I

can read pity in his eyes. 'You were the biggest treasure in her box, Genie – the cause of most if not all her happiest moments. I told you that she would never have held a grudge, poppet. She simply wasn't capable.'

I nod because it is too difficult to speak.

When I confessed the truth about the argument to him on the morning of the barbecue, David had said the same thing – he had told me that I was being silly to even acknowledge such a thought. But still, I had not listened; I had not been able to hear him. I needed to hear it from Anna herself.

'It feels like she's died all over again,' I mumble.

Either David doesn't know how to reply, or he's battling with his own emotions, because for a while, neither of us says anything. The smell of burgers is overpowering the scent of shampoo in my still-damp hair, the paper bag still on the floor just inside the bedroom door.

'You should eat,' I say eventually, shuffling up into a sitting position. 'You must be starving.'

'I will if you will,' he offers, and I shrug. Food feels like an impossibility, but I can't remember the last time I ate. The morning feels like it happened in a different lifetime. The Genie that ate a toasted bagel and drank a coffee all those hours ago is another person – a different girl to the one sitting on this bed now.

It comes as quite a surprise to me, therefore, that I am ravenous. The cheeseburger is gone in five large bites, and I make short work of the fries, too. David watches on, nodding in approval, and breaks his own dinner up into pieces before popping each morsel into his mouth. It is such a simple thing, sitting and eating a meal together, but it's comforting, and it doesn't take long for the food to do its trick. I start to uncurl and relax, one yawn stretching into the next until my jaw cracks with the effort of being open.

I still have Bonnie's story to read, but when I say as much to David, he looks at me aghast.

'Why don't you sleep on it?' he pleads. 'Just for tonight. There's only so much a person can take in one swipe.'

'How could I ever sleep?' I protest gently. 'I'm going to make a cafetiere of coffee, and then I'm going to read it. And anyway,' I call over my shoulder as I head towards the kitchen area, 'what could possibly shock me more than the things I have already seen – and read – today?'

It takes me two hours.

Transfixed as I am by the story unfolding on Bonnie's scribbled pages, I don't notice the sky outside lose its glow and turn dark. When David points out that I'm shivering and fetches me a blanket, I barely notice. The coffee goes cold, my hair turns crinkly as it dries, and I bite first one nail, and then another down to the quick as I read about my eighteen-year-old mother's arrival in London, about how she found a job, met a boy, fell in love, trusted him and others who let her down. I try to imagine what it must have been like to be so far from home – this home – away from parents who had yearned for a child for so long. I picture Bonnie's loneliness, and her naivety, and her innocence – I find common ground where I don't expect to, and experience pangs of sympathy, and of understanding.

When the story takes me inside the house belonging to the professor and his wife, and shows me the shelf of baby books, the truth hits me with such force that I gasp, and looking up I find that David's gaze is already on me, and that he is waiting to answer any questions that I might have.

'You were a university professor?' I prompt, and watch as his features contort into an apologetic grimace.

'Yes, for a time. I gave it up before you were born, though – started teaching at a secondary school instead.'

'Why?' I ask, but before he can answer. 'No, don't tell me – you didn't want to risk any news of me getting back to Seth?'

He frowns at that, as if puzzled.

'No – God, no. We all tried to find Seth. After Bonnie found out that she was pregnant, I tried everything I could to find him, but he'd vanished into thin air, like Evangeline's train. We later discovered that he had been using a false surname. He stole a lot of money from Lavender's family. I'm afraid he was a bit of a crook.'

'Nothing that she didn't deserve,' I grumble, but David merely sighs.

'Lavender was very young then, too,' he points out.

'Seth was a master manipulator. He had all of us fooled in the beginning – including me.'

'Still,' I say, 'she hardly deserves a bloody medal.'

He chuckles at that, and when I raise an enquiring eyebrow says, 'You never used to swear – not even a "bugger". You must have picked that up while you've been out here.'

From Kit.

'So,' I say, reaching for my coffee, only to recoil when I realise how cold it is, 'what happened next?'

'You mean, after Seth disappeared?' David checks. 'Sorry, I don't know how far through the story Bonnie got.'

I pass over the last few pages, watching as he reads. When David used to read me bedtime stories as a child, he would change words and replace them with others that he thought worked better, and I wonder if that is what he's doing now. Another of those authorly tics over which he has no control.

'How did Bonnie go from getting pregnant by Seth to giving their child – giving me – to you and Anna? She doesn't say how it happened,' I say, leaning forwards as David lowers the papers into his lap. 'I know you two were friends, but I still don't understand the logistics. And what about Seth? Where does he fit into the story? Did he ever know that Bonnie was pregnant?'

The colour has been slowly leaving David's face ever since I started talking, and now he looks almost translucent.

'There is another chapter to this story,' he says, lifting the sheaf of papers. 'Something that Bonnie did not have time to write down.'

'Right . . .' I reply, my skin starting to prickle with unease. I have seen my adoptive father look many things – angry, upset, disappointed, happy – but I have never seen this expression before. If I had to guess, I would say that he is scared.

'This is something I should have told you a very long time ago, but there is a reason I didn't. There are many reasons, in fact. But now I think it's time you knew. Really, you should always have known.'

'David,' I say, hearing the tremble in my voice, 'just tell me, please.'

'It's about your father,' he says, his eyes glistening behind his spectacles.

'You mean Seth?' I reply, but any confidence I feel is obliterated by the next look he gives me.

'No, Genie.' It is barely a whisper. 'I mean me.'

44

We ride out together on the second afternoon of the new year.

Me and Anna would often do the same thing, both of us itching to get back in the saddle after a lazy New Year's Day spent lounging on the sofa, me recovering from a hangover and her simply happy to flop down beside me, a bowl of crisps or popcorn balanced on the blanket across our knees. The second day of January was when we would tack up, head out, and trade resolutions, making each other laugh with our absurd proclamations that yes, this would be the year that we gave up chocolate, or learned another language, or – in my case – stayed in a relationship for more than three weeks.

I cherished those times, but that doesn't mean I can't take some pleasure from this one. Bonnie may not be Anna, but she is here, and she is willing to talk and to be honest with me. And what a place I am in, too. Even on its most glorious days, Cambridgeshire has no hope of competing with the awesome beauty of New Zealand, and today the sun seems to be shining even brighter than usual, just for us. Bonnie wrote in her story that she craved an escape from this place, but I cannot imagine ever feeling that way – even as a teen-ager. Maybe there was a deeper reason for her wanting to go?

This is just one of the questions I want to ask her – and will ask her – but I am waiting for the right time. Being here in New Zealand has reminded me of the importance of slowing down, and of allowing things to take place when they naturally should. My time with Anna may be over in one regard, but my memories of her are as far-reaching as the unblemished sweep of sky above the mountains – she will only ever be lost to me if I stop letting her in.

'Thank you for agreeing to this.' Bonnie throws a timid glance in my direction. She has pulled her long dark hair into a braid, the rest squashed under a skull cap, and rather than jodhpurs, she is dressed in a pair of grey leggings that are streaked with dirt, and a sweater bearing the logo of the Rolling Stones. The overall effect is thrown-together, slightly chaotic and charm-ingly reminiscent of Tui. Bonnie is up on a large bay called Brian today, while I have been permitted by Tui to ride her beloved Keith.

'Just take good care of him, OK?'

I had promised that I would, although in truth, the robust little pony is doing a sterling job of looking after me. Despite my Grand National-style race through the undergrowth on Ekara two days ago, it still feels strange to be up on a horse again, and Keith seems to realise this. When Bonnie and I rode through the river a few minutes ago, he didn't even stop to splash me with his front legs, which I know is his party trick.

'That's OK,' I tell Bonnie, ducking to avoid an overhanging branch. 'It feels good to be out – I was starting to get cabin fever in the apartment.'

After David and I had talked the other night, I had been so overwrought that I didn't feel able to face the world – at least not for a while. I had shouted and raged at first, then cried yet more tears. I felt as if I had both lost and gained, and I am still struggling to make sense of how I feel about it all.

'After I had you and came back here,' Bonnie says, clicking her tongue against her teeth to distract Brian from eating the grass, 'I rented a room in Auckland for a month and spent almost the whole of it completely alone. I don't think I have ever felt so lonely, or so utterly bloody miserable.'

I get the impression that she wants to say more, so I remain quiet, and for a few moments the only sounds are the birds in the trees and the horses' hooves on the stony path. Keith has been noisily blowing the dust from his nose since we left the yard, and now he stops to rub his handsome head along an outstretched foreleg.

'I couldn't go home right away,' Bonnie explains, looking down at her reins. 'I needed time to heal, both physically and in here.' She taps the side of her hat. 'I was an idiot, though, because I thought that I was strong enough to cope by myself, and I wasn't.'

'That sounds familiar,' I allow, thinking of how I hid indoors after Anna's accident.

'Do you know what my single biggest regret is, after leaving you behind?' she asks, and I shake my head.

'No.'

'It was not telling my parents about you. By the time I had grown up enough to realise that they would have supported me – and you – no matter what, it felt like it was too late. They would have insisted that I fly back to England and bring you home, and I couldn't do that. I didn't want to go back on my promise to David and Anna.'

'Do you think they would have liked me?' I ask, my voice so small that I am amazed she hears me.

'Loved you,' she says sadly. 'I'm not religious or anything like that, you know, but I like to think that if there's any way of them looking down on me, then this would make them happy – seeing us together in this way after all this time.'

'And Anna, too,' I agree, whereupon Bonnie gives in to a deep sigh.

'Anna was such a darling,' she says.

'You must have been close, the three of you,' I guess, and Bonnie nods.

'We were. David was a saint and Anna did everything for me. I never doubted for a second that she would be an amazing mother – a far better one than me.'

I start to say something, only for my words to falter, and Bonnie brings Brian to a standstill, waiting until I have caught up.

'Go on,' she urges.

'I can understand why you wanted to help them,' I begin, 'but I still don't get why you didn't want me. Why didn't you want to keep me?'

It is such a big question that my voice cracks, and I fight for several seconds to keep the tears at bay. I cannot cry any more – there has been too much of that already.

'I was scared,' Bonnie confesses. 'I know it sounds pathetic – and it is – but it's the truth. I was scared of letting down my parents, scared of proving everyone right when they warned me that I wasn't cut out to take on the big, wide world. I was scared that I wouldn't be a good mother, and that you would be unhappy. I was even scared that I wouldn't be able to love you in the way that I should, but of course I did. I loved you from the first second that I felt you kick.'

'Did you ever think about me?' I ask.

'Every day,' she says simply.

'And did you ever think about coming back?'

'Every day.'

'But you never did.'

'I told myself that you were happy, that you were better off with the parents that you had. I watched as David's career skyrocketed, and I imagined the life you must have, all the opportunities and the nice things. I thought it would be cruel of me to disrupt all that. It was only when Tui came along that I realised how much I had given up, how much I had lost. But by then you

343

were a teenager, and I was a world away, with a new baby – it felt impossible.'

'Anna was going to suggest that I meet you,' I say. 'Right before she died – in fact, the day before. She wrote about it in her diary. And she gave me your ring on my twenty-first birthday, although I never knew then that it belonged to you.'

'The jade-stone ring?' Bonnie says, perking up.

'Yes. But I lost it. It fell off in the river when I waded in to rescue Beavis.'

'Well then,' Bonnie flicks her eyes in my direction, 'I guess it found its way home, then.'

I know she's waiting for me to add a 'just like me' to the end of that sentence, but I can't. Not yet. There are still too many things that I need to have clarified.

'Is there somewhere we can stop for a bit?'

In the end we double back on ourselves and pick a spot not far from the river, where the horses can have a drink and there are plenty of trees under which to shade from the sun. Pulling up our stirrups and unbuckling the girths, we ease the saddles off Brian and Keith and spread the thick cloths on the ground to sit on. Mine is dappled with sweat and covered in chestnut hairs, but it saves me from getting white dust all over my jodhpurs.

Bonnie pulls off her boots and socks and dangles her bare toes in the cool water, telling me a story about a film crew who flew a crowd of white stallions all the way over from America to shoot a dramatic scene for a movie, only for every single one of them to come to a

344

stubborn halt at the river's edge. They had learned not to enter water back in Florida because of alligators, and no amount of clever coercion would convince them otherwise. In the end, she explains, they had to paint some of the local horses white and use those instead.

I watch as Keith grazes his way half-heartedly through a patch of grass, his tail flicking away flies and his ears drooping contentedly to each side like those of a seaside donkey.

It is difficult not to study Bonnie's face, to spend time scrutinising each of her features in turn. Some – like her eyes and heart-shaped hairline – are exactly the same as my own, while others are totally different. Her nose is larger and her lips fuller, but I notice that we both twirl our hair around a finger when we're nervous.

'You know, nobody ever suspected that I was adopted when I was growing up,' I say, drawing Bonnie's attention away from the merrily tumbling river. 'I always thought that was weird, because to me I felt like it was obvious – as if I was wearing a badge or something.'

'I felt the same way about being a mother,' she says, tossing a pebble into the water. 'I could never understand why nobody knew, why nobody worked it out. I think I probably resented my parents for not somehow seeing it, but they never did.'

'What about Simon?' I ask, and Bonnie turns to me in surprise.

'You met him?'

I nod.

'He knew I was hiding something, but he gave up asking eventually. He's not a bad person – our relationship ended because I never gave it a chance. I know that.'

'Don't you ever get lonely?' I want to know, but Bonnie laughs.

'Hardly! I have Tui, and the horses. And Kit has been my live-in tenant for years now.'

At the mention of Kit, I feel a tightness spread across my chest.

'I'm not very good at relationships,' she continues, looking at me apologetically. 'I guess I just don't trust most of the men I meet.'

'I'm not surprised – not after what Seth did. It must have been so hard for you at the time, finding out that a man like him could have fathered your baby.'

'He was a shithead,' Bonnie pronounces. 'But what he did to Lavender was arguably worse than what he did to me.'

'Good,' I say firmly, but just as David did, Bonnie shakes her head.

'I don't hold a grudge against her. We were all so young.'

I still haven't asked her about that night – the chapter of her story that she didn't get around to writing. David has told me only the headline facts as he remembers them, but I want to hear it from Bonnie, too – I need to hear it from her. Lifting first one foot up, and then the other, I remove my boots and socks and dip my feet into the water beside hers. We both have long second toes, and apparently the same shade of dark red nail varnish.

'David told me,' I say, deliberately not meeting her eyes.

She sighs, just once, perhaps drawing in breath to give herself courage.

'I guessed he would.'

'He told me it's mostly all a blur, what happened, but that enough happened.'

'That's about the size of it.'

Another pebble disappears with a plop into the river.

'How did it happen?' I press, desperate for details yet fearful of finding any out.

'I always liked him, as you know, and we had grown closer since I moved in. He was missing Anna and I was upset about Seth cheating on me. We got drunk, it just happened. Or, it started to, and then David stopped. He said he couldn't go through with it, that he was sorry, but he loved his wife.'

'And afterwards?' I prompt.

'We just carried on as normal, never spoke about it. For the first few days, it was a bit weird and embarrassing, but after a while, we went back to being friends again. And then Seth disappeared. I hated the guy, but still loved him, and when I did the test a few months later and realised I was pregnant, I went racing off to find him only to learn that he'd scarpered, and that the police were after him because he'd stolen money and all sorts from Lavender.'

'Bloody hell,' I say, though I'm not actually that surprised.

'I don't even know if I would have told Seth that I was expecting, if I had managed to track him down,' she continues. 'But I doubt he would have been very happy about it. That man's life began and ended with him – he was the focal point of everything. He would have made a useless father, because he was very selfish.'

'And David was a better choice?'

'Not only that.' Another sigh. 'While it was less likely that David could be your father, there was a chance – we both knew that. After I had tried and failed to locate Seth, I went back to the house in search of David, only to find Anna instead. She had come back to make things right, and suddenly she's dealing with me, crying all over her and telling her about the baby.'

'Did she know?' I ask. 'About you and David?'

Bonnie nods, her expression haunted.

'She had to know. I don't think she ever would have agreed to it all had there not been a chance that David really was your father. They decided not to find out for sure because it was more fair, more equal, but as far as the official channels were concerned, you really were his.'

'His name is on my birth certificate,' I say, even though I know she is well aware of the fact.

'Yes, and perhaps that is exactly where it belongs.'

'Do you really think David could be my real father?' I ask.

'What I think,' says Bonnie, putting a tentative hand on top of mine, 'is that he already is.'

'But can you see him in me?' I implore. 'Can you see any trace of Seth?'

'It was so long ago.'

I can tell that she is being deliberately vague.

As a child, I was so often told how much I looked like my dad, and all those times I dismissed our similarities. Like him, I enjoy reading, but that could just as easily have come from Seth, who was studying English when he met Bonnie. David had dark hair, but so does Bonnie. His skin is fair, but Seth was blond, so presumably he would have had a similar complexion.

'You could do a DNA test,' suggests Bonnie, breaking a dry twig into several pieces then wiping the residual dirt on to her leggings.

'David said the same thing.'

'That would give you a definitive answer, if that's what you need. And you would be well within your rights to find out,' she says.

'I need time to think,' I tell her. There has been too much information to take in over the past few days, and not enough time to act.

'That's fair,' she agrees, bringing her feet up out of the water. 'Shall we start heading back?'

'There's just one more thing,' I say, reaching for my socks. 'You said before that you were too scared to come back to England and find me, and that you had no idea about the accident until you got there?'

'That's all true.'

'What was it that made you get on the plane, then? And why, after all this time, did you write down that story for me?'

Bonnie turns her face so it's pointing towards the sun, her shadow falling away behind us.

'That,' she says, 'is a whole other story entirely.'

45

Bonnie

It was the new tumble drier that did it.

If it hadn't been for that rogue bra getting tangled up in the bedding, and the underwire melting so that it dug into her side, Bonnie may never have found the lump on her left breast. At first, she told herself that it must be nothing, then convinced herself that it would go away by itself. As the weeks and then months went by, however, the lump stubbornly remained where it was, and eventually, Bonnie could ignore it no longer.

'You can get dressed again now.'

Dr Kenyon got up from the stool she had been perched on and made her way back to her chair. Bonnie watched from the curtained-off corner of the consultation room as the doctor tapped away at her computer keyboard, only to curse in irritation and bang the mouse against her desk.

'This machine is even older than I am,' she explained, to which Bonnie quipped back, 'Not a day over twenty-five, then.'

Dr Kenyon, who had celebrated her fortieth birthday that summer, smiled amiably across at her patient.

'I think we should perhaps test your eyes for you, too,' she said. 'While you're here.'

Bonnie and the doctor knew each other well, the former having spent a lot of time in and out of appointments with Tui when she was still a child. They had spoken frankly about Bonnie's entire medical history, which of course included her first pregnancy, and the fact that the doctor knew so much about Bonnie's life had made approaching her about the lump less daunting. Dr Kenyon had been as brisk, frank and professional as she always was, and organised for a biopsy to be done at the earliest opportunity. The lump, meanwhile, had lurked uncomfortably like a thorn in Bonnie's side, goading her. She had watched her mother succumb to breast cancer, and was terrified at the prospect of the same fate.

In true Bonnie Moon style, however, she had told no one about either her lump or her fears. Tui would not understand, and even if she did, it would only scare her. Kit was a friend, but not someone that Bonnie confided in about anything this personal, while Simon was now far too busy looking after his new family. She had handled things by herself before, and figured that she would handle this latest crisis, too. Bonnie had actually believed that she was doing a good job of remaining strong – and certainly she looked as if she was. Nobody would ever have guessed that something serious was troubling her.

When the biopsy results had come through, however,

and Dr Kenyon had summoned her back to the clinic, Bonnie had fallen to pieces in the waiting room and almost bolted back home to the stables. She had decided there and then that cancer was not an option, that she would not tolerate so cruel a twist. Finding out a few minutes later that the lump she had found was, in fact, just a cyst after all, had made Bonnie weep all the harder. She had come so close to allowing time to run out, and while she had never been superstitious in her life before, she took this scare as a sign that she must seek out her lost daughter – and that is exactly what she did. Following a relatively simple operation the following week, Bonnie had fired up the ancient computer in the office at Koru Stables and booked herself the first available flight over to England.

'How have you been feeling since the op?' Dr Kenyon asked now, sipping from a half-empty bottle of water.

Bonnie pictured the puckered scar under her arm.

'Fine. A bit sore right after, but nothing for a while now.'

'Good.' The doctor nodded in satisfaction. 'And no other lumps or bumps anywhere they shouldn't be?'

'Well,' Bonnie said lightly, 'I did eat a lot of stodgy British food while I was away, so there may be a few around my middle.'

Dr Kenyon swept a frowning eye from Bonnie's neck down to her sandals, and scoffed.

'It was a bit foolish of you,' she said, turning back to

the old monitor, which had begun humming like an idle bus, 'to scarper off abroad like that before the stitches were even out.'

'I know.' Bonnie did her best to look sheepish. 'But it didn't feel like it could wait. Finding the lump and going through the terror of it being potentially cancerous, it made a few things fall into place for me, you know? It was just a cyst this time, but next time it might not be. I realised that I'd been a bloody wimp for long enough, and that I should go and get things done while I still could.'

'And did you?'

For a moment Bonnie thought about Genie, and the ride they had gone on together the previous day, how much they had already shared with one another, and how understanding her daughter had been. She was an incredible young woman, she really was, and even though Bonnie had had no part in raising her, she still felt proud. Genie was her girl, and what a wonder she was.

'You know what, Doc?' she said. 'I really think I did.'

The centre of Queenstown still bore witness to the parties that had rampaged through it on New Year's Eve. Bonnie took hold of Tui's hand as they weaved in and out of high-spirited tourists and hopped over a discarded pink cowboy hat. Having left England in such a hurry, Bonnie had forgotten the promised new shoes for Tui, so they were going to choose her some now.

'What colour are you thinking?' she asked her daughter, as they stared at row upon row of trainers, sandals, flip-flops and boots. Tui's forehead was furrowed in concentration – this was not a decision to be taken lightly.

'Red,' she announced. Then, catching sight of an ultra-shiny brogue, 'Or silver.'

'How about all the colours of the rainbow?' suggested Bonnie, holding up a particularly eccentric wellington boot.

Tui nodded solemnly.

'I don't think so, no.'

'Maybe not the right shoes for school,' agreed Bonnie, grinning as Tui dissolved into bellows of deep, throaty laughter.

'I think these,' she said, surprising Bonnie by selecting a rather sensible blue pair with a good sturdy heel and neat set of gold buckles. 'The same as Evangeline's shoes in my books.'

'Oh, yes!' Bonnie was enchanted. 'So they are – aren't you clever?'

Tui had knelt down to examine the display shoe, her hands twisting together with excitement on her lap.

'Come on.' Bonnie ushered her to her feet. 'Let's try them on, shall we?'

When the assistant had returned with a fresh new pair in a box, however, Tui started to fret, her moans growing louder as the man attempted to slide one on.

'What's the matter, darling?' Bonnie was unconcerned. Tui often communicated her dislike of things through sounds rather than words as she searched for the right ones to use.

'I hate my school, that's all,' she announced, her voice shrill.

The assistant, who was now struggling to work the buckle, glanced up at her and smiled.

'You absolutely don't hate school,' Bonnie reminded her. 'You love it.'

Tui bit down on her own hand, her temper now on the verge of making a full-blown appearance, but Bonnie, who was well accustomed to such displays, merely laughed it off.

'Why do you hate school, Tui?' she asked gently. 'Is it because Beavis can't go with you?'

'No.'

'Is it because you'll miss Mummy?'

'No,' Tui said, sounding calmer. The assistant had valiantly got one shoe on, and was now pulling scrunched-up bits of paper out of the other.

'Oh, I know!' Bonnie slapped a hand against her head. 'It's because you'll miss Genie?'

'I love her so much,' Tui whined. 'I want her to live with us in Kit's room.'

Bonnie pulled her daughter against her in a half-hug.

'Maybe she will one day,' she said. 'But for now, I'm sure if we asked her very nicely, then she would come and pick you up from school tomorrow with me. Would you like that?'

Tui agreed that she would, cheering up almost

immediately and getting up to lope around the shop in her new shoes.

'Genie?' The assistant turned to Bonnie. 'That's an unusual name – is she one of your daughter's friends?'

Bonnie watched as Tui came to a halt in front of a full-length mirror, into which she gazed with her wonderful lack of self-consciousness, smiling her wide, pure-hearted grin and finding only delight in her reflection.

'Her big sister,' Bonnie said, thinking then that she might never have felt as happy as she did right now, in this very moment. 'But Genie is her best friend, too.'

46

I find the note pinned to the door of the apartment.

David and I had just spent the afternoon wandering through Queenstown, trying to find ways to talk to each other. Every time I look at him, it becomes a study, as I search his face for clues that we could be related by more than a fraudulent birth certificate. I am still swinging unsteadily on the rickety bridge between outrage and relief, and the relentless effort it is taking to prevent my shaken-up emotions blowing skywards, like a cork out of a bottle, has left me feeling drained.

When David suggested that he return to his hotel and leave me to my own devices for the evening, I agreed with perhaps too much enthusiasm – but then I figured that maybe he needs some time alone to reflect, just as I do. There is too much to digest for it all to be resolved over the course of a few days, and I am still grappling with the concept of a birth mother – let alone a biological father.

My ride out with Bonnie the other day felt like a tonic, and I found myself opening up to her much more than I had expected. Either she is adept at listening and being sympathetic, or she is making a special effort because of who I am. Either way, it doesn't really matter – I am still consoled by the fact that she will eventually become a friend. It is so strange. I came here prepared to dislike the woman who had, as I saw it, abandoned me, and now I cannot imagine my life without her in it. When she told me about finding that lump, and believing for weeks that she had cancer, it made me go cold all over. And it makes perfect sense that a scare that momentous would have prompted her to finally seek me out, just as Anna's death had been the catalyst for me attempting to locate her. I hate that she had to go through something so frightening alone. The thought of losing another mother is simply too much to bear, and Bonnie's confession made me realise just how important she is to me – and always will be now that we have been returned to each other.

I am chasing these thoughts and more around in my mind as I walk up the steps of the apartment, and in my preoccupation, I don't even see the note until my hand is almost on it.

At first, I simply stand and hold it, immobilised by an irrational fear that it somehow must be bad news, and not wanting to face it. Telling myself not to be such a coward, I lean back again the wooden railings, take a breath, and open the envelope.

Genie,

By the time you read this, I'll be on the road to Welly. I didn't want to just bugger off without at least telling you why, because

359

even though we haven't known each other all that long, a lot has happened. A lot of bloody drama. I saved your life, for one thing! Nah, I'm only pulling your feathers out — I would have done that even if I didn't like you much. Probably.

I know I told you before that I wasn't that keen on moving away. The yard might be out in the wop-wops, but it's always felt like a home to me, especially since I started renting with Bon. But Allie has been so patient, waiting here for me to feel ready all this time. The thing is, I didn't want to leave Tui. I know she has her mum and Simon, but she needs someone else — someone who can look out for her, who understands her in the right way, you know?

I have watched the two of you scamps growing closer every day, and when the truth all came out last week, and I realised that you weren't just Tui's mate, but her sister, it dawned on me that she doesn't need me as much any more. And that's a good thing. Tui deserves someone like you in her life, a person who can love her in an uncomplicated way. And I can tell how much you love each other, just as I know that if you give it time, you'll totally fall head-over-weird-Shire-horse-shoes for Bonnie, too. The three of you are cookies cut from the same dough, so I'm glad you've ended up finding each other. And there is no reason why you can't all be happy now — no reason at all.

As for me, well, I made a promise a long time ago to a girl that I have loved for a lot of years, and now, I guess, it's time for me to put her first.

Watch out for Griff, won't you? Now that me and Allie aren't there, he'll be after a new drinking buddy. At least, that's what he'll tell you to get you out on a date with him.

Oh, and remember what I said about the sun and the shadows. Let misery make its home in the darkness, and seek out your future in the light.

Kit x

Even though I can barely see his words through my tears, I am also smiling. In the few minutes before I read Kit's note, I hadn't known for sure what my plans were – if I would stay here in New Zealand or venture home to England. But now, thanks to his note, I do. I guess that really, the truth has been creeping up on me for some time now, and that it simply needed someone else to state what Kit would probably call the 'bloody obvious'.

It has been so long since I have been able to picture Anna and not see an expression of hurt on her face, but now when I conjure her up in my mind, my beautiful mum looks content. She would have been happy for me – Kit was right. All Anna would ever have wanted for me is happiness, in whatever form that might be. Kit has taught me how to start making sense of her death, while meeting Tui has shown me that there is way more for me to do. Hiding away from the world is no longer an option – I need to be brave for my sister, but more than that, I want to be courageous for myself, too. Because I am allowed a look-in – I am also important, and loved, and wanted by those I care about.

For all these years now, I have resented a mother who gave me up – but what Bonnie really did when she left me behind was provide me with more love. With Anna and David, I had an extra helping, more than Bonnie was capable of offering at the time, and yet that young, scared girl never stopped caring about me. Far from having less than those who I perceived to be 'normal' people, I have, in fact, had far more. I've just been too blind and self-centred to realise it until now.

It occurs to me then that if Anna had never died, I might not have made it here. I may not ever have met Tui. Even if Bonnie had sought me out when she did, who is to say I would have listened? Would the allure of a half-sister have been enough to tempt me as far away as New Zealand, or did I have to come face-to-face with Tui to really understand how intrinsic she is to my life, and to my future?

Asking myself such questions is as silly as a dog chasing its own tail – because how can I know? It could all be part of life's grand plan, or it could be nothing more than a series of coincidences. The only thing I know for sure is that I am here now, and at last I have all the facts I need. And the truth, no matter how much like cuddling a cactus it might be, is as good a starting point as anyone can hope to find. From here on in, there will be no more dark spaces around me, and I can make my way forwards with hope in my heart.

I read Kit's note again, snuffling with laughter at his gentle teasing, and his typically Kit-like turns of phrase. I am going to miss him so much – I already miss him.

My thoughts have strayed often to that evening we

spent on the balcony in Oamaru, giddy on a mixture of whisky and close encounters with penguins. The breeze rolling in from across the water had lifted my freshly shorn hair and flattened it across my cheeks, and Kit, his eyes never leaving mine, had reached over to tuck the errant strands behind my ears. Such a small gesture, but one that had triggered a surge of feeling within me. I have told myself up to now that my reaction could be blamed on simple loneliness, or on alcohol taking its toll – but far from fading away, that yearning I experienced has only increased. Even as I got angry with Kit for pushing me to ride, all I really wanted was to fall against him again, just as I had on the pier amongst the seals, so that I might draw comfort from his strength, and find solace in his arms. I knew there was a chance that he would leave, but I have dared to hope that he would stay – not for me, but for himself, because I think Kit cherishes this small and exquisite corner of New Zealand even more than I do.

As he says, though, Kit made a promise a long time ago, and so he must honour it. He wouldn't be Kit if he didn't, and if he wasn't, I would not love him as much as I do.

Because I do, of course.

I love him.

47

Six weeks later . . .

February has heralded the arrival of autumn in Glenorchy, and every morning when I reach the yard, the outdoor school is littered with red, gold and amber leaves. One of Tui's favourite pastimes is to run through them at high speed, before gathering up handfuls to throw in the air for a delighted Beavis to jump up and catch. The little dog has increased both in size and amounts of fluff, and when he curls himself up for an afternoon nap in the corner of Keith's box, it's almost impossible to discern which end is head and which is bottom.

Bonnie is out with the midday ride, while I have promised my sister a jumping lesson once the mucking-out is complete. I am also keeping half an eye on the time, because Hayley is due to arrive this afternoon along with her new boyfriend . . . Billy. My two best friends started dating not long after I flew out here, with Hayley confessing rather cautiously that it had started as a drink to cheer Billy up after I friend-zoned him, then progressed to car-park snogging after he beat her at six consecutive games of pool.

'I let him win, obviously,' she had added, and I had laughed.

Hayley was worried that I would feel weird about this development, but that could not be further from the truth. I am genuinely thrilled for them, and even more thrilled at the prospect of winding them up about their new couple status when they get here. David, who bumped into them in the pub recently, told me that they make quite the striking duo. He and I still talk most days, but there's a lingering uneasiness there and we rarely stray on to the topic of him being my real father. And while I believe things between us will settle down eventually, it is definitely going to take some more time.

Slotting the pitchfork back on its hook and propping my hosed-down wheelbarrow up against the wall, I venture across to the hay barn in search of Tui. I have enjoyed working here every day with Bonnie, getting to know her better, but it is the weekends I relish the most, because that's when I get to spend quality time with my exuberant half-sibling.

'Come on, Tu!' I call up into the rafters. 'Keith is not going to tack himself up, you know.'

I hear a muffled 'Jeez' followed by a screech of laughter, and then Tui's bare feet come into view.

'Beavis,' I say, addressing the dog as he follows his mistress, 'have you been eating Tui's socks again?'

Tui starts giggling, bouncing from one bale of hay down to the next on her bottom and hiccupping with amusement.

Spotting her discarded boots, I pick one up and give it a sniff.

'Ugh!' I cry, wrinkling up my nose. 'You didn't tell me these were made from fish skins, cheese and poo, Tui.'

Still snickering as she staggers to her feet, Tui swipes the boot from my hands and starts to put it on sans sock, tumbling into me on her unsteady foot.

'Oh no,' I tell Beavis, 'Tui is drunk again.'

Such is Tui's mirth that she is still laughing when we emerge from Keith's stable ten minutes later, and I'm forced to make her count calmly to twenty before helping her to mount. Watching how much she is coming on continues to be the unrivalled highlight of my time here in New Zealand. She has spent hours up in the saddle while I instruct from the ground, taking her right back to basics and starting with her seat and leg position, before progressing to sitting trot, rising trot, and finally, a week or so ago, tentative cantering. Keith seems to know that he has a very precious cargo up on his back and behaves accordingly, barely flicking an ear when Tui gets carried away and starts flapping her arms, or her legs, or both consecutively. Today, we are going to tackle jumps again, and this time I want her to ride over them without being led by me – a big step.

'Very good, Tu!' I praise, as she pops over a tiny cross bar. 'But next time, remember to bend over forwards from your middle, as if you're bowing to the queen.'

'Okaaay.'

'And bring your hands up along Keith's mane, as if you're going to tickle his ears.'

'OK, Gee-nie.'

After she has successfully cleared a row of small jumps, I prop the poles up a fraction higher, flicking the lunge whip through the air to encourage Keith forwards. There is a dicey moment when Tui loses a stirrup after the first fence, but she manages not to fall, and even slots her foot back into place without any assistance from me.

'You're doing so well,' I tell her. 'You'll be winning the Grand National in no time.'

'What?' she bellows, looking down at the pony's outside foreleg to make sure she's rising to the trot at the right time.

I am just about to explain what the Grand National is when Tui interrupts me with an excited shriek – one that is loud enough to send an alarmed Keith veering off course and cantering skittishly towards the gate. Assuming that he will stop when he reaches it, I don't bother to give chase, but the next second the determined pony has taken an almighty gazelle-style hop into the air and cleared it by inches. Tui, to my total astonishment, not only manages to stay in the saddle, but remembers to fold forwards, too.

'Bloody hell!' I shout, throwing down my whip and hurling myself across the muddy ground. If Keith has decided to bolt, he could be halfway across the yard by now. What will Bonnie say if Tui goes missing again – and on my watch?

Fumbling with the bolt on the gate and swearing in earnest as I round the corner at speed, I skid across the concrete of the yard and almost collide with the errant Keith's toffee-coloured back end, which has thankfully come to an abrupt stop not far from the tack room.

Panting with relief, I lean against his warm rump for a moment to catch my breath, my hand already reaching up to reassure Tui, then step out into view and almost fall right over in shock. Because standing there, holding Keith's reins and looking at me with both endearment and bemusement on his face, is Kit.

'Lost something?' he asks.

'Wh—' I begin.

Tui is scrambling to get down so she can give Kit a hug, and seeing her flail, my body immediately moves into action, but my mind is spinning more than a gymnast's ribbon. Kit told Bonnie that he wouldn't be back for a visit until Easter at the earliest, so what is he doing here now? And why didn't anyone warn me, so I could at least have put on some make-up? I am horribly aware of the smears of dirt on my cream jodhpurs, the Mickey Mouse on my T-shirt, and the unflattering grey hairband pushing my unwashed locks off my face.

Kit, by contrast, looks good enough to eat off toast. He is wearing snugly fitting black trousers and a moss-coloured shirt that sets off his pale mint eyes. I want to tell him how good it is to see him, and how glad I am that he is here, but I can't seem to dredge up any words at all.

'Kit!' Tui is now on the ground and has thrown herself heavily into his arms – so heavily that he staggers back a few paces, laughing as he rights himself. Beavis, who had been dozing in one of the open stables, hurtles across to join them, his little body writhing with pleasure as he leaps up and licks Kit on the chin.

'Now this is what I call a welcome,' he jokes, glancing at me. Still unable to move or speak, I stare back, wondering how I have got through the past six weeks without him. I have missed Kit every single moment, and now that he's here, I want to fling myself against him just as Tui has done, and beg him never to leave again. But I don't. I *can't*.

'I'll just . . .' I say hesitantly, forcing myself to move. 'Just see to Keith. I'll, er, be back in a minute.'

Once in Keith's box, I shut and bolt the half-door behind me and lean against the wall, giving in to a smile so broad that I can feel it pulling my skin taut across my jaw.

This is a good thing. I am happy to see him. So, why am I hiding in here like a fairy-tale ogre?

By the time I have untacked and rubbed down Keith, Bonnie has returned from her ride and the yard is full of tourists needing assistance. I am only too happy to help them, but despite ferrying tack and returning borrowed hats, I make sure that I know where Kit is at all times. Tui is still dangling off him like a spider monkey, gazing at him with all the awe and adoration that I feel, yet am unable to show. Bonnie, too, looks happy to see her old friend, but I also clock her exclamation of surprise as she greets him. Clearly, my mother did not know that Kit was going to turn up today either.

My phone beeps with a message. It's Hayley, informing me that she and Billy were delayed in Dubai, and as a result, they have missed their connecting flight out of Melbourne, causing them a day's delay. Flicking my eyes in Kit's direction yet again, I am ashamed of how relieved I feel to unexpectedly have the evening free.

I'm just tapping out a quick sympathetic reply when Bonnie joins me. She is sporting flattened hat hair from her recent ride, but looks aglow with happiness.

'I can put that away for you,' she says, removing Merlin's saddle from my arm. 'You're taking the rest of the afternoon off.'

'What?' I ask, puzzled. 'Why? I told you I didn't need any time off yet – and anyway, my friends aren't coming until tomorrow now.' I hold up my phone.

Bonnie fixes me with one of what I have learned are her 'Mum knows best' stares.

'Even more reason to take advantage, then,' she says, and this time I see the hint of a glint in her bright blue eyes.

'But . . .' I protest, as she turns to go, 'I don't have any plans. I don't even know what I'd do.'

Bonnie's expression is loaded with undeniable suggestion, and she looks first towards Kit, then back at me.

'Oh, don't worry,' she says, her tone light and teasing, 'I'm sure between the two of you, you'll think of something.'

48

'Where are we going?' I ask Kit, fastening my seatbelt as he puts the jeep into gear.

'You remember that other big hill I once told you about?' he says.

'Queenstown Hill?' I recall, and he gives me a one-handed thumbs-up.

'That's the fella. I thought we could climb it.'

'Any particular reason why?'

'That's for me to know.' He gives me a sidelong look.

'And me to find out?' I counter hopefully.

'All in good time, you little lamp dweller.'

'Well, that's a new one.'

'Really? Have you never heard your name before?'

It's nice to have fallen back into an easy exchange of banter with Kit, and the back-and-forth asides continue in light-hearted earnest as he drives us along the highway towards town. I tease him about the photo he sent to Bonnie while she was still in England, of me and Tui beside the penguin statue in Oamaru, telling him that really, he is the reason I was outed. When I ask after Allie, he tells me that she is well and loving life in the city, but doesn't elaborate further than a vague 'I had a few days off' when I ask what prompted this visit.

'Do you love city life, too?' I ask, turning my head towards the window to take in the blue sweep of Lake Wakatipu. No matter how many times I see it, I am always moved by its quiet beauty. When Kit doesn't reply straight away, I glance back at him, noticing again how smartly he is dressed, and how neatly he's brushed back his tight black curls.

'It certainly looks good on you,' I tell him, gratified when he grins across at me.

'I don't think that's Wellington,' he says. 'I reckon it's being back here again.'

'I'm glad it's working for one of us,' I joke, plucking unenthusiastically at the material of my scruffy T-shirt. 'If you'd agreed to pass by my brand-new flat, I could have run in and got changed.'

'There was no need.' Kit slows down to allow two elderly ladies clutching walking sticks to cross the road. 'You look fine as you are.'

Unsure whether he is winding me up again, I say nothing, but it's impossible not to feel cheered just by hanging out with him again. I had forgotten how easy he is to be around, and how alive he makes me feel.

The trail up to the top of Queenstown Hill begins on the immediate outskirts of the town centre, not far from where the pair of us ventured the first time we went out on an afternoon alone. The weeks spent working daily at the stables have strengthened my muscles and improved my fitness, and this time I don't find the first part of the climb as arduous as I did before. Similarly to the Tiki Trail, the path here is also shaded by vast Douglas firs, but there are fewer roots to trip over this time, and we see fewer people on our way up.

Kit continues to natter away to me as we walk, pointing out curious stacks of flat stones, a tiny doorway that someone has carved into the stump of a felled tree, and all the birds that flit and fly from bush to branch above us, singing to one another almost as sweetly as Tui does to Beavis.

As the path continues to snake upwards, Kit points out a sign set back amongst the sparse undergrowth.

'"Queenstown Hill",' I read aloud. '"This hill was once known as Te Tapu-Nui, a hill which signifies intense sacredness." That's good to know.'

Kit chuckles.

'Your Maori needs a bit of work,' he says.

'Hey!' I exclaim. 'I'm trying my best here.'

'I'm so glad you decided to stay,' he says then, his finger brushing the gentlest stroke along the underside of my arm.

Taken aback by both the change in subject and the jolt that ricocheted through me at his touch, I mumble something incoherent in response.

Kit drops his hand.

'Say that again.'

'I'm glad, too,' I tell him, wanting to add that I stayed partly because of him, because he helped me to be brave, and to accept the things that I could not control.

374

But it feels wrong to crank the dial around to serious when we're only just settling back into playful.

After a few contemplative minutes, the trail widens and the stony ground gives way to a fine, sandy dust. We have reached the first stage of Queenstown Hill's summit, and I can see a bowl-shaped sculpture on the edge of the pathway. It has a circular base made from wide, tightly packed slabs of stone, while its basin-like top has been constructed from twisted strips of metal.

This time Kit reads the sign.

'"The Basket of Dreams",' he announces importantly. '"The Basket's spiral of steel follows you inward, to reflect, to draw inspiration from the mountains, lake, and from those who are with you. Outward, to dream, for the future. Time flies, eternity waits."'

'Wow,' I remark. 'Sounds serious.'

'It's pretty bloody beautiful, don't you think?' he asks, and I agree that it is. The truth is that the more I stand here and gaze at it, the more I find pleasing about it. The steel is warm to the touch, and the view beyond it nothing short of miraculous. The green mountainside rushes down to greet the vivid blue of the sprawling lake, while in the distance the Remarkables sit huddled together like giant's teeth – a great, toothy grin smiling up at the heavens.

'Let's go right to the top,' Kit says.

It is tough going, and my thighs burn in protest as we scale the final stretch of path, but the view alone makes the struggle worthwhile. It feels like we are above the sky itself up here, the two of us. Clouds float across the endless puddle of blue sky like bubbles in a bathtub, and the far horizon shimmers with dancing light.

'Seat?' offers Kit, tapping the dry earth with his boot.

I ease my bag off my shoulder and sit down. It is a relief to rest my legs for a moment, and I sigh with pleasure as I stretch them out in front of me.

'So,' says Kit, who has lowered himself down next to me.

'So,' I reply, looking from the view to him. There is so much wisdom in his wide-set eyes, such nobility in the strong line of his jaw, and the smooth expanse of his forehead. His lips are parted, and I can see the tantalising tip of his pink tongue. Reminded of how I longed to kiss him in Oamaru, I glance away guiltily, back towards the view.

'Thank you for coming up here with me,' he says. 'I know you probably had other things you would rather be doing.'

'Nope,' I say truthfully. 'I am very happy to be here, albeit a little bit mystified as to why you invited me.'

Kit deflects me again by asking about my visa. My tourist one expires in March, but Bonnie is already looking into a family application, which will allow me to stay longer. The goal eventually is to become a resident, and my spirits lift up a notch as I explain to Kit just how much of a home New Zealand has already become. David understands and has given me his blessing, as well as promising to visit as much as he can. The benefit of being an author is that you can work from anywhere in the world, and he is planning to take full advantage of that fact.

'I love this place,' I say dreamily, gazing out at the shifting clouds. The lake is pitted with tiny bright sails, the only sound the caressing whisper of the wind.

Beside me, Kit moves one of his big legs and dips his free hand into the pocket of his trousers, extracting a small drawstring pouch.

'What's that?' I ask.

'A present for you,' he says. Then, when I widen my eyes in surprise, he adds in a murmur, '*Ahakoa he iti he pounamu* – although it is small, it is greenstone.'

Fumbling as I untie the tiny knotted string, I turn the velvet sack upside down and tip the contents out into my flat, open palm.

'Oh, wow,' I say, taking in the fine gold chain and the jade-stone swirl at its end. 'It's so beautiful.'

'It's a koru,' Kit explains, lifting the necklace and holding it up so I can see the symbol. 'It's supposed to represent a silver fern unfurling.'

'It's the same as the "O" of Koru Stables,' I say in wonder.

'That's true.' Kit looks almost nervous now. 'But it also symbolises new life beginning, and peace, and strength, I guess. I wanted to get you something to make up for you losing your mum's ring in the river that day, but if you don't like it then—'

'No!' I protest, taking it from him and clutching it against my chest. 'I love it. I really love it!'

'I did look for your ring,' he adds, as I lift my hair and fasten the necklace. 'But I couldn't find the bloody thing.'

He looks so contrite that I have to laugh.

'You know, that ring never was my mother's,' I say. 'Well, it was, but not my adoptive mother's. It was Bonnie's all along – she gave it to Anna to give to me.'

'Maybe that's why you didn't need it any more,' he suggests. 'Because after that day, you had Bonnie herself. You had the real thing.'

'You know,' I tell him, still fingering my necklace in delight, 'I have been thinking a lot about what I really need lately. I was only a child when I found out that I was adopted, and it became so intrinsic to who I was, and who I became as I grew up. I'm ashamed to admit it now, but I was such a victim. I wrote myself into this role as a forgotten, abandoned child, and it warped me. David knew it, and I guess that's why he created all those Evangeline stories in the first place, in order to show me that a person is only defined by their actions, rather than their situation. Whenever I was acting up or being resentful, he would ask me what Evangeline would do, and I hated it, because I knew that she was better than me, and less bitter than me. But all he was really trying to do was chivvy me out of my self-pity. I should have followed Evangeline's lead, but instead I retreated into the shadows, and it took coming here, and meeting Tui and Bonnie and – ' I pause – 'you, actually, to make me realise what I really needed.'

'And what was that?' Kit asks, his voice low.

'Me,' I say simply. 'I just needed to be me.'

Kit smiles at that, and for a moment or two, neither of us says anything, content to simply take in the scenery and close our eyes against a re-emerging sun.

'Thank you so much for this, by the way,' I say, turning to look at him again, enjoying the sensation of simply seeing him there. I pick the necklace up off my chest, tracing my thumb around the spiral shape of the koru symbol. 'I can't think of a better present – there is literally nothing better that you could have given me.'

Kit looks amused.

'Nothing?' he says, tilting his head to one side. 'Nothing at all?'

'You still haven't told me,' I say, talking to mask how thrown I am by the potential meaning behind his words, 'why you're here – and why we're on the top of this hill.'

'I used to come up here with my pa,' he says, so wistfully that it douses any vestiges of my imagined flirtation. 'We would sit here for hours, watching the clouds drift by, and he would tell me all the old Maori stories, trying his best to instil in me all the wisdom that he had learned from his own father.'

'He did a good job,' I say softly, but Kit shakes his head ruefully.

'Nah – I mean, I reckon I get by OK, given the fact

I'm only strictly half Maori. But next to that man, I'm still only a beginner. I make mistakes all the time.'

'Everybody does,' I point out. 'Look at me! And what about my parents – both sets?'

Kit fixes me with a steady gaze.

'Bon told me about David,' he says. 'About the possibility of him being your dad after all.'

'Mad, isn't it?'

He nods. 'Just a bit. Do you reckon you'll find out for sure? You know, do a DNA test or something?'

If he had asked me only a day ago, I would not have known how to answer, but for some reason, I realise now that I do. And that probably, I have known ever since David told me the truth about his one night with Bonnie.

'I don't need to,' I reply. 'If the last few months have taught me anything, it's that family are the people you choose to have in your life. David is my dad – he has always been my dad, and that is good enough for me. I don't need a test to confirm or deny what I already know. In fact, as soon as we get down off this hill, I'm going to call and tell him just that.'

Kit is smiling again, this time with what looks an awful lot like pride.

'You know what?' he says. 'I reckon my pa would have really liked you.'

'And my mum, Anna, would have loved you,' I say, unable to stop a wobble sneaking in amongst the words. Kit puts one of his big hands over mine.

'Still hurts, huh?'

I can only nod.

'I broke up with Allie,' he says then, so casually that at first I think I must have misheard.

'What did you s—' I begin, only to yelp in alarm as my bag slithers away over the steep edge of the hill.

'Shit!' yells Kit, diving over sideways just as I do the same, both of us making a furious grab for the strap. With a resounding thud, our heads collide and we reel upwards, the mischievous bag held up in the air between us.

'Ouch,' laughs Kit, as I rub my brow. 'You really know how to ruin a bloke's big moment, don't you?'

'Me?' I exclaim, still rubbing.

'You,' he concurs, wiping dust off his trousers.

'Well, I'm very sorry,' I retort.

'Be quiet,' he chides. 'I'm trying to do my big speech over here and you're making it impossible.'

'Sorry,' I reply, feeling all of a sudden ridiculously giddy. If I were Tui, I would be bouncing up and down on my bottom by now.

'You wanted to know why I came back?' he prompts, to which I nod, unable now not to beam at him. For once, the staggering landscape has lost its captive audience, because all I want to stare at is Kit.

'When I got to Wellington, I tried really hard not to think about home,' he says, chewing at the corner of his thumbnail. 'Allie had found us a place in a nice part of town, and everyone was really friendly and all that – but it just felt, I dunno, empty somehow, you know? Like there was a space around me that nothing and nobody there could fill.'

I swallow, the hairs on my arms standing up with recognition.

'Me and Al, we'd been together so long that it had become a habit, and once we took away everything else that we knew – all our friends and family, our jobs – we found out pretty quickly that we didn't have all that much in common any more. I mean, I love the girl, and she loves me, but neither of us loved each other in the right way, you know.'

My mind flickers to Billy, to how much affection and respect I have for him, and how much I wanted to love him in the other way, but could never quite get there.

'I am a stubborn old mule,' Kit goes on, pushing his foot through the dust. 'Because I'd said I would go to Wellington, I did, even though I knew deep down that it wasn't what I wanted. So, I gave it a whirl, but it was never going to work.'

'Is Allie OK?' I ask.

'Oh, yeah.' Kit nods in earnest. 'Better than OK, in fact. Once we'd had the chat, she told me she felt relieved. We had been arguing so much – even before we left here we'd been doing that. It was sad to be ending something, but we both knew by doing so, we would be opening ourselves up to something even better. She's happy in Welly. Like, really happy. I would never have left her by herself up there if I didn't believe that.'

'I know you wouldn't have,' I agree. 'You're just too . . . well, you, to do that.'

'When I wrote you that note, I didn't tell you the whole truth,' Kit says then.

'Oh?'

'I told you that I was feeling sketchy about going because I was worried about Tui, but that was only half the reason. Fact is, I didn't want to leave you either.'

My heart is fluttering so fast now that I am afraid it might carry me right off the top of this hill.

'As it turns out,' he says, picking up both my hands, 'Tui is not the only girl that I can't live without. And I'm not just saying this because I'm not with Allie any more. I'm not on the rebound; I know how I feel. It slinked up on me, but it was only when I got to Welly and I couldn't see you every day that I realised just how much I wanted to see you – how much I needed to be around you.'

He is gabbling now, but I feel powerless to stop him. All I can think is that I love this man. I have never been in love before now, but I love Kit. I know I do, because suddenly it feels as if the sun has been put there just for us, the sway of the trees is actually the world sighing with contentment, and even the darkest corners of my heart have all at once been bathed in wonderful light.

'I guess what I'm trying to say, in the great big idiot way that only I can, is that I came back here for you, Genie. I gave you that necklace because I want to be part of your new start, and because I know how much you have been hurt and are still hurting, and I want to be here to help you through it. Because there are going to be some tough times ahead, and days where you want to tear down the world because Anna is not in it, but on those days I will be here. If you let me, if you want me to be?'

Before I can say anything, Kit has moved his hands up to my face, his thumbs wiping away my tears as they begin to fall, his voice telling me not to be upset, and that everything is going to be all right. What he doesn't realise is that, for once, I am not weeping because I am sad, but because I am happy.

'I'm sorry,' I say, my voice strangled by sheer, unadulterated happiness. 'I'm not upset.'

Taking an enormous breath to steady myself, I rub furiously at the mess that my face has become and rest my head against his shoulder, drawing him in and relishing the wonderful, solid Kit-ness of him.

I hear him start to say something, but unable to make out exactly what, I lift my chin to face him, my lips colliding with his.

'That's better,' he says, leaning forwards a fraction more until his nose is touching the tip of mine. 'Now I have you right where I want you.'

I could ask him what he means by that, or I could tell him that I have never felt more at peace than I do now, on this spot and in his arms. I could say that if the Basket of Dreams below us really is spinning outward for eternity, then there is only one man that I would want to be with for the ride.

But I don't say any of those things, because Kit is already kissing me. On and on we kiss, dissolving into each other until my limbs begin to buckle and my heart pounds with joy, only breaking off when we have to in order to breathe, and to look at each other in bewilderment, searching for and finding the love reflected right back.

Kit runs a tentative hand through my hair, allowing himself a small sigh as he whispers some more beautiful and mysterious words into my ear.

'That's another Maori saying, isn't it?' I murmur.

He pulls me closer.

'It's what my pa said to me right after he told me that he was sick. And he said it right here, right on this spot. Now, I want to pass it on to you.'

He falls silent, and as I wait for him to continue, I remember how small I felt when I arrived here, how insignificant in a country overflowing with so much life and vitality. But rather than diminish here, I have flourished. I have grown and I have blossomed; I have forgiven and I have fallen in love – with my family, with Kit, and with myself.

'Come on, then,' I say. 'Tell me what it means.'

'It means,' he says, bending his head to kiss me, 'that life is not forever, but love is.'

Acknowledgements

Heartfelt thanks to you, my dear reader. Thank you for choosing this book when there are so many out there in the world, and thank you for choosing to keep on reading, too. Us writers would be nothing without our readers, and it is to you that we all owe the greatest debt of gratitude. If you would like to chat to me about anything I have written/am writing, please come and find me on Twitter and Instagram @isabelle_broom, or on Facebook under Isabelle Broom Author.

Of course, it takes more than one person to bring a novel out into the world, and this time I have an entire Hobbit hole full of people to lavish my love on. To my agent, Hannah Ferguson and the team at Hardman & Swainson, thank you for all your support and for continuing to believe in me. To my chanting monk (ha!) of an editor, Tilda McDonald, you know this story would be a shadow of its completed self without your wisdom, patience and brilliance – you are INCREDIBLE. Thanks also to Laura Nicol, Helena Fouracre, Jess Hart, Sarah Kennedy and Sarah Bance, plus the rest of the awesome team at Penguin Michael Joseph. You are all heroes.

I used to list all my writer colleagues and old-school friends separately, but with publishing folk being as amazing as they are, the two groups now just crowd happily together under the same big umbrella. I could not possibly list everyone here, but I would like to especially thank Sadie, Ian, Tamsin, Ranjit, Gemma, Sarah, Colette, Carrie, Katie, Vicky Z, Graeme, Kimberley Atkins, Cesca, Cressida, Katy, Rachael, Jo, Roxie Cooper, Cathy, Nina, Kirsty G, Fanny, Tammy, Sara-Jade, Louise C, Claire Frost, Hannah R, Basia M, Sophie Ransom, Whittlesticks, Ali Land, Giovanna and Tom Fletcher, Jade Beer, Rosie W, Adele P, Tasmina, Karen, Lisa Howells, Kay Ribeiro, Corrie 'MOFN' Heale, my Queenstown crew Ross Greer, Josh, Griffin, Aman and Emily Durber, and Mr Edward Wears – aka the greatest tea maker of all time. All the colour, laughter, emotion and wisdom in this book comes from you lot.

To all the bloggers, reviewers, early readers, booksellers, competition winners and book champions far and wide – don't ever stop doing what you do. You are all legends of the highest order who deserve three scoops of hokey-pokey ice cream with added chocolate sprinkles.

It is no real surprise that the stories I choose to tell always come back to family, because I have a pretty amazing one myself. We have faced some tough times over the years (perhaps especially in the past few), but my god have we learned a lot in the process. I can't think of any people I am more proud of or love more. Thank you for teaching me about what matters most (and for looking after the dogs while I go gallivanting

388

off on research trips to far-flung locations). This book, however, belongs most of all to you, Mum. Thank you for being so funny, witty, big-hearted, brave and for cheering me on when all this being-an-author malarkey was nothing but a far-off dream. As Kit would say, we bloody well did it – again!

He just wanted a decent book to read ...

Not too much to ask, is it? It was in 1935 when Allen Lane, Managing Director of Bodley Head Publishers, stood on a platform at Exeter railway station looking for something good to read on his journey back to London. His choice was limited to popular magazines and poor-quality paperbacks – the same choice faced every day by the vast majority of readers, few of whom could afford hardbacks. Lane's disappointment and subsequent anger at the range of books generally available led him to found a company – and change the world.

'We believed in the existence in this country of a vast reading public for intelligent books at a low price, and staked everything on it'
Sir Allen Lane, 1902–1970, founder of Penguin Books

The quality paperback had arrived – and not just in bookshops. Lane was adamant that his Penguins should appear in chain stores and tobacconists, and should cost no more than a packet of cigarettes.

Reading habits (and cigarette prices) have changed since 1935, but Penguin still believes in publishing the best books for everybody to enjoy. We still believe that good design costs no more than bad design, and we still believe that quality books published passionately and responsibly make the world a better place.

So wherever you see the little bird – whether it's on a piece of prize-winning literary fiction or a celebrity autobiography, political tour de force or historical masterpiece, a serial-killer thriller, reference book, world classic or a piece of pure escapism – you can bet that it represents the very best that the genre has to offer.

Whatever you like to read – trust Penguin.